TALES OF THE
SHADOWMEN
Volume 8: Agents Provocateurs

TALES OF THE
SHADOWMEN

Volume 8: Agents Provocateurs

edited by
Jean-Marc & Randy Lofficier

stories by
**Matthew Baugh, Nicholas Boving, Matthew Dennion,
Win Scott Eckert, Martin Gately, Micah Harris,
Travis Hiltz, Paul Hugli, Rick Lai, Joseph Lamere,
Olivier Legrand, Jean-Marc & Randy Lofficier,
DavidMcDonald, Chris Nigro, John Peel,
Dennis E. Power, Pete Rawlik, Joshua Reynolds,
Frank Schildiner, Michel Stéphan** and **Michel Vannereux**

portfolio by
John Gallagher

cover by
Jean-Claude Claeys

A Black Coat Press Book

Table of Contents

Tales of the Shadowmen *normally features French fictional characters, but this charming story by our regular contributor Matthew Baugh spotlights some Italian ones, mostly the duo of Don Camillo and Peppone, created by the great Italian writer Giovanni Guareschi (1908-1968). The Don Camillo books were the basis for five Italian-French co-productions in the 1960s, which starred Fernandel as Don Camillo and Gino Cervi as Peppone. Cervi also played a remarkable Maigret on Italian TV. Welcome to the sun-drenched Po Valley where Don Camillo and Peppone are about to encounter the most extraordinary visitors...*

Matthew Baugh: *Don Camillo and the Secret Weapon*

The Po Valley, Late August, 1952

It was midnight and Don Camillo was in bed when he heard a pounding at the church door. He grumbled as he made his way downstairs. When he opened the door, he saw Mayor Peppone and Smilzo, supporting another man between them.

"What do and your henchman want at this hour?" Don Camillo asked.

"This man is ill," Smilzo replied.

"There's no need to wake me for a man who's had too much to drink," the priest said. "Let him sleep it off in one of your homes."

He started to shut the door when Peppone caught it with one of his big hands.

"That's no way for anyone to behave," he said. "Not even a priest. This man isn't drunk; he's really in bad shape and he needs help."

"Very well," Don Camillo said, brushing the mayor's hand away. He swung the door wide and gestured for the men to lay the stranger on a little bench in the vestibule.

He looked the stranger over. He was perhaps 40, tall and lean, with an intellectual look to his face and the cut of his beard. He was dressed like a businessman from Rome, but Don Camillo thought that he was a foreigner. He saw that his shirt was bloody and there was a fresh bandage on his side.

"This man's been shot," Don Camillo exclaimed.

"It's good to know that our priest isn't blind," Smilzo said with a smirk. His expression faded as he saw the scowl Peppone was giving him.

"Come on, Father," the mayor said. "The doctor is out of town; besides he hasn't half the experience removing bullets that you had in the War."

Don Camillo grunted and led the way to the sacristy where they laid the man on the credenza where Don Camillo kept his vestments. The priest tore open the man's shirt and gently began to remove the bandage. He hesitated as the man groaned.

"Can you hear me?" he asked.

"I can hear you," the man said in accented Italian.

"How were you injured?"

"A hunting accident," the stranger replied, keeping his eyes shut.

"Would you like some brandy to dull the pain?"

"That would be welcome."

The surgery took the better part of an hour and nearly half of Don Camillo's best bottle of brandy. When it was over, the stranger lay unconscious as the priest cleaned the long fisherman's knife and the pair of forceps he had used.

"With that accent of his, I should have sent for vodka instead of giving him brandy," he said.

Peppone and Smilzo shared a guilty look at each other.

"Wherever he's from, you did him an act of Christian charity," the mayor said.

"Which means he's no longer my responsibility," Don Camillo replied. "You can take him back to your house or the People's Palace to recover."

"Why can't he stay in the church?" Peppone demanded.

Don Camillo fixed a fierce stare on the mayor.

"That was a pistol bullet I just removed, which means this was no hunting accident. When a Russian shows up—"

"I think he's Bulgarian," Smilzo interrupted, then lowered his gaze as both men turned fierce expressions on him.

"When a *Bulgarian* shows up in our little village with a bullet in him," Don Camillo continued, "he's clearly been up to no good. I suspect he's a Bolshevik agent of some kind and that's why you're so keen on my helping him."

"Suppose he is what you say," Peppone said. "You are still obliged to care for the helpless."

"Not when he's one of yours, Comrade Mayor," Don Camillo said. "This wayfarer is clearly better off in the hands of his own kind. Take him to your community center."

"But he is on the run," said Smilzo, which earned him another withering look from Peppone.

"Father," the mayor said, "This man wouldn't be safe in the People's Palace."

"I am not hiding a fugitive from the police for you."

"It's not the legitimate authorities who are after him," Peppone said. "These will be secret police; assassins..."

"What secret police? Whose assassins?"

"Whose do you think? The Americans, the French, the British."

"That's your affair."

"Father, he needs sanctuary," Smilzo said.

8

"Sanctuary?" Don Camillo shouted.

"You must give it to him," Peppone said.

"He hasn't asked for sanctuary."

"I'm asking for him."

"You can't do that!" Don Camillo shouted, throwing his hands in the air.

"Why not, when he needs it and can't ask himself?"

Don Camillo's face turned red and stomped out of the small room into the chancel where he turned his eyes to the crucified image of Christ.

"What is the matter, Don Camillo?" Christ said.

"They are asking me to give sanctuary to a Communist agent!"

"Sanctuary is the right of every man."

"But Lord, he doesn't even believe in you," Don Camillo said.

"Yes, but *you* believe."

"But he is a *Communist!*"

"Don Camillo, you know that I am not interested in politics," Christ said. "I only care about mercy."

"Some people don't deserve mercy, Lord," Don Camillo replied. "This man is bound to be up to something that will bring death and terror to the whole world."

"The Good Samaritan did not pause to check the background of the injured man he found," Christ said. "Mercy is not only for the deserving, but for all who are in need; otherwise it would not truly be mercy."

"Yes, Lord," Don Camillo said, lowering his eyes. He stepped back into the sacristy where the three men waited.

"Very well," he said. "He shall have sanctuary, but there is something I need you to do."

"What is it?" Peppone asked.

"The bishop has received special incense made with myrrh and blessed by the Holy Father himself. All the churches are to use it for the Feast Day of St. Joshua. I was going to pick it up tomorrow, but if I am to play nursemaid to Comrade Spy here…"

"Don't worry Father," Peppone said. "Smilzo will take his truck and pick it up."

Smilzo looked surprised and annoyed but kept his mouth shut, and Don Camillo smiled.

Anita looked up as the dark-haired man entered the office. He was younger than Mr. Hawthorne's usual visitors, and handsomer. She took in the tall, lean frame, the blue-gray eyes, dark hair cut short, all neatly in place except for one stray piece that fell across his right eyebrow. Out of practiced habit, her gaze flicked to his left hand and she saw it was ringless.

The man noticed her glance and smiled. There was something cruel about his mouth and sent a thrilling shiver through her.

"*Buon giorno, signore*," she said with a smile. "*Come posso aiutarla?*"

"That's not a Roman accent," he replied in English. "Are you an American?"

"You caught me," she replied switching to his language, and pouting. "I guess all those Berlitz classes didn't do me much good after all."

"Have you lived in Rome long?" the man asked, leaning on the girl's desk.

"Only a few weeks, she replied. "I'm still getting the lay of the land, so to speak."

"I'd be happy to help you with that."

Hawthorne heard the voices from the outer office. It sounded like an animated conversation and he wondered if his receptionist had forgotten her place again. He pressed the intercom button and was rewarded with the sound of girlish giggles over the speaker.

"Miss Hutchens," he said in his iciest and most proper tone, "is that the man from London?"

"Yes, Mr. Hawthorne," she said.

"Then send him in, please."

The door opened and the agent entered, winking at the girl as he did.

"I see my secretary has caught your eye, Commander," Hawthorne said as the door closed. He looked over the younger man, disapproving of his short sleeves and casual air. In contrast, Hawthorne wore a Savile Row suit and reeked of the exclusive clubs of London.

"Why an American girl?"

"I lost my regular secretary and this one's on loan from the American Embassy. God save us from these girls who come to Rome looking for romance."

The agent smiled sardonically and took the seat that Hawthorne indicated.

"Could I interest you in some tea?"

"No, thank you, sir."

"Scotch then?"

"Of course."

Hawthorne poured the amber fluid into two glasses and added ice. The agent took his and sipped it.

"Very good, sir," he said.

"Old Pulteney, 12-year old," Hawthorne said. "A bit hard to come by in this place, but you must be used to that sort of thing. A field agent has to deal with all manner of hardships."

"Quite."

"I'm sure you've heard about the unpleasantness here," Hawthorne continued. "Seems one of the GRU chaps managed to get hold of some restricted research. He was making off with it when two of our chaps caught him on a train heading through the Po Valley. There was a bit of a tussle and the man got away, though not before taking a bullet."

"Where do you think he is, sir?"

Hawthorne took a map from a nearby bookcase and unrolled it on his desk.

"The incident took place here," he said, stabbing a point on the map with his index finger. "The closest towns are Brescello, Pontaratto, Boretto, and Viadana, so we think he's in one of those."

"But you haven't been able to find him?"

"He's very clever," Hawthorne said. "Besides, the Communist party is strong in the area, so there are plenty of people to help him hide out."

"What did he take?" the agent asked.

"Are you familiar with biological weapons?"

"Germ warfare and all that?" the agent said. "Nasty business."

"Quite so," Hawthorne agreed. "This chap's got the microfilm of our best research on a 'Satan-bug' we've been working on. No vaccine, infectious as all blazes, and better than 99 percent fatal."

"Good Lord," the agent said, his suave façade slipping for a moment. "Is there such a thing?"

"Not yet, but he's got our research," Hawthorne replied. "That's going to set us back at least ten years, I'm told. Worse than that, the Russians may develop it first. It's your job to see that doesn't happen."

"I'll do my best, sir," the agent said, recovering his nonchalance. "I don't speak Italian, though."

"I've arranged for a translator to accompany you." Hawthorne hit the buzzer on his intercom. A moment later the door opened and a girl of 18 or 19 entered. She wore her blonde hair up and concealed her figure with a loose sweater; still, she was very attractive.

"This is Miss Kant," Hawthorne said.

The Agent raised an appreciative eyebrow and lifted his glass in greeting.

Avakoum Zahov woke to find himself in a narrow bed wearing an oversized nightshirt. He started to sit up only to wince at the pain in his side.

"Lie still, Comrade Spy," a voice said. "You are not healed yet." He looked up to see a massively-built priest with a long face and a set of teeth that would have looked more at home in a thoroughbred's mouth. The priest set aside the breviary he had been reading, and took a puff on his cigar."

"Am I to take it that you bandaged my wound, Father?"

"Your 'hunting accident,' yes."

"Then I am in your debt," Zahov said.

"I am not sure that I want you in my debt in my debt, Comrade Spy."

A sardonic smile appeared on Zahov's lean face. "You're not too proud to smoke my Havanas," he said.

"I only took half of them," the priest said, taking another puff. "As a good Party member, I was sure you wouldn't mind the equal distribution of wealth."

Zahov closed his eyes and chuckled.

"You took the bullet out of me?"

Don Camillo nodded and took another puff of the cigar.

"Thank you," Zahov said.

"You're not trying very hard to hide that you're a Russian agent," the priest said.

"I'm not," Zahov said with another smile, "but you've decided that I am. Clearly you searched me, or you wouldn't have my cigars. Did you find anything else of interest?"

"Just this," the priest held up a small film canister.

"Ah," Zahov said. "May I confess a little sin to you, Father?"

Don Camillo took the cigar out of his mouth and frowned. "Are you going to ask for absolution for spying on my country?"

"Not exactly. I work for a design house. That film is all of next season's fashions from our competitors in Rome."

"A Soviet designer?" the priest said, smiling ironically.

"No, Father," Zahov replied. "I was born in the Soviet Union but my secret love was always fashion. I defected years ago. My employer is in Clerville. When our Princess Ann visited here this summer, she fell in love with your fashions so these are sure to be a sensation."

Don Camillo harrumphed.

"It's the truth, Father," Zahov continued. "I'm no spy, but I will get in trouble if I'm caught. They might even send me back, and I'm sure you wouldn't want that on your conscience."

"If you're not a spy, you're certainly smooth enough to be one," Don Camillo said. "Fortunately for me, your allies here are not so glib."

Zahov studied the priest more carefully. Despite his rustic appearance, the man was no fool. He wondered briefly about finding a way to overpower him and taking the microfilm, but swiftly decided against it. Don Camillo was a big, powerful-looking man, and he was wounded. Besides, he would hate to injure someone who had probably saved his life. Fortunately, the mayor seemed to trust this man. That must mean that, even if he was not a part of their cause, he had integrity.

"So, what will you do, Father?" he asked.

"I told Peppone and his gang that I'm putting you out just as soon as you're fit to travel. This film, whatever it is, stays with me."

He crossed to a heavy bureau, placed the film in a drawer and locked it.

"That seems an extreme precaution," Zahov said.

"Perhaps I'm doing you an injustice, Comrade Spy. Sometimes a cynic like me forgets how harmless Comrade Stalin and his friends are."

Eva Kant slipped into the bathroom, leaving the Englishman sitting on the bed, cleaning his gun, a little Beretta .418. They had checked into a hotel in Parma to use the central location as their base of operations.

12

She smiled just a little as she undressed for the shower. The Englishman clearly wanted her, but was chivalrous enough to wait. She'd had to deal with the other kind before, the kind who thought wanting automatically entitles one to take. She didn't think the Englishman was one of those, but she tucked a little pistol in the folds of her towel, just in case.

She thought about the Englishman as she showered. It might be fun to give in to him; he was handsome and she liked dangerous men. Still, for all his fascination, he struck her as the kind who got tired of a woman quickly once the pursuit was over. She would much rather find a man who was dangerous to the rest of the world, but faithful to her.

Emerging from the shower, she dried off, then wrapped her hair in a towel and bundled up primly in an oversized bathrobe. She knew the Englishman was hoping for something else and smiled with a touch of regret.

This wouldn't be the last time she disappointed him.

The first two towns yielded nothing, but Miss Kant thought she caught a flicker of a reaction from the mayor of the third when they showed him the photo of Avakoum Zahov.

She studied the man carefully. The mayor—Peppone was his name—worked as the town mechanic and blacksmith. He was a big, thickset man with hands that liked like they could tear a deck of cards in half, or pull a horseshoe straight. She also noticed a portrait of Garibaldi on the man's office wall and another of Lenin, which was more than enough to judge his political leanings.

"I've never seen this man before," the mayor said, and she translated for the Englishman.

"I'm certain that's true," the Englishman replied, speaking slowly enough for her to translate. "We are certain he's found refuge somewhere in this town, though. If you hear anything, please tell me at once. This man has stolen valuable military secrets and anyone who shelters him faces the severest penalty."

"Of course," the mayor said.

When they had left, they climbed into her car, a black Jaguar XK120 which he insisted on driving.

"The next village?" Miss Kant asked.

"No," he replied. "Just the top of that hill ahead, and get my field glasses out, would you? There's something I'd like to see."

When the Englishman and his pretty translator had left, Peppone sat at his desk, fuming. After several moments, he called for Smilzo.

"Yes, Chief?" the younger man said as he entered.

"That man who was just here is a British agent," Peppone said. "We need to get the Bulgarian out of town before they discover he's hiding in the church."

"We're sunk, Chief," Smilzo replied. "Don Camillo will turn him over in a second."

"Don't be an idiot," Peppone countered. "The priest gave his word and he's not going to break it. I just don't want him getting into trouble over this; it would be on my head. Get over to the church and warn him."

"Right away, Chief," Smilzo said.

Eva Kant watched as the Englishman lay on his belly in the tall grass of the hill overlooking the town, studying the mayor's house through his binoculars. She noticed a smile touch his cruel lips as a man came out the front door and hurried down the street.

"What is it?" she asked, knowing the hunter has caught scent of his prey.

"They've got him in the church," the Englishman said.

Don Camillo opened the church door to an attractive young couple. The woman was a pretty blonde, the man lean and dark, and both carried an air of danger about them.

"Can I help you, my children?" he asked.

"We are looking for this man," the girl said holding out a photo of Zahov.

"Yes, when that buffoon, Smilzo came to warn me, I figured you wouldn't be far behind."

The girl seemed surprised but relayed his words to the man, who made a brief reply.

"You will surrender him to us," she translated.

"Of course not. He has received sanctuary here."

She translated this to the man who scowled and said something.

"He says this is a very serious matter," the girl said.

"I agree," Don Camillo replied. "Matters of canon law are very serious indeed."

"In this instance, the laws of the state must take precedence over those of the Church."

Don Camillo shrugged. "You will have to take that up with my bishop. If he agrees, then I will certainly turn the man over to you."

The girl related this to the man, who nodded his head impatiently and said something else.

"Can you take us to see him, at least?" she asked.

"Of course," Don Camillo said.

Avakoum Zahov was struggling with the lock on Don Camillo's bureau when he heard the footsteps on the stairs. He recognized the priest's heavy tread and knew he had only seconds. He twisted the piece of wire he had kept hidden in the lining of his shoe and felt the lock give. He opened the drawer and grinned when he saw the little film canister. He pocketed it, shut the bureau and managed to get back into bed just as the door opened.

Don Camillo was followed by a dark-haired man with the look of a professional agent and a lovely blonde girl.

"Comrade Zahov, isn't it?" the man asked, speaking English with a British accent.

"It is, though I don't believe we've, met," Zahov replied in the same language.

"Pity," the Englishman said. "Still, we'll have some time for pleasantries. Give me the microfilm and come along like a good chap, won't you?"

"But I am in the custody of this good priest."

"You know as well as I do that's not going to make any difference."

"Father," Zahov said, switching to Italian, "this man says that I am his prisoner whether you like it or not."

That was enough to send Don Camillo into an angry tirade. He waved his hands and shouted at the Englishman, not seeming to care that they didn't speak the same language. As he did, Zahov managed to palm the film canister, then caught the blond woman's eye. She nodded and did a masterful job of maneuvering herself closer while translating Don Camillo's ranting. When he was confident that neither the British Agent nor the priest could see him, Zahov slipped the canister into the girl's hand.

The one-sided conversation soon subsided with the British Agent assuring Don Camillo that he would do nothing until obtaining the bishop's permission. With that, he and the girl left.

Zahov felt a tide of relief wash through his body. If this worked, he had accomplished his mission and only the secondary task of escaping with his life remained. Almost immediately, he felt a new fear. As smoothly as he had passed the film, the Englishman might have seen it. Zahov rated him as an extremely dangerous man and knew that his mission was still in danger.

"What is it, Comrade Spy?" Don Camillo asked.

"I am just hoping this all comes out as it should," Zahov said.

"Well, it is a good thing that the Lord listens even to the prayers of the Godless," Don Camillo said.

That evening, as Don Camillo was saying mass for the feast of St. Joshua, Zahov heard footsteps on the stairs. The room was dark and he imagined the Englishman coming back to take him… though he wouldn't have expected the Agent to make so much noise. He moved to a spot behind the door and waited.

A moment later, the door opened and the muzzle of a shotgun poked through. Zahov grabbed the barrel and the arm that held it then stepped forward, ignoring the fresh pain of his wound, to turn his body in a judo throw. The gunman rolled across his hip and crashed to the floor, leaving him holding the shotgun. There was a second figure on the landing and Zahov pointed the weapon at him.

"Please, Comrade," Peppone said, dropping his own shotgun and raising his hands. "We are only here to protect you."

Zahov looked down and saw a stunned Smilzo lying on the floor. He lowered the shotgun and chuckled, wincing as the action caused him pain.

"It seems we had the same idea, Comrade Mayor," he said.

"Yes," Peppone said. "I can't see that Englishman giving up so easily."

"He doesn't," said a voice from the window. Zahov spun to see the blond woman and the Englishman, each wielding a pistol, looking in. Zahov dropped his weapon and the pair entered through the window.

"That's an interesting version of sanctuary," the Englishman said, nodding to the shotguns. "Now, let's have the film and we'll go."

"That is not going to happen, my dear," Miss Kant said from behind him. She also spoke in English and had turned her pistol on her companion, who raised his hands and allowed Zahov to take his pistol.

"*Et tu*, Miss Kant?" the Englishman asked, and Zahov marveled at his coolness.

"They paid better," she said. "I'm afraid you had lost even before we came here this evening. Zahov slipped me the film when we were here before. It's on its way to Moscow now."

"Bravo, darling," he said. "And now what do you plan to do with me?"

At that moment, they heard heavy footsteps on the stairs. A moment later, Don Camillo entered, still wearing his vestments and carrying a censor. He looked around the room taking in the people and the guns without changing his expression.

"My room is getting very crowded," he said.

"I'm sorry to have subjected you to this, Father," Zahov said. "At least, it's over now."

"It is," Don Camillo replied. "I took it upon myself to end it."

"*You* ended it?"

"I did. I have disposed of your microfilm."

The fumes from the censor reached Zahov's nostrils and he noticed something was wrong.

"That isn't incense," he said.

"Burning film!" Miss Kant said.

"Burning film!" the Englishman repeated in his language. He grabbed the censor and burned his hands getting it open. Inside were the twisted, half-molten remains of the microfilm."

"It's a sin to destroy property," Don Camillo said, "but whatever this secret was, I'm sure it was something nobody should own."

"Indeed," Zahov said. "It was a disease-weapon that could have meant the end of humanity."

"I didn't know," Miss Kant said, turning pale. "How diabolical. But that means that the container I sent to Moscow..."

"Rare myrrh, blessed by his holiness, the Pope," Don Camillo said. "I hope that Comrade Stalin's Politburo appreciates the extravagance."

Zahov began to laugh.

"What do we do with him?" Smilzo asked, gesturing to the Englishman.

"Let him go," Zahov said. "I feel well enough to travel, if Miss Kant will consent to drive me. He won't catch us if we have his car."

"*My* car," Miss Kant said.

"The priest did what?" Hawthorne shouted into the phone.

"Burned the microfilm, sir," the British Agent repeated with infuriating calm.

"And you say the girl and Zahov got away?"

"I can go after them if you want, sir."

"No," Hawthorne said, letting quiet resignation replace the anger in his voice. "No, I suppose there's not much point to that."

"There is one thing you could do, sir."

"Yes?"

"I don't have a good way to get back to Rome," the agent said. "Could you send your secretary around with a car?"

"Lord forgive me," Don Camillo said as he cleaned up remains of the censor. "I misused the bishop's gift and stank up your house with burning cellulose."

"You are forgiven," Christ said. "There is no incense as sweet as a prayer for peace."

After her dramatic defeat at the hands of Arsène Lupin in the conclusion of Countess Cagliostro *(available in a new translation from Black Coat Press), Maurice Leblanc told us that Joséphine Balsamo returned to London to lick her wounds. Nicholas Boving, a new contributor to* Tales of the Shadowmen, *reveals what she did there in a high-spirited sequel to* The Prisoner of Zenda *entitled...*

Nicholas Boving: *The Elphberg Red*

London, 1897

"It's called the Elphberg Red. There's a silly legend that says, so long as the stone remains in the family's hands, there'll be an Elphberg on the throne of Ruritania."

"But you set no store by legends of course." Rudolf Rassendyll's lips had the hint of a smile.

Colonel Sapt frowned like the very devil and made a good deal of harrumphing noises. He glared at Rassendyll. "Lot of damned silly nonsense, if you ask me. Still, if the word got out." He got up quickly and strode to the window overlooking the square. "But you see how it might look, don't you? I mean to say, the people there; good fellas, but willing to believe anything." He turned. "Good God, Rassendyll, they still believe in vampires!"

He slumped against the window frame. "Damn Rupert. Always short of the ready, but I never thought he'd sink this low."

Rassendyll took a thin cheroot from his case and lit it with some care. "And Prince Rupert could make great capital out of it, could he not?"

Sapt snarled. "He might use it to bring the Elphbergs down. With Michael dead and buried these years past, he's in line. God knows what would happen to my country if he called the castle in Strelsau home."

Rassendyll could see he was at his wits' end.

"I need hardly tell you that if this were to be made public, the consequences would be, to say the least, unfortunate." Sapt looked even more than usual like a red-faced walrus.

"And you have no idea where he is?"

"In England. That is all I am sure of."

Rudolf Rassendyll smiled. "I think we can narrow that down to London. He has to fence it, and besides, he's hardly likely to isolate himself from the fleshpots."

Sapt looked suddenly as if a weight had been lifted. "You'll do it then?"

Rassendyll laughed. "Did you doubt it?"

Sapt strode to the fireplace and tugged the bell rope. "This calls for a bottle, and later, we'll dine in style if this place offers anything worth eating." He leaned against the mantelpiece. "I still say the wrong Elphberg is on the throne."

Rupert of Hentzau, resplendent in white tie and tails, sat sprawled across an armchair, one leg beating time to some imagined tune while he held a cut crystal glass of brandy in his hand. He took a drink and called out impatiently.

"Devil take it, Josey, but you're taking an uncommonly long time. At this rate, we'll miss the last act, let alone the first."

Long heavy brocade curtains parted and a woman came into the sitting room. She was tall, beautiful with her honey blonde hair swept up and crowned with a thin circlet of gold inlaid with emeralds. Her dark-green silk dress, cut low at the bosom, swept low to the floor. Joséphine Balsamo, a.k.a. Countess Cagliostro, stood poised, her entrance complete, awaiting the appreciation of her audience.

Prince Rupert of Hentzau sprang to his feet, went quickly to her, bowed over her hand and kissed it. "Countess," he said. "I would wait 100 years for a moment such as this."

Joséphine flicked him negligently with her fan. "Flattery was ever your strong suit, Rupert, but have a care you do not overplay it."

Rupert shrugged. "I am what I am." He took his evening cloak from the back of a chair, threw it carelessly around his shoulders and offered his arm. "One assumes the, er, package is secure?"

"Do not worry yourself on that score. Now, let us find out whether this new work of Signor Puccini lives up to the fuss being made of it. What is it called, *La Bohème*?"

Fog swirled thickly making faint glowing halos of the gas lamps as the cab driver carefully picked his way along the street. Rassendyll drew on the cheroot between his gloved fingers and blew smoke with a force that belied his calm appearance. Finally the clip of the horse's hooves stopped and the cabby called out.

"221B, Sir."

Rassendyll got out quickly, tossed his cheroot into the gutter, paid the man generously for his skill at finding the destination under such difficulties and, for a moment, stood looking up at the lighted windows. He mounted the steps and knocked on the door. If the man he was about to ask for help could not assist him, then he had a much greater task ahead of him.

A grey-haired woman in her sixties answered his knock. She smiled, inviting his question.

"I have come to see Mr. Sherlock Holmes," Rassendyll said.

The lady shook her head. "Mr. Holmes is not here, sir. Perhaps you would leave a message?"

Rassendyll had a sense of great let down. "That is most unfortunate. I come on a matter of great urgency. When will he return?"

Again the lady shook her head. "I cannot say, sir." She stood aside, gesturing him inside. "But perhaps the doctor can help."

"The doctor?"

"Doctor Watson, sir. He is Mr. Holmes' associate."

The woman took his cloak and hat then led the way upstairs.

The bluff soldierly man stepped forward, hand outstretched. "I am John Watson," he said.

"Rudolf Rassendyll."

Watson gestured to a cheerful coal fire blazing in the hearth. "Please be seated, Mr. Rassendyll. I regret Mr. Holmes is away on a mission of some delicacy, but perhaps I may be of assistance. I have some experience with his methods." He took a decanter from a table. "Perhaps something to ward off the chill?"

Rassendyll frowned and was about to decline when he realized he had nothing to lose, and the man might be able to help in some way. Glasses filled, the doctor sat on the opposite side of the fire.

"May I know the nature of your problem, Mr. Rassendyll?"

Rassendyll sipped the brandy. "A certain very valuable gem, the property of a great lady, has been stolen. I have reason to believe the thief is in London."

Watson remained silent. He knew more information would be forthcoming and that it would come in its own time. The clock on the mantel struck the half-hour. His guest shrugged.

"Doctor, I must insist on your absolute discretion before expanding on my brief statement."

Watson spread his hands as if to say that such a request was completely natural. "Most of Mr. Holmes' clients have similar stipulations. We, that is, he and I, have never betrayed a trust."

Rassendyll sized the man up, liked the cut of his jib, and relaxed.

"You will of course know of Queen Flavia of Ruritania?'

Watson smiled. "One of the most beautiful women of our time."

Rassendyll nodded. "Indeed. And perhaps you are also acquainted with Prince Rupert of Hentzau?"

Watson's expression changed immediately. "Little enough, but the man sounds a damned rogue."

"Add murderer and thief to that, Doctor."

"You paint a pretty picture, Mr. Rassendyll."

A coal settled in the grate, making a rustling sound. From outside in the street came the steps of someone hurrying to their own fireside. Rassendyll took the bull by the proverbial horns.

"There is an enormous rose-coloured diamond, The Elphberg Red, part of the royal regalia. Suffice to say there is a legend to it and whether it contains truth matters not." He snapped a look at Watson. "Rupert has stolen it and it must be returned. The possible repercussions are unthinkable. He is in London to fence it; of this much, we may be reasonably sure." He got up, went to the window and looked out onto swirling fog, the faint glow of a streetlamp a lone reminder that another world did indeed exist.

"A night for crime and treachery, Doctor." He turned back. "Is there no way to contact Mr. Holmes?"

Watson looked slightly put out. "None whatever. But as I said..."

Rassendyll returned to the fire. "Forgive me. But there is much at stake, possibly even the continuance of the Elphbergs on the throne of Ruritania."

"That is indeed desperate news." Watson got up and refilled their glasses. "As I said, I have some considerable knowledge of Holmes' methods. I would be honored to assist in any way possible."

"You are kind, Doctor, but I feel we two may not be enough. I have had dealings with Hentzau in the past, and he is not to be taken lightly."

"Then we shall call in reinforcements."

Rassendyll frowned. "This must not get out, Doctor. Secrecy must be maintained at all cost."

Watson nodded. "Of course. But Holmes speaks highly of Inspector Mackenzie. He calls him one of Scotland Yard's finest." His mouth twitched in what might have been of amusement. "Holmes has also what he is pleased to call his Baker Street Irregulars; a group of urchins who earn a few honest shillings now and then by providing him with information."

"With regard to payment of a fee, there is no limit."

Watson got up. "Mr. Holmes has a set fee, sir. And I am merely his confidant and sometimes aide."

Rasendyll also arose. "I feel somewhat heartened, Doctor. I confess that finding Mr. Holmes unavailable was at first glance a blow, but I begin to see why he places such trust in you." He finished his drink. "When shall we meet? Time is of the essence."

Watson saw his guest to the door. "The Irregulars, I can set upon the trail at once. I assume it unlikely Prince Rupert is in London under his own name?"

Rassendyll smiled thinly. "He has the nerve of the devil, and an opinion of himself to match. I think you will find master Hentzau as himself."

Watson held out his hand. "I shall send Mackenzie a telegram tonight. Return here by eight tomorrow morning and we shall see what we shall see." He looked out of the doorway into the fogbound night. "I doubt you will find a cab Mr. Rassendyll. Is your hotel far?"

Rassendyll smiled. "I am a Londoner as you, Doctor. I have a town house within walking distance in Hyde Park Square."

Rupert threw his cape onto the back of a chair, held his arms out to Countess Cagliostro and waltzed her across the room as he sang an aria from *La Bohème*. He spun her once more and let her gently down onto the chaise.

"Champagne, my love?"

The lady smiled. "One needs something to chase away the chill and fog of this accursed country."

Rupert undid the wire on a bottle of Bollinger '89. The cork popped slightly and he expertly poured the wine into two glasses.

"This will bring life back to your cheeks."

Joséphine looked at him from beneath lowered lashes as she sipped. "If I did not know better, I might think you were mocking me."

Rupert raised one eyebrow. "And that would never do." He swallowed his wine and refilled the glass. "Damn me, but what a partnership we make, Countess. There will be no stopping us now."

The lady wagged a finger in admonition. "Have a care. The gods punish hubris."

"You sound like one who has had experience."

"Perhaps I have. I have found the past has a way of insinuating itself into our lives." Joséphine put her unfinished glass on the table at her side and got up. "And now, I am going to bed. Italian opera exhausts me."

Rupert laughed. "It is rather emotional, isn't it?" He bowed. "I shall remain here and think of the brilliant future before us."

The Sun shone from a sky that had no memory of the previous night's fog when Rassendyll arrived punctually at 8 a.m. to find another had beaten him. Watson introduced Inspector Mackenzie; a lean, grizzled, dour-faced Scot with an Edinburgh accent. He wore a scar on his face, a souvenir from the Milchester incident when Lady Melrose's necklace was stolen.

"I have given Mackenzie the gist of the problem," Watson said, "and Mrs. Hudson will bring us coffee shortly."

Mackenzie offered a dry, strong hand with a firm grip, and cut straight to the chase. "What d'ye ken of this Hentzau fellow?"

Rassendyll held his hands out to the fire for the morning was cold despite the brightness.

"More than I care to, Inspector. We crossed swords, literally, a while back and I was lucky to come away with my life. Suffice it to say he's a rogue and will stop at little."

"And he has this," Mackenzie flipped open a small notebook. "This Elphberg Red." A thin smile split the narrow lips. "It must be a gae great bauble to stir up such interest."

Mrs. Hudson entered with a tray bearing coffee and biscuits. She placed them on the table, checked the fire and left without a word. Mackenzie watched her.

"A fine woman that," he said. "She kens when conversation is of value or not."

Watson raised an eyebrow. "She would surely be glad to know that," he said.

Mackenzie appeared not to hear. "And ye say yer man is in London? What makes ye sure of that, Mr. Rassendyll?"

"He is known to be in England, Inspector, and from what Dr. Watson has told me, the best receiver of stolen goods is in this city."

Mackenzie nodded slowly. "Aye, his name is Baird, a slippery customer and I've yet to feel his collar. He pretends to be in business as a money lender."

Watson spoke up. "I have set the Irregulars to keep a watch. Right now, they're headed by a cocky young lad named Wiggins."

"And what might these, er, Irregulars, do that London's finest cannot?"

Watson lit a cigarette. "Be invisible for a start, Inspector. They're not different than 10,000 other young ruffians, to look at. Baird won't even notice them. They go everywhere, see everything and overhear everyone."

Mackenzie seemed less than impressed. "And I suppose we then just wait till yer man Hentzau obligingly turns up wi' this bauble in his pocket?" He grunted his disbelief. "Ye'll wait a long time I'm thinking."

"Not if we drive him there," Rassendyll said.

"Ye'll have to find the man first."

Rassendyll laughed. "A man like Rupert won't skulk in dark corners, Inspector. He loves the good life, the theatre, gambling, women, horses, good food." He turned to Watson. "Half the Irregulars on Baird and half on Hentzau, and two guineas if they find him within 24 hours."

Raffles put his hand on Bunny Manders' shoulder and guided him to a corner table in the dining room. There was a twinkle in his eye that spoke of no good to come.

Manders felt his stomach lurch. It had been months since the affair at Milchester Abbey and Lady Melrose's necklace, and they'd made enough from that to take them through the rest of year without thought of further banditry. But a bored Raffles was a dangerous Raffles, ripe for any devilment.

"I have just bumped into young Crowley," he announced.

Manders suddenly found his appetite dwindling. Raffles sat back with that particular sleepy expression his friend mistrusted.

"Guess what he told me."

Manders' answer was somewhat stiff. "I am not a mind reader."

Raffles leaned forward quickly and conspiratorially. "He was at the opera last night and was just leaving after the second act when he bumped into a fellow he was damned sure was Prince Rupert of Hentzau, complete with a stunningly beautiful lady on his arm he recognized as Countess Cagliostro."

Manders relaxed. He had no idea who this Prince was and said so. Their fish came and with it a bottle of Montrachet. Raffles held forth on the news from the Test in Melbourne until it was served.

"Ruritania, Bunny. There was a coronation a few years ago rather marred by dark scandal. It seemed this Rupert had a hand in some plot to overthrow the king. All hushed up of course. And now he's in London."

"I fail to see what this has to do with us."

Raffles sighed. "Don't be so dense Bunny. If young Rupert is in London, then can skulduggery be far behind? And I mean to find out what." The sleepy expression returned. "Joséphine Balsamo, Countess Cagliostro, is also known to be a pretty successful thief and antagonist of Arsène Lupin, a Frenchman somewhat after my own heart."

Manders was determined not to take the dangled bait. "So a harum-scarum prince and a known thief are in London to take in the opera. Does this instantly make them suspect?"

Raffles drank some of his wine. "Instantly, Bunny, instantly. The charming prince has expensive tastes and is known to be notoriously hard up. *Ergo*, they are either here to acquire or to dispose of valuable items; most likely the latter."

Manders pushed the plate away. He waited, keenly aware he had not heard the last of the recalcitrant prince. He nevertheless fell into Raffles' trap.

"I imagine we will not be the only ones aware of this Hentzau."

Raffles gave another of his deceptive sleepy smiles. "Verily hast thou spoken, oh, Bunny. There could indeed be a positive cavalcade on his trail as we speak. It is therefore up to us, or rather me, to pip them at the post."

"I may disapprove, but I shall be in on this, Raffles."

Raffles shook his head firmly. "No, Bunny, old chap, this one's a solo affair. Prince Rupert has a reputation not to be trifled with and won't think twice about pistols and sword play."

"Dammit, this is England," Manders protested.

"And Hentzau has scant regard for the laws of any land."

"Then, why tell me anything if you do not mean me to help?"

Raffles laughed. "To see your face Bunny." He became serious. "And to know that you would still risk all if I asked."

The fat man with greasy ringlets and a stubborn growth of beard lowered his jeweller's loupe. He looked at his would-be client and shook his head.

"Not worth my while," he said, sucking yellow teeth. "This stone. It's too well known. It'll 'ave to be cut, and then it'll lose half its value." He pushed the pink diamond across the counter. He sighed massively and theatrically. "Tell you what, I'll take it off your 'ands as a good will gesture for," he cocked his head, waggling his hand from side to side, and mentioned a sum.

Rupert of Hentzau, dressed for the occasion in a wide-brimmed black felt hat, a cloak with the collar raised and a black scarf covering the lower part of his face, snatched the stone angrily. "You damned blackguard, it's worth ten times that. I've a good mind to..."

He carefully brought his temper under control. The fence, Baird, narrowed his eyes and replied softly in the accent of Bow Bells.

"Have me horsewhipped?" He jabbed a dirty finger with a blackened nail on the counter. "Do that, my Lord, and there's not a dealer in Europe will touch you. As for worth, well, it's worth what someone's prepared to offer. You won't get a better offer than mine."

Rupert took a deep breath. "Split the difference then and be damned."

Baird didn't answer, merely kept his bloodshot gaze fixed on the prince. It was a standoff, and for once Rupert of Hentzau knew he'd met his match. He stowed the diamond in his waistcoat pocket, swung and strode to the door and stopped, half out of the opening.

"You're a damned thief, Baird."

The cockney chuckled. "It takes one to recognize another, my Lord."

Rupert slammed the door and strode angrily into the night.

Rupert of Hentzau was in a foul mood. He stormed into the sitting room where Joséphine Balsamo reclined on a chaise, reading *Wuthering Heights*.

"One gathers matters did not go so well."

Rupert made a noisy show of pouring himself a brandy, banging the decanter and rattling glasses. "That thief Baird tried to rob me."

Joséphine laughed delightedly. "Such delicious irony. What will you do?"

"I've a mind to put a pistol to his head and take what I want."

"Not one of your better thought out schemes. He may steal from you, but threaten violence or steal from him and no fence in Europe will touch you."

Rupert drank brandy. "The blackguard threatened as much. Your suggestion?"

"Give him a night and day to think about it, then return and take what he offers. He knows the value and is greedy. It would be a coup for him."

Rupert rounded on her angrily. "A coup? The man's a grubby little Shylock."

Joséphine shrugged. "Even Shylock had a reputation to maintain."

Rupert laughed then shook his head in admiration. "Dammit, my dear, what would I do without you?"

"Very well, I imagine. Now bring me some champagne."

"Why wait 24 hours? The longer we delay, the more chance of being found out. Besides, London begins to bore me, and England is so wet and cold." He gave her champagne. "How does a palazzo in Venice sound?"

The Countess looked at him over the rim of her glass. "Who can possibly know we are here?"

"That damned old fool Sapt will know I have the stone."

Balsamo shrugged. "He can say nothing. Disclosure would be disastrous." She eyed him speculatively. "Would you announce it?"

Rupert did not answer. Instead he went back to the hypnotic flames as if to find an answer. Then he straightened and turned and smiled. "It would damned well serve them right. But Sapt won't stand still." He stopped as a thought hit like a lightning flash. "My God! I wonder if...?"

Joséphine lifted a fine eyebrow. Rupert shook his head. "Let us see if the old fool is such a fool after all."

Watson sat hunched disconsolately in his armchair. He growled. "It's at a time like this I wish Holmes were here."

There was a knock on the door and Mrs. Hudson came in. She handed a folded note to Rassendyll.

Rassendyll thanked her, read the note and passed it to Watson. "Speak of the Devil. It's from Holmes. How did he...?"

Watson scanned the paper, obviously torn from a pocket book, and shook his head. "I find it better not to ask: it is less puzzling that way. Blackheath. Hmm. There are many houses thereabouts, I wonder which one..."

Rassendyll smiled. "I imagine he wishes us to do something towards the solution, no matter how small." He glanced at the clock. "When do you expect news from young Wiggins?"

Mrs. Hudson reappeared to announce Mackenzie. The Inspector went to the fire, held out his long, bony hands to the blaze and sniffed inelegantly.

"This Hentzau fella is holed up in a big place on Blackheath," he said. "It was the place owned by Sir Osbert Geld, the banker ye ken, until the scandal sent him running for foreign parts." He turned to face the others when his news produced no effect. "Someone's beaten me to the punch I gather."

Watson held out the note. "The Master has spoken. A mere snippet gleaned from God knows where."

"Aye, well, he has the right of it." His hands warmed he stuck them under his coattails and put his back to the flames. "It seems to me, sirs, that ye have the makings of rendering Scotland Yard superfluous with yer knowledge."

"Not a bit of it, Mackenzie," Rassendyll said firmly. "There's likely to be desperate work afoot and the assistance of officialdom will be most necessary."

Mackenzie seemed a trifle mollified but his demeanour lacked conviction.

"So what's to be done?" Watson asked.

At that moment, Wiggins came in, flowed by a flustered Mrs. Hudson in a vain attempt to preserve decorum. At Watson's frown, the boy pulled himself to attention.

"We found 'im, sir," Wiggins announced. "'E's got this posh place up on Blackheath. There's this lady with 'im. Good looker she is an' all."

Watson's frown deepened. "That's enough of that, boy. Just the facts, they're all Mr. Rassendyll and I require."

Wiggins tried to look suitably chastened but failed miserably. "We 'ung about all day, sir, an' all evening, an' perishin' cold it were too, and I ain't 'ad no supper nor no breakfast. Then late last night 'e went out and straight to Baird's." The boy hooked his thumbs in his vest in a cocky gesture. "Stands to reason don't it. I mean, Baird's the biggest fence."

Mackenzie rubbed his hands together. He gave Mrs. Hudson and imploring look. "I suppose there's nae chance of a cup of tea, Madame?"

Mrs. Hudson nodded, scooped the breakfast dishes from the table and disappeared, a woman with a mission.

Wiggins' confidence had slipped a notch as he looked apprehensively at Rassendyll, who raised an eyebrow. "That is all?" he said.

"Well, he came outa Baird's place with a face like a box of frogs. Right put out 'e was, sir, or so it seemed. He shouted something but I couldn't catch the drift."

"Sounds like Rupert can't get his price."

Watson looked alarmed. "Dash it all, Rassendyll, then he may go elsewhere."

Mackenzie shook his head. "Nae, Doctor. He'll be back. He'll be greedy and a bird in the hand, ye ken?"

Rassendyll put his hand in his pocket and took out a gold sovereign. He gave it to Wiggins and very deliberately placed the other on the mantelpiece.

"Insurance, young man. The other is yours when the job is done."

"What else, sir?" It was hard to tell if the lad was put out or eager.

"You are our eyes on this man. The denouement will be soon, but until that time, I want an hour by hour report on his movements. Use the others as runners, but you stay put. If you lose him..."

The inference was not lost on the young man. He grabbed his prize and scuttled from the room. There was an exasperated shout from Mrs. Hudson as his boots thudded down the stairs and the door slammed.

Rassendyll smiled. "Now, gentlemen, we need a plan of action. Rupert obviously still has the stone. The Irregulars will keep us posted. I suggest if nothing unforeseen occurs, we make our play tonight."

"Why so soon?" Watson asked.

"The forecast is for half a gale with rain to match. We could break in with sledge hammers and crowbars with no one the wiser." Rassendyll looked out of the window onto the rain-sodden street below. "Can you be back at dusk, Inspector?"

"Aye. And I'll bring reinforcements."

Rassendyll objected. "Inspector, much as I admire the London Bobbie, we need as few feet clumping around as possible. Hentzau is no fool, and if I were he, I'd be keeping my weather eye open. He knows time is not on his side."

After the Inspector had left, Watson said, "I still wish Holmes were in on this."

Rassendyll turned. "This calls for brute strength, Doctor, not brains. Though I feel, between us, we have enough of that commodity. Rupert still has the stone, and it is safe to assume it is in the house. Our task is simple: to enter, demand the return of the stone and leave."

Watson did not appear convinced. "You make it sound so simple."

Rassendyll smiled. "Surely not difficult for a man who has been through the Second Afghan War?"

Watson opened his mouth then closed it and shook his head. "You're as bad as Holmes. But I was an army medico, not a soldier."

"And carried a revolver. Incidentally, bring it tonight. Rupert can play rough and I don't imagine he'll hand his prize over without objection."

"Dash it all, Raffles, you can't keep me out of this you know."

Raffles shook his head. "Don't you see, Bunny, rogue Rupert of Hentzau may be, but he's still from one of Europe's royal families. There's nothing to stop him holding us at gun point for the police to take off in irons. And who do you think a judge is going to believe: us or a prince of royal blood?"

"But he'd be caught with the stuff," Manders protested.

"It would disappear, Bunny, and things like jewels don't take much hiding, and no amount of protest on our part would bring them to light." He threw his Sullivan into the grate and lit another. "No, Bunny. We'd be detained at Her Majesty's pleasure in durance vile until we were both old men."

"Then, for God's sake, why risk it, Raffles?"

Raffles was suddenly serious. "I have a feeling there's more to this than just a few baubles. Rupert may be a rogue, but he's not small minded. Master Hentzau plays for big stakes, and I mean to find out what they are."

Rassendyll parted the curtains that looked out onto Baker Street. Wind-driven rain washed across the yellow gaslight of the street lamps, and on the far side, sheltering in a doorway, he saw the huddled form of one of the Irregulars.

"Holmes must be a hard task master if his lads are out on a night like this."

Watson knocked the dottle from his pipe and started to refill it. "Not Holmes: Wiggins. He'll have put the fear of death in them."

"Speaking of whom, it would seem that Rupert hasn't moved."

Watson struck a match. "Probably has more sense. This isn't weather for a dog, let alone man." He lit the pipe and glanced at the clock. "Baird will have shut up shop anyway."

Rassendyll took a cigarette from the box on the mantel. "If I were a thief this kind of weather would be Heaven-sent. Think of all the miserable Bobbies lurking in doorways instead of keeping an eye open."

A growl came from the doorway. "They better nae be if they want to keep their positions. And they ken the ways of the thieves as well as you seem to, Mr. Rassendyll."

Rassendyll greeted Mackenzie warmly. "Your arrival is well-timed, Inspector. In another hour, we shall set out of our adventure, meanwhile Watson has insisted on a toddy to keep the night chills at bay, a provision with which I am heartily in agreement."

Mackenzie as ever felt the need for the fire to chase the cold from his lean, gaunt frame. "Could ye nae have ordered a better night for this—what did ye call it—adventure?"

Rassendyll chuckled. "It couldn't be better if I had ordered it. You could drive a coach and four into the driveway at Blackheath and not raise an alarm."

Mackenzie grunted. "Better not to think of it as an adventure. If this man Hentzau is as bold as ye seem to think, then he's not likely to take our attention lightly."

"Exactly. And that's what makes it an adventure."

"I think Mr. Holmes would not share your opinion, Mr. Rassendyll. He kens well that the criminal class can be dangerous when cornered."

Rassendyll smiled. "That's the difference, Inspector. Hentzau is not of the criminal class; he merely behaves that way when it suits by disregarding the law as being an impediment."

"I suppose that's because the man's a gentleman," Watson said drily.

Mackenzie was not impressed. "It's my opinion that when a gentleman goes bad, he's the worst kind of criminal: ruthless and cold-blooded."

Rassendyll laughed. "But at least, he's polite about it."

Watson fed bullets into his revolver and snapped it shut. He gave Rassendyll an inquiring look. "You are unarmed?"

"Never had the need for one in England, Doctor."

"Then let us hope this adventure doesn't end up in gun play."

Mackenzie was not impressed. "If it does and ends in a death, then someone'll answer for it at the end of a rope."

Rassendyll shrugged on his ulster. "Gentlemen, we are to reclaim a jewel for lady. Whatever has been said, I doubt Rupert will descend to shooting."

Watson pocketed his revolver. "I shall go and engage a hansom." And with that announcement he left.

Mackenzie put on his greatcoat. "A fine man, the doctor. A wee bit unimaginative, ye ken, but ye couldna find a better man if the situation gets a mite rough."

"Then let us follow him."

Mackenzie strode to the door. "As a great man himself is won't to say, the game's afoot."

Within a short time, they had crossed the river at London Bridge and were heading at speed along the south bank. Deptford passed and, shortly thereafter, the great Observatory at Greenwich. At that point, the city thinned and they were into a sprawling suburban tracts of new villas and unmade roads with the driver slowing to a walk as he sought to find his way without the aid of streetlights.

Finally, Mackenzie gave a short bark of triumph and called to the driver to stop.

"We're close, gentlemen," he said. "It's shanks' mare from here on."

Watson checked his revolver for the tenth time since leaving Baker Street and lit a lantern, in the light of which Mackenzie studied a street map.

"Ah, there it is, Lucknow Lane."

Watson grunted. "Let's hope it is misnamed by association and this does not turn into a siege."

Mackenzie folded the map and stuffed it in his coat pocket. He pointed. "Half a mile that way, gentlemen, and we shall find out the truth of it."

"Still, the name has unfortunate connotations," Watson said.

Mackenzie refused to be impressed. "I'm a cynic. Seen too much of life. Are ye a cynic, Mr. Rassendyll?"

"Not a bit of it, Inspector. Life may bowl us a corker once in a while, but there's always another innings."

"Until there isn't."

"And then, I dare say I shan't much care. What d'you say Doctor?"

"If you're looking for information on the afterlife, you've come to the wrong man. Try one of those damned theosophists."

Wind lashed the trees that lined the roads and the rain, having earlier been no more than an annoyance began to come down in earnest. Rassendyll pulled up the collar of his Ulster and remarked cheerfully that it was perfect.

And then, Mackenzie, who had been leading, stopped, holding up his hand for silence. "Better douse the glim Doctor," he growled, pointing to a large house looming through the darkness and rain.

Rassendyll took a binocular from an inside pocket and focussed it on the one lighted window. Watson stood at his side. "Anything?" he asked in a hoarse whisper.

Rassendyll shook his head and then gave an exclamation. "Yes. There. And there it is again."

Mackenzie shook the water from his bowler and wiped his face with a large handkerchief. "What?"

"The silhouette of a woman, Inspector. And there she goes again. Let us keep going."

The last 200 yards were through a mere tunnel of trees starkly eerie in their winter drab. Rassendyll stopped abruptly and gripped Watson's arm. "Did you hear that?"

"In this weather? You think we are followed?"

Rassendyll shrugged. "In this part, at night, who knows what is abroad."

They crossed a bridge and a while later came to the back of a garden.

"This is the one," Mackenzie said.

There was a garden gate that gave onto a lawn. There was still just the one light to be seen.

"At least we know someone is at home," Watson said.

Mackenzie eased open the gate with the care of a housebreaker, although a kick from a mule would not have been heard, and the three made their way across the lawn until they stood in the poor shelter of what appeared to be a gardener's shed.

The Inspector teetered on his heels. "Yon looks a gae easy crib te crack, Mr. Rassendyll. But o'course, it's breaking and entering and I'm a police officer."

Watson reminded him the reason for their being there in the middle of a filthy night and that he had reasonable grounds as they believed an international jewel thief lived there and had stolen goods with him.

Mackenzie chuckled. "Aye, Doctor, I was but having a moment's fun. We'll need to spread out to find a way in. You, Doctor, take the left and I'll go right. Mr. Rassendyll, as ye saw the lady, maybe ye can find a way to her boudoir. We'll meet back here in…" He glanced at his watch, "…ten minutes."

The three men moved out of the shelter of the shed eaves. Rassendyll ran lightly across the open space, paused for a second in the lee of a lilac bush, then made for the back wall. He looked up and realized the climb would be easy, with little risk as there was a scullery roof with access from a rain barrel, and then some very convenient pipes that must run from a bathroom. The problem would be to open a window without making the most unholy row. And the woman was upstairs, doubtless about her toilet. He prowled a little more then returned to the rendezvous. Watson was before him and, a moment later, Inspector Mackenzie slid out of the darkness.

"Anything, Mr. Rassendyll?" he said, again removing his bowler and wiping his face.

"An easy climb, but I'm afraid of noise."

"Doctor?"

"There's a cellar window ajar. I doubt I could make my way through, but you're a wiry chap, Mackenzie. You'll slip through like a ferret and can open a back door."

"What about the front?" Rassendyll asked. "If we flush them from the back, they could make a dash for it."

"Aye, they could," Mackenzie said, "and run into the arms of my men. Besides, the horses are stabled."

Watson frowned. "I thought we agreed this was to be a three-man show."

Mackenzie shook his head. "Did ye seriously think I'd go in with a pair of amateurs—begging your pardon, Doctor—when this is police work?"

Rassendyll grasped his arm. "They must stay out of sight, Mackenzie; this, I insist on. Hentzau may open up to us as he's a braggart, but flood the house with bobbies and he'll imitate the clam."

"Dinna ye worry. They have their orders. If the birds are flushed they'll nab them, but nothing else unless I call." He held up a silver whistle. "This will bring them running."

The silhouette passed the lighted window again. "I wonder who the lady is?" Watson mused.

Mackenzie grunted. "Probably some doxie." Then he became businesslike. "Doctor, do ye help me through that window, and do ye take yer post agin the back door yonder Mr. Rassendyll."

It was a night to be snug before a fire, with one's feet on the fender, a glass of whiskey and a good book; not contemplating housebreaking and a possible dangerous confrontation to boot. But whatever the others may have felt, Rassendyll relished the near future: his avowed intention being to return the stolen gem to its rightful owner. True, the Elphberg Red did not in fact belong to the Queen, but in his mind, she was true ruler of Ruritania, as she was indeed the queen of his heart, and therefore any deed done was for her alone.

It was as these thoughts and emotions chased through his mind and heart that the heard the bolts shot in the door and, a moment later, it opened to reveal the lean, saturnine features of the Scotland Yard Inspector. Mackenzie beckoned him in.

"So far, all's well."

Rassendyll and Watson followed Mackenzie along a flagstoned passage into a large, well-equipped kitchen. Watson gestured with the barrel of his revolver to a white painted door. "That must be the way into the main house," he whispered. "I wonder what the layout is."

Mackenzie answered. "The front will house the reception rooms and there will be other doors to the dining room, a library or study, a family sitting room and a breakfast room. There will of course be an imposing staircase." From the tone of the inspector's voice, it was apparent he had little time for what was popularly described as the *nouveau riche*.

Rassendyll cut in. "There will be an upstairs sitting room. I expect to find Rupert there if he has a lady with him."

"Then that must be our target," Watson said firmly.

Mackenzie imposed a restraining and experienced hand on the doctor's eagerness. "Not so fast. We must hae a plan or we'll find the birds flown." He frowned fearsomely in a way that no doubt struck fear into his subordinates. "First, we shall ascertain that the ground floor is unoccupied."

"There'll be lights under the doors." Rassendyll said.

"Aye. Unless yer man has already tumbled to us."

Rassendyll smiled. "You couldn't hear a brass band above this storm."

"That's as maybe, but many an enterprise has failed because of carelessness. Doctor, do ye check the front rooms while Mr. Rassendyll covers the others. Meantime, I shall start for the upstairs and try to get the layout. Do ye then join me, and no matter what ye may think, silence is the watchword."

It was as Rassendyll had said, and, within five minutes, all three were on the upstairs landing. Mackenzie pointed along the corridor to a door under which a strip of light showed.

As silently as burglars, they crept towards the light, Watson and Rassendyll standing at the ready on each side of the door, Mackenzie grasped the brass handle, twisted hard, threw the door open, and all charged in.

The room was empty.

Watson swore. Rassendyll swore. Mackenzie scowled horribly, but forbore to swear on account of his strict Calvinist upbringing.

Evidence of the room's recent occupancy was shown by the electric light still on, two half-full champagne glasses on a small table and a cheroot in glass ashtray from which arose a thin spiral of smoke. Mackenzie held up his hand in a peremptory command to halt. Rassendyll, who was at his elbow said, "Damn it, we've been..."

"Caught like rats in a trap."

The voice, languid and drawling, came from the far corner where a Chinese screen had been placed. The three men started and turned. Rupert of Hentzau emerged with a revolver in either hand. He jerked one meaningfully.

"Doctor Watson, is it? Please do not be so foolish as to try to attempt to fire your weapon, but rather place it on the floor and kick it to me. As you can see, you are outgunned, and I am a very good shot."

Watson, who had not survived an Afghan War without knowing there were times when a strategic withdrawal was the sensible option, did as he was told. At that point, Joséphine Balsamo also appeared, and in her hand was a revolver, smaller and more ornate, having a pearl handle, but deadly nonetheless. She motioned to Mackenzie.

"The chair by the fire, if you please."

The Inspector's face was a mask. "How did ye..?"

The Countess shrugged. "A small bell connected to the kitchen door. Simple, yet effective."

Mackenzie was crestfallen. "Caught like a damned..."

"Amateur? I agree." Rupert said and sauntered forward. He stuck one revolver into his waistband and retrieved his cheroot. He took a pleasurable draw, inspected the glowing end and smiled at Rassendyll.

"My God! It's the play actor. You gave me the Devil of a lot of trouble last time; not going to do it again are you?"

"Not if you return a certain lady's property."

"And which lady would that be, and what property?"

"Rupert, the jig, as they say is up. I know you have the Elphberg Red."

"Then you know a lot more than I." He turned to Joséphine. "By the way, may I introduce Joséphine Balasamo, Countess Cagliostro. My dear, this is Rudolf Rassendyll who is by way of being a thorn in my side, again."

Rassendyll acknowledged her with a slight bow. "You have fallen into bad company, Countess."

"So how did you know?" Rupert asked.

"That you had stolen the Elphberg Red?" Rassendyll shrugged. "Sapt, of course."

Rupert barked a short laugh. "Maybe the old fool isn't such an old fool after all."

"Just out of interest, where have you been since the debacle at Zenda?"

"Took a change of scenery for my health. Sapt made Strelsau a little warmish for me." He took another draw on his cheroot, his eyes fixed on Rassendyll. "I heartily recommend Rome."

There was some heat in Rassendyll's reply. "Pity I didn't finish you the first time." He took a step but stopped quickly as Rupert raised his revolver and shook his head in warning. "Just how did you get the stone? And it's useless to deny you have it."

Rupert shrugged good-naturedly. "Oh, well, as you said, the jig is up I suppose. Yes, I have the damned stone."

"Which I intend to return to its owner."

"Ah, the fair Flavia. Pity about that; you'd have made a lovely couple; much better than that feeble object she's saddled with."

"How did you do it?"

"Get the stone? Well, would you believe I was passing the jewel room on my way to see Rudolf with a view to squeezing him for some of the ready, and there it was, just begging to be removed. There wasn't a guard in sight. You know me, play actor, always ready to oblige. So I popped it in my pocket and by the time the thing was missed, I was across the frontier."

"You'll never get it out of this country, and no fence, not even Baird—oh yes, we know about your abortive trip to see that gentleman—will touch you now, not with Scotland Yard in close attendance."

Rupert eyed Rassendyll speculatively as he stroked the barrel of his revolver. Then, with a laugh, he spun it like a western American frontier gunfighter.

"I'll take that chance when it comes. Very well, play actor, but you're going to have to fight me for it. If you win, I'll hand it over calm as you please but, if I win, your two dogs must stand aside."

Watson growled. "Not a chance of that, you rogue."

Rupert ignored the outburst. "Do we have a bargain, play actor?" He pointed to the pair of rapiers on the wall above the mantel.

Rassendyll frowned. "This is London, Rupert, not Zenda."

"Hang the geography, Rassendyll. We have a history, you and I, and it must end one way or the other tonight."

Rassendyll's face was a mask with no emotion showing. And then, with a quick nod, he said, "Very well."

"And you'll call off the dogs?"

Rassendyll turned to Watson and Mackenzie. "Even this game has rules, gentlemen, and I look to you to abide by them."

"Yer a damned fool man," Mackenzie cried out. "If a crime is committed, I canna ignore it."

"No crime, Inspector. A fair fight is all, and none to be the wiser unless you tell."

Watson cut in. "I agree with the Inspector; you're a damned fool, Rassendyll."

Rassendyll's eyes narrowed. "Do I have your word?"

Watson nodded. "My word on it."

"And yours, Inspector?"

Mackenzie looked surly as a dog from which a meat bone has been stolen. But he, too, nodded, though with obvious reluctance. "Aye. My word."

Rassendyll turned to Rupert. "Then it would seem we have an agreement. Is it to be a gentleman's duel or a free for all?"

Rupert smiled. "A free for all, of course. Definitely a free for all. But we'd better clear the room because I still can't get used to this fighting with furniture"

Rassendyll shook his head. "Free for all, remember."

Rupert shrugged, strode to the fireplace, took down the rapiers and unceremoniously tossed one, point first. Rassendyll dodged as the sword missed him by a hair and stuck, quivering into the back of a chair. He wrenched it out and made a mocking *en garde* salute.

For a few moments, they circled like dogs, wary of one another. Rupert swished his blade with a viscous hiss. "Not quite as much room as at Zenda."

"At least, you don't have a moat to swim."

"Damn it, Englishman, you've interfered for the last time." And with that, Rupert made the opening lunge.

As a fight, it lacked finesse, for the rapier lends itself to a style of swordplay more robust and vigorous than the épée. Rassendyll and Rupert of Hentzau were both first class blades, but they were not engaged in a duel for sport, but a fight they both knew could very well end in serious injury or even death.

Blade slashed upon blade, the ring of steel harsh as each man sought to break through the other's defence. But neither gave an inch, both evenly matched and familiar with each other's ability as a result of their duel some years earlier.

Rupert skirted behind a chair, grabbed the back and hurled it at Rassendyll, who dodged and sent it smashing against the wall near the Countess.

"Have a care," he said. "You might hurt the lady."

Rupert lunged by way of an answer and the point of his sword nicked Rassendyll's left arm, which instantly sported a splash of blood. Rupert grinned triumphantly.

"The first cut won't hurt at all; the second only makes you wonder..."

Rassendyll slammed home an attack that surprised his opponent with its violence, forcing him to leap onto a table to escape the slashing blade. Rassendyll aimed at cut at Rupert's legs but he jumped then leapt from the table to a couch, vaulted the back and stood panting.

"...what the last will feel like. Tell me, play actor, do you feel the blade as it slips between your ribs?"

Rassendyll advanced into the center of the room, his sword point circling as he sought his target.

"You'll be able to tell me, Hentzau. What would you like as an epitaph?"

Hentzau came from behind the couch. "Something heroic, but the time's not yet ripe."

There was an attack, an engagement, Rassendyll was insistent, forcing Rupert back, but he recovered quickly.

"Well, well," he said, a flush of effort on his face, "you've been practicing since we last met."

They attacked simultaneously. The blades clashed, slid and the hilts locked as it became a contest of strength and not skill. Inexorably, Rassendyll pushed Rupert back until his knees found the couch. Across the room, the Countess raised her revolver. Watson saw her and gathered himself to charge, when there was a crash and the distinctive sound of breaking glass.

"What was that?" Rupert said between gritted teeth.

"The storm breaking a window," Rassendyll snarled.

With a supreme effort, Rupert threw Rassendyll away, leaped the couch and stood, listening, his hand up.

"Dammit, but I don't think so. Joséphine, check the safe, now."

The words were hardly out of this mouth when the Countess had run from the room. Rassendyll approached the couch, his blade pointing in extension. "If this is one of your tricks, I swear..."

Rupert threw down his rapier and raised his hands. "No tricks, play actor."

Mackenzie made a dash for the table and scooped up Rupert's revolvers, while Watson recovered his. Rupert watched helplessly, shrugged and reached for the box of cheroots on the mantel. He lit one with a taper from the fire and calmly blew a stream of smoke.

"Round one to you, play actor," he said.

Rassendyll disagreed. "A knock out, Hentzau."

There was a cry of rage, a slammed drawer, the sound of angry feet and then the Countess stormed back into the room.

"We've been robbed, Rupert! The stone is gone!"

Mackenzie was onto the news quick as a flash. "I dinna believe ye. Show me where the bauble was."

The Countess glanced at Rupert. He shrugged and drew on his cheroot again. "Dammit Rassendyll, but I've a nasty feeling we've been had."

A minute later, Mackenzie returned. He held a scrap of paper. It was an anonymous note to the effect that the Elphberg Red would be restored to its rightful owner.

Mackenzie frowned in puzzlement, then his brow cleared and, for the first time, a thin smile creased his lean face and he gave a wheezy chuckle.

"My God. Played with a straight bat. What an innings. And I was clean bowled for a duck." A second later, the humor had been replaced with determined intent. He took a set of handcuffs from his coat pocket and gestured at Rupert. "It will save a deal of bother if ye'll come quietly."

"On what charge, Inspector?"

Mackenzie stopped. "Why, robbery of course."

Rupert raised one eyebrow. "Of what?"

"That jewel, what d'ye call it, the Elphberg Red."

More smoke plumed into the room. Rupert was all cool assurance. "Show it to me and I'll come quietly as you wish."

Rassendyll placed his rapier on the table and helped himself to a glass of champagne. "Much as I hate to agree with an irredeemable blackguard, he has a point, Inspector. Just where is the aforementioned item?"

Rupert smiled broadly, savouring the moment. "Then, where's the crime?"

"I damned well know ye did it," Mackenzie persisted. "What say ye, Mr. Rassendyll?"

Rassendyll shook his head. "Knowing's one thing, Mackenzie, proving it another. I regret it, but no judge would give us court time on this one. And after all, he is a Prince of a royal house."

Mackenzie was justifiably furious. He pointed a lean finger at the Countess who had recovered her humor and managed a sneering chuckle.

"I know of ye and yer reputation," Mackenzie growled. "Ye're a thief, Countess." He spun to face Rupert. "And ye, sir, strike me as worse, for there are few things worse than a traitor. But as Mr. Rassendyll has been good enough to point out," and there, Mackenzie's tone took on an edge of sarcasm, "ye have committed no provable crime in this country so far and I must let ye go. But I warn ye both; think long and hard before ye consider gracing our shores again."

"Better consider mending your ways, Hentzau," Rassendyll advised.

"No, play actor. I lapsed into virtue for too long and wound up damned hard up. Probably have done something rash if it hadn't been for Joséphine."

"You don't call the theft of royal gems rash?"

"Hardly. Who was going to tell, the delectable Flavia or that pathetic king?" he grinned. "You missed out there. Think what we could have done as a team with the country ours. Dash it all, Rassendyll, a rogue can no more change his nature than a leopard his spots. Conscience and I have irrevocably parted; the divorce is absolute."

"Then, stay out of England if you know what's good for you, or Mackenzie here will have you in irons."

Rupert's mouth curled dismally. "I imagine the same goes for Ruritania. Pity, I had visions of returning like the prodigal son."

Watson cut in. "Australia has a better climate, or America might appreciate a man of your talents: you could try for politics."

The three men returned to Baker Street. Rassendyll was very low in spirits, not at all helped by the misery of a gale-blasted night, because he saw himself as having failed in his promise. But more than that, he believed he had failed the Queen. The others tried to cheer him up in that at least the stone had been taken by an 'honest' thief who had declared his intent to return it and so the Elphberg line was safe.

Rassendyll was only partially satisfied. "And if not, what of the legend?"

Mackenzie was his usual pragmatic self. "A stone is a stone, whether it be big, small, a jewel or a pebble on the shore. It has no life and canna affect our destinies a whit."

"What was that humor you found in a straight bat?"

Mackenzie brightened somewhat and a smile creased his face. "Yon princeling may deny he has the gem, but I've a shrewd suspicion who has."

Rassendyll's mood jumped a notch. "The arrest him, man, arrest him."

Mackenzie shook his head. "As ye said yerself, knowing's one thing, proof another; and proof may be a long time coming."

A few days later on the other side of Europe, Colonel Sapt entered the Queen's drawing room to inform her that the British Ambassador, Sir Edward Lytton, begged an audience on a matter of importance. The Queen inclined her head in acknowledgement, and, a moment later, the ambassador, looking somewhat uncomfortable, entered carrying a finely crafted wooden box. He bowed and presented it to the Queen.

She opened it. It contained one perfect blush pink rose.

Sir Edward cleared his throat. "A rose for a rose, Your Majesty," he said in a gruff voice that plainly said he thought the whole thing damned nonsense.

The Queen inhaled the scent "It's beautiful. What is it called?"

Sir Edward cleared his throat again and it seemed his collar had grown too tight for he flushed to match the flower. "I believe it is The Pink Panther, Your Majesty."

The Queen gave an exclamation of surprise, for under the rose, nestled on a soft cushion of pure white silk lay the stolen diamond.

"How came you by it, Sir Edward?" the Queen asked in a soft voice.

"Fella gave it to me Your Majesty. He wouldn't give me his name, but I never forget a face. Dash me if I didn't think it was a chap named Raffles. Sure I've seen him at Lords, playing cricket don't you know. Devilish cunning slow spinner. A useful bat as well."

And with that Sapt tactfully eased Sir Edward towards the door. The ambassador continued in a monologue.

"Can't understand what all the fuss is about, it's only a stone." Sapt asked him what he preferred and he said thoroughbreds, though his young grandson Charles was showing an uncommon interest in his mother's baubles, which he sincerely hoped was a child's passing fancy.

The Queen watched them fondly. She thought that men such as they might not pass her way again.

Then she looked at a photo in a silver frame. It was of a man who could have been the king. It was signed "Rudolf."

Flash fiction—short-short stories—have always been welcome in Tales of the Shadowmen. *Matthew Dennion, who previously contributed untold tales of Judex and the Nyctalope, now focuses on the character of the deadly Madame Atomos, whose saga is currently being translated and published by Black Coat Press. In this vignette, the indomitable Japanese comes face to face with another nightmare created by the Atom...*

Matthew Dennion: *The Most Dreadful Monster*

Los Alamos, 1963

A single ray of sunlight cast a small modicum of illumination in the dark abandoned bunker. Madame Atomos sat in one of the two chairs in the former shelter as she awaited the delivery of the "package." She smiled as she mused how this location was the official birth place of the weapon that had ravaged her country and propelled her towards her destiny. The damage the Americans had wrought on Japan with their atomic bombs was unbelievable—and unforgivable.

The explosions themselves had killed tens of thousands, but the blast was only the first stage of the death the Americans had wrought on her homeland. The next two stages were by far the worst. The people who had died initially were the lucky ones; those just outside the blast range had died a slow, painful death from radiation burns and poisoning. Their bodies betrayed them and decayed like some form of advanced leprosy as their inside tore themselves apart. Yet, even these people were fortunate compared to the people who suffered under the third consequence of the nuclear attacks; the rise of the *daikajiu.*

Atomic mutant beasts had awakened, changed by the radioactive fallout, and ravaged Japan for years. Madame Atomos had watched as Gojira, Rodan, and beast after beast rose from the bottom of the sea and the bowels of the Earth to prolong the effects of the Americans attack. Her fury continued to build as she recalled these events. She stood and shouted: "The *Dakaiju* are not the most terrible monsters created by radiations; I, Madame Atomos, am the most terrible monster born of the nuclear fire, and soon, I shall bring pain and suffering onto America far beyond that of any monster!"

Outside the bunker, she could hear the sound of a car screeching to a halt. A door was pulled open as one her men shouted orders. She composed herself, as she realized her guest had arrived. The door flew open and several of her henchmen dragged a man into the room. He had a black sack over his head and was still in his pajamas.

Madame Atomos addressed her followers: "The extraction went as planned? He is unharmed?"

"Yes, Madame, we broke into his house at night, and drugged him in his sleep. He should be starting to regain his senses soon."

"Good work. Tie him to the chair and remove the blindfold. I will deal with him personally."

Today was the day that she would use the weapons of America's past to destroy one of them and the weapons of its future to destroy them all.

The man was tied to a chair and the bag removed from his head. He was tall and thin, with brown hair and eyes. His head lolled from side to as he regained consciousness.

"Good morning, doctor," said Madame Atomos. "You may be wondering where you are, what has happened to you, and why you are here." She slowly walked up to the man and looked down into his eyes. Then, raising her hand, she slapped him across the face. "To answer the first question, we are at the testing grounds for the first atomic weapon. I chose this place as it holds significance to both of us on several levels. This is the spot where your country, and, more specifically, scientists like you, created the tools that have brought much suffering on my county and my people. On a personal level, in a sense, this is where my life truly began—and yours will end."

The scientist mumbled something, but Madame Atomos slapped him again in response.

"Vermin! You will speak when I give you permission to speak! Anyway, I doubt the sedative you were given has yet worn off to the extent of allowing you to speak." Her voice softened. "To answer the second question, my followers have drugged you and brought here so that you may decide how quickly you will die for your sins. You see, doctor, there is still enough radiation in this area to cause a human to become afflicted with radiation poisoning. My men and I are immune to these effects. You, however, are not so fortunate."

The doctor mumbled something slightly louder than his previous attempt at speech, for which he was struck again.

"Swine! You will learn to speak only when I command you." Another slap quickly came snapping the man's head to the side. As to why you were brought here, the answer is simple. You have created a new weapon far more deadly than the hydrogen bomb. As such, I hold you just as responsible for the destruction of my homeland as I do those who created the H-bomb. By now, your body is starting to take in all of the radiation that is still floating in the air. Your choice is simple: divulge the secrets of your weapon to me and we will kill you quickly, or remain silent and strapped in that chair until the radiation slowly corrodes your body from the inside out."

Madame Atomos laughed as she walked around the man. She grabbed him by the collar, her eyes filled with rage, and slapped him again with each word she spoke: "DO I MAKE MYSELF CLEAR, DOCTOR?"

She straightened her posture and lowered her voice "Now what do you have to say to my proposition?"

The doctor took a deep breath and slowly raised his head, panting as he spoke. Madame Atomos saw his eyes flash green. Inside them was a rage in them that far exceeded even her own.

"Don't make me angry," growled Bruce Banner. "You wouldn't like me when I'm angry."

Madame Atomos realized at last she was not the most dreadful monster born of radiation.

In his contribution to our two previous volumes, "Is He in Hell?" and "Nadine's Invitation", Win Scott Eckert has begun to tell stories centered on the fateful meeting at Wold Newton (or Would Newton as it was spelled then) as conceptualized by Philip José Farmer and his followers in general, and Sir Percy Blakeney and his family in particular. This latest installment takes place after the fall of the meteorite and sets in motion a new series of dramatic events yet to come...

Win Scott Eckert: *Marguerite's Tears*

Blakeney Manor, Richmond, 1798

It's hard to believe Marguerite is dead."

Violet Holmes' voice came through the door separating their chambers, and Siger Holmes, not for the first time, cursed propriety. It was dammed inconvenient—bordering on ludicrous—to conduct a conversation with one's wife through a closed door.

"Yes, my dear," Siger replied. "And yet, Lady Blakeney had been in slow decline ever since that winter at Sir Percy's place up in Would Newton."

"You blame yourself."

"Of course. I am to blame. I am—was—her physician after all."

"Sir Percy does not hold you responsible," Violet said gently. "There was nothing you could do."

"I am not entirely certain that's the case," Siger said.

"Well, I am. You know that Marguerite began to wane soon after that strange rock from the sky came down near our carriages. I've often wondered if there was a connection with the rock's blazing light and heat. Perhaps we should not have alighted to examine it so closely."

"And yet, no one else seems to have suffered," Siger replied. "In fact, with the exception of poor Marguerite, we are all the picture of health, you included."

"That is true," Violet conceded. "And even Marguerite delivered healthy twin boys shortly thereafter."

"Indeed. And a baby girl for Sir Percy the year after that." The infant, Violet Yvonne, was named after Siger's wife. "All this despite the fact that she appeared to waste away more and more each year. No, my dear, I find it impossible to believe this rock conferred any deleterious effects upon those of us exposed to it. I and the others have discussed this at length—"

"The others?" she interrupted. "You mean, the men. You rarely discuss it with us women."

Siger's impatience got the best of him. "Would you be averse to opening the door in order to facilitate this conversation?"

"Siger! You know that's impossible. We are guests here. The servants—"

"Surely the servants' discretion is above reproach. Sir Percy's personal arrangements are hardly conventional—he and Marguerite and your sister Alice are, or were, inseparable—and yet, he has managed to avoid the scandal which you so evidently dread. It logically follows that the servants are unwaveringly loyal, or extraordinarily well paid to keep their silence, or both."

"You and your logic..."

"Indeed. My logic. You cannot be heard, on the one hand, to defend the propriety of separate bedchambers for husband and wife, imposed upon us by Society, and on the other hand, to decry Society's rules of conduct governing what is discussed in so-called 'polite company.'"

Siger heard Violet laugh softly through the door. It was a familiar argument, and not one carried out in a spiteful manner.

"No, my love," she said, "you cannot distract me with sensibility. I'll stay in my own chambers tonight."

"Good night, then, my dear. Do not be alarmed at the pipe smoke under the door. I am afraid sleep shall elude me for some time to come."

"That wretched pipe."

"Yes, yes, Sir Percy teases me as well for my plebeian habits, but nonetheless, it is to be the pipe. The *haute ton's* snuff holds no sway over me."

With that, Violet retired to her bed. And Siger Holmes paced his chambers like a caged tiger, filling the room with a dense blue smoke.

Earlier that evening, Siger Holmes had paced in a similar fashion. It was a habit for which Sir Percy Blakeney regularly chided him, filled with mock worry that his friend would wear an irreparable path in his expensive Persian carpet.

Not tonight.

Sir Percy hadn't the energy, nor the inclination. He had cheated death, laughed at it cavalierly, as the Scarlet Pimpernel.

And now Death had caught up with him, taken his beloved Marguerite.

"Who will be at the service?" Siger asked.

Sir Percy didn't respond, but waved a handkerchief listlessly in Fitzwilliam Darcy's general direction. Percy's friend answered: "Everyone who is anyone. Did you have anyone in particular in mind?"

Siger's grey eyes fastened on Darcy's. "Yes. Colonel Bozzo-Corona. And his man Lecoq."

"They will be in attendance," Sir Percy spoke up. "Are you still on about that?"

"Yes. Our plans, as discussed in the conclave at Would Newton, have not exactly unfolded as intended."

"The Colonel seems to have done his part," Darcy said.

"And yet, I observed Lecoq meet with Countess Carody at the Calyx Bar in Paris, the month before they were all present at the conclave," Siger said. "We never discerned their purpose."

"Perhaps..." said Darcy.

"No," Sir Percy replied. "Their meeting may have been illicit, but not in the manner you imply. The Countess does not prefer the company of men. In fact, she was quite enamored of Alice—and Marguerite."

Darcy reddened at Percy's frank description. "And yet, we have never discovered anything else untoward. The Colonel and Lecoq appear to have executed their portion of our plans. Lupin's half-brother made great gains in Italy—"

"And schemes to invade our shores next. He is a wild card," Siger said.

"The Colonel can control him," Darcy said. "Despite our uneven successes thus far, the game is far from over, and in all events, Countess Carody was never a player."

"Wasn't she?" Siger challenged.

"Certainly not," Darcy said. "She was merely a guest of Marguerite's at Would Newton, for a simple holiday diversion. She had no part in planning the course of larger matters."

"With all respect, Darcy," Siger replied, "you no longer undervalue your own wife's contributions to our efforts, and we've seen the depths of strength displayed by Marguerite, and Alice, and my own wife Violet. I suggest we not make the mistake of underestimating the Countess."

"This gets us nowhere," Sir Percy interjected. "I am retiring for the evening. Good night, my friends." He left Siger Holmes and Darcy and they sat in silence before the crackling fire.

Finally, Siger bid Darcy good night as well. He withdrew to his chambers, aware that a long and sleepless night awaited him, for the tangled threads that tickled at his brain refused to be ignored.

Logic.

Sir Percy's offhand comment earlier in the evening had set Holmes' mind racing. "In fact, she was quite enamored of Alice—and Marguerite," the baronet had said.

Was Countess Nadine Carody was involved in Marguerite's demise? Lady Blakeney had taken a turn for the worse every time the Countess had come to visit.

What was it about the ethereally beautiful woman?

He puffed fiercely at his pipe and reviewed what was generally known of the noblewoman. Ravished by Martinovics radicals. As a result, she refused to have anything to do with men, or so the story went. Rich. Anti-Revolutionary. She was well-travelled, having crisscrossed Europe from Ireland to the Carpathians, and perhaps beyond.

Holmes filled his pipe bowl again and focused on his personal observations. The Countess kept several female servants, utterly silent, utterly obedient, whom she used in the most unusual ways. She was often seen wearing a long red scarf about her neck. Her skin was pale to the point of transparency, and her flesh icy to the touch…much as Marguerite's skin and flesh became, as she continued to waste away.

The Countess' servants also shared these characteristics.

Coincidence?

Perhaps, but it was the only thread he had.

Childhood stories, legends, arose from the depths of Siger's memory. He pulled on a dressing gown, lit a candle, and made his way down the curved marble staircase and through the dark manor house to Sir Percy's vast library.

As Holmes stepped lightly through the double doors, the shifting candlelight sent shadows flitting across the shelves of books which filled three walls of the chamber, two stories high. Where was the area devoted to mythology? Ah, there it was. The *Ruthvenian*.

He slid the heavy leather tome from the shelf and set it on a reading table inlaid with gold leaf. The candle flickered and almost went out as he blew the dust from the volume.

Holmes flipped the heavy parchment pages until he found the section he wanted: the Carpathians.

Siger Holmes was a man of medicine, of science. Still, he had heard the story of the adventure Sir Percy, Alice, and Marguerite had had as they battled the wizard de Musard. It was an unbelievable tale, but he did not disbelieve them. The alternative was mass hallucination, which he deemed impossible. Rejecting the impossible, only the improbable remained.

Nonetheless, what he read in the *Ruthvenian* challenged his vaunted logic.

And yet, in some strange way, it was logical.

His great brain continued to process the legends and reconcile them with the facts as he knew them. He reviewed all the evidence, all the options, and discarded the impossible.

Logic told him that whatever remained must be the truth. The dark tome told him how to confirm his theory.

The candle sputtered again, and almost went out.

He shivered.

The following night, after the somber service and burial, two shrouded figures advanced on the gravesite.

Siger Holmes and the Duke of Holdernesse pitched their shovels at a feverish pace, while taking care to be as silent as possible. Siger had first approached Darcy for assistance, but the latter had declined, calling the plan an abomination.

A cold rain had fallen throughout day. Despite this, Marguerite's funeral had been well attended, as expected. The eleventh Baron Tennington, the Duke of Holdernesse, M. Delagardie, Fitzwilliam Darcy, Drummond, even the Prince of Wales. Others who had also been to the conclave at Would Newton had come. Some were key players, others had danced on the periphery. Colonel Bozzo-Corona was there, of course, with his man Lecoq, as were Balsamo, Kramm, de Winter, and Gerolstein. Sir John Gribson, or Grebson—Holmes couldn't quite remember—was there; the man was a distant relation of Holdernesse, if Holmes recalled correctly, and he noted that with the startling grey eyes and coal black hair, the family resemblance was indeed quite marked.

Lupin had come, no longer posing as a coachman as he had at Would Newton, and despite the heaviness of the occasion, Sir Percy and Alice had taken the opportunity after the service to pull him aside privately and castigate him for his half-brother's lack of cooperation and, indeed, antagonism.

The Frenchman, however, had only shrugged helplessly at his inability to influence his half-sibling.

There had been myriad others in attendance, none of whom had had anything to do with Sir Percy's winter gathering at the East Yorkshire village a few years back. Charles Bingley, Lord Richard Selwick, and George Knightly numbered among them.

One of these was a large, powerful-looking man who stood apart from everyone else. He was bearded and hazel-eyed with a Roman nose, and like Sir Percy, he affected the dandy's quizzing glass. Upon noting Siger Holmes' observation, the man grinned broadly at him and gave a slight Germanic bow. Then he produced a mother-of-pearl and silver snuff box which was inlaid with elaborate symbols and seemed to shimmer and fade in and out of focus. He took a pinch, inhaled deeply, and sneezed loudly, sending clouds of the ground tobacco pluming in the air and causing those near him to sneeze in turn. He blew his nose into a silk handkerchief, which he then stuffed back up his sleeve.

The man's inappropriate demeanor struck Holmes and he had resolved to seek him out after the service, but when he had done so, the man was nowhere to be found. Holmes had quickly forgotten about him as his thoughts turned again to Countess Nadine Carody.

Tellingly (to Holmes at least), the Countess had sent her regrets, although of course, if she had come, propriety would have dictated that she gather at Blakeney Manor with the rest of the women rather than attend graveside. Sir Percy and Marguerite's children, Hélène, Jack, George, and Violet, also remained at the manor in Alice's care, along with Percy and Alice's own children, Percy Armand and newborn twins Serena and Suzanne.

Holmes presumed that his sister-in-law Alice and Sir Percy would marry as soon as decorum allowed, although neither of them would really ever fully recover from the loss of Marguerite.

The physician and Holdernesse continued to dig at Marguerite's grave, and despite the cool night air, sweat trickled down Holmes' forehead into his eyes.

He paused to remove his cloak and toss it aside, and then resumed the night's grim work. The soft but heavy loam slowly grew into a pile at the graveside.

Finally, they hit the hard surface of the casket lid, and the two men pulled it open. Holmes slid the shutter of his lantern aside and shone the light into the coffin.

It was empty, as Holmes had expected.

He felt wet droplets land on his cheek and looked up. The day's rainclouds had parted hours ago and the night was clear. He cried out and Holdernesse also looked up into the crystal night.

Two dark blurry shadows flitted across the stark white of the Moon and disappeared.

Holmes aimed the lantern at the coffin again. Tiny droplets of fresh crimson blood now stained the white linen lining.

The men were silent, and after a while Holmes realized he was involuntarily holding his breath.

"Will you tell Sir Percy?" Holdernesse asked.

"No, I don't think that would be wise," Holmes replied. "He's been through too much as it is."

The two men began shoveling cold earth back onto the empty casket.

Darcy was right, Holmes thought, *it* was *an abomination*. But the abomination was the beautiful, deadly Countess Carody. "Woe to her," he whispered to himself, "if she shows herself in England ever again."

The "Books of Shadows" are, in the vernacular of 1950s comics, "imaginary" books, books that never existed, at least not in our reality. In this volume of Tales of the Shadowmen, *we are proud to launch what we hope will be a regular feature in our series: imaginary book covers by various talented artists, creating the shadows of books that we wish had been written, but never were. We start the ball rolling with British artist John Gallagher...*

John Gallagher: *The Books of Shadows*
(text by Jean-Marc Lofficier)

1. RETOUR EN ATLANTIDE – Pierre Benoit.
Before he decided to return to Atlantis, and probably die at the hands of Queen Antinea, Saint-Avit left a notebook recounting his earlier adventure. After finding it, the French Foreign Legion decides to send a rescue party, led by François Gérard. His expedition falls into a trap and the soldiers are killed, except for Gérard. He, too, resists Antinea's charms, and manages to organize a successful native revolt. Antinea dies falling into a vat of boiling orichalc.
What if...? In 1921, Benoit had learned of the plans for an unauthorized sequel by a writer named Georges Granjean and decided to beat him to the post by releasing his own sequel, Retour en Atlantide, *in 1922, setting aside* La Chaussée des Géants *(tr. as* The Giants' Causeway*) on which he had been working.*

2. DELIRIUM CIRCUS – Jean-Claude Forest
After escaping from planet Lythion, Barbarella and Pygar the blind "angel" find themselves in the souk city of Scolopandra on Venus. There, they come across Gipsie-Yoyo, the mysterious queen of the Space Gypsies Zargazoum, the owners of the interplanetary Delirium Circus, and become involved in her quest to locate the "bottomless treasure chest" of her people.
What if...? In 1964, three years after his best-selling Barbararella *graphic novel, Jean-Claude Forest became the editor of a short-lived comics magazine named* Chouchou. *He was toying with the notion of creating a new character, Bébé Cyanure, but instead chose to write and draw this sequel to* Barbarella, *introducing the Delirium Circus, which played a major role in the next episode of the series.*

3. JUDEX CONTRE BELPHEGOR 1: LE CRIME – Arthur Bernède
4. JUDEX CONTRE BELPHEGOR 2: LA VENGEANCE – Arthur Bernède
1935. As official ceremonies take place at Mont Saint-Michel to celebrate its new status as a historic treasure, the French President is mysteriously assassinated under impossible circumstances: shot by a ghostly apparition. Meanwhile, Micheline du Bec, the fiancée of Judex's son, is kidnapped. A 50-year-old Judex

is forced toagain take up the mantle of crime fighter. His investigation reveals the mastermind behind the murder and the kidnapping: Simone Desroches, a.k.a. Belphegor, a ruthless, amoral scientist who is seeking the location of the Sword of the Archangel Michael who slew the Dragon of the Apocalypse. Micheline is the key to finding the Sword, hidden on the Mount by her ancestor.

What if...? The manuscript for Judex contre Belphégor *was found unfinished (except for a few pages) in the papers of Arthur Bernède upon his death in 1937. Written 20 years after Judex and 10 years after Belphégor, this mythic encounter between two "monstres sacrés" of the French cinema immediately became a best-seller. Plans to film it were abandoned due to a disagreement between the heirs of Bernède and those of Louis Feuillade (co-creator of Judex).*

5. DOC ARDAN: L'ILE DES LANGUES BLEUES – Guy d'Antin

Doc Ardan pursues the mysterious criminal mastermind Doctor Natas to the prehistoric Island of the Blue-Tongued Death where he and his men fight for their lives against terrifying monsters created by the diabolical doctor.

What if...? Doc Savage *had been translated into French in 1939 under the name of* Franck Sauvage, l'Homme-Miracle; *its author was not listed as Kenneth Robeson but Guy d'Antin, a pseudonym of writer Guy d'Armen, who had already penned the adventures of Docteur Francis Ardan serialized in the magazine* L'Intrépide *in 1928-33. When the Nazi occupiers forbade the imports of American comics and pulps (such as* Flash Gordon, Superman, *etc.), the French publisher of* Franck Sauvage *released one final issue, written entirely by d'Armen and loosely based on the cover and blurb of the original* Doc Savage *adventure* The Land of Terror, *but had the name changed to Doc Ardan.*

6. LA RESURRECTION DE FANTÔMAS – Marcel Allain

A new Fantômas spreads terror! Equipped with the latest technology, controlling seemingly limitless resources, this deadly supervillain is the world's latest public enemy no. 1. The grandchildren of Juve and Fandor, the men who fought the original Fantômas, are soon drawn into a web of murder and deceit. They must find the answer to the true identity of the new Fantômas before Paris is utterly annihilated by his proton bomb.

What if...?In 1964, Gaumont released the first of three Fantômas *movies directed by André Hunebelle, starring Jean Marais and Louis de Funès. In it, Fantômas was portrayed as a mysterious black-clad mastermind who hid his features behind a spooky green latex mask. Marcel Allain, who was 78 in 1963, was hired to write a novel to introduce this "new" Fantômas to the public, which he did with* La Résurrection de Fantômas. *Allain had plans for a sequel, which became the inspiration for the third film,* Fantômas contre Scorland Yard, *but the book was left unwritten because of his poor health and ultimate death in 1969.*

7. LE SECRET DE MADAME ATOMOS – André Caroff

Now in her rejuvenated body, Madame Atomos is intent on reconstituting her criminal organization, destroyed by her enemies. Using her earlier experiments with spiders, she creates a new breed of deadly giant arachnids to blackmail the South American Republic of Pindorama. But Smith Beffort and the Green Dragon squad are determined to stop her.

What if...? When Fleuve Noir cancelled his Angoisse *imprint in 1974, André Caroff's latest Madame Atomos novel,* Le Secret de Madame Atomos, *was left unpublished, even though a cover had already been commissioned. The book was eventually released in a limited edition by a group of fans the following year.*

8. LES VAMPIRES 2 - Louis Feuillade

Mysteriously back from the dead, Irma Vep must first reclaim the leadership of the Vampires, now in the hands of the dwarf Luciferox. Then, she puts in motion a plan to blow up the Butte Montmartre to steal the gold bullion of the Banque de France. Once again, journalist Philippe Guérande must come to rescue of the police, and help Commissaire Durandal stop the Vampires.

What if...? The relative failure of Tih Minh *(1918), in which the remnants of the Vampires gang conspire to avenge Irma Vep's death, convinced Feuillade that the public wanted the "real thing" and he immediately put a sequel to* Les Vampires *into production, scheduled for release in 1920. This time, Irma Vep would return, again played by Musidora. Unfortunately Feuillade's loss of his job as artistic Director at Gaumont in 1918 meant that the marketing of the film was somewhat neglected by his successors, and* Les Vampires 2 *was not a success. All copies of the film (as well as other films by Feuillade and Musidora) have been lost.*

ARTHUR BERNÈDE

JUDEX contre BELPHÉGOR

PREMIÈRE ÉPOQUE : LE CRIME

"LES ROMANS MYSTÉRIEUX"
ÉDITIONS JULES TALLANDIER

ARTHUR BERNÈDE

JUDEX CONTRE BELPHÉGOR

DEUXIÈME ÉPOQUE : LA VENGEANCE

"LES ROMANS MYSTÉRIEUX"
EDITIONS JULES TALLANDIER

MARCEL ALLAIN

LA RESURRECTION DE FANTÔMAS

A. FAYARD EDITEURS

ANDRE CAROFF

LE SECRET DE MADAME ATOMOS

ANGOISSE

EDITIONS
"FLEUVE NOIR"

Other than his brilliant espionage novel, Rouletabille chez Krupp *(scheduled to be translated by Black Coat Press), Gaston Leroux only delivered cryptic hints about Rouletabille's other secret missions undertaken for the French Government just before and during World War I. Our latest contributor, Martin Gately, fills in the blanks left by Leroux by imagining a clash between Rouletabille and a German Agent on American shores, a clash which will have consequences that will be felt in modern times...*

Martin Gately: *Leviathan Creek*

New Jersey, July 1916

Joseph Rouletabille had a few hours to kill before his appointment with the French Ambassador to the United States and his fantasy had been to pass the time by dipping his toes in the cooling waters of the Atlantic. However, this was the hottest day, *so far*, of an oppressive heat-wave and it had driven thousands of the inhabitants of New York City to Spring Lake Beach on the New Jersey Shore with much the same idea. There was scarcely room on the beach for another soul; and the golden sands seemed more than two thirds concealed by the pseudo-geometric placement of picnic blankets upon which families feasted from their lunch pails.

In the hazy far distance, a good portion of the milling throng bathed shoulder to shoulder in the azure sea, while the hundreds who couldn't even get near the water just stood there trying to catch on their faces the moisture that rode in on the mild breeze. Rouletabille was thankful that he'd had the good sense to discard his usual tweeds in favor of a light linen suit. An obviously polite, yet rather overweight, lady in a summer dress eased a few inches along a wooden bench on the promenade so that Rouletabille could perch precariously on the very edge. Naturally, sitting in such close proximity to the fairer sex, he did not seek to light his pipe lest he spoil her enjoyment of the ice cream cone she was so ardently devouring. Ah, but what he would have given for a flagon of chilled French country cider! So much more refreshing than the tasteless suds that the Americans chose to call beer.

Then, it happened. Suddenly everything was different. The sound and mood of the packed beach altered. First, there were the screams, high pitched screams; the simultaneous screams of scores of women mixed with the outraged cries of men; then, the sound of retching, followed by the foul, sour smell of vomit on the air. Strangest of all, like a twisted parody of Moses' parting of the Red Sea—the crowd itself parted—what had been a tight wedged mass of humanity divided to make way for two men who carried a deathly pale human form towards the promenade. Great arterial gouts of blood hosed onto the sand. The injured man's life drained away from the bloody stumps that had been his legs with every step his rescuers took.

A middle aged man ran towards them shouting, "Tourniquets! Quickly!" He pulled off his belt and another man did the same. They tightened the belts around the two ragged transfemoral injuries and lifted the poor fellow into a commandeered horse-drawn wagon. As they did so he shuddered and went limp... The corpse was soon transported at breakneck speed towards the nearest hospital.

Only a single thought inhabited the mind of Rouletabille, *What had done this?* He fought against the tide of people evacuating the beach and soon found himself by the water's edge. A girl of about 19, wearing a one-piece cotton swimming costume, stood looking out to sea and shielding her eyes from the glare of the Sun with one hand.

"Do you know what happened to that man...the man with the terribly injured legs?"

"He wanted to see the red canoe. There was a red canoe capsized in the water. When he swam over to it, something got him... bit away his legs... A shark? A barracuda? I don't know," she answered, her voice quavering with shock.

Rouletabille scanned the waves, shielding his eyes from the sunlight in the same fashion as the girl. Could a fish really sever a man's legs? Cut through muscle and bone? It seemed totally unbelievable.

"Look!" she cried pointing. "You can still see the canoe..."

She was right. Rotating gently in the surf about 15 meters away was what appeared to be a dug-out canoe of pinkish red hue, almost crystalline in appearance. The rip-current dragged at it and it disappeared from sight.

The girl started to sob and walked away, but Rouletabille could not take his eyes from the ocean.

"The sea has teeth, I think," said Rouletabille to himself.

With his striking pure white beard and glinting jade colored eyes, Jean Jules Jusserand was foreboding in appearance, and yet avuncular in manner. Dwelling behind those eyes was a commanding, powerful dreadnought of an intellect. Indeed, Rouletabille was aware that the Ambassador had just been nominated for the Pulitzer Prize for History, but that sort of thing can be so very difficult to work into the conversation without appearing to be a fawning sycophant. Jusserand reached over his desk and liberally replenished the crystal brandy bloom in Rouletabille's hand.

"You still look a little pale, my young friend. Are you sure you are sufficiently recovered to receive the details of your mission?"

"Of course, Monsieur. I am more than a little preoccupied by what I saw...and intrigued to see if I can solve the mystery of the red canoe."

"Rouletabille, you must not allow yourself to be so distracted. Your mission here is vital to the future of France, and while the task is easy enough to explain, its execution will require the full dedication of your intelligence and skills."

"My apologies, Monsieur, I have something of an addiction to solving impossible puzzles, but I understand full well that a higher duty calls me now."

"Quite so, your mission is two-fold. Firstly, a ring of German saboteurs is operating unhindered here in New Jersey at present. Their base of operations is the summer residence of the German Ambassador; so, you see, it is not for the taking of sea air that I, myself, have temporarily moved to Spring Lake. The mastermind of the sabotage is likely to be the senior military attaché: a former U-Boat commander known as Mors, but that is a matter for you to fully determine."

Rouletabille pressed the tobacco firmly into the bowl of his pipe and lit it. "What has been the nature of the sabotage thus far?" he asked.

"The main targets have been armaments and pharmaceuticals bound for Europe. They have successfully planted small bombs on ships carrying munitions and stolen and destroyed consignments of salicylic acid from which analgesics such as aspirin are made. But they are not always successful, an attempt to make off with 2000 ampoules of morphine was thwarted by security guards and I have reports that the same men also hijacked a barge loaded with salt...presumably an error..."

"The agents of the Wilhelmstrasse are fallible mortals, I assure you."

"Secondly, your mission is not merely to bring an end to these attacks but to turn them to our advantage. The perpetrators must be exposed in such a way that it furthers French interests and increases the likelihood of American entry into the war," explained Jusserand.

The Ambassador pulled open the drawer of his bureau, removed a gilt-edged invitation card and handed it to Rouletabille.

"There is another factor to be taken into consideration, another piece on the chessboard of diplomacy and espionage that you and I inhabit. His name is General Herbert Brown and he could prove a powerful ally. He is a confirmed Francophile and, even though he is formally retired from the army, he still has the ear of the President in matters of foreign policy. Here is an invitation to a function at his mansion tonight. Be sure to attend it. He lives on Ocean Way just outside town."

"Monsieur, this is a costume ball! I will have no time to obtain suitable attire..." complained Rouletabille.

"You will find a most appropriate costume in a white box on your bed upstairs," Jusserand informed him.

"I've not yet established my cover..." spluttered Rouletabille. "How will I convince them that I am the new cultural attaché?"

"My dear fellow, I should not worry over much about that. Everyone will assume that you are a spy."

Rouletabille approached the mansion on Ocean Way already wearing his cloak and mask and with the invitation clutched in his gloved hand. The costume had not been the only thing in the white cardboard box. There was also a small collapsible Kodak camera and an 1892 Lebel revolver with a small carton of ammunition (the only tools that the French government seemed to think it necessary to issue to intelligence agents).

At the door, an immaculately uniformed powerfully built black man of about 25 eyed him suspiciously before admitting him to the party after a careful scrutiny of the invitation. Inside, the revels seemed at full-throttle: maids circulated with trays overloaded with champagne glasses, handing drinks to a profusion of men dressed as knights, cowboys, highwaymen and even apes, with women masquerading as mermaids, witches and angels (amongst other things). The young spy had only stepped a few yards into the palatial entrance hall when he was accosted by a man in his mid-sixties with steel grey hair wearing the dark blue uniform of a Civil War era Union soldier. He fixed Rouletabille with a glare, as if trying to see through the mask he wore.

"Well, what have we here… a gatecrasher? You are the only one of my guests that I do not recognize, sir," said General Brown. "Who are you?"

"I am the Phantom of the Opera," said Rouletabille as he secretly sweltered beneath the mask and woolen cloak on such a hot night.

Brown laughed and then said quietly, "Your accent and choice of get-up mark you as one of Jusserand's boys. That means we should get on just swell. Let me get you a drink; my wife's got a craze on some new cocktail, it's got a whole bunch of fellas on their backs already. You're gonna love it."

"Elena, meet the Phantom of the Opera," chuckled Brown. The tall woman dressed as a Roman Empress turned from her mixing table. Rouletabille judged that she must be approaching seventy but she was still one of the most elegant and strikingly handsome women that he had ever seen; there was a vibrancy and joyfulness about her that the mere process of aging had failed to diminish.

Mrs. Elena Brown proffered Rouletabille a mauve colored drink in a frosted cocktail glass. "This," she intoned with a voice redolent of the uppermost echelons of English aristocracy, "will blow your little socks off. Gin, lemon juice, and crème de violette with maraschino—the general effect is like an army of archangels massaging your tonsils. It's called an *Aviation*."

Three glasses later Rouletabille understood what she meant. He sat down quietly in a corner under the fronds of a potted palm waiting for his system to find some way to metabolize the violet flavored lava he'd been drinking. Then something caught his eye, a man in a naval uniform wearing a domino mask was stealthily skirting the edge of the party crowd…making his way ever so nonchalantly towards a duck egg blue colored door in an alcove in the far corner.

The man pulled from beneath his tunic a golden cylindrical object roughly the size of a fountain pen. A flash of iridescent liquid sprayed out of the tube into the door's lock. Then, a moment later, the man opened the door; stepped into the room beyond and, just as swiftly as he had opened it, shut the door behind him.

It occurred to Rouletabille that he alone had just witnessed this fellow pick the lock by squirting some sort of concentrated acid into it. Now, if he were to catch this miscreant, General Brown would doubtless look upon him most beneficently.

As casually as he could, the spy eased his way through the revelers until he got to the door. Unhesitatingly, he pushed it open while tugging the Lebel revolver out from under his cloak. The stranger in the domino mask had been busy. A large oil painting of Abraham Lincoln had been swung to one side by way of its hinged connection to the wall. Behind the painting was a steel wall safe with a combination lock. The man had connected something that was perhaps some form of electrically-powered stethoscopic listening device to the door of the safe; he turned the combination dial waiting for the tumblers to click. With the earpieces of the device in place, he was quite oblivious to the presence of Rouletabille.

"I hate to interrupt your concentration, Monsieur, but I've been meaning to ask you, what is that costume you are wearing?" exclaimed Rouletabille in an unnecessarily loud voice. This caused the masked man to whirl around. Suddenly a pistol of unusual, almost futuristic, design was in his hand.

"This is how I usually dress," said the masked would-be thief in a German accent so guttural that it set the Frenchman's nerves on edge.

Rouletabille was conscious that the door had opened behind him, but he was unwilling to give the German even a momentary advantage by looking away; instead, he kept his revolver calmly leveled at him.

"What's all this?" said General Brown. "Not so much a Mexican stand-off as a Franco-German one." The General interposed himself between the two men and Rouletabille saw that he held a massive long-barreled Colt Dragoon revolver.

"I caught this gentleman trying to break into your safe," said Rouletabille.

"So I see. I expect you've had no time for introductions... Monsieur Phantom, allow me to introduce Kapitan Mors of the Imperial German Navy. Captain Mors, this man is a French agent and perhaps it would therefore be best if you did not learn his name, nor see his face. At least, not tonight; tonight is for fun. Have you tried my wife's new cocktail?"

"Do not mock me, General," spat the German. "The contents of that safe are your property only by chance. By rights, it should be mine! It was never Smith's! It should never have been yours... I, and I alone, am the true heir to Captain Nemo."

"When I think you are in the same league as Nemo, my friend, I'll let you know. But for now, if you're done shouting, the party is outside…if you're *not* feeling sociable, I'll unlock the French doors out into my garden and you may take a hike. Either way, if I catch you in here again, I'll shoot you through the head. And I never miss." Brown stepped forward, produced a key from his pocket and opened the doors.

Still covering General Brown and Rouletabille with his odd pistol, the German officer backed out into the garden's inky shadows.

"Well," said Brown after a moment, "he's gone. I guess you'd like a crack at the safe. I'd much rather the French had access to its contents than the Germans. The papers inside were given to me for safekeeping by the President himself—though who may see them is at my discretion. They once belonged to Cyrus Smith and any engineer or scientist in your country would give his right arm for a look at them."

"Since you were once cast away with Captain Smith on that most mysterious of South Pacific islands, I can hazard a guess what might be inside," murmured Rouletabille in awe.

"You've got five minutes, then I'll drag you back to the party. I never met one of Jusserand's men who didn't have a nifty camera…please take pictures and leave the originals."

"But, General, I am no safecracker," explained the young man desperately.

"Oh, you'll figure it out," said Brown with a wink.

As Brown left, Rouletabille took off his mask and cloak and turned up the gaslight in the room to maximum. This was a forlorn hope. How was he supposed open the safe with no training…no idea at all how it was done? About the only thing he knew was that most modern British and American safe combination locks had to be rotated five times past a certain number clockwise, four times anticlockwise past the next number and so on until a single clockwise rotation past the final number was reached. He'd seen secretaries in embassies lose their tempers with combination locks even when they knew the numbers.

He swung the oil painting of Lincoln back over the safe door ready to give up before he had started and return to the party. The old man looked down at him with those kindly eyes and seemed to exhort him to try harder. Wait a minute…could it really be so simple?

Rouletabille looked around, the synapses of his brain opening and shutting fiercely like sparking electrical connections. From the bookshelf, he pulled down an old sea atlas and turned up the pages for the South Pacific and scanned the area around New Zealand. He could see no mention of what he was looking for… the atlas was too old, it predated the return of Captain Smith and his companions… but it had to be here somewhere in this room.

Rouletabille opened a cherry wood cabinet and found inside a collection of reasonably modern rolled up sea charts. He went through the same process again, looking minutely at the tiniest features of the South Pacific; looking for what once had been Lincoln Island: the island upon which Brown, Captain Smith, Pencroff, Gideon Spillett, Neb Dobey and Smith's dog Top had been stranded. Finally, he found what he was looking for... 1617 miles east of New Zealand: Ernest Legouve Reef—a scattering of fang-like rocks just peeping above the surface of the ocean—all that remained of the "Mysterious Island" following the cataclysmic volcanic eruption. The reef was subsequently charted by a French ship around the turn of the century.

Using a nautical rule and ready-reckoner, Rouletabille did his best to calculate the latitude and longitude of the reef. It had been a long time since a friend had taught him the rudiments of navigation during a Channel crossing, but he estimated the location to be 35° 12'S 150° 40'W. The 150 in the middle was the problem. Since there would be no 150 on the dial, Rouletabille would have to assume that this would be a 15 and hope that Brown had decided the same.

He swiftly turned the dial five times past 35 clockwise then even quicker, four times anti-clockwise past 12. No longer daring even to breathe, three times clockwise past 15 and finally twice anticlockwise past 40. Nothing happened. Rouletabille could hear the door starting to open behind him. He had lost his chance! What embarrassment he would now face before the remarkable old General. The ignominy of it... Wait! The additional zero from the 150, perhaps it should be accounted for at the end of the combination. It was surely worth a try. He rotated the dial past 0 clockwise, just one solitary turn.

There was an audible click from the mechanism and the thick steel door eased open. Without pausing to turn to see who had entered the room, he removed the sheaves of paper from the safe and spread them on the desk in preparation for photographing them.

"I can see that the next time I set a test for the most famous detective in France, it will have to be a more difficult one," laughed General Brown. "Forgive my pretence of not knowing the Great Joseph Rouletabille... Of course, Jusserand told me who he was sending to my house."

Rouletabille carefully examined the drawings and blueprints from the safe. The first set were drawn in pencil on pages torn from a small notebook; they were intricate technical drawings of air pumps, torpedo tubes, some kind of combined periscope and camera obscura, water tight doors... and so on. Then the larger blueprints, these were orthographic projections and cutaways of a massive submersible vehicle...no prizes for guessing which one; the blueprints were marked *NAUTILUS*. The next set was completely different—silvery white ink on pale gold paper. The illustrated vehicle was like an elongated bullet on disc-shaped metallic wheels. Rouletabille took out his miniature camera, loaded the flash with magnesium powder and started shooting.

"The designs on the goldleaf parchment are by Robur, the self-proclaimed 'Master of the World,'" explained Brown. "Captain Smith was one of the few men to meet both Nemo and Robur. And Smith was an incredible engineer himself, he was able to hold his own; gain their respect."

Rouletabille turned over two drawings that were pinned together, one was one of Nemo's blueprints the other on the gold paper of Robur. In essence, what they showed was broadly similar – a long cigar-shaped craft with a metal riveted hull and wide nozzles at the rear. The differences between the two seemed largely aesthetic. Robur had drawn octagonal portholes, Nemo's were hemispherical. Rouletabille had no idea what the drawings were supposed to be of.

"What are these?" he asked quizzically.

"Hmm. First Nemo, then Robur and now Mors. All of them trying to develop the same thing—a craft that can escape the atmosphere of the Earth and head out to other planetary bodies. And where Nemo and Robur failed, Mors, I'm sure, will one day succeed. C'mon, let's get back to the party."

Rouletabille had expected to wake up in his quarters at the French Ambassador's summer residence. It took a few minutes for him to realize that he was still at General Brown's mansion on Ocean Way. Worse than that, it felt like the inside of his skull had been stuffed with coarse grade wire wool and fishing hooks; and that a violet flavored lizard had nested in his desert-dry mouth. Too many Aviation cocktails had left him trapped in a black vortex of a hangover. He climbed uneasily out of bed and poured water from a fish-shaped majolica jug into a blue glass tumbler. Just after his second swig, there was a perfunctory knock at the door. Before he could answer, General Brown marched cheerfully in wearing a robe and slippers.

"Ah good, you're awake," said Brown as he threw a blue and grey striped swimming costume onto Rouletabille's bed. "Get changed. We're going swimming...I expect you have a sore head and it'll do you a world of good."

"Swimming? In the sea? I saw a swimmer with his legs bitten off yesterday..."

"I swim every morning in summer and have never seen a glimpse of a shark. Hell's Teeth! I swam practically every day at Shark Bay on Lincoln Island without trouble. Anyway, I daresay most sharks don't bite harder than the average dog."

Rouletabille shrugged mentally. The problem with senior military men was they expected everyone to do everything that they said. He reached for the swimming costume.

Rouletabille and Brown exited through the garden onto the beach. It was only around 6 a.m. but the temperature was already pushing 75 Fahrenheit, it would be back in the 90s later in the morning. The young black man who'd admitted Rouletabille to the mansion last night was sitting on a driftwood log nursing a type of Marlin Model 1893 rifle—a variant with an extremely long barrel fitted. It occurred to the detective that it was the sort of weapon a sniper or an assassin might choose.

"This is Neb Jnr.," explained Brown. "He's my guardian angel. I relax when he's around because I know no harm will come to me."

Neb Jnr. nodded to Rouletabille and then pushed down the lever-action of the rifle as if to signal that he was ready for any eventuality.

The two bathers walked into the surf, which seemed almost icy when compared to the growing heat of the day. As the cold water hit his calves, every muscle in Rouletabille's body tensed and his headache suddenly worsened, but then as he strode further and finally began to swim, the vise of pain clamping his skull slowly released.

"What further can you tell me about Captain Mors?" asked Rouletabille. "If he is a disciple of Nemo—who despised imperialist aggression—then why is he allied with Germany? Surely he should have forsworn allegiance to a nation-state?"

They paused to tread water and Rouletabille became aware that the morning tide was churning the sand and carrying in great swathes of seaweed. Visibility under the water was much reduced and, if there was a shark swimming beneath him right now, he would never know it.

"Mors is a complicated character. He'd love to be like Nemo, but circumstance has dictated against it. A few years ago, he built a unique airship that was impervious to rifle and artillery fire. It was fitted with a ram and, for a while, he lived the Nemo or Robur lifestyle, calling himself 'The Air Pirate' and wrecking a few ships and balloons to very little purpose. But what Man could not bring crashing to Earth, God did. His airship was caught in a colossal storm in the Pyrenees and almost completely destroyed. He wasted his fortune attempting to salvage it and is now reduced to being a mere agent of the German government. Nevertheless, do not underestimate him, he is a quite brilliant man; though his eccentricity will be his undoing—he tells me he never removes that domino mask, like some penny-dreadful villain."

As Brown spoke, something caught Rouletabille's eye, a white spherical shape in the sky that was passing across the bay and losing height rapidly.

"Is there a weather station near here?" asked Rouletabille pointing.

"I think there's one over in Hunterdon County, but that's no weather balloon," replied Brown.

As the balloon came lower, Rouletabille could not help but agree. It carried no barometric instrument package, but rather a nest of cylindrical tubes festooned with electrical wiring. His heartbeat quickened with horror as he realized what the balloon's burden was strangely reminiscent of. In his mind's eye, he could see both the electric stethoscope and pistol belonging to Mors. Yes, they were all products of the same frustrated genius.

As the droplets hit the sea, part of Rouletabille's brain refused to accept that this was anything more than a rain shower. Why then was the rain red? Why then was it spraying down from the device slung beneath the balloon? It was blood. And every instinct screamed to Rouletabille that it was human blood. What terrible message was Mors trying to send after his humiliation yesterday?

Rouletabille looked towards Brown and saw that his hair and face were covered in bloody spatters. The two of them were swimming in a crimson slick.

"Let's get back to the shore!" shouted Brown.

A crack of rifle fire from the beach drew their attention. Neb Jnr. had shot the Marlin in the air and was now frantically pointing to something in the water; something that lay directly between the swimmers and the shore. As the brownish grey finned back broke the surface, the detective prayed that the thing sharing the sea with them was something harmless. He remembered reading about how the largest sharks were quite innocuous—they ate the tiny things that floated on the surface. Unfortunately, his memory had been seized by raking talons of fear and was refusing to divulge the proper name for these tiny things. He was also concerned that the shark wasn't really big enough to be one of the harmless giants of the ocean. It was perhaps three or four meters long, at most.

He clung desperately to Brown's assurance that the bite of a shark was no worse than the bite of a dog, but with progressively less and less conviction that it was really true. His whole perception of the nature of sharks had shifted in less than a day. He'd thought them to be weak in every sense: weak jawed, cowardly, stupid… Something that might nip at a man's flesh in error, but incapable of taking away his legs in a deliberate attack. What if they were as cunning as wolves, or if their instincts were so perfectly adapted to survival in the hostile environment of the sea that it gave the illusion of tremendous guile? After all, what was intelligence but an appropriate response in any given situation?

His momentary reverie was broken by another report from Neb Jnr.'s rifle. The bullet blasted through the shark's dorsal fin tearing an untidy fist-sized hole more-or-less dead center. It was admirable shooting from that range—and what the Devil was he using for ammunition!—but he wanted to exhort Neb Jnr. to aim lower. The horrifying leviathan was hardly likely to die from having its fin shot; it was like shooting an axe-wielding maniac in the earlobes.

Without warning, Neb Jnr. unleashed a barrage of shots from the Marlin. Judging by the impact splashes as the bullets hit the water, Rouletabille guessed that the marksman had struck the shark in the nose or the top of the head. The great fish zigzagged away at astonishing speed heading out into the deep.

A few minutes later, Rouletabille and Brown were helping each other out of the surf.

"I need a drink," decided General Brown.

"I never want another Aviation as long as I live," declared Rouletabille.

"Who's talking about those silly cocktails? What we need is Kentucky Bourbon," said the old man.

"Let me shake you by the hand, Neb," requested Rouletabille. "You are the finest shot I've ever seen."

"But then, you never knew my father," smiled Neb Jnr.

"It's a pity that my guardian angel isn't going to be with me for much longer," explained Brown. "He's secured a position as a police officer over in Bay City."

"I'd been meaning to ask you, Monsieur Rouletabille, seeing how you're a famous detective, if you'd maybe give me a few pointers on that line of work," asked Neb Jnr.

"My dear friend, by the time I've finished with you, they'll want to make you Captain of Detectives; and probably your descendants too," laughed Rouletabille.

"My little Harold plays cops and robbers already…" added the future policeman.

Rouletabille looked back at the sky and the water. The balloon that had lost height so suddenly was now regaining altitude as if guided by an unseen hand.

In the following days, operating from within Jusserand's summer domicile, Rouletabille placed himself at the centre of a web of surveillance on Captain Mors. Embassy "cultural staff," and paid informers dogged his every movement while Rouletabille kept himself carefully out of sight, planning to bring himself into play only at the final confrontation.

Mors' movements and clandestine meetings with his subordinates suggested that a major event was planned for sometime in the next few weeks, probably around the end of July, something that would take place in the vicinity of New York Harbor. In addition, Mors was now in the habit of taking a prolonged early morning voyage in a small sailing skiff. Rouletabille deduced that Mors was making a rendezvous with a U-Boat, possibly the one that he had previously commanded. The question was, how to maximize this information to further French interests. A U-boat operating in US territorial waters could always claim it was there due to navigational error…it would have to be caught involved in the act of sabotage. It was really just a matter of giving Mors enough rope with which to hang himself; if Mors went too far and committed an extreme act the game was essentially over—the Americans would enter the war. Yet if Mors' efforts were too ineffectual, his masters would put him under pressure to do more. Rouletabille did not envy Mors' position. Conversely, if Rouletabille uncovered a plot that meant likely death or injury to US citizens, he would be duty-bound to thwart it, even if that meant delaying American participation in Europe.

Rouletabille had also become very interested in sharks. Reports from ships arriving on the eastern seaboard indicated that there was a veritable plague of sharks about ten miles off the coast. The public mind had formed a link between German U-Boat activity and the presence of the sharks. In the popular imagination, the predators had come to feast on dead and dying sailors. The war was on America's doorstep, yet it was the sharks that everyone most seemed to fear. Coastal tourism was now blighted. Rouletabille could walk along the promenade alone, paddle in the waves to his heart's content... The concession stands were empty and abandoned. It seemed like the town was dying.

On the wall next to his desk, Rouletabille had thumbtacked a map of the New Jersey shoreline. Ostensibly, it was for marking the surveillance of Mors, but he had also placed on it the locations of the two shark attacks that had taken place, albeit the first attack had been erroneously (if not bizarrely) attributed to a turtle. Charles Vansant was the first victim; killed in the early evening of July 1 at Beach Haven, Long Island. Over 40 miles from the second attack, that on Charles Bruder at Spring Lake on July 6—the attack that Rouletabille himself had witnessed. Finally, the detective had marked the private strand of beach to the rear of the Brown mansion as well as some possible launching places inland for the murderous balloon.

It seemed apparent that this attack was merely an attempted assassination of General Brown, revenge for his humiliation of Mors the previous evening. The ingenious method of luring a shark to that location by way of the controlled balloon dropping human blood into the water was breathtaking in its audacity and infuriating since it left no physical evidence that might link Mors to the crime. Rouletabille had cogitated on the attacks for days now and concluded that the red canoe, like the balloon, was a device for attracting the sharks to where humans were bathing. Something that would go largely unnoticed by people yet would be an irresistible siren call to the largest and most dangerous of sharks... Mors was therefore responsible for all the shark attacks. And that was something that the detective had felt to be true from his first day here, even when there wasn't a scintilla of evidence to support it.

There was a brisk knock at Rouletabille's door and Pierre Galpin, the administrative under-secretary, strode in.

"Monsieur Rouletabille! We have just received word that, earlier today, there was a further shark attack. This one was on some young boys at Matawan."

Rouletabille consulted his wall map. Matawan was on Raritan Bay, only just south of New York.

"Do we know yet the exact location of the attack within the bay?" he asked the under-secretary.

"Monsieur, the attack wasn't in the bay—it was miles inland in a river creek."

"What! That is surely impossible... I must go there at once. Tell the Ambassador I am commandeering his chauffeur and roadster on urgent business."

Minutes later, Rouletabille was running down the residence's cantilevered staircase taking the steps two at a time. Outside, he could see the Ambassador's yellow roadster with the engine already running. Then he heard Jusserand's booming voice call after him:

"Rouletabille! Attacks by sharks are not your affair!"

"They are when they are economic warfare!" he called back, not even bothering to slow down.

When Rouletabille got to Matawan Creek, they were already planning to dynamite it. The place was not at all what he had been expecting. A muddy, shallow and narrow creek, lined with reed beds and thick with flies, probably no more than 15 yards across at its widest point. It was also a good ten miles from the sea.

Earlier that day, a group of boys had been swimming in the dirty brown water. The shark had taken one of the boys and the body had not been recovered. Nightmarishly, a 24 year-old man called Stanley Fisher had waded out to try and find the boy's body and also become a victim of the shark. He was now dying at the Morgan-Lovell Infirmary in Matawan. It seemed appalling to Rouletabille that the boys had nowhere better to swim... they'd probably gotten into the habit of cooling off in the creek during this sapping hot spell. Yet, who could guess that a monstrous sea creature would, or could, venture so far upriver.

A boatman called Thomas Swann was holding court on the bank of the creek talking to a couple of Matawan newspapermen. Rouletabille noted that Swann reeked of whisky, which would be a minor point were he not also handling dynamite. He had a stick of dynamite in his left hand and a box of matches in his right; between the two hands, he was trying to wrestle a match out to light the magnesium fuse. Rouletabille had only had some basic demolitions training but the fuse looked very short. There were also onlookers, including children, scant feet away.

"Yeah, I seen a shark alright," began Swann. "They laughed at me then, said I was an old soak. They ain't laughin' now as little Lester got ate."

"So you actually saw the shark swimming upstream? How do you account for a salt water shark in a freshwater creek?" asked one journalist.

"Bull Shark that's all. They's well known to swim in rivers. Ain't no mystery. It was a monster though; mebbe fifteen or twenny feet long."

Swann lit the fuse and the sudden fizz as it took startled him. He tossed the caramel-colored stick away reflexively, but it only flew about three yards then struck the tops of some reeds and fell to earth at the water's edge. There were two girls in pinafore dresses only a few feet from where the dynamite had come to rest. Rouletabille leapt forward—a child had already died today and he would damned if any other innocents would die while he could do something about it. He grabbed the stick and hurled it hard and low across the creek. It span through the air and went about ten yards before hitting the water; it exploded almost the second it touched the surface generating a broad fountain of muddy water.

The shockwave disturbed a metallic object that lay just under the water's surface. It was a long segmented pole that seemed to run the full width of the creek. It rose up in the swell and then disappeared again. Rouletabille was puzzled by this sight immediately. Once again, the nerve endings inside his brain were firing furiously; theorizing, constructing explanations and dismissing them just as quickly. Was the pole the top of some sort of barrier, a net or an underwater fence? And if so, on which side of the barrier was the shark?

Rouletabille crouched by the water and scanned the surface of the creek. He nearly jumped out of his skin! The head of an enormous shark suddenly protruded from the swirling brown water not eight feet from the bank. The jaws extended as if trying to escape from the creature's head and snapped at him twice. The shock of seeing its pink fleshy maw and triangular teeth was more terrifying and alarming than it had been when he was actually swimming in the sea with such a creature the other week.

The beast broke the surface heading downstream towards the pole barrier. Rouletabille saw the dorsal fin quite clearly. The jagged hole in it was unmistakable. This was the same shark that Neb Jnr. had blasted with the Marlin rifle. His heart was beating so fast it was starting to hurt; it felt like every muscle in his body was soaked with adrenaline.

Knowing what little effect Neb Jnr.'s rifle had had, Rouletabille did not pull the Lebel from his shoulder holster. Instead, he yanked out the camera and hoped that the creature resurfaced. The shark's head came out of the water again as it rammed into the pole. He clicked the shutter and hoped he'd managed to capture it on film. The shark dove and there was a thrashing as if it was fighting its way through something then it was gone. One thing was for sure, Swann had exaggerated its length. The great fish could not have been more than about twelve or thirteen feet at most (to use the Imperial measurements which Rouletabille personally disliked).

"Wow!" said one of the journalists as he approached the young detective with notebook in hand. "You sure are a man of action! And if that photo comes out, the *Gazette* and just about every paper on the East Coast will want to buy it off you...who are you anyway?"

"Oh, I'm just a tourist...but I really don't like publicity," lied Rouletabille, who then tried to melt away in the crowd but ended up jogging back towards the roadster to escape the newsmen.

He returned to complete his investigations at 6 a.m. the following morning. The bank of the creek was deserted now. His first port of call was the metal pole that traversed the width of the water. It was slim, telescopic and made out of a light steel alloy. It was attached to a motor that was half buried in the mud and atop the motor were both a timer and some sort of wireless radio receiver. The purpose of this arrangement was to extend a fine metal net across the creek. The barrier could probably be set to be deployed at a certain time of day (perhaps to match the tides?) or to keep captive or release the imprisoned leviathan by radio signal. The shark had wrecked the net by ramming it after the dynamite had gone off. Rouletabille suddenly felt nauseated. Those boys had not been subject to a terrible cruel whim of nature...the shark had not stumbled upon them while they were swimming. They had gone swimming in the shark's enclosure.

Rouletabille looked upstream where something had caught his eye. Of course, Matawan Creek was still tidal at this point and now it was low tide. This revealed something that he had not seen previously: a metallic disc perhaps four feet or so across, like a wide flat buoy sitting in the water, presumably anchored in place. It had the look of one of Mors' inventions. There was also a decaying, leaky row boat tied up to a post in the reeds.

He unhitched the boat, jumped in and pushed it away from the bank with its rotten oars. Nearing the disc, he reached over the side and laid his hands on it, bringing the boat's movement through the water to a halt. The disc had a section with a hinged lid. Rouletabille half expected it to be locked or welded shut, but it wasn't. He lifted it and saw that inside were open compartments packed with salt. A small electrically powered Archimedes screw type arrangement fed the salt gradually into the water. It was a device to salinate the shark's enclosure. From this, two things were apparent: the saboteurs had not stolen that consignment of salt in error, and, secondly, the creature held captive here was no mere Bull Shark; it was something larger, more deadly and something quite without the ability to exist in freshwater. Rouletabille headed back to the bank.

Rouletabille stood in the crowd at Raritan Wharf watching the little man with a mixture of curiosity and admiration. He was probably no more than five feet four inches tall and sported a droopy walrus moustache. One thing was for sure, he exuded, or perhaps broadcasted, a palpable aura of utter fearlessness. Amongst the onlookers were the same Matawan journalists that Rouletabille had encountered during the incident with the dynamite several days before.

"Yes, ladies and gentleman, I had no fear of the King of Beasts when I worked as a lion tamer so I certainly have no hesitation in taking on that jackal of the sea—the shark."

"Mr. Schleisser," began one of the journalists, "will you be hunting for the creature alone?"

"No, Monsieur Joséphin of the French Fourth Estate will accompany me. He offered a considerable sum for the privilege, but I've invited him to give that money to the family of the little boy who was killed in the creek."

It seemed strange to Rouletabille to hear his former name, his *real* name used, that name belonged to a different life. It had so little connection to him that it might as well be an alias.

"Monsieur Joséphin provided a photograph of the creature that has allowed me to identify it as a Great White Shark, the most dangerous man-eater in the ocean. It is not an adversary that I will be underestimating... and I will not be satisfied until I have defeated it."

Schleisser and Rouletabille climbed down into the little boat that Schleisser had hired for the expedition. It was scarcely bigger than the decayed row boat that he had used when he examined the salination disc. Rouletabille took up the oars with a steady determined stroke and the two men slowly moved away from the wharf into the choppy waters of Raritan Bay.

After about half an hour they traded position and Schleisser started to row. He instructed Rouletabille to break open the first of a series of three sealed zinc pails that were stored in the stern. Rouletabille recoiled at the appalling odor as he took the lid off.

"Chicken guts!" he laughed. "Just throw it all over the side…sharks cannot resist blood. Soon we'll probably be surrounded by 'em. Including the big son-of-a-bitch that you saw in the creek."

In fact, it was nearly an hour before the shark arrived. Rouletabille lay dozing with his hat over his face. His first thought was that they had collided with another boat, so sudden and powerful was the impact. He leapt up and looked down into the water. The shark seemed to just be hanging in position relative to the boat about ten feet down. He dragged the Lebel from beneath his jacket, adopted a stance with his feet wide apart to steady his aim and then fired. He saw his bullet corkscrew through the water leaving a tight spiral of bubbles and then go wide. He took his time and aimed again, this time the shot clipped the front edge of the shark's pectoral fin. This was ridiculous! How many revolver shots might it take to kill it? Fifty? A hundred? He had four left in the cylinder and twelve more in the box in his jacket pocket.

Schleisser jostled him out of the way. The lion tamer's arms were filled with a lead weighted wide-gauge fishnet which he hurled down into the sea very accurately towards the great fish.

"That peashooter's no use! We gotta net him and row to the shallows…find a way to beach him"

The weighted net caught on the top lobe of the shark's tail and on its right pectoral fin. This drove it to the surface and allowed Rouletabille to confirm its identity. Yes, it was the shark with the damaged dorsal fin that he had encountered twice before now. The shark's mouth clamped onto the sternpost and started splintering the timber.

My God, it's eating the boat, thought Rouletabille.

The fish's wide brownish gray head was high out of the water and thoroughly occupied with destroying the boat. Seawater overtopped the gunwales and started to swamp the craft. Rouletabille held the end of the Lebel's barrel against the coarse sand-paper skin of the shark's head, trying to make some sort of calculation as to where its brain might reside. He fired twice, punching neat bloody holes, but there was little other discernible effect. He dropped the gun and grabbed one of the oars. Leaning the oar against the deck at about 45 degrees, he kicked hard just above the blade, while yanking the top of the oar towards him. The last two feet of the oar sheared off leaving a sharp, spear-like point. Wielding it high above his head, Rouletabille brought the broken oar down like a harpoon and pierced the beast through its left gill slits.

As he encountered resistance, he plunged and pushed the point further, shoving on hard through the spiracle openings—the shark equivalent of a gizzard—and then by blind chance tearing through the aorta. He'd had no idea that a shark's heart was so far forward, but the frenzied spray of blood into the ocean revealed he must have hit the most vital organ of all. The shark immediately stopped moving and started to sink. Schleisser hurried to cut it from the net.

"Help me get this net off him or he'll have us in Davy Jones' Locker!" he shouted with astonishing cheerfulness.

As Rouletabille assisted the little man, he looked up at something crossing his field of vision; another Great White, this one only about seven feet long, was starting to circle the boat. Schleisser saw it too.

"We killed one, we can kill another. It's the business we're in."

Just over two weeks later, Rouletabille was in a boat again, a motor launch crossing New York Harbor. This time, he was not looking for sharks. Mors himself was his quarry. And tonight was the night when, according to every scrap of intelligence that they had, that Mors would bring his plans to fruition. It was the early hours of July 30 and, like Mors before him, Rouletabille was heading for Bedloe's Island. The launch docked inconspicuously out of sight on the east pier where he was met by a single US Marshal.

"Is Mors definitely still on the island?" he asked the Marshal.

"His sailing dinghy is still tied up. He's been creeping around for hours thinking we haven't noticed him. Right now, he's up somewhere inside Lady Liberty."

Rouletabille sighed. Mors' plans had once seemed obscure to him, but now they were all too obvious. He meant to destroy the Statue of Liberty, that symbolic gift from the French to the American people. It would have to be rebuilt and that would deflect valuable men and materiel away from the war effort. He wondered if Mors now regarded American entry to the war as simply inevitable. Either that, or he had figured out a way for someone other than the saboteurs to take the blame.

"Do you want the arc lights on?" queried the Marshal.

The temporary lighting that had been installed for the recent July 4 celebrations was apparently still in place.

"No thanks, keep it dark. I'll use a bulls-eye lantern when I really can't see what I'm doing."

Rouletabille jogged towards the colossal plinth then headed inside. He could hear booted footsteps echoing from above. Mors was somewhere high above him still ascending the narrow spiral staircase. Rouletabille removed his shoes and crept silently upwards. In his overworked imagination, he saw Mors carrying a small but incredibly powerful bomb, perhaps no larger than an attaché case, perhaps derived from Professor Stangerson's disassociation of matter experiments—something that could level this entire island.

Rouletabille entered the statue's crown and swiftly flashed around the beam of his bulls-eye lantern. The chamber was empty, Mors was in the highest possible part of the statue, the Torch of Liberty. Rouletabille pressed onwards up the ladder that rose 40 feet through the statue's arm. He cast his light out onto the torch viewing gallery while also covering the visible area with his revolver. A lone figure in a full-dress German naval uniform was standing out on the torch balcony platform.

Mors turned to greet Rouletabille as he stepped out into the fresh air.

"Ah, the little phantom who has hounded my trail these last few weeks and slain my pets... You've come to observe my little experiment, eh?"

"I've no time for pleasantries, Mors. How long until the explosion?" demanded Rouletabille.

"It will be any moment now... Certainly within the next 90 seconds..."

"Then let's get out of here! Do you want to die when the statue is razed?"

"Your arithmetic is poor, detective. While I'd hardly say this was a safe distance, 100,000 pounds of TNT and three million pounds of munitions couldn't demolish Lady Liberty from so far away."

"What are you talking about? Where is the explosive device?"

"Why, on the Black Tom Pier amongst the dozens of railroad cars packed with dynamite... Where did you...?"

Over on the Jersey Shore, the gates of Hell opened. A pearlescent dome of white fire, hundreds of yards across, appeared for a split second and then consumed itself... It transformed into billowing black and red burning clouds; and the clouds, in turn, started to form something shaped like a titanic tree of ebony smoke which towered thousands of feet over Jersey City. The Black Tom Pier was the logistical node for all ammunition and explosives heading to the European theater. Only a madman—or a genius—would've set a bomb there. Rouletabille cursed himself for disregarding the possibility.

"You are insane!" screamed Rouletabille, though he could hardly hear his own words over the deafening booms that were agony to his eardrums. "You could not have calculated the effect; you might've destroyed the city!"

"Nonsense! I know exactly what I am doing..." shouted Mors.

And at that instant a wall of debris engulfed Bedloe's Island like a January fog. What might've have been a railroad tie struck the fine copper work and glass of the torch platform. Rouletabille felt suddenly nauseous and realized that his scalp was very wet; the wetness dripped into his eyes, then the platform deck lurched violently upwards to meet his face as his knees gave way.

When Rouletabille awoke on the U-Boat, the solution to the "Mystery of the Red Canoe" lay immediately in front of him. Accommodation on the submarine must have been at a premium, and he lay on a camp bed in the refrigeration plant, which was not currently in use. Beside him were a small wooden canoe and some buckets which still held a bloody residue. Mors' men had used the canoe as a mould to create a small gory iceberg which could be set on the incoming tide to attract sharks to bathing beaches. The man-eaters would follow it like homing pigeons.

A few minutes later, the steel door to the plant swung open and Mors swaggered triumphantly in.

"Your injuries have been treated with medicaments of my own devising. You will heal swiftly and with no scars," he assured the detective.

"Am I your prisoner?" asked Rouletabille.

"No. I have a proposition for you... American entry to the war has always been inescapable, and now I have fulfilled my patriotic duty to the Fatherland by perpetrating the greatest act of sabotage the world has ever seen. I intend to take no further part in this war. In fact, I intend to leave the Earth completely. Especially since my superiors will assume from my radio silence that this craft and all in it were consumed by the Black Tom Pier explosion. But I need your assistance..."

"You want Nemo and Robur's plans for the outer-space craft," concluded Rouletabille.

"Only for the purposes of checking certain calculations regarding the hull stresses that will be experienced as we leave the gravity of Earth. I have a duty to protect the lives of my crew in this hazardous endeavor."

"I thought you needed the designs to construct such a ship."

"No, my ship, *The Meteor*, is already built and stands ready on one of my secret island bases."

"I see. I can provide you with the blueprints on the proviso that you cease to participate in this conflict; but that is purely on the basis of my own country's national interest and the orders that I am compelled to follow. I must tell you that, if it was a matter of my personal discretion, I would seek to bring you to justice for the appalling crimes that you have committed—most especially causing the death of an innocent child. And if I could not obtain justice, I would settle for mere revenge."

"The death of the boy is a source of great regret to me... and while I cannot undo it, if you come with me now, I will try to prove my good intentions for the future."

And so, Mors and Rouletabille ascended to the U-Boat's deck. Lashed to the deck were two huge cylinders, each almost 25 feet long. Rouletabille initially mistook them for immense torpedoes.

"This was to be the next phase of my war on the United States. Each tube contains an immature Great White Shark in a chemically induced torpor. Inside, nutrients and hormones will grow the predators to fantastic size, and they will be anthrophagous—they will specifically seek out humans as their main food supply. This weapon I will sacrifice as a gesture of goodwill. The growth process cannot be stopped. The devices are booby-trapped and impossible to open prematurely or sabotage—sometimes I am overly cautious—but I will allow you to set the control mechanism so that the cylinders won't open until decades in the future, rather than in a few months as I would have. And if we dump the sharks here, they are many miles from the nearest resort in any event—there is nothing but fishing ports here."

Rouletabille knelt down and turned the stiff metal control wheel almost as far as it would go. Six hundred and ninety months... The torpid sharks would surely be dead by then, and if they weren't, then hopefully this craze for sea-bathing would be over by three quarters of the way through the 20th century. The German then stabbed at a glowing blue control stud and the cylinders fell into the sea, the backsplash momentarily inundated the deck.

Mors gestured to the small sailing skiff that was moored aft.

"You can use that to get ashore. I won't be needing it anymore. Rendezvous with me here in a week's time and bring the spacecraft plans...After that, I can assure you that you will never see me again... I shall be leaving this sphere or dying in the attempt."

"Very well. I hope for your sake that you are a man of your word, Captain Mors."

"I am a German officer."

At these words Rouletabille just bit his lip.

The detective climbed down into the skiff and then Mors untied it.

"Head for the lighthouse," instructed Mors.

Rouletabille turned the boat so that the prow faced the Amity Point Lighthouse and set sail. He could just make out the twinkling lights of the little township beyond.

In the first installment of "Slouching Towards Camulodunum" (published in Tales of the Shadowmen No. 7), the great Occult detective Sâr Dubnotal, on the trail of the sinister Helen Vaughan (from Arthur Machen's The Great God Pan), met the adventuress Becky Sharp, whom Micah Harris previously featured in "The Ape Gigans" in Tales of the Shadowmen No. 3 and "The Scorpion and the Fox" in Tales of the Shadowmen No. 6. While the Sâr and his associates seek to punish Helen, Becky is after her because the evil sorceress stole her child. Unfortunately, one of the Sâr's friends, the artist Pickman, turns out to be a traitor—and a Ghoul—foiling the plot. Dubnotal and Becky, already at odds, feel increasingly frustrated as the prospect of capturing the elusive Helen Vaughan grows more elusive. Now, read on as Becky is finally ready to reveal how she met her foe...

Micah Harris: *Slouching Towards Camulodunum* *(Part Two)*

(*from an idea by Mark Schultz*)

Bath, Colchester, and Cornwall, 1917

III. The Testimony of Rebecca Sharp.

"I suppose that when I take my dying breath, I will still be cursing the night I first laid eyes on Helen Vaughan. If only I had not walked into that tavern, choked with soldiers just about to head off to France. But foresight is a luxury those struggling to make it through the day can ill afford.

"I am not proud to say that I was there to barter my flesh with men who knew it may be their last night in their homeland forever. You must understand, gentlemen, how dire my circumstances were. I was with child; I dared not approach the father—and, please, do not ask why. Suffice it to say, the circumstances of our parting meant any future reconciliation quite out of the question.

"Nevertheless, I could not let our child die or be born sickly and weak for lack of nourishment. So I was in that tavern, surveying the room for the means to insure I would eat that night, and that was when my eyes were compelled to linger on Helen Vaughan...

"No one else in the tavern saw *it*, or they most certainly would have immediately fled the establishment for France and the comparative safety of the trenches.

"At her shoulder was an impish little satyr, and it was revolting: the sallow skin of its man's torso with pink dugs stretching thin to the waist, the veins bulging on the purplish, pulsating sacks at the base of its horns, the jaundiced eyes that stared with utter contempt at the mass of humans about it, the nastily tangled fur of its legs...

"It was the same type of beast I saw at Pickman's elbow this very evening. That was how I knew he was allied with Helen. And I reasoned that his glove concealed that which, unlike that satyr, would otherwise be visible and which he did not wish to be seen...

"I can see the inevitable question in all your faces: 'how is it that you perceived something that we talked about—and that walked about us—and we could not?' I do not know for certain, gentlemen, but I strongly suspect that it has something to do with the lingering effects from my pregnancy. Though I had seen such things before that night in the tavern, I had no such visions before I conceived.

"I'm certain that it had nothing to do with the father. My body went through a preternatural change in its make-up—again, do not ask—some time before I met him."

She allowed herself a slight, wry smile. "Believe me: you would all be astonished by how my youthful beauty belies my true age.

"It would seem entirely logical, then, that the heightened state of a human body, no longer merely '*a little lower than the angels*,' would have its own brand of prenatal quirks and unexpected side effects. Some women get flat feet; I saw monsters.

"I had not asked for this burden, but it was what caused me to linger my gaze longer than I should have on Helen Vaughan. To take note of a face that would have otherwise remained indistinct amidst the constant shifting of persons in the low lighting of the tavern.

"Well, I found my Jack for the evening, and we retired to the alley behind the tavern to transact business. Unfortunately, this soldier was not so intoxicated that he disregarded my swollen abdomen which my clothing had so far concealed. With a look of shock and revulsion on his face, he began to beat me and did so until I lost consciousness.

"When I awoke, Helen Vaughan was over me, palpating my body—trying to ascertain that I was still alive, she claimed, though I'm sure now she was trying to take any money or valuables off my person. I have no doubt that she would have strangled me in my weakened state and then continued her pillaging, except that my eyes opened on her ring, and I blurted out in my confusion:

" 'The goat man on your ring—was it he at your shoulder?'

"Her hands hovered over me. 'You saw him?' she asked after a moment.

" 'In the tavern.'

"Astonishment froze her facial features, and it was only when her hands dropped to my person and touched my abdomen again that her halted expression resolved into the sweetest, solicitous-of-my-health, smile.

" 'My sister,' she said.

"She gathered me up, took me to her own run-down lodgings, and nursed me back to health. During this time, she asked me repeatedly the identity of my baby's father, but I would not expose him to her so that she could blackmail him or charge him a ransom for our child. After a time, she mentioned it no more.

"I was not stupid, gentlemen. I knew she was trouble, but I had no other friend. I shudder now at how much like Helen my latest reversals had made me; I have never been a saint, but I had believed the love I had of one man, and the love I had for the one whose child I bore, had somehow redeemed me. Now, with no chance of recourse to either, I quickly warmed to Helen Vaughan's considerate ministrations. I found my bitterness and rage, tempered in a furnace of helplessness and despair, commensurate with whatever black, vile abscess festered inside her where a human heart would beat—at least to the point that when I was sufficiently recovered, we began to work as a team. Helen would seduce the soldiers and bring them to her private place and, together, we would rob them. I struck many of them over the head until they lost consciousness—repeatedly so, if need be--each time seeing the face of the soldier who had so beaten me.

"I am not proud of my behavior, gentlemen. But unless your life has ever ebbed into so dark a place that no beam of light can penetrate it, pray, do not judge me.

"With the money we had thus accumulated, Helen suggested that, since my delivery was now near, we move to her home village of Caermaen. Though a scandal had caused her to flee from there—the cause, I suspected, of the nasty scar around her neck of which she would never speak—she assured me that many years had passed, and her appearance was much changed.

"There, Helen often took me walking along what had been her favorite childhood haunt—the Roman road. It was on such a promenade in the winter months that I went into labor. And it was Helen who delivered me there as the pains of labor came nigh to wrenching me out of this world. My agonies sent me teetering on the edge of it, and the nightmarish one that enveloped me.

"As I pushed, I saw on my breast a horned succubus, leering into my eyes. I could actually feel its weight on my chest, choking my breathing—that's how close I came to its hellish abode. As Helen tore my child from my body, I could see behind her, surrounding us, a crowd of horned, wretched, twisted things. I could make out every detail of their perverse anatomies: from the crusted matter caking the rims of their yellow eyes to the sickening pinkness of the dugs rowed over their foul abdomens. *And my child, not I, was the subject of their intent focus!*

"Like that of a crowing cock compelling what ghosts have walked the night back into purgatory, my child's first cry banished those monsters from the periphery of our world and returned them completely to their own sphere. The darkness that had hung over the whole dreadful proceedings suddenly passed, and I could feel a soothing sense of normalcy rush over me in the twitter of winter birds and the wind in the trees that surrounded us.

" 'Helen,' I weakly croaked out, hearing my child's continuing cries, 'I... want to see... my baby.'

"But helpless on my back as an upside down tortoise, I could see only an empty sky, and now even the child's wailing had suddenly gone silent.

"My heart thudded mightily against my ribs as I tried to wrench myself up from the ground, but I was too weak after my ordeal.

" '*Helen!*' I shouted. '*Bring me my baby!*'

Only then did she lean into my field of vision, but without my child. As she switched my papers with her own and slipped her ring on my finger, she said in mockingly sweet tones:

" 'Relax, Becky, darling. It's a girl.'

"And then, I saw the large fragment of ancient Roman masonry rushing down upon me.

"You now understand, Sâr Dubnotal, the origins of that groove you found atop my head. My skull was sufficiently crushed, or you can be sure that Helen would not have left the job half-done. Nevertheless, I possessed a resilience she could not suspect, and I retained enough consciousness to hear that witch chanting to my child as she walked down the old Roman road:

"Old King Cole was a merry old soul

"And a merry old soul was he;

"He called for his pipe, and he called for his bowl

"And he called for his fiddlers three.

"And then the red mist that hung over my eyes darkened, and I knew no more.

"I know not how many days passed before I was found on that deserted road. Fortunately, no one checked my papers or recognized the ring until I was taken to a doctor, for Helen was not remembered fondly by the good people of Caermaen. I was told that, as I laid unconscious in hospital, I was saved from suffocation by pillow at the hands of some grieved parent whose child Helen had ruined years before.

"The village doctor, who had no love for Helen either, still insisted that any punitive action be delayed until my swollen features healed enough to see if they could be recognized. He realized that I might be Helen's victim, that she could very well have schemed to switch our papers, in hope that the locals would bury *me* in an unmarked grave for *her* past sins. They would thus serve their enemy's further purpose by erasing all evidence in the event of an investigation into my disappearance.

"I believe now there was a second reason: the fear that Villiers and Clarke might learn—as they indeed did—of her resurrection. I am certain this fear was why she chose the anonymity of a guttersnipe's existence for so long. Thus, the need of a new identity—*my* identity—to move more freely about England and reunite her followers.

"Of course, when it became apparent that I was indeed yet another victim of Helen Vaughan, the locals took pity on me and nursed me, though all expected me to die. Even with my preternatural ability to regenerate, a year passed before I was able to leave Caermean in pursuit of my child. Yet another year went by before I again heard that cursed song from that upstairs window on Great Gualteney Street

"Once before, about six months after I left Caermean, I had a near reunion with my Annie and Helen. In one village, I learned of the arrival only a month before of a woman of an unsettling mien leading a toddler by the hand. Both were dressed in filthy and disheveled clothing. The authorities were so bold as to take the child from this unfit mother and place her in an orphanage five miles away.

"Naturally, I rushed to the site, and as night fell, I saw the glow of a conflagration on the horizon. I found the orphanage on fire. No children survived the night. They laid on the ground, burned black, some of them so much so that..." here, Becky shuddered, "...that the skin had split open in places."

"Dear Lord," Clarke said.

"I shall never forget," Becky said, "how the pain that would not release them to the relief of death twisted their little faces into the most ghastly of grimaces. It was as though, their voices failing to convey the depths of their pain, the flesh itself was wailing.

"The faces are so etched in my memory, gentlemen, because I did not know—*could* not know—which one of these wretched figures, as I ran from one to the other, might be revealed as my child. I was forced to study each of the agonized little girls in hopes of recognition of a facial resemblance that their disfiguring made impossible.

"I swooned at the news, upon the breaking of day, that Annie had been removed from the orphanage by Helen, and that the witch had set the blaze to conceal her latest abduction of my child by creating the impression she had been consumed in the flames. I had this account from one of the authorities who interrogated the orphanage handy man. Helen had seduced him into aiding her, but he swore he had no idea of her full plan until she put a knife in his back and then began setting the fire. But he survived both blade and blaze. That the woman was Helen was clear from his description of the nasty groove around her neck."

"The Sâr, Clarke, and I, are all very familiar with the events of this last episode in your story, Miss Sharp," Villiers said. "We three have been on Helen's trail since Sâr Dubnotal came to London with his letter from our late, esteemed associate Dr. Matheson. The Sâr wished to examine Helen's remains to add the description of such a creature to his repository of occult knowledge. It was then that we discovered that her body had vanished. Since only Clarke and I knew where she was buried, and the full range of her dark powers were unknown to us, it was all too possible that she had resurrected herself. Our subsequent investigation confirmed this horrible truth.

"That search led us, too, to that orphanage a few days after its burning, after reading in the papers that the villagers were certain it was the work of the 'devil-woman' who sought revenge for the taking of her child. That Helen Vaughan had reproduced was perhaps more frightening to contemplate than her reincorporation.

"Miss Sharp," Villiers continued, going on one knee so that he could look her in the eye as he warmly clasped her delicate hand between his two, "Helen Vaughan is the spawn of a human woman and an entity from that hellish dimension you glimpse on occasion. After hearing your story, we are much relieved to learn that Providence has apparently rendered her sterile. When she saw you were pregnant, and that you could see the satyr—well, those were the circumstances of her own mother and father. When you steadfastly refused to divulge the paternity of your baby, it only confirmed what she already suspected: here was a child of a similarly abominable conception by the same sire, and being of her own perverse lineage—her chance for a daughter.

"Clarke, if you would bring my valise…"

Once his partner had delivered it to him, Villiers opened it and took out a stick with a metal noose on one end. "We thought this sufficient to destroy her, and if Sâr Dubnotal had not arrived with Dr. Matheson's letter, requesting to see the remains of this foul creature, we would have never known she had resurrected. It appears you have paid the price for our folly."

"She suffered by this garrote?" Becky asked, sniffing.

"Much agony."

"*Très bien*," Becky said. "Please, might I hold on to it? It would be such a comfort."

An expression of both puzzlement and distaste immediately registered on Villiers' face at her request. Still, he said, "Of course," folded her hands about the stick, and rose to his feet.

Sâr Dubnotal had listened intently to Becky's tale, and while Villiers talked, he had withdrawn into a deep state of meditation over her story. He suddenly snapped his fingers, as though to awaken himself from his own trance, turning the attention of all assembled upon him.

"Miss Sharp, do you still have Helen's ring on your person? Yes? If you would be so kind as to hand it to me… Ah—thank you."

Sâr Dubnotal held the ring out, pinched between thumb and forefinger, so that the satyr's head could be seen by all. "The nursery rhyme, Miss Sharp. Have you ever thought that it might have some special significance to Helen Vaughan?"

Becky slowly shook her head from side to side. "I must confess I have not."

Dubnotal now examined the inscription inside the ring band. "Here 'tis written, *DEVOMNODENT-MAVORS CAMVLOS*. The first part translates roughly 'Nodens, the god'—of the abyss, in this case. That, then, is the identity of the satyr on this ring, though the name 'Pan' is by far more common. The second part of the inscription gives yet a third and fourth title: *MAVORS CAM-VLOS*, or Mars-Camulos. Camulos was a Celtic god sometimes depicted, satyr-like, with the horns of a ram and who, through the syncretism of the Roman invaders, became identified with their Mars.

"As to the significance of that tormenting nursery rhyme, Miss Sharp, it is a palimpsest through which we can still discern the pagan under-text: King 'Cole' is Camulos. We may assume that his pipe is for smoking, but the fact that he calls for three fiddlers indicates it was originally musical pipe*s*—*Pan* pipes.

"If this still seems mere speculation to any of you, let me add this to remove all doubt: the oldest city in England, built by the Romans, was named Camulodonum after Camulos. Today, it still bears his name, though softened—just as in that nursery rhyme—to Colchester. It is inevitable that Helen will retreat to her father's house."

"Then, that is where my child..." Becky began, her voice choking on a sense of hope she wasn't sure she could trust.

Sâr Dubnotal reached down and firmly gripped her by her shoulders. "Be strong, Miss Sharp, for not all of what I'm about to say will be comforting: Helen is taking her to Colchester—to meet Camulos."

IV. Out From the Abyss

"But do not despair," the Great Psychagogue added. "Helen Vaughan's arrogance and manipulative schemes have already given us the keys to her undoing.

"Villiers! Clarke!" he said. "Go immediately to the train depot, and obtain a list of every train station along the railways from Bath to Colchester. Have dispatched a telegram to all the stationmasters describing Helen Vaughan and ordering they place highly visible wanted posters for her, with your names prominently attached to each in large block letters.

"The dispatcher will be reluctant to do what you ask, of course. Therefore, take this signet ring of mine and have him describe it via wire to the County Somerset railway superior stationed at Cad Green. This man is in my debt for services rendered on his behalf in the Affair of the Leprous Bodhisattva."

"But... why would we want Helen to know we are on to her?" Clarke asked. "Even if we make it impossible for her to travel by train, and slow her progress..."

"Exactly, but my reason is twofold: you two are the only men Helen Vaughan fears, so she will take every precaution now that you are on her trail, most certainly including a disguise. You see, she does not have the option of turning back. I now recognize our earlier guest Yeats' poem about the return of a beast-man as the record of a prophetic—if distorted—dream. Based on his poem, I suspect this meeting of Helen with her father at Colchester will be a uniquely tangible one. Her cult, which is surely gathering there to join her for this event, will be alerted to expect her arrival incognito.

"Miss Sharp, I return Helen's ring to you. Keep it safe, for it, along with the papers she placed on your person, will aid in your passing yourself off as your enemy, thereby granting us ingress into this vile Sabbat.

"Villiers and Clarke, little Jacques and his Eustache, will go with you. Once that you see the telegram is dispatched properly, all of you will board the next train to Colchester. But first, make a second request of the Somerset railway superior. For my sake, ask if he will prepare an alternate schedule for all trains arriving at Colchester for the next 48 hours. It should place them two hours behind their actual arrival. *This* schedule is to be presented to any who might request it—except those whose duty is to see that the trains arrive safely. Helen's cult will be monitoring your pursuit, and this will grant us an element of surprise. Jacques, I suppose I need not remind you to bring your box? I thought not."

At that point, Naïni entered the room.

"Naïni, has Rodin received due recompense?"

"He has, master."

"Then justice has been served. Rudolf, Annunciata: normally I would dispense this detail to Naïni, but I have need of him elsewhere. To you, I'm afraid, falls the unpleasant task of disposing of Rodin's remains."

A stunned Rudolf opened his mouth but was mute, his face contorting with more and more revulsion as the exact nature of this grim detail settled in.

Annunciata, however, immediately found her voice: "Please, master! Wouldn't I be more useful channeling his spirit—something more along my line?"

"If I may," Aytown injected. "One theory of Basil Hallward's disappearance that we…" he nodded at Randolph and Tate, "…have investigated was that his murderer could have disposed of his body through dissection in a tub and then an application of acid."

"Yes," the Sâr replied. "That was my exactly my idea in having Rodin taken to the room adjoining a water closet with bath. Messers. Aytown, Tate, and Randolph—though I'm sure you wish to personally take the battle to Vaughan—you would best serve all our interests here. But be assured, your friend Beardsley *shall* be avenged, and you all will be witness to it.

"Your investigation into Hallward's disappearance has, no doubt, made you familiar with the milieu of such men who might discretely provide us with such items as we need in the matter of Monsieur Rodin. Will you be so good as to obtain them? And aid Rudolf in their administration? Poor Annunciata over there has actually managed to exceed her usual pallor—altogether, quite remarkable. Feel free to retire to your room, my dear Annunciata. And, for pity's sake, be careful of *which* WC you visit over the next 48 hours.

"In the meantime, Miss Sharp, Naïni, and I will board the earliest train to Colchester. Hopefully, the circulation of the wanted poster will force Helen off the railways sooner than later and allow us to arrive first, delaying her inevitable challenge of our ruse. This should give us plenty of time..." here, a smile parted the lips of the Great Psychagogue, a smile which, though slight, was weighted with foreboding, "...to do some damage of the irreparable sort."

The turbaned man who identified himself as "Severus el Tebib" and the cloaked and hooded woman calling herself "Helen Vaughan" strolled through the midsummer's eve twilight that had now enveloped Colchester. A giant draped under cape and cowl followed. Fresh dew shone on the grass, and the stars themselves seemed just minted. The night air was soft and all nature insouciant on the cusp of its dissolution.

"I still do not quite understand," the woman under the hood said, "why Helen has waited two years to deliver my baby to that thing she believes is Annie's father."

The three were passing an ancient oak which the locals had mentioned was 750-years old. At the sight of it, Severus el Tebib thought again of Yeats poem that he had, on more than one occasion over the last 48 hours, regretted not committing completely to memory.

"It was not given to her to choose the moment of his coming," he said. "Take a lesson from the oak, Miss Sharp: should it be sawed off at the trunk, you would see concentric rings, one for each year of its 750 years of growth. The past, you see, is not simply done; it is yet present inside of that tree. Its cross section is both a chart of Time and a symbol of its cyclic nature.

"Camulos, I suspect, was here, in the deep time before men, but at some point was locked out. In the revolving of the ages, it seems there are certain junctures that could be propitious for his return. Among the natives in Africa, there is a similar tradition of *L'mur-Kathulos*, while the South Seas Kanakas look to the gyring consolations as the harbinger of *Tulu*.

"Miss Sharp—are you trembling?"

"Just the chill from the evening dew," she said and even her voice shivered. "Please, go on El Tebib—or should I just say, 'Doctor?'"

"According to Mr. Yeats, the last propitious moment for Camulos was approximately 2000 years ago. But at that point, Camulos was forced into slumber; the human race was granted an extension to allow for the grace of Christ to take global effect—which would have been sufficient to lock out Camulos forever. Well... to see what we did with that opportunity, I submit for your consideration the 'blood-dimmed tide' of 'the war to end all wars.'

"But I rather think this time around we are set against Camulos' coming as God's appointed conspirators. A motley lot to be sure, but then, so were Christ's first disciples."

"I suppose I fill the spot of the woman taken in adultery, then?" Becky asked, her smile sardonic beneath her hood.

The Sâr's cheeks burned under his beard. "It was perhaps... not so much an analogy as an *induction*, Miss Sharp."

"I understand all you have said so far, Doctor—believe me, far more than you could ever suspect. But why are you certain that the cult of Helen Vaughan is gathering at the old castle?"

"Like a tree, a building may retain past time in its present: a phenomenon responsible for more than one haunting I have investigated. Now, that castle is built on the foundation of the burned temple of Claudius, erected contemporaneously with the rise of Christianity, which Yeats sets as the *terminus a quo* of the epoch which the arrival of his 'rough beast' will end. Within Colchester Castle, all time from the beginning of Christianity's spread throughout the world unto this very moment is present: as it contains the *terminus a quo*, it is the most apropos point for the inauguration of the *terminus ad quem*."

Sâr Dubnotal touched Becky's elbow while holding up his other hand at Naïni and nodded slightly at one of the Australian soldiers who currently filled Colchester Hospital. The trio stopped to watch the soldier angle up a telescope on its tripod. Nearby a large searchlight set on the ground.

Becky drew the hood down lower so that her eyes were veiled as the Sâr said, "Excuse me, sir. You seem to be surveying the constellations—may I ask you for what purpose?"

"I'm not stargazing, if that's what you mean," the soldier answered without looking at who addressed him, his face grimacing with the effort of keeping his eye properly attached to the viewfinder. "The first Zeppelins that bombed England last year chose a route in this vicinity for their return to Germany. Makes sense they might come back this way."

"I see. Goodnight, sir. And thank you for your efforts on all our behalves."

The soldier grunted something, still without looking at who addressed him, steadfastly intent on searching the skies.

Now, they came at last to Colchester Castle. How they had obtained the use of the facilities, the Sâr did not know, but he felt certain it had more to do with some mundane form of blackmail or coercion than any occult "hostile current."

Bearing electric torches, three muscular men in evening wear were quickly making their way across the lawn toward them. Naïni's cape rustled as he began to move it back to give his long, massive limbs freedom, but the Sâr raised the fingers of one hand. "Not yet, Naïni. Not until we see there is no other recourse."

Still, the cloaked giant had to do no more than stand there for the men to stop short of the trio. They were armed, and their hands were already at their holstered revolvers in case Naïni should begin to encroach upon them.

"Who are you?" the leader of the guards demanded.

Becky alone stepped forward. Her heart was racing, for if Helen had somehow managed to beat them here, things were about to get much more difficult.

She extended her hand from the long sleeve of her cloak, letting her wrist dip to display Helen's ring. "I am Helen Vaughan," she said. "Behold the ring that bears the visage of my great sire, god of the abyss, lord of fortresses. Surely you were told that the pursuit of my mortal enemies Villiers and Clarke necessitated I come in disguise? Was this identifying effect not described to you? Does anyone without my birthright dare wear it? Do any of you fools dare come between me and my father?"

The guards now were more cowed by Becky than Naïni. The leader took tentative steps toward her while the other two hung back. He did not dare touch her hand to lift it, but instead bent and held his electric torch near.

"My lady!" he gasped in awe and quickly stepped away. "I will run ahead to announce your arrival. My men will escort…"

"Fool! Do you not see that I already have an escort? And no one shall know I am here until *I* deign to reveal it. All of you return to patrolling the grounds."

"Well played, Miss Sharp," Sâr Dubnotal said when the guards were out of earshot.

The threesome finished their approach without further impediment. Upon entering the main chamber of the castle, they found before them men and women from England's and France's highest societies, dressed as though they were attending the symphony.

"Dilettantes and elitists," the Sâr said, sniffing contemptuously. "These fools all think they are attending nothing more than a glorified version of table rapping or *planchette*. They play with strange fire in the decadent idleness of the privileged, heedless of what they are about to unleash. *Sur vous, le Déluge.*"

From behind Becky, a salutation delivered in an effete, urbane intonation: "Helen! Is it you? Here at last? It has been too long since 'Mrs. Belmont' held court over her infamous Ashley Street salon, eh?"

"Do not turn," the Sâr hissed under his breath.

The immaculately dressed man with his trimmed goatee the color of ash was now upon them. The whites of his eyes were shot through with tiny red tendrils, and the crevices of his crow's feet had reached his cheeks. Still, the wreck of a once devilishly handsome face was discernible under a now sallow complexion.

"Helen! Surely you have not forgotten your most devoted admirer, Harry? It's Lord Henry!" As a jaundiced hand reached for her shoulder to turn her, the Sâr imposed himself between Becky and the aristocrat.

Lord Henry withdrew his hand but did not step back. "Swarthy heathen! You dare come between me and a friend I thought I would never see again?"

"I dare nothing less! You, sir, certainly know of the trauma which she suffered and how she changed form into a writhing obscenity at the point of expiration. Perhaps you have not heard that, since her resurrection, she has not been able to completely assume full human form—and such human features as she retains have been misshapened. Even her vocal chords have thickened. She ventures out, silent and hooded, to spare herself the humiliation of the involuntary shock and revulsion that could not help but strike even the closest of friends."

Lord Henry's hooded pupils shifted from Sâr Dubnotal to the giant who loomed protectively over the turbaned doctor. Still, he stood his ground. "Do you think me a fool? That I would just take a stranger's word?"

"Harry," Becky croaked as she turned and extended her arm, her hand thrusting from the sleeve of her cloak.

Lord Henry gasped. "The ring!"

"Do you wish to examine it?" the Sâr said. "Helen told me beforehand to grant this dispensation only to her closest friends to assure them, under these extreme circumstances, that it is indeed her."

The Great Psychagogue reverently removed the ring from Becky's still extended hand, then placed it in Lord Henry's palm. As he held it close to his bloodshot eyes, Henry said, "This craftsmanship cannot be reproduced today—and there is the inscription of the names of her father. Only she and her nearest associates—of whom I am one—knew what was written on the inside of the band. And she wore it only on special occasions, keeping it at all other times in a place known only to her. It was not on her person when she died. We thought it either pilfered or its location lost with Helen."

He returned the ring to the Sâr, who placed it back on Helen's finger. "My dear Helen," Lord Henry began, "I am so sorry for your misfortunes. Forgive me for adding to your distress. But we must announce your arrival!"

Sâr Subnotal held up his palm. "It is Helen's wish not to reveal herself until her father restores her former glory at his advent, and she takes her place at his left hand."

"Of course," Lord Henry said. "And please—you are?"

"Severus el Tebib—you may call me 'Doctor.'"

"Quite. Please, Doctor, accept my apology. You and this..." he nodded at Naïni, "...giant are her escorts, then? Ha! Few would be inclined to engage in fisticuffs with this bruiser, eh?"

"Villiers and Clarke would be most hesitant to attempt to murder her again with such a bodyguard, yes."

"Our spies have reported they are bearing down on us—in the company of a monstrous hound and its master, a most untoward dwarf I once had the displeasure of knowing. Although it was obviously something of a stretch for him, we of Helen's salon sought to school him extensively in the secret knowledge, but he could only see it as a short subject. When it became clear our investment in him was one of diminishing returns, he—and his flea-bitten cur—were expelled from our company.

"No matter: they will all arrive too late. I assume, now that Helen is here, I may order those who have assembled in the Roman cellar to begin the summoning?"

"Immediately," the Sâr replied.

"Sâr!" Becky said when Lord Henry was out of earshot. "What are you doing? Why are you hurrying this on with Helen and my child not yet arrived?"

"We could only revive his suspicions by not agreeing to what Helen Vaughan has expressly come to do. But be at ease, Becky, and let me concentrate. I have not before attempted hypnotism on quite this scale, but the wills of these people are as thin and pallid as their inbred blood."

Sâr Dubnotal swept his gaze back and forth over the lengthy table where the idle rich had all gathered, until he made eye contact with a dandy. In an instant, the current of mesmeric magnetism rushed across the room, and the man was held by Severus el Tebib's will. After a pause, the man began arranging his dishes, cutlery, and other dining implements into diagonal lines, then did the same with the dinnerware of whom sat at his right and his left. Baffled, they stared as he rose, compelled to carry on this task around the entire table, raising ires as more than once his leaning over his fellow diners put an elbow in someone's face.

Sâr Dubnotal now strolled across the room to the table. As the rest of the group looked up at him, he threw open wide the floodgates of his eyes and the rapacious force that swept out took them all.

In a moment, all returned to their idle chatter, unmindful of the Doctor as he withdrew and the dandy as he continued on his mission.

"What exactly did you do?" Becky asked.

Sâr Dubnotal smiled and slightly raised his hand. "Watch," he said.

Becky noticed that, as people tried to return the dishes and other utensils back to their proper places, they could not lift them despite what turned into strenuous efforts.

"Hypnotic suggestion," the Great Psychagogue explained. "Those diagonal lines form sigils wedged into Camulos' point of ingress. The sigils will snare him between our world and what lies behind it until his moment has passed, and he must return fully back into the abyss."

"But if someone you didn't hypnotize enters the room?"

"Other than Helen and whoever accompanies her, no one else will. Lord Henry would not have begun the summoning unless the coven was complete. He was only awaiting Helen's arrival, which you were kind enough to supply. I dare say, when the real Helen comes, she will not take time to count the silverware, and those who are with her will be too intent on their mistress to care how the table is prepared. As for Lord Henry, upon his return to the chamber, should he move toward the table, he can be persuaded to do otherwise easily enough."

"*What the deuce does that mean?*"

They all startled at Lord Henry's exclamation, but he was still out of ear-shot of their lowered voices, his attention riveted on the action across the room.

Henry had now reached the Sâr's group. "What on Earth does Monsieur N*** think he is doing? Why, he has become as fantastical in his behavior as Doctor Johnson! I'll put an end to this before he disrupts..."

"*You will do no such thing, Lord Henry,*" the Sâr commanded—and the force of his words struck Lord Henry stock-still.

"What the deuce? Who... who are you? Who are you *really*?" Lord Henry said as his voice trailed into a whisper.

"The one who knows all that you have done in public and private over a lifetime that has lingered far too long in this world. I know by name those you have corrupted, and their loved ones to whom you have dealt a lifetime of woe with no cause but to satisfy your vanity and contempt.

"You who have sown the vile seed in the field of innocence, know that the reaping is at hand. *The axe is already laid to the roots.* I will deal with you personally, Lord Henry. Your only choice is this: shall you suffer the fell stroke now or tomorrow, or the day after tomorrow? In a fortnight or next month? But be sure of this: *I shall not tarry!*"

Lord Henry's knees dipped and his face blanched. Even here, amidst the cult, he knew he was not safe.

"Retire to that corner where you will be under the watchful eye of my manservant. Speak to no one, nor move one muscle. Be as still as if you were posing for a portrait. I trust I am clear. Naïni, if you will."

"You frighten me, Sâr Dubnotal," Becky said as Naïni escorted Henry. "And that is not an easy accomplishment."

He smiled down at her. "Rebecca Sharp, the downtrodden and innocent victim shall never have cause to fear me—only the guilty."

"That is most comforting," Becky said as she withdrew her face even deeper into the folds of her hood.

"*All rise for the Advent of Our Lady of Pandemonium!*"

Four figures stood in the castle doorway which remained open, framing them against the night sky. The stars had gone out in the wake of Helen Vaughan, leaving behind the four a dark void that went on forever. The three men who had intercepted Becky, the Sâr, and Naïni made a guard about her. She stood hooded and cloaked, radiating a malicious self-possession. With a haughty toss of her head, her hood fell to her shoulders. Her hair was fire and her face a mask of porcelain most adamantine. And in her arms, she cradled a small child.

Sâr Dubnotal's hand was already reaching to restrain Becky. But he found her to be the epitome of composure. She stood as straight and regal as did Helen Vaughan. Only then did the Sâr think to look for Lord Henry, who, at the announcement of Helen's arrival, had stopped on his way to the corner. Now he was grinning triumphantly at Sâr Dubnotal as he brushed by Naïni and strode toward them.

But the Great Psychagogue displayed no concern. It was clear he considered both Lord Henry and his moment of triumph beneath contempt. "Reduced to hiding behind a woman's skirts, Lord Henry?" he asked out of the corner of his mouth as the dissipated aristocrat stopped beside him.

Henry shot the Doctor a sour look, then shouted, "Helen! I have found out three impostors among us! And this wench has gone so far as to dare impersonate you!"

He reached to pull away Becky's hood, but Naïni had followed and his hand shot out and enveloped Henry's frail one. He winced as he felt and heard something snap.

"Manners, Lord Henry," Sâr Dubnotal said, shaking a finger at him.

Henry fell back, gingerly working the fingers of his injured hand while cradling it in the other.

Then, for the first time, Helen Vaughan spoke: "All this is known to me."

"It would appear the guards have licked the red off Lord Henry's confection," Sâr Dubnotal murmured to Becky.

Helen put out her arm and flicked her wrist in an imperious gesture that ended with her forefinger pointing at Becky. "Let me see the face of she who has dared try to supplant the chosen daughter of Nodens, the Handmaiden of Chaos!"

All heads turned toward Becky as she calmly drew back her hood and smiled at the woman whose status as an enemy outstripped any adversary she had faced before.

Helen's eyes widened on reflex, and Becky was gratified to see the "chosen daughter of Nodens" look at her with a disbelief that was almost awe. But she quickly resolved her expression into one of a smiling, sinister dominance.

"I see you still have my ring," Helen said, slightly craning her head forward.

"I see you still have my child," Becky said, still smiling.

"Yes," Helen said, making a point to lower her head to the face of the child in her arms and smile as though she might coo. Then Helen looked up at Becky. "I am so happy that, in your final moments—and you may be sure you will most certainly be dead this time—you might see what good care I have taken of your baby. I hope, since your eyes shall close forever on this sight, it might keep your eternal rest peaceful."

Sâr Dubnotal remained silent. He was watching Becky for her reaction. Her shoulders had not slumped, nor had she ceased to smile. Her countenance showed no sign of defeat. Becky was up to something which she had not shared with him. As Helen Vaughan was presently neither concerned with him nor Naïni, El Tebib bided his time.

Until the opportune moment presents itself, thought the Great Psychago-gue, *discretion dictates that I leave this one to the ladies.*

"Now," Helen continued, "bring me my ring. While I hold your child, you will kneel before me and place it on my finger. Come, wench! And if you fail to keep your hands before you, you will be shot on the spot!"

Becky, serenely obedient, proceeded to do as told and soon stood before her archenemy. But she neither moved to kneel nor to remove the ring from her hand.

"The ring!" Helen demanded.

Becky's gaze bore into Helen's eyes as she continued to remain still and si-lent.

"Do you want to die now, cow? No—you're too much of a survivor for that. What is wrong with you? *Say something!*"

"I'm going to kill you, Helen."

Helen's head jerked as though stunned by a slap, but immediately she turned this slight tremor into a spasm of a haughty laugh. "I do not die easily," she said.

"Why, Helen," Becky said with a guileless smile, "why ever would you think that I want it to be easy?"

Becky's right arm now dropped to her side, and from its sleeve slipped the end of the stick with the metal garrote which Becky had told Villiers she had returned to his valise. The necessary haste to carry out Sâr Dubnotal's orders had not allowed for reflection on Becky's earlier, odd regard for that instrument of death until he, Clarke, Jacques, and Eustace were on their train to Colchester.

Upon sight of that metal noose, the imperious mask of Helen Vaughan cracked. She looked from the garrote into a face whose expression made clear that, despite her current unwinnable circumstances, nevertheless, Becky would, somehow, inevitably, manage to squeeze her throat by that noose until the wires touched.

Helen's hand went to the scar which the clasp of her cloak concealed. "Kill her!" she screamed at her guards. "Kill the bitch now!"

"*I think not!*"

Sâr Dubnotal's voice stunned the guards as though the mystic had hurled a thunderbolt across the room. In the next moment, they were again grabbing at their weapons. But the moment that the Sâr had purchased was enough.

A large, airborne hound thrust through the still open doorway and struck full on the guard on Helen's left, sending him down before he could remove his gun. The dog's jaws clamped onto his throat. As their trajectory carried them past the guard on Helen's right, the dwarf atop the hound sliced the razor-honed edge of his sword across the man's throat.

Helen, her features contorted by shock, fell back, shoving the remaining guard behind her off balance and out the door. He dropped backward on to the steps and the angle and impact of the fall broke his neck. For the first time, the child in Helen's arms began to cry.

Becky pushed forward, grabbing the staggered Helen by the upper arms. She wrenched her forward, so that, though cradled by her enemy, Becky felt for the first time her baby against her breast. "Let go of my child, bitch!" she snarled.

The jostled Helen cast a desperate glance over her shoulder toward the open doorway, only to see her archenemies, Villiers and Clarke, standing there, shoulder to shoulder. Villiers held a revolver on her.

"You're not going anywhere, Helen," Clarke hissed. "Except when Villiers and I send you back to Hell."

Then all simultaneously heard for the first time a rumbling which, in all the excitement, had begun gathering itself below the threshold of their hearing. Now it seemed a sudden, apocalyptic blast that made the castle around them tremble.

Helen's chin rose as a look of smug satisfaction reappeared on her face. "You hear that, you fools? That is the footfall of Camulos! He has come at last!"

Though worry could be seen in the faces of her enemies, they did not retreat, and she could not pass through the door and the longed-for reunion with her father. Then, with a sneer, Helen threw the tiny Anne over Becky's head.

Wide-eyed, Becky immediately turned her head over her shoulder and Villiers instinctively lunged forward for assistance. This was the opening Helen needed. She bolted out the door. Clarke caught her, but Helen scratched her nails across his face.

Clarke fell back, cursing Helen, as she ran onto the castle lawn.

Becky watched as a squalling Annie landed, knocking her head against the leg of a chair in the process. Livid, Becky bit into her lower lip so that it bled.

"Oh, that's the limit!"

Becky shot out the door, Sâr Dubnotal's shouts to her drowned out by the rumbling that had descended upon them all—not that his commands would have been heeded. She hit the lawn in a run and found Helen standing there looking up, her mouth agape at what she saw:

Three zeppelins, aloft over the castle grounds, like airborne whales migrating through a starless sky. It was the pulse and throb from their engines that shook the castle.

Becky, however, remained heedless of what was above. While her enemy stood slack-jawed from the false note of her demonic father's arrival, Becky tackled her, the momentum behind her run yielding an impact that thrust the air from Helen's lungs.

Becky quickly turned Helen on her back and mounted her. As her knees bore into Helen's ribs, she brought the back of her hand like a cudgel to her enemy's mouth, bursting her lips. Helen winced, as Becky again drew back her hand...

But the sudden flash of spotlights from the ground arrested her, their beams of brilliant white aimed at the zeppelins, but revealing something *more...*

Glimpsed only in diagonal cross sections by the sweeping streaks of light angled into the sky, *Devomnodent-Mavors Camvlos*, the Great God Pan, loomed so large that his goat's head reached the altitude of the zeppelins; it seemed he might catch them on his giant horns and toss them out of the sky, or, by a few quick thrusts, burst them like a child's party balloons.

The sharp, frantic cries in German were faintly audible even over the oppressive droning of the zeppelins. The risk of opening their floodlights to direct their fire meant losing what cover of darkness they retained. And their committed, slow drift combined with a limited ability to maneuver placed them, quite literally, on the horns of a dilemma.

A vicious metallic chattering heralded machine gun fire—their only defense—which followed wherever the beacons from the ground revealed the giant straddling Colchester with one hoof planted on the foothold of the castle. Ground fire followed, but no one could be certain if it was aimed at the Germans or Camulos.

Curiously, whatever parts of his massive anatomy which at any moment were outside the band width of each spotlight were simply *not there*, as though the beams rubbing over him in their passing erased what was seen as soon as it was revealed. There was complete lack of presence in their wake until the lights swept over in cross sections again.

Even in the light, Camulos appeared composed of no more than the motes of dust swarming in the beams. It was said that the world would dissolve with the weight of Camulos' glory as he placed his hooves upon it, but it was *he*, rather, who was rendered ethereal...

...for the diagonal bar Sâr Dubnotal had decreed lodged against the door to the abyss had held!

Helen was forced to glimpse her father's near advent upside down as she lay flat on her back under Becky. "He's not coming through!" she wailed.

"Allow me to offer my condolences," Becky said and brought down upon Helen's mouth a large rock she had found within reach, smashing her front teeth.

"Sauce for the goose, eh, Helen?" Becky said with a smile. She tossed the stone aside and clamped Helen's mouth closed, angling her head back. "Swallow, Helen! I want those teeth lodged in your throat!"

But Helen fought. In her paroxysms, her esophagus swelled and rippled like an engorged boa constrictor.

"Choke!" Becky ordered, digging her knees into Helen's ribs. "Very well, then," she said, withdrawing the garrote from her sleeve, "this has proven fairly effective before..."

Despite her distress, Helen's bulging eyes immediately took note of the garrote, and Becky was rewarded by the sheer fear in her adversary's eyes. But before she could get the noose over the still-convulsing Helen's head, Naïni's powerful arms locked around her and yanked her up.

"What are you doing? Let me go, you fool! Are you trying to save her now?"

"Miss Sharp!" Sâr Dubnotal's thunder clap of a voice caused her to immediately cease her struggling. She saw now that, along with the Sâr and Naïni, Clarke, Villiers, Jacques and a growling Eustace, had also arrived. The latter two were guarding Helen, who was on her knees, spewing out teeth.

"Why did you stop me?" Becky wailed bitterly.

"Miss Sharp, you must remember you are not the only one Helen Vaughan has sinned against. Others have suffered grievously as well... Would you rob them of their share of vengeance?"

And then, for the first time, Becky noticed Annie was cradled by the Great Psychagogue.

"Annie..." her voice trailed off softly. She slipped free of Naïni as he relaxed his grip, and, for the first time, Becky took her daughter into her arms.

"I have examined her," the Doctor said, "but only cursorily so due to the circumstances. I will be much more thorough later. But she seems perfectly sound physically. In fact, she is developed beyond a child of two. It seems little Annie at an early age will blossom into young womanhood, where I suspect she shall remain for an indeterminable period of time. All due, no doubt, to her mother's own preternatural defiance of the aging process.

"Now, my friends, the zeppelins have gone, and Camulos, his moment now passed, has vanished in their wake. It would appear Pan has been cuckholded by an upstart, particularly 20th century kind of evil. In any event, while there is still general confusion, let us remove hence, before the interference of the authorities somehow grants Helen Vaughan a succor she must assuredly does not deserve."

V. The Judgment

Helen Vaughan was transported by surreptitious route to a concealed estate Sâr Dubnotal maintained in Cornwall, his base for whenever his battle against the principalities of darkness brought him to England. It was here, surrounded by those whose friends had been destroyed by Helen Vaughan, that the Great Psychagogue pronounced her sentence.

He sat upon a raised judgment seat, Helen Vaughan bound before him. Standing and watching were her accusers: Becky with Annie in her arms, Clarke, Villiers, Jacques with Eustace—and his little box of tremors—and Aytown, Tate, and Randolph. Seated to the side were Ruldolph, Annunciata, Naïni, and three detectives on permanent retainer to Sâr Dubnotal. These three had managed to obtain a list of the names of the children who had perished from Helen's act of arson. At the end of the voicing of the charges against her by those present, each detective, by turn, read aloud the names of 50 silent orphans.

"Helen Vaughan," Sâr Dubnotal said when they were finished, "you have inflicted anguish not only on your victims—whose sufferings were blessedly cut short when death removed them from your hands—but also their survivors, who will endure a deep and abiding anguish for the remainder of their lives. Were we to execute you now, they would still not be free of you. If the end of their suffering will not come quickly, then neither shall yours.

"Therefore, it is my decree that you will fulfill your boast to not die easily. Jacques, come forward. And Naïni, if you will now perform what I instructed you to do earlier."

The dwarf commanded Eustace to stay, then approached the throne, bearing the thumping box before him. He stood before Helen and flashed a nasty smile up at her. Naïni knelt between Helen and Jacques as the dwarf removed the box's lid.

Up jumped two small, rubicund objects which Naïni's great hands snatched out of the air like grizzly paws catching fish leaping from a rapids. Naïni rose and turned. At the sight of what the Hindu now held, Helen Vaughan's eyes widened and her face paled.

"I believe you recognize these shoes, Helen," Sar Dubnotal said coldly.

Thrusting to be free of Naïni's hands were tiny red ballet slippers—and within them, tiny white feet. Holding one shoe in the pit of his arm, Naïni's fingers dislodged its mate's foot, which hit the floor and skipped frenziedly scattershot over the room. The other foot soon followed.

"Open the door, Rudolf," Sar Dubnotal commanded. "Allow them the dignity of at least attempting to rejoin their mistress's other remains before the residual enchantment fades and they begin to decompose."

Rudolf did as told, and the feet that had been throwing themselves against every wall in their imbecilic dance immediately ran out.

"*Au revoir, mes enfants*," Jacques said, as his tiny hand rose to a salute, wiping away a single tear in the passing.

The red shoes, now free of the tiny feet, seemed to have grown in Naïni's hands. And Helen Vaughan contemplated them in horror.

"Ah," said Sâr Dubnotal. "I see you also recall that whosoever wears these ballet slippers cannot stop dancing until another removes them. Did you think Jacques would not tell me how Minuette's tiny heart failed after you placed them on her feet? How your laughter mingled with that of your guests while she begged you, her most cherished friend, for help? And how, for the amusement of subsequent salons, you would open the trunk in which you kept her corpse and send it prancing even in the advanced stages of decomposition? And that it was only Jacques' sword that released Minuette from this continued indignity, this *violation* to her person.

"In the hour you purposed to commit this abominable atrocity, it was you who decreed your own sentence. These shoes will drive you ever on like a fury, Helen, until your heart stops from exertion. Of course, your heart will beat far longer than Minuette's little one did under the same duress—but it's all a matter of proportion, wouldn't you say?

Now Sâr Dubnotal said to Rudolf: "Bring the saddle, reigns, harness and bit."

"What... for?" Helen whispered.

"Why, Helen—did you actually think we would just set you loose?" Sâr Dubnotal said. "To be rescued by the first fool whom you would most assuredly murder at the earliest opportune moment and then begin a new reign of terror—the focus of which would, no doubt, be innocent Annie there?

"It is my sentence, then, that while propelled by the red shoes, you be repeatedly ridden 'round the coasts of Britain, from the drowned lands of Lyonesse to the regions of the Hebrides and back again—until you expire."

"Oh, saddle me up!" Becky said and would have passed Annie into poor Villiers' arms right then, except he was so stunned by such an instantaneous shedding of maternal instinct that his hands were rendered torpid.

"Miss Sharp!" Sâr Dubnotal said. "You have already enjoyed the privilege of crushing the face of the woman who crushed yours and taking back the child she claimed as her own. You must see to Annie and leave to others the administration of justice for Helen's sins that are not against you. Do I have to ask you which is more important?"

Becky gathered Annie back to her and tucked her head in token abashment, yet her hooded eyes could not conceal the gall of resentment therein.

"I already have riders stationed along the shores of this isle," the Sâr said, as his gaze bore down on Helen like the most pitiless sun. "You will be ridden until death, at which point, the shoes will be removed, and you will be dismembered, your body burned, and your ashes scattered into the ocean.

"Ah, here is Rudolf. You will now be shod and saddled, and then you will be ridden to the first station by Naïni..."

Helen's mouth dropped. "That giant... atop me? How can you expect me to go even five feet under the Hindu without falling to the ground, unable to rise?"

"Helen, the sentence of the red shoes punishes you only for what you did to Minuette. But the children of the orphanage cry out as well for justice from the ground where they lay in prolonged agony. The children for whom a single comforting touch against their blistered skin was rendered into a hornet's sting. Do you dare say you deserve one less such touch of encouragement?

"Therefore, when you fall, you will receive a goad until you rise—one for each child who died in the orphanage to which you set fire. No more; no less."

Helen's jaw dropped. "But there were 150 children in that orphanage! Your sentence is too cruel, Sâr Dubnotal!"

"Helen Vaughan," Sâr Dubnotal's voice roared down upon her so that she dipped at the knees and clasped her hands over her head, "you who never showed mercy to your victims, who mocked them in their agonies that were the fruit of your corruption… you dare accuse *me* of cruelty? Beware lest *having whipped you with whips, I whip you next with scorpions.*

"Yet this mercy I will grant you. If, while you might still rise, you choose to end your torment, whether it be two feet from where you now stand or 20 miles, you have but to lie there, endure how many of the goads remain, and you will be immediately beheaded. And when the goads are finished, upon my word, Helen, you shall have no more or no less than what your transgression has decreed—should you choose to go two feet or 20 miles more—you will have but to say 'enough.' Whether until your heart bursts or while it may yet beat on another day, or week, or month, you, Helen, shall decide the length of your agonies; a dignity you never allowed any of your victims."

"But what… what do you mean by 'goads?'" Helen asked, her voice small and trembling.

"Jacques?" Sâr Dubnotal said and turned his head toward the little man.

Jacques again grinned toothily up at Helen as he reached into his pocket and produced a leather pouch from which he took two mean-looking, barbed objects.

"It has been my experience," said the dwarf, "that nothing will drive the Devil out of this woman like a fine set of spurs."

From the eldritch magic of Helen Vaughan to the enchantments of the Orient, it is but a small step. Travis Hiltz returns to the mysterious sect of the Ubasti, last seen in Tales of the Shadowmen *No. 6, with a story featuring a cast of magical heroes, including a remarkable version of the Wandering Jew, perhaps the most definitive incarnation of this character, as created by the great Paul Féval in the eponymous novel published by Black Coat Press...*

Travis Hiltz: *In the Caves of the Serpent*

Afghanistan 1919

The riders came over the hill just in time to see the plane crash.

Francis Xavier Gordon, formerly of Texas, used his riding crop to prompt his camel to greater speed, knowing that they would be no help to whatever poor souls had been in the plane. All he'd be able to do is drag the bodies from the wreckage and give them a decent burial.

The plane looked to have been a Bristol, but the collision with the rock face and the subsequent fire had rendered it into a pile of scrap wood and twisted metal.

The other rider caught up with Gordon, but stayed on his camel. He was a young Bedouin, and while fearing nothing that walked the Earth, the infidel's flying machines seemed unnatural and a deliberate attempt to antagonize the Prophet.

Gordon climbed down from his camel and walked cautiously towards the wreckage. He got close enough to feel the heat of the flames. He was not a tall man, compact, with wide shoulders. His hair and thin mustache were midnight black, while his eyes were a piercing sky blue. Gordon wore a traditional head-dress, but the rest of his clothes were khaki and European in style. One callused hand rested on the butt of his pistol. His face gave away none of the emotions that played across his eyes.

With a shake of his head, he turned to his traveling companion.

"Masa, once the flames die down, we can see about taking care of the bodies," he said. "Keep the scavengers away and hope the smoke doesn't attract any bandits."

"Um...Effendi...?" Masa, said, pointing towards the wreckage.

Gordon spun, gun in his hand.

Out of the wreckage crawled a figure. It quickly threw away a smoldering aviator's helmet, revealing a cascade of auburn hair. Struggling to her feet, the wounded aviatrix limped towards Gordon, holding her side with one hand and attempting to beat out the ignited bits of her flight suit with the other.

She was a tall woman, with features a bit on the masculine side. Despite the method of her arrival, Gordon noted that, underneath the soot and bruises, she wore a self-satisfied grin on her face.

"Mister Gordon, I presume?" she asked, coughing.

"You all right?" Gordon asked, unsure what to say under the circumstances.

"Aside from putting the lie to the adage that 'any landing you can walk away from being a good one,' yes, I think so… Um… Could you do me a favor…?"

"What?"

Pulling her hand away from her side, she revealed a jagged gash that cut through, not just the flight suit, but also the flesh beneath. Broken spikes of rib poked through the bloody wound.

"…Catch me."

She pushed the bones back into place. There was a wet, grating sound and a groan escaped from her clenched teeth, as she swooned.

"Masa!" Gordon shouted, over his shoulder, moving awkwardly with his new burden.

The young Bedouin ran to join him. Gordon lowered the injured aviatrix to the stony ground. Once he had a free hand, he gestured to his companion to hand him the canteen and his cloak.

Masa bunched up the cloak into a crude pillow, while Gordon began to bathe the woman's wounds.

"Effendi, how is she still alive?" Masa asked.

"Good question," the Texan replied. "Wish I knew. Is this the British agent we were to meet? I was expecting a man…"

"I was expecting… (cough) to be a man… hmm… By the time I arrived," she muttered. "So we're both disappointed."

"Lie still," Gordon advised. "Where's the pilot?"

"You are gazing upon her," she replied, struggling to sit up. "Up until the point I was shot at, the flight was going swimmingly," she explained, pausing to hack and spit a blob of bloody phlegm.

"You were shot at?" Gordon asked. "Who shot at you, Miss…?"

"Orlando. Are you the renowned El Borak?"

"You're the English agent?" he asked.

"You sound disappointed."

"This is no place for a woman."

"Really? A group of men alone in the mountains? Seems the perfect place."

"Who shot at you?" Gordon repeated.

"No idea," Orlando replied. "I was trying to read the map. Next thing I knew, my windscreen cracked. The next shots must have hit my fuel line… and here we are. Are you my guide?"

"Are you all right to travel?"

"I'll live."

"Then, on your feet," Gordon said, offering Orlando a hand. "We are wasting daylight."

Gordon took the lead, with the wounded Orlando on the second camel, young Masa walking along besides, leading it along the thin, rocky trail.

"I don't suppose you'd care to tell me where we are going?"

"We need to put distance between us and the crash," Gordon replied, without looking back. "As well as reach a vantage point... see if we can get a look at who is hunting you."

"Clever," Orlando nodded. "I could have used someone like you at Hastings."

Gordon shook his head and encouraged his camel to pick up the pace. Masa walked along, doing his utmost to avoid eye contact with his passenger. Whether this was due to her being a half-naked Englishwoman or the strong suspicion that she was insane was anyone's guess.

Once up in the hills, Gordon left Masa and the camels, and crept to a jagged ledge overlooking the wreckage.

After several moments, a pair of men crept out of the desolate foothills and approached the remains of Orlando's plane. Gordon watched them walk around the wreckage, occasionally poking it with the long staffs they carried. Still and silent as the stones around him, he studied them at length.

"Tall fellows, aren't they?" Orlando commented.

"Thought I told you to stay with Masa," Gordon said, without looking away from his quarry.

"Oh, you assumed I was going to listen?' Orlando mused, patting the pockets of her ragged coverall. "How quaint."

She extracted a thin, brass telescope and peered down at the duo. Her forehead wrinkled in concentration and her chatter faded into silence.

"What?" Gordon asked.

"What, what?" she replied. "I didn't say anything..."

"That's how I can tell it must be important, you aren't talking."

"What can you tell me about them?" Orlando asked, handing the Texan her telescope.

"Nothing that marks them as any specific tribe or outlaw band," Gordon explained. "No steeds or markings on their clothing..."

"What about the walking sticks?"

"Interesting. Afghanistan isn't known for a surplus of wood. They have carvings on them."

"I know," Orlando muttered. "I've seen them before, but I can't remember where. Curse, my cluttered brain. Memory is always a bit dodgy when I'm transitioning..."

Gordon cocked a curious glance at his traveling companion, but decided that further questioning of Orlando would be fruitless.

"They've come from the east," Gordon said, instead. "Don't like that."

"Why? What's out that way?"

"Nothing."

"Nothing?" Orlando asked. "There really is a place where the Earth just falls away into the void?"

"It's mountains and barren rock and if whoever is hunting you came from there," he explained, handing back her telescope, "then our task just became more difficult."

"How so?'

"This might be a good time to swap stories," Gordon said, settling against a rock and crossing his arms. "Ladies first."

Orlando's reply to Gordon's stern look was an appreciative smirk. She brushed at the lap of her tattered flight suit, as if it was the skirt of an evening gown.

"I am in the employ of the British government," she began. "There is a …man, of my acquaintance who has gone missing. I believe he has been abducted and I traced him to this charming little corner of the world. I was told if I needed a guide in Afghanistan, I should call on El Borak. Imagine my surprise when The Swift One turns out to be a short cowboy…"

"Short…?" Gordon muttered, scowling at Orlando. "So, as you've been tracking this acquaintance, someone has been tracking you…"

"…And they seem more successful at it than my own humble efforts," Orlando commented.

"That's the other thing," Gordon said. "They hunted you down quickly."

"Well, that's not something I'm inclined to worry about," Orlando shrugged. "Catching me and holding me are two very different instances, as you may be fortunate enough to find out. So, why are these mountains causing your brow to furrow?"

"They are some of the most desolate miles, not just in this country, but in the world. It's one of the few stretches of ground in Afghanistan that no one is fighting over because no tribe or government wants it. Let's get back to the camels, before Masa starts to worry."

Keeping low, they retraced their steps. Masa acknowledged their return with a brief nod. Gordon's gesture told the native that they were going to be heading back onto the trail.

"So, the ones hunting me are from a place where no one lives?" Orlando pondered. "That's positively zen, when you think about it."

"I didn't say no one lives there," Gordon told her. "The men who choose to make it home have nowhere else to go: outlaws and outcasts, Followers of the white wolf, or Ubasti…"

"Ubasti…?"Orlando muttered. "Hadn't thought about them in ages…"

"You've crossed paths with the Ubasti before?" Gordon asked.

"A long time ago," she replied, as she climbed, gingerly due to her wounds, onboard her camel. "In my headstrong youth, I accidently seduced a sacrificial virgin and slew a giant snake... They've held a bit of a grudge since... You are looking at me like I'm a lunatic again..."

"You're facing away from me."

"Am I wrong?"

"No."

Masa shot Gordon a questioning look, and the compact Texan shrugged in reply.

The young Bedouin shook his head and taking the reins of Orlando's camel followed Gordon's through a narrow alley of rock.

"Allah watches over children and fools," he muttered, as they trudged along.

"Well, that's both of us covered then," Orlando smirked.

Gordon led them through the foothills. His plan was, if the hunters were unaware that they themselves were being hunted, they would lead them to wherever Orlando's friend was being held captive. His instincts told him it wouldn't be that easy. Something about the cloaked men nagged at him. He was familiar with most of the tribes of the area, as well as having crossed paths with many of the rebels and mercenaries that operated in this part of the world. His current quarry fit none of them. They wore no adornments and carried no weapons, beyond their staffs.

"Too many questions," he frowned, shading his eyes with one hand, and peering across the stony wasteland that awaited them. The mountains were jagged stumps of rock, lined with paths that looked as though they'd been gouged out by the claws of some huge beast. No traces of habitation. No water, smoke or even a circling vulture to hint that life could exist here.

"It's like gazing at the surface of the Moon," Orlando said, riding up next to him.

"Which, I suppose you've visited," Gordon muttered.

"Twice. Any idea where they're going?"

"No."

"Any idea where we're going?"

"There," Gordon replied, pointing toward a nearby peak. "Your hunters are heading east. There are several shadowed spots that look to be caves. That'll give us shelter."

Orlando nodded her approval.

"Will we be able to keep my new admirers in view?" she asked.

"Hard to say." Gordon said. "There are too many caves and hidden trails. We need to keep moving."

"Where have I seen you before...?" she whispered, chin on hand, as she peered down at the distant figures. "I really need to start keeping a journal..."

Hours passed. The trio struggled to keep their quarry in sight, sometimes losing them, then miles on, catching a faint glimpse. As dusk was approaching, travelers and camels were worn down by this game of hide and seek.

Masa stumbled and Gordon could tell the camels would soon begin grunting in protest; he decided it was foolish to push on further.

The night was cloudy, with a knife's blade crescent of Moon, so finding a cave, he decided to risk a fire.

Masa sat, huddled against the kneeling camels, in the back of the cave. Orlando and Gordon sat across from each other, hunched close to the small fire. The eccentric aviatrix was contentedly munching on a strip of dried meat.

"Tasty," she commented, wiping her mouth on a tattered sleeve. "I'd probably regret asking what animal it came from, so I won't bother. What's our next move?"

"That depends on you," Gordon replied, quietly. "Without some answers, Masa and I will be returning home."

"What?" Orlando asked, surprise causing her usual clever cynicism to slip. "The fabled El Borak is going to abandon me in the wilderness? The stories I'd been told…"

"…Don't include any mention of my being a blind fool," Gordon interrupted. He did not raise his voice, nor change his expression, but there was something in his tone that caught Orlando's attention. "I grew up in the heart of Texas cattle country, not a place known for soft living, then joined the army and spent the war here. I fought alongside Lawrence. 'El Borak' isn't something I picked to impress the natives; that name was given to me when I was accepted as a warrior of the tribe. I do not shy away from a challenge, once I have taken it on."

"Well, then…"

"But, neither am I some fatalistic mercenary. My trust and loyalty must be earned. I cannot complete a task without information."

"I have given you information!"

"You have babbled incessantly," Gordon corrected, "and thanks to the law of averages, there was the occasional bit of useful information. We are now in the wilderness and the only hope of continuing is for you to be honest with me about why you're here."

For several minutes, the duo merely stared across the fire at each other, Orlando pensive and obviously struggling internally. Gordon's face might have well as been carved from oak, so little did his expression give away. Orlando chewed her lip for a moment, then returned Gordon's look with a rueful smile.

"…And before you start concocting another silly story hinting at your being hundreds of years old," Gordon said, 'let me tell you, I don't care."

"Well, then, ask what you need to know," Orlando suggested. "I myself enjoy the coy banter, but if you prefer to do without, so be it."

"Are you really an agent of the British government? I'm finding it hard to believe you and Lawrence came from the same place."

"Yes, I am in the employ of Her Majesty's government, and have been for...quite some time. My position is more of a freelance nature. I think of myself as a courier, of sorts, but have also been referred to as a troubleshooter..."

"You sure it wasn't troublemaker?"

"I thought we were going to avoid witticisms?" Orlando mused. "While Her Majesty's government has made use of my services, in this case, I am making use of theirs. My missing friend is practically unknown to the government. This search is my own undertaking. He is an old friend, and in his own way, an important and powerful man. His abduction has grave consequences for not just this little country, or even England, but the world at large."

Gordon nodded absently and then hunched forward, elbows on his knees.

"We won't be able to take the camels any further. They make it easy for us to be tracked and there's no way to gather more feed. Masa can stay with them. You and I will go ahead, on foot. I'd like to head out before daylight."

"That's it?" Orlando said, blinking in surprise.

"Was I supposed to make an impassioned speech?" Gordon asked in reply. He stood up, wiping his hands on his pant legs. "Get some rest. We need to head out in a few hours."

Orlando awoke suddenly. Years of experience told her something was wrong. She lay, unmoving, her back against the cave wall, a thin saddle blanket draped over her. There was a whisper of movement and a hand was clamped over her mouth.

"Stay quiet," Gordon breathed in her ear. "Your friends have found us."

Orlando opened her eyes, taking a second to adjust to the gloom. Gordon was crouched down at her side. Glancing towards the cave mouth, she caught a glimpse of a shadow moving, and a faint sound of gravel underfoot.

"Let them come to us," Gordon whispered, passing her his knife, under her blanket. He then lay down and gave a decent impression of a man deep in slumber.

Orlando, her eyes closed to slits, watched the hunters. There looked to be a half-dozen rough-looking tribesmen, all wrapped in black. As they crept forward, she could make out a tall figure, holding a familiar looking staff, standing in the cave's entrance, silhouetted by the faint moonlight.

Again, a strand of memory, far in the recesses of her brain was pulled a bit closer to remembrance.

The intruders moved about the cave like a breeze, coming closer. Orlando could feel Gordon tense; yet, she, herself, felt more eager than anxious.

During the course of her life, Orlando had learned there were only two constant elements: the first was a skill young women didn't boast of, the second was fighting.

"Come at me, if you're hard enough…!" she shouted, as she leapt to her feet. "I still can't believe Will kept that in… I told him, I was joking…"

The robed intruders crept closer, drawing from the folds of their clothing various weapons. Orlando strode, almost casually towards them, like she was doing nothing more dangerous than going for a walk in the park.

Within seconds, her knife was protruding from an attacker's eye socket and she'd snatched up his scimitar. The swing of the scimitar was followed by the crack of a collarbone. Orlando frowned in annoyance as she struggled to pull her weapon free. Another outlaw rushed forward, taking advantage of her distraction. Without looking up from her grisly task, the heel of her hand drove straight into his Adams apple.

Gordon was momentarily stunned by his traveling companion's switch from eccentric to skilled killer. He grabbed a stick from the fire and thrust it forward in order to keep their attackers from tackling Orlando en masse.

"Masa!" he barked, over his shoulder. "My belt!"

Masa grabbed and tossed it. Gordon caught the belt, yanking his six-guns from the holsters and then in one fluid motion, spinning and firing. Four shots and four outlaws fell. Orlando was busy with the last two. There was no way Gordon could take a shot, without risking hitting her. He turned his attention to the outlaw's leader, the tall man draped in black.

Gordon fired and, with an almost lazy gesture, the tall man swung his staff, which sparked as he swatted the bullet away. Across the cave, Gordon could see the thin opening, around the tall man's eyes that was the only hint that there was a man underneath all that black fabric. Those eyes seemed to draw in and then reflect whatever light was around. It was as though two candles had suddenly been lit. Gordon's gaze locked with that of the tall man, and the Texan found himself feeling light-headed and struggling to keep his numbed hands holding his guns.

"Damned if I'm letting some bit of desert hoodoo stop me," Gordon muttered, through gritted teeth. He dropped one six-gun, and, using both hands, brought up the remaining one, struggling to hold it steady. Trembling with the effort, Gordon took a bead at the spot between those two hellish eyes. The single shot rang like a cannon through the cave and as the tall man dropped. His remaining followers then lost all interest in the fight and battled to escape.

Orlando, now wielding two scimitars, cut down the last of the attackers.

Gordon was reloading his guns as he moved about the cave. The Texan crept up on the limp form of the tall man; kicked aside the rune-covered staff, and using the barrel of his gun, pushed aside the black hood. The face was thin, pale and weathered, like white leather. Even in death, those eyes seemed to glow with an inner light; Gordon could feel a throbbing in his temples.

"Well, that went as well as could be expected," Orlando said, peering over his shoulder. "Oh my…!"

"What?" Gordon said, turning. His eyes then grew wide and he whipped his guns away from the corpse and at her.

"I must look a fright," Orlando said.

A dagger protruded from her right shoulder, another from between her ribs. A large chunk of her left ear was missing, as well as a long strip of flesh from her forehead. The ragged remains of her clothes looked like they'd been used as cleaning rags in a slaughterhouse.

"We need to talk," Gordon said, cocking his six guns with his thumbs.

"Yes, we do," Orlando nodded. "I've remembered where I saw the markings on that staff."

"I don't mean that," Gordon said, his guns still steadily pointing at Orlando.

"You mean me?" she asked, tapping at her bloody chest with a bloody fingertip.

'What are you and why aren't you dead?" Gordon asked, his tone quiet, but no less dangerous.

"That, like so much about me, is a very long story…"

"Edit it to a small one."

"I see," Orlando sighed, her forehead creasing in thought. This caused her to wince. "I can't die, and believe me, a great many people have put that theory to the test. The how of it is a bit vague, even to me, but it's a gift and a curse, depending on my mood. Needless to say, Her Majesty's government finds the idea of an indestructible courier worth putting up with my…eccentricities. I also have a talent for attracting and dealing with the unusual. When we reach the part of the map that reads *here, there be dragons…*, I'm the one they send to explore."

"We are off the map, as far as I'm concerned," Gordon muttered, lowering his guns. "Suppose I shouldn't shoot my 'native guide.' What about him?"

Gordon gestured at the dead man. He watched Orlando out of the corner of his eye, as she studied the body, until she began to pull the various bladed weapons out of her body. Some odd gentlemanly streak made him think she deserved a bit of privacy.

"I knew I'd seen those runes before!" she muttered.

"Forgot that for a moment," Gordon interrupted, brusquely. "What is he?"

"What do yiu mean?'

"There's something… wrong. If I look at him for more than a second, half my brain is telling me to run and the other half thinks I haven't put near enough bullets into him. Is he…like you? Is he a man at all?"

Orlando dropped the knives on the cave floor and stared at the dead man. After several seconds, she dabbed at the corners of her eyes with her knuckles. She then turned to peer with equal intensity at Gordon.

"You are a singular man, Mister Gordon. Not a man in a thousand would have noticed what you did about him… I wouldn't have noticed it, and we would have most likely walked to our deaths. I misread what the runes on the staff meant..."

"They're used by the Ubasti," Gordon said. "Seeing them, up close, I remembered I've seen them before, carved in the walls of one of their old meeting places."

"Actually," Orlando said, picking up the black staff. It was wood, but worn to a glass-like smoothness by age and use. "The runes are Lemurian."

"Lemurian?"

"Lemuria... The dark sister to lost Atlantis," Orlando mused. "That takes me back..."

"Yeah, yeah, I've heard stories, about how the Ubasti aren't just a bunch of fanatics, but come from a long line of evil wizards, stretching back to the sister city of Atlantis," Gordon grumbled. "There's no magic here..."

"No?" Orlando asked, taking his chin between her thumb and finger, turning him to face her again. Before his eyes, he could see her wounds closing, till there was nothing but soft, smooth skin beneath the streaks of drying blood.

"We are talking about the Ubasti," Gordon grunted, extracting himself from her grip.

"How did they find us?" she asked.

"After we lost sight of them after the crash, they doubled back and spotted us. After that, it was easy to lead us where they wanted, dropping out of sight, then showing themselves just enough to keep us following. By the time night fell, they had us running in circles for hours, tired and easy prey."

"And how long have you known all this?" Orlando asked, with a mischievous smirk.

Gordon shrugged, holstering one of his guns.

"On the trail, once you stopped talking, I had time to think. As much as you prove there are things in the world beyond this Texas boy's understanding, there are some basics you can always rely on. These men are outlaws, not mystics."

"I wouldn't be so sure," Orlando said, kneeling down next to the tall man's body. She muttered under her breath, guttural words in no language Gordon recognized, then reached forward and tapped the corpse in the center of its forehead. The corpse's features swirled and rippled, like the surface of a pond hit by a fierce wind. When it stopped, the corpse had a new face, an inhuman face. The skin scaly, the eyes larger, set farther apart and a dingy yellow, the nose was now two slits in the skin.

Gordon flinched, his finger tightening on the trigger.

"What the Hell is he?"

"They have many names," Orlando said, in a quiet, grim tone, "but, I prefer to call them Serpent Men."

'Not sure I care what his name is," Gordon replied. "What is he? What kind of monster is stalking us?"

111

"No one is entirely sure where they came from," Orlando said, resting a hand on Gordon's shoulder. "Some say that, as people believe men grew from apes, the Serpent Men grew from the dinosaurs. Some say they are the bastard children of a particularly vile god. They may have to come to this world from another world, or even another universe..." She shrugged. "What is known is that they were the source of power of the high priests of Lemuria, and so, are the sires of the Ubasti."

Gordon walked away from the body and sat, in the opening of the cave, upon the rocky ground. His hands hung loosely against his knees. He stared out into the night.

Orlando covered the Serpent Man's face, then got to her feet and walked over to Gordon.

"I understand that this may be difficult to absorb," she said. "I have been there and will understand if you need me to shut up and leave you alone..."

"No," Gordon said, not looking away from the night sky. "There's no time. Whoever sent these men will miss them. We can't stay here."

He got to his feet and peered around the cave for several moments, taking in the remnants of their camp, the bodies of their attackers and the form of Masa, huddled in the rear of the cave, struggling to keep the camels and himself, calm.

"You left one alive?" he asked.

"Yes, short fellow with a badly trimmed beard."

"Good, I'm going to need to talk to him in a minute."

Gordon spent the next several minutes going over the corpses, gathering up a good-sized pile of weapons and supplies. He then dragged the bodies and dumped them in a pile at the mouth of the cave with the Serpent Man. When he was done, he yanked their prisoner up into a sitting position and used some of their rapidly dwindling water supply to splash his face till he woke up.

The dirty outlaw sputtered and blinked, gasping in surprise at the sight of the bodies of his comrades and that his intended victims were now his captors.

He grumbled in a Turkish dialect and then stubbornly clamped his jaw shut.

"You understand him?" Orlando asked.

"Enough for what I need," Gordon replied. He grabbed the bandit by the front of his robe and cracked him, twice, across the face with the butt of one of his guns.

He growled a question in the bandit's language. When he received no reply, he struck several more times and repeated the question, until the violence and the night's defeat crumbled the last shreds of the bearded man's defiance. The bandit spat blood and mumbled a reply. Gordon repeated what he said, and nodded grimly.

"What did he say?" Orlando asked.

"We need to travel to the Mouth of Naga," Gordon replied. "It means..."

"Snake, yes, I've heard it before. Another cave?"

"A cave where demons dwell," Gordon said. "Or so he says."

"After the events of this evening, I think we can trust that he's not speaking metaphorically."

"How many of these Serpent Men are there?" Gordon asked.

"I don't know," she shrugged. "They used to be armies, but were cut down. I thought they'd gone the way of the dodo; I haven't encountered any since... for quite some time."

"The Mouth of Naga is further to the east, between two peaks. I'm guessing we have some hiking to do."

Soon, Gordon and Masa had the camels repacked, saddled and standing in front of the cave.

"We will need to find water soon," the young Bedouin said.

"You should be fine, as soon as you get to the well at Hakim's Rest."

"Sahib?'

"You are heading back, Masa," Gordon told him. "Take the camels, after you've watered at Hakim's, go on to the old fort. There will be scouts there, either from the tribes or the military. Let them know where we've gone."

The two men locked gazes for a second; while separated by years, skin color and places of birth they had forged a bond, in this hard country and on the battlefield. There was no need for sentimentality or drawn out good-byes.

"Allah watch over you, El Borak," Masa nodded.

"And you."

"That's all well and good," Orlando interrupted, "but these might help in case the Prophet is busy elsewhere." She had a rifle and gun belt slung over her shoulders and was dragging the body of one their attackers along.

"Good thinking," Gordon nodded. "Set up a couple of the dead men on the camels and from a distance it looks like we are all leaving. Let me help."

Soon Gordon and Orlando were hunkered down behind some rocks, watching young Masa lead the corpse-loaded camels back the way they'd come.

"I'm sure he'll be fine," she said.

"He will," Gordon replied, simply and got to his feet. The duo was weighted down with weapons and supplies they had liberated from their attackers bodies.

With silent determination, they hiked across the barren rock, wanting to make as much progress as they could before sunrise left them exposed to their pursuers and the unforgiving Sun. Hours and miles passed and found them at the base of the twin peaks and still undetected. Gordon decided on a brief rest, before the ascent. Having lived the life of a soldier, and then a Bedouin, he was able to survive on brief snatches of sleep, even when his pillow was a rock and his blanket the night sky. So, it startled him, when he was roused from a deep slumber, by a hand shaking his shoulder. Orlando's face was inches away from his own, and she was peering with concern into his eyes.

"Are you all right?" she asked.

'What... um... just... sleeping..." he muttered in reply.

"You were walking away from camp."

"What?" he exclaimed, looking around.

He now stood amongst a gathering of boulders and stones, yards from where he'd been sleeping.

"Do you sleepwalk?" Orlando asked.

"No. Never... but, this hasn't been a typical day. With everything I've seen, not surprising. Just dreaming and..."

"Dreaming? About what?"

"I don't know... bits and images," he said, rubbing at his weary eyes. "Doesn't matter."

"It may matter more than you think. We are off the map, Mister Gordon. What was your dream?"

Gordon frowned at her and then shrugged.

"I was walking... someone was holding my hand... I heard music... singing."

"Who were you walking with? You need to remember," Orlando coaxed him.

"It was a... a young girl... her dress was old-fashioned and pretty impractical for hiking the mountains. Any help? Is it an omen of doom?"

"Hardly," Orlando said, relaxing and sitting upon a rock. "In fact, it may be the opposite. Where was she taking you?"

"What's this all about? It's just a dream, wasn't it?"

"No, it was a hint, a trail of bread crumbs perhaps. When she let go of your hand, where did she go?"

"That way," Gordon pointed, his voice equal parts annoyance and anxiety. The duo turned, and could just make out a thin trail, going up amongst the rocks.

"She was real?" Gordon asked, looking back at Orlando.

"In a way. Don't be worried. She likes you, that's a good thing."

"It's a good thing that a... ghost... is rummaging around in my mind?"

"She's not a ghost, per say. That implies she's dead. This little girl is more... um... a kind of... something else... difficult to explain."

"Coming from you, that's almost funny."

"Very droll. Let's gather our things. If you have any more dreams or visions, let me know."

"What is she doing here?" Gordon asked, as they returned to their makeshift campsite. "Not really dressed for the terrain. More like she's going to a party."

"She's generally more concerned with watching over her father than fashion," Orlando said, tucking various weapons into her belt.

"His daughter?" Gordon muttered. "Her father is your missing friend?"

"Yes."

"You know some unusual people," Gordon said, shouldering his pack and heading up the narrow trail.

"You have no idea," Orlando said, following.

The trail twisted its way up the mountain, narrowing in places till they had to struggle to squeeze between rocks. Several times, they had to push through their packs and then work through a gap. There was no instance where it was wide enough to walk side by side. Conversation was impractical. They traveled nearly three quarters of the way up before they reached a clearing and were able to rest and stretch out a little.

"Lord, much more hardship to my clothes and I'll be rescuing Issac *au naturel*," Orlando commented, as she ruefully attempted to repair the tattered remains of her flight suit.

Gordon nodded absently, as he checked his weapons and began emptying out his knapsack, keeping only the most essential items.

"We have more important things to worry about," he said, gesturing over his shoulder.

Orlando looked up. There was a thin line of sunrise, starting to light the sky. It tinted the surrounding rock blood red. On a ridge above the duo, was the mouth of a cave with two formations of rock that hung down like the fangs of a serpent.

"The Mouth of Naga," Orlando murmured. "Ancient cults do so love their symbolism. Do we look for a servants' entrance or just stroll right in?"

"I don't see any guards or sign of movement inside the cave," Gordon said, pulling out one of his six-guns. "Not sure where to go until we find another breadcrumb."

Gordon tucked his knapsack in a crevice between rocks, keeping only his gun belt, extra ammunition, scimitar and a water skin. Orlando followed his example, though all her weapon choices were swords and knives.

The duo made their way, stealthily, to the Mouth of the Naga. The area was deserted, and aside from some faint footprints, Gordon could find no sign of habitation.

"Did our informant send us to the wrong place?" he wondered aloud. "Or is it a trap?"

"Or are they up to something and decided we aren't worth worrying about?" Orlando added. "Not a comforting thought in the bunch."

Thin crevices in the cave roof allowed in trickles of light and, as they moved deeper into the cave, the walls became coated with lichen that gave off a faint glow.

They soon came to a passage that forked into three separate paths. Gordon studied the area, looking for some clue to tell them where to go next.

"Anything?" Orlando asked.

'Somebody's been this way," the Texan replied, straightening up. "They dropped a coin. Looks foreign."

"A one-*sou* coin," Orlando said, snatching it away from him and running her fingers over it. "Which branch was it nearest?"

Gordon pointed to the left tunnel and Orlando strode down it.

"Are we back to not explaining anything?" he asked, catching up to her.

"I thought we were at the point where any fantastic thing that occurs, you'd accept as a clue."

Gordon shrugged and they continued on their way.

"Do you feel that?" Orlando asked, pausing and pressing her palm against the cave wall.

Gordon stopped, closed his eyes and listened to his surroundings for several second. When he opened him, his expression was concerned. "Some kind of hum," he said.

"Exactly."

"Like someone trying to lull a child to sleep."

"No! It's... something wrong." Orlando said, her features tainted with anxiety. "Like the noise of a great machine, about to break or... the approach of a predator, gliding ever closer. We need to... I don't... Crom, it makes my teeth itch..."

"We need to stop for a moment and think," Gordon said, grabbing a hold of her arm, struggling to calm her down as well as quell his own rising fear. The idea of what could frighten a woman that could shrug off plane crashes and multiple stab wounds was deeply worrying.

Orlando hugged herself, dropping her sword, and peering about the tunnel nervously.

"Look at me," Gordon snapped. 'Whatever we are hearing, it seems to be two different things. I think the girl... what's her name...?"

"Lotte," Orlando muttered.

"I think that I'm hearing another trail of breadcrumbs from Lotte, and it's keeping me from feeling whatever is affecting you."

"I ... don't... know... feel... something... wrong..." Orlando muttered. "May just be my wounds catching up with me... but no, there's something..."

"Then we'll follow my trail and hope we're moving away from whatever is affecting you." Gordon said. Orlando nodded distractedly and walked along. The tunnel was wide enough for them to walk side by side. Gordon hooked his arm through Orlando's to steer her along. The glow from the walls dimmed and grew as they walked.

Gordon split his attention between his surroundings and keeping an eye on his companion. Her dazed condition was cause for concern, but Gordon also noticed something wrong about her face. Her features were a bit man-ish before, but they seemed to have coarsened further and her shoulders seemed broader. It was one more puzzling thing for Gordon to add to the ever-growing list he'd mentally compiled since meeting this unusual woman.

If they survived this mad quest, he planned to sit down with Orlando and a very large drink in the hope she would answer any of his questions.

"What was that?" Orlando asked, suddenly. She came to a halt and ran her hands over the wall. "Skittering behind the walls... it's following us... or me... what if that's it... you can't hear it because it doesn't want you...!"

"Stop it!" he snapped, giving her a shake. "I haven't tramped this far just to have you turn into some weepy damsel. Get hold of yourself!"

"Are you going to slap me and then explain it was for my own good?" she asked, a trace of her old self peeking through.

"No, surprisingly enough, for the first time since I've met you, I don't have the urge to hit you."

"Not even to put me over your knee and teach me a lesson?" she asked, her voice sounding teasing and tipsy.

"Not as such," Gordon said, starting to walk again.

"Shame."

Fifty feet down the tunnel; they spotted the first openings in the walls. Most were small side chambers, used for storage. No sign of the phantom horror Orlando seemed convinced dwelt behind the walls. Several had stout, ancient-looking wooden doors.

"Wait," Orlando said, pressing her ear against one of the doors. She ran her fingertips down the wood. She repeated this ritual on every door they encountered.

Several seemed to have symbols carved into the wood and one had a palm-sized metal disk hammered into it. She paused before a door, smaller than most they'd seen, the wood so weathered as to be black. Three runes were carved into it and when Orlando spotted them, she smiled.

"Coin," she said, not looking away from the door, merely holding out her hand. Once Gordon had complied, she tapped it against the door. The wood rang like a tapped crystal glass.

"Is that good?" Gordon asked, looking from the door to his companion's smile.

"No, it's terrible news. Things are worse than I imagined."

"Then why are you grinning like a lunatic?"

"We found him," Orlando breathed, not looking at Gordon, but placing a hand against the door. "I know you are in there, Issac. Why, is the question?"

She lowered her head, and closed her eyes. Gordon could soon hear her murmuring under her breath. He couldn't make out the words. Some of it reminded him of Latin, a few fragments of an Arabic dialect and then some Chinese.

There was a click and the door swung open, revealing a cavernous, well-lit chamber, and two startled guards.

Using all the built up tension of the trip through the tunnels, Gordon leapt past Orlando, his scimitar pierced the chest of one, while, with an almost casual movement, he put a bullet through the head of the other. They stepped over the bodies and into the chamber. It was a cathedral of stone. The light Gordon had noticed came from the center of the room, and he got his first look at the only surviving occupant: the man whose abduction had set him on this mad quest.

There were four stones, marking the corners of a wide square, waist high and worn down into nearly smooth podiums. Each stone had a lit candle upon on it, thick as Gordon's arm and giving off both bright light and greasy smoke. Within this roughly formed square, someone had drawn a slightly smaller circle on the cave floor. As they drew closer, Gordon saw that there were in fact three circles; between each one was a scrawl of runes and symbols. In the center of the circles, a man was pacing, an extraordinary-looking man. He was close to seven feet tall, with a white beard that reached to his waist. His clothes looked as though he had purchased them some time during the 1700s and worn them continuously since. His long coat had dusty brass buttons and wide cuffs. He carried a gnarled walking stick that was nearly as tall as he was. As he turned, Gordon caught a glimpse of something moving along next to the bearded man, like a shadow, but rather than being the shadow of a tall man, it looked to be the shadow of a child. He changed his path and walked towards Orlando, only to stumble backwards, as though colliding with an unseen wall. He shrugged and then resumed his pacing.

Gordon closed the door, in case the gunshot attracted attention. He stayed back as Orlando walked up to the nearest candle. In this ancient chamber, surrounded by the obvious trappings of some kind of mystic ritual, he felt a bit lost. There was a sense of age and power about the two other people in the room. It made Gordon feel like the only child at an adult's party.

Orlando peered at the symbols within the circles, her forehead wrinkled in thought, while a slight smile played around her lips.

"I find myself both impressed by the amount of effort this trap must have taken and horrified by what their plan must be," Orlando mused. "At the same time, I'm embarrassed on your behalf, Issac, for having fallen into it."

"I have become lax and arrogant in my powers," the bearded man replied, not slowing his pace around the circle. "I should have trusted in my friends, rather than feel that the lone path was the one to take. We are in a grave situation, but at the same time, it gladdens me that you and my daughter were able to put aside your differences and come to my rescue."

"Well, Lotte still declines to chat with me; it was only the trust inspired by my traveling companion that allowed us to get this far. And don't think I'm the only one to notice your absence; MacLeod, Sâr Dubnotal and Doctor Omega have all been on your trail. Now, what are we going to do about all this...?" She gestured at the candles and circles. "They knew what they needed to hold you, Issac; there's at least a half dozen spells and rituals mixed here. The symbols within the circles are taken from a dozen languages, at least one that even I can't recognize... hmmm... maybe... no, I was never one for spells... let's try something undramatic and straightforward..."

Orlando brought her right foot forward and scuffed across the circles. The candles flared brightly and the wax spat and crackled like bacon grease on a hot griddle, then slowly the symbols in the circles faded away and the tall man, a smile struggling to get through his beard, stepped over the now impotent barriers.

Orlando rushed over and the two shared a joyous, if chaste hug.

"Thank you, old man," Issac said to her.

"Any time, youngster."

"Can someone tell me what's going on?" Gordon asked. "Are we done?"

The two separated, and Orlando took the bearded man by the arm and led him over to where Gordon stood guard by the door.

"First things first," she said. "Issac, may I introduce Francis Xavier Gordon of Texas, a.k.a. El Borak, without whom, this little rescue wouldn't have been possible. Mr. Gordon, this is one of my oldest and dearest friends, Issac Laquedem, who you may know by his sobriquet, The Wandering Jew."

"I have really taken all the nonsense I can stomach from you," Gordon said, before pausing to look from one to the other. "You're serious?"

"While a great many of the legends that have gathered around me are mere stories," Issac said, in a tone that reminded Gordon of every preacher and teacher he'd ever heard. "I am quite real, and I am in debt to the House of Gordon."

Issac offered his hand and Gordon re-holstered his gun in order to shake. The tall man's grip was firm, yet dry as parchment.

"Um...don't mention it,"

"I'm almost afraid to ask this next question," Orlando said, "but the Ubasti and their mentors are up to something terrible, aren't they? I can feel it. These tunnels are saturated with it... What is going on?"

"The Brotherhood of the Naga have always had congress with dark gods," Issac said, gravely. "They believe they have found a way to pierce the celestial barriers and summon one to this world."

"Gods?" Gordon said, anxiously. "Lord, this gets stranger every time one of you opens your mouth."

"Shush, for a moment," Orlando said, patting his arm. "Let your elders speak. How are they going to summon... whatever horror they're after, and why kidnap you?"

"Any dark ritual requires a payment of blood," Issac intoned.

"Blood? From you?" Orlando exclaimed. "Better chance getting blood from a stone."

"So, the story about you being immune to Earthly weapon is true?" Gordon asked. "I'm going to guard the door. You two can sort this out..."

"Poor boy," Orlando smiled. "I have pushed him off the deep end and asked him to hold an anchor."

"He has a noble spirit," Issac commented, "but, yes, the Naga believe they have a weapon that will draw blood from even myself."

"Ridiculous," Orlando scoffed. "I've seen you shrug off mystical blades and wade through gunfire like it was spring rain. It would take a unique blade to... Oh, dear bawd! A Hattori Hanzo blade! How in the world could they get their scaly hands upon a Hanzo sword? There can't be more than six left in the world... I know I went through quite a bit to acquire mine and was heartbroken when I lost it. Unless... It's my sword, isn't it?"

The Wandering Jew nodded gravely.

"Of course, it would have to be. I had it for nearly a century; it's been bathed in holy fire, tasted the blood of immortals and dragons. I could shave God's whiskers with that sword. If anything could draw your blood..."

"Only a drop is needed."

Orlando nodded, lost in thought.

"Get you out and my sword back from an army of fanatics and inhuman mystics, without them using it to draw any of your blood," she mused. "Tricky, but not impossible. Mr. Gordon...?"

"I heard that last bit," he said, moving away from the door. "There's movement in the tunnel. Large group coming this way."

Gordon looked about the chamber, taking in the sole doorway and the lack of anything that could be used as shelter. "Humph," he said, "we can't hold out here, so, have to fight our way free. This one sword is the only weapon they have that can cut you, Issac?"

The Wandering Jew nodded.

"Then, I'd say our best bet is if I help Issac fight his way out of the caves and Orlando concentrates on getting her sword back."

"Somehow I was expecting more strategy," Orlando said.

"My daughter shall lead us out," Issac said, placing a hand on Gordon's shoulder. "And with such a warrior by my side, we shall be free of this place."

All three turned at the sound of hammering on the door.

"It's back," Orlando breathed, anxiously. "That... feeling... that thing is back...!" She hugged herself, her glance darting about the cave.

"Settle down, grandmother," Issac murmured, patting her gently. "You are stronger than this. It is but the merest sliver of the Naga's dark god intruding upon this world. Once free of this cave, we will be free of its grip."

"Grandmother?" Orlando fumed. "If you were my kin, I'd box your ears for failing to respect your elders..."

"You two can bicker once we are in the sunlight," Gordon snapped. "They'll be through that door in minutes. Are we ready? Issac, I've got a spare gun..."

"Then keep it where it will do the most good," he replied, gripping his staff, tightly. "Immortality has made me a poor shot."

The heavy door cracked and the topmost hinge was wrenched free of the frame. The shouts and blows from the other side grew louder.

"Once the way is open," Issac said to Gordon, "My Lotte will lead us out. Stay close and follow where I go."

"Fair enough," Gordon said, drawing his six-guns.

The other hinge broke and the door fell, kindling by the time it hit the floor. A wave of killers poured through. There were dozens of them, mostly dirty and battle-scarred men, but scattered through the group were the Serpent Men of Lemuria. Feeling no need for disguise their hideous faces, partly men and partly snake, they snarled and spat as they lead their human followers on.

Gordon stepped in front of the immortals.

"Now this, I understand," he said, then shifting to a tribal dialect. "Come, you miserable dogs! Let El Borak hasten your journey to Hell!"

His guns were aimed and fired faster than the eye could follow; all who stood in the cave understood how he had earned the title The Swift One. Twelve shots and twelve men fell, their comrades leaping over the bodies to reach their quarry. The first group went down on one knee and raised their own firearms; this allowed a second group to aim and fire, over their heads.

"Damn," Gordon muttered, frantically racing to reload, while bracing himself for the first impact. As the various pistols and rifles fired, ringing like fireworks across the cave, Issac stepped forward, pushing Gordon behind him. As the sound of gunfire died down, Gordon could hear another noise, like a handful of coins hitting the pavement and then he noticed, wide-eyed, bullets landing at the tall man's feet.

"Raise your arms!" Gordon barked, and then reached around the Wandering Jew to continue firing. They soon had an additional barrier of dead bandits to protect them, as the hordes kept pouring in.

With a high pitched battle cry, Orlando raced past, a scimitar in each hand. She launched herself at a trio of Serpent Men, screeching like a banshee, hacking and stabbing. When they had fallen, she pushed her way through, to reach the next grouping, as she searched frantically for her sword.

Gordon struggled to keep track of her, not wanting to impede her progress by accidently shooting her. Isaac used his staff to push back the attackers, as he and Gordon slowly made their way to the doorway.

The Texan had to pause, as the metal of his six-shooters had grown almost too hot to hold onto. He clubbed down a bandit with the guns, and with one smooth motion, shoved them back into his belt, and drew his extra guns, one from the back of his gun belt, the other from a shoulder holster.

Orlando hacked the head off of a Serpent Man, wiped blood and scales from her eyes, and then shouted with triumph, as she spotted the reptilian mystic who held, instead of the usual black staff, a white and silver Japanese katana. Symbols had been scrawled down the blade in what looked like blood.

She batted aside bandits and pointed one of her scimitars at the katana wielding Serpent Man. "*En garde!*" she snarled. "You sword-pilfering bastard!"

She leapt; both swords high above her head. With a hiss of rage, the Serpent Man stabbed Orlando through the chest and struck her in the temple with a scaled fist. The weight of her body wrenched the sword from his grip and she hit the floor with a wet thud, followed by the metallic noise of her swords falling to the stone floor.

"Grab my shoulders!" Issac shouted.

Gordon obeyed. The tall man charged into the crowd, his staff and invulnerable body knocking aside blades, bullets and bodies, until he'd reached Orlando. Issac scooped her up and hunched up his body, like a line backer and pushed the remaining way through the doorway and into the tunnel. As soon as they were through, Gordon let go, spun and fired through the doorway.

"Quickly, Gordon," Issac said, striding down the tunnel. "Lotte says we must hurry. It's closing in on us!"

"What is?" Gordon asked, racing to keep up with the Wandering Jew's long strides. Neither his age nor the burden of Orlando's limp form seemed to be slowing him down.

As they raced back through to the fork in the tunnel, something loomed out at them. It filled the tunnel, yet was no more than an indistinct shape, a massive shadow given substance. As with the disguised Serpent Men, Gordon's attempt to look at it made his eyes water and his temples throb. He fired several shots, which caused the shadowy form to flinch, but more from surprise than hurt.

Issac lowered Orlando gently to the floor and strode to face the shadow. It flowed and wiggled, like seaweed tossed by waves or a multitude of twitching fingers. He scraped the tip of his staff against the stone floor and the ancient wood raised sparks.

"Your followers have fallen and your chosen weapon is ours. Go back from whence you came!"

"Whence?" a faint voice asked. "Really?"

Gordon and Issac both turned, in time to see Orlando struggle to her feet. She was coated with blood and gore, one of her eyes was swollen shut, her right ear was a ragged scrap of skin, a dagger protruded from her right thigh, her coverall was now just a few scraps of filthy cloth, stuck to her body by the blood and the katana blade protruded out of her back.

"You'll never intimidate an elder god using words like 'whence'," she muttered, and then spat blood. She grasped the hilt of the Japanese sword and with a scream of pain, yanked it free from her chest. She took a few unsteady steps toward the vague form that loomed over them, seething hatred coming off of it in waves like heat haze.

"I am Orlando! I have walked this world since its infancy. I have seen empires fall. I have seen kings and gods rise and fall, and helped both to occur. I have walked, seduced and fought my way across this globe. It is my world and I want you off it!"

With a savage arc of her sword arm, she slashed at the shadowy shape. Its shriek of pain echoed through the cave and across the surrounding mountains. Gordon dropped his guns, clapped his hands to his ears, and fell to his knees. Issac rushed to the entrance of the cave, cradling the trembling form of a ghostly child.

As the god's cry of pain, and its very form, faded from the cave, Gordon fell over and lay on his back, struggling to catch his breath and get his eyes to focus.

A bruised, bloody, androgynous face came into his field of vision.

"Rest," Orlando said, her voice weak and hoarse. "Issac will watch over us... Move us to a safer place. You have gone above and beyond, Mr. Gordon."

"You all right?" Gordon slurred. "Sounds like this... last time I speak to you...?"

"We... we will speak again... but, my body needs to heal and for that to happen... I'm going to change. You may not recognize me or wish to speak to me."

"I don't...?"

"Just know," Orlando said, gently touching his cheek, "that you are a true friend and I am in your debt. Another time, my thanks would've been of a more amorous nature... for now, all I can give is thanks..."

She slumped out of his line of sight and, despite his struggles to move, his worry for her was no match for the swirling in his brain and the darkness washed over him.

When Gordon opened his eyes, the sky he found himself staring into was blue-black and shining with stars. He felt weak and heavy, but it was the heaviness one felt after a deep sleep. He raised himself up and pushed aside a rough blanket. He'd been sleeping on the ground. Judging from the nearby peaks and the stars, Gordon could tell they were far from the Serpent men's cave.

There was a small fire in the center of the clearing, and a figure in robes and a headdress tending it. The form turned, revealing it was a man. A white man that smiled upon noticing Gordon awake, with a smile that Gordon had last seen on a different face.

"You?" he croaked, surprise and a dry throat keeping him from completing the question.

The man leaned forward and offered Gordon a sip from a water skin. He then caught a glimpse of a silver and white sword tucked into the man's sash.

"We were wondering how much more of your life you planned to dream away. Let me help you sit up. Would you like some stew?"

He spent the next several minutes fussing over Gordon. Only after the Texan was sitting comfortably and slowing sipping watery stew did the other man sit back and smiled that odd, familiar smile at him.

"Don't bother to speak. I've done this so many times before. I am not Orlando's brother, I am Orlando... Oh dear, sorry, my fault for telling you when you had a mouthful. Let me get you a cloth."

"I'd say that's impossible," Gordon said, wiping the front of his shirt, "but, after today, it's seems a worthless phrase. It's really you?"

"In the flesh."

"How?"

"Immortality is a funny thing. Isaac is invulnerable to practically everything. I, on the other hand, can be hurt, but heal remarkably quickly. In some cases, my body receives more punishment than it can handle and things... rearrange. When that happens, sir becomes madame, and vice-versa."

"Where's Issac?" Gordon mumbled.

"Unfortunately, he can only stay in one place for so long," Orlando shrugged. "Otherwise, he'd be known as the Staying-in-one-place Jew."

"He really is the Wandering Jew?"

"Actually, he is *a* Wandering Jew," Orlando said. "But, yes, the stories you've heard are, for the most part, about him."

"But, you're older than him?"

"If we play 20 questions," Orlando said, getting to his feet, "you'll miss your chance to see Issac. Come along."

"What?" Gordon said.

Orlando hooked his arm through Gordon's and they strolled up to the ridge that surrounded the clearing.

A figure strode off, across the rocky terrain. Tall as he was, his shadow seemed to stretch out behind him for miles. Gordon wasn't sure but when he squinted, he swore he could see another small form, walking at Issac's side.

Just as they were about to start down a slope, the smaller form paused, turned and waved.

Then father and daughter were lost to sight.

Harry Dickson began his literary life as a third-rate, unauthorized Holmesian spin-off created in Germany and published in Holland, Belgium and France, under the title of "The Secret Files of the King of Detectives." *Then, Jean Ray took over the editorship of the French-language edition and turned the character into a new archetype of Occult Detective. One of the few adversaries who returned for a second battle with Dickson was the pretty Georgette Cuvelier, a.k.a. The Spider (or* "Madame Spider"), *herself the daughter of one of Dickson's earlier foes, Flax. In this tale, Paul Hugli describes how one Spider eventually led to the creation of another...*

Paul Hugli: *Sleep No More*

Marion, California; 1932

We are Property.
Charles Fort

Barreling down Coast Highway, the Daimler convertible's radio blared a tune by *Bobby Rose & the Rosettas*. Behind the wheel, Richard Wentworth navigated effortless, his calf-skin gloved hands at ten-and-two, his gray-blues eyes glancing in the rear-view mirror. In the distance was a Mediterranean Revival manor on the hill, shimmering in the morning fog burn-off.

William Randolph Hearst, its owner, had named the manor *La Cuestra Encantable*—the Enchanted Hill—but to most, it was known as San Simeon, or, simply, the Castle. The latter brought a smile to Wentworth's face. His Uncle Cyril—of Wentworth Steamline Co.—had christened his flag-ship liner, *The Wentworth Castle*, in honor of, or perhaps in spite of, the newspaper magnate.

The evening before, Wentworth and his paramour, Nita Von Sloan, had been entertained at the Castle. Just a small get-together—only 50 or so—though neither Doug, nor Mary, nor any other A-listers were present. They still had managed to enjoy a swell time. Wentworth entertained the guests with a virtuoso performance on his Stradivarius, while Marion Davies shone with her sparkling personality—though not her Shakespearian recital, no matter how loud William Randolph had applauded. Wentworth was enthralled with a young ingénue, Iris Meredith, who had just completed a bit part in *Hat Check Girl*; while Nita chuckled over the good humor of radio-singer Warren Hull.

Everyone had had a grand time slinging gossip, especially speculations on the recent robbery of a costume warehouse. It was strange; who would want to steal a load of film props from DeMille, Chaney, and others. There was surely no market, no collectors, for the stuff.

After the beautiful people had tired of such speculations, they had gathered on the terrace, searching south, hoping to catch sight of the "Ghost Lights of Guadeloupe," dancing across nearby Nipomo Beach. The Lights hadn't been spotted in months, and remained a no-show that night, much to the disappointment of the gathered idle-rich.

Looking away from the rear-view mirror, Wentworth glanced toward the ocean, his eyes falling on Nita—the smooth oval of her face, her shining, glistening blue eyes, the tresses of her chestnut hair blowing freely in the breeze.

"Some party, Nita dear?"

"Yes, Dick," she replied as she lit a *Camel* with the slim, silver lighter Hearst had presented to Wentworth as a gift. "What was that about 'rosebud'?"

"I'm sure I don't know," he replied with a wry smile.

By the time the Sun was high overhead, the Daimler was far from the coast, traveling through the Diablo Range of Central California. Then, the sizzling summer heat began to take its toll on the motorcar. Its radiator hissed for water. The gas gauge was gargling for petrol. Pulling off the Paso Robles highway, Wentworth drove the demanding auto down an oak-lined, quiet road. The town sign declared: *Marion. Elevation: 573 feet. Population: 1,543.*

"Marion?" Nita read.

"Well, at least, it isn't Rosebud."

They both laughed as he guided the Daimler through Main Street, and immediately realized something was queer. All the businesses appeared closed. Surely, not even a sleepy little town like Marion rolled up its sidewalks at one in the afternoon. Yet, all the non-descript, brick-and-mortar buildings were silent; the badly maintained asphalt street was generously littered with leaves and discarded newspapers.

"They could use some civic pride," Nita said, as Wentworth coasted into a Texaco Station, and cut the engine.

"Or a new mayor."

"Perhaps you should run, Dick."

"What? I'm all for charities, but..." He stopped short when he notices a tower in the valley, just pass the end of town. Constructed of wood, rising 100 feet into the air, it appeared to look every bit like an oil derrick, which wasn't that uncommon anywhere in California. Yet, something was strange about this one: atop was a 20-foot diameter greenish-copper ball.

"Wonder what that is?"

"It's a virilium assimilator," replied a woman, walking out of the Texaco station.

"You don't look like a Service Station attendant," quipped Wentworth.

And she didn't. She was an attractive brunette, though it was difficult to confirm as she wore large, round eye-glasses and a conservative gray ankle-length skirt with a matching jacket over a white blouse. Her hair was tied back in a serious bun; her feet nestled in sensible black shoes.

"My name is Georgette Cuvelier," she said, managing a smile which appeared both seductive and condescending at the same time.

"Are you with the Welcoming Committee?"

"You might say that."

Wentworth was about to make another glib remark when he heard a *click* behind him. He glanced in the rear-view mirror and froze. Standing on the Daimler's rear end were two ugly goons dressed in the garb of Ancient Dynasty Egypt: bare-chested, head cloth, white linen kilt and sandals. Plus, each toted a non-Dynastic Tommy Machine Gun, both pointed at him.

"Is it Halloween already?" Wentworth inquired.

"Yes, and I'm the Shadow," Georgette said, leveling a .45 automatic at Nita's head. "Now, get out. Both of you. On the driver's side. No tricks."

"Dick," Nita said. "What should we do?"

"I suggest we do as the lady says," replied Wentworth. He opened his door and slid out. When he leaned back in to help Nita, the butt of a Tommy Gun came crashing down on the back of his head.

And all went black as a widow's gown.

"Rosebud," Wentworth mumbled as the cobwebs coalesced in his head. "Nita"

Groggily, he managed to sit up on his bunk, holding his throbbing head in his hands, moaning as he rubbed his temples. Then, reality came crashing down: "Nita!" he repeated.

He bolted to his feet, his eyes scanning the room. But all he saw was the bareness of his fifteen-by-fifteen cell: a bunk, a toilet, a sink. The bleakness of his cage and his situation was interrupted by a low humming melody floating through the barred window. He couldn't place to tune at first. Then it dawned on him: *Amazing Grace!*

Climbing on his bunk, Wentworth gripped the iron bars of the window, and looked out across the deserted street. Standing in front of Martin's General Store was an young, raven-haired girl dressed in a blue sun-dress, spotted with yellow daisies, wiping the accumulated dust and grime from the showcase window with her white cotton glove, peering in at the revealed goodies on displayed: a variety of toys and, especially, a cherry-red bicycle, the Grand Prize for a sweepstakes drawing which never took place: *Guess the Correct Number of Marbles... Win a Brand-New Schwinn Red Chief!*

The girl closed her intense blue eyes tight, her brows furrowing, eyebrows almost meeting, her mouth fixed in a grimace as she concentrated on the cat's-eyed marbles in the large pickle jar. The marbles rolled, bounced off one another, back-and-forth in her mind as she calculated the volume of the jar, those of the marbles. Adding. Multiplying. Vectoring. *The correct number of marbles is...*

"Natty! Natty! Ah, there you are!" an attractive, slender, thirtyish brunette called. "You know you're not to be out here. Not now!"

"But, Mama…"

"No buts, Little Girl," the mother said. "We must go!"

"Halt!" a booming voice commanded. "Turn around!"

Trying to hide her fear, the mother turned, shielding her daughter behind her. "We were…"

"There are no excuses," the hulking figure dressed as an Egyptian soldier began. Then, the man realized who he was talking to. "Sorry, Mrs. Saunders. I hadn't realized it was you. Still, you and Natasha, shouldn't be out here. Not now. The procession is about to begin. Don't you hear the loudspeakers?"

"Yes, but my daughter…"

"You must return home at once," said the guard without compassion, waving his Tommy Gun.

Before being led off, Natasha glanced back at the jar of marbles as the correct number flashed before her eyes: *672.*

At once, a small fire seemed to spontaneous ignite amongst an accumulation of dried leaves and litter in the gutter.

No one noticed except for Richard Wentworth from his cell window. But he had no time to ponder this, as the hypnotic *Amazing Grace* was suddenly replaced by a monotonous blare of heralding trumpets.

Down Main Street crawled a royal procession, led by heralds, who gave way to a stretch litter carried on the burly shoulders of six beefy men dressed only in kilts and sandals, walking lock-stepped, their faces blank, expressionless masks, though their eyes glowed an eerie purple haze.

Upon the litter, on a golden throne under a sun-shade, sat a thirtyish man ensembled as the Living God—as Pharaoh! Upon his head sat the Double Crown of Lower and Upper Egypt. He held in his hands, crossed over his heavy chest and broad collar of gold, the regal flail of ebony and gold enamel, and the bejeweled scepter of Majesty. Glistening in the last of the setting sun's glory was a golden arm-band embossed with a highly-stylized obsidian swastika, set within a circle of pearl, surrounded by a square of crushed rubies.

"Nazis!" Wentworth hissed. "Why did it have to be Nazis?"

This was entirely different than the Pathe' Newsreels he'd seen. There was no real fanfare, no cheering crowds, no *Seig Heil*s, just a *faux*-Pharaoh being carried towards the end of town.

Towards that weird "oil rig."

Abruptly, the booming loud-speakers and the heralding trumpets ceased. Yet, the procession hadn't ended. Slowly down the street rolled a dozen brand-new, shiny white garbage trucks, following after the Pharaoh.

Before Wentworth had a chance to ponder this odd juxtaposition, he heard some scrapping on the wooden floor and a man demanding: "Let me go, you blundering Fascists!"

Jumping off his bunk, Wentworth rushed to the door as a pair of neo-Pharaonic Nazi guards tossed the man on the floor of the adjoining cell, slamming the door shut behind him.

"Where's Nita?" asked Wentworth, thrusting his arm through the bars, trying desperately to grabs one of the guards.

His attempt fell short and the guards just laughed at him and left.

The other prisoner rose to his feet, dusting off his beige trench-coat. Picking his brown fedora from the floor, he shook off the dust before plucking down over his head, tilting it just-so to the right. Beneath his coat he wore a rumpled brown suit, vest, white shirt and black tie. He turned and said:

"You're Richard Wentworth, aren't you?"

"Er, yes. How did you know?"

"The society pages," the man said, offering his hand through the adjoining bars. "My name is Dickson, Harry Dickson."

"Commissioner Kirkpatrick has mentioned you," Wentworth said, shaking the proffered hand. "He referred to you as some kind of 'American Sherlock Holmes.' Perhaps you can tell me what's going on?"

"It's not at all elementary."

"Probably not. My friend Nita Van Sloan has been kidnapped and I have been tossed in this hole. And some Nazi-cum-Pharaoh is parading through the streets. Plus there's a girl named Natasha who seems to be able to start fires with her mind. I don't see a connection."

"It's a long and convoluted story..."

"We don't seem to be going anywhere, so why don't you start at the beginning," Wentworth said.

The two men settled down on their separate bunk, and the detective began:

"I was hired to solve what initially seemed to be two separate cases, yet they both dove-tailed here, in Marion." He drew in a breath, slowly let it out. "First, my friend Leo Saint-Clair asked me to check into the rumors of an Egyptian cult, here, in California..."

Wentworth nodded. "Ever since Carter discovered Tut's tomb, the world has had a case of Tut-mania. A few years back, a business associate of mine stopped a crazy Egyptologist who thought he was the re-incarnation of the Boy-King."[1]

"Yes, Saint-Clair was involved in that, I believe. But that wasn't an isolated incident. There have been other cases: a re-animated mummy named Imhotep. In England, Dr. Anton Phibes used the Curses of Pharaoh to murder the doctors he thought responsible for the death of his wife... I, myself, encountered Living Mummies hiding underground in Scotland... It's been maddening..."

---

[1] See "Death to the Heretic!" in *Tales of the Shadowmen* No.7.

"Amazing," Wentworth said, shaking his head. "But what's going on here? Who is that Georgette broad, and the Nazi who dresses himself up as a Pharaoh?"

"Georgette Cuvelier," Dickson said with what Wentworth thought was a degree of infatuation, "is the daughter of the late Professor Flax, once known as the 'Human Monster.' She, too, is a criminal mastermind known as *L'Araignée*—the Spider. I was surprised to see her here, because her talents lie in the iron-fisted rule of her criminal web, not mixed up with Nazi thugs."

"I still don't understand what's going on, but I don't know if I really care. I only care about finding Nita."

"Before I was caught snooping around by Georgette and her men," said Dickson, ignoring Wentworth's plea, "I discovered that the man calling himself the Living Pharaoh is one Tang-Akhmut, a Copt who took his religion a tad too seriously, and is connected to some cult known as the Temple of Love, which is just a cover for his real masters: the newly-elected Chancellor of the National Socialist Party, a man named Adolph Hitler, and his henchman, Heinrich Himmler. They both dream of heralding the supremacy of the Aryan race."

Wentworth took in the info with a nod. "I thought that Schopenhauser's theories claimed that the 'White Race' superiority was due to a harsh, demanding environment which led to the evolution of a racial ideal: tall, blond and blue-eyed 'supermen.' But I also seem to recall that Hitler and most of the rest of his Nazi horde are far from blond and blue-eyed."

"They still believe themselves to be the Master Race. The highest civilization on Earth since the ancient people of India and Egypt."

"Thus the King Tut bit?"

"Exactly."

"But why are they here?"

"Best as I can determine, this cult is an off-shoot of the Vril Society, whose origin is centered in the Occult, and which is said to have received secret revelations dealing with ancient and future mysteries, and the coming of a New Age. Lots of dogma, esoteric nonsense about the Holy Grail, the Spear of Longinus, and God knows what else." He took a breath and continued: "They also believe in magical violet-black stones, and something called the Black Sun, powered by crystals containing an unknown element they called *Vrilium*, an isotope of radium."

"Appropriate. The symbol for radium is *Ra*."

"As in Amon-Ra, the Egyptian God... I hadn't thought of that."

"And does any of this have anything to do with that derrick with the odd metallic ball on top?"

"A failed experiment by Nikola Tesla. Have you heard of him?"

"Wentworth Enterprises has conducted some experiments dealing with Tesla's theories and applications."

"That tower, out there, was built by Tesla in 1923, for some type of experiment, but was abandoned."

"What type of experiment?"

"No one knows," Dickson said, re-positioning himself on his cot. "And Tesla has been mum on the subject. Some believe he was trying to repeat his Wardenclyff experiments to provide a universal power source. Others say he was trying to contact Mars."

"And this girl, Natasha, I saw outside the window, with the power of pyrokinesis... Who is she?"

Dickson huffed out. "This brings us to my second assignment, this one for the Secret Service, which surprisingly meshed with my first investigation. Albert Einstein..."

"The E-equals-em-cee-squared guy?"

"Uh-huh. He's fled to the U.S.—to Princeton, in fact. He made a request from the U.S. government. He wants them to find his illegitimate daughter, Liserl, who was born out-of-wedlock, and put up for adoption. The Secret Service managed to track her to Serbia, where she was raised by an aunt. She married a young military man who died towards the end of the Great War, leaving her with a baby daughter to raise. Then—*poof*! —the trail dried up. That is, until she turned up here on the arm of Tang-Akhmut."

"So this pyrokinetic kid is Einstein's granddaughter?" Wentworth said, rising to his feet, rubbing the nape of her neck. "Well, that's just peachy." He turned back to the cell's barred window, glancing out the deserted street as the last of the daylight shadows crept down the asphalt.

"We've got to get out of here," said Dickson.

"Agreed, but I knew Houdini and you're no..."

"No, I'm not, but my dad was an illusionist," Dickson said from outside his cell. "I can get us out of here..."

Suddenly, an elderly man appeared. His face was wrinkled, jowls hanging, his hair a grayish-white. He wore a white doctor's smock, a stethoscope slung around his neck. "Sorry," he said, "I thought you might need my help."

"Who are you?" Dickson said, staring into the old doctor's surprisingly alive, intelligent blue eyes.

"My name is Dr. Fairchild. I took care of the guard," said the old man, jangling the now useless jail keys. "Do what you must. I have my own important business to attend to."

He then turned around and left, surprisingly fast for a man of his age.

Glancing into the main office, the two escapees saw the Egyptian-garbed "sheriff" passed out across the desk, the remains of a spiked cup of coffee spill being absorbed by the green blotter.

Quickly, they rifled the gun racks. Dickson opted for a pair of .38 revolvers, while Wentworth selected a pair of .45 automatics, shoving boxes of ammo into his pockets.

"I don't have much experience with hand-guns," Wentworth said, studying the .45's barrel absently.

"Just be careful."

"Now what, Dickson?"

"Obviously, my dear Wentworth, the game's a foot."

"You've spent way too much time in the England."

"Tut-tut, Old Man."

Dr. Fairchild darted quickly, stealthily, keeping to the shadows, as he circumvented Main Street, hurrying down a dark alley, stopping at a storm cellar. A quick glance told him he was alone, unobserved. Opening the door, he descended the creaking stairs, into the small basement, only lit by a low-watt, bare light bulb hanging from the ceiling.

On a wooden work bench lay a man of about 25, his face and hands blistered. Unconscious. Perhaps comatose.

"Bobby," the doctor said, rubbing the man's hand with aloe. "What have they done to you, my brother?"

Wentworth and Dickson met no resistance as they ran down the street, arriving at the place where the pharaonic parade had gone. And what they saw there froze them:

A double row of giant golden sphinxes—five on a side—looking as if they weighed five tons each, created a pathway toward a 14-foot high, 30-foot wide, pylon, a gateway dominated with a giant relief of Rameses in his chariot, smiting his enemies.

"*The Ten Commandments*," Wentworth said, shaking his head.

"What?" Dickson asked.

"*The Ghost Lights of Guadeloupe*," Wentworth added, picking up a chip of the outer casting of one of the sphinxes, rubbing it between his fingers. "It's concrete, not stone."

"What?" Dickson repeated, his eyes taking in the wonders of the pylon and the Tesla Tower in the near distance. "What Ghost Lights?"

Wentworth relayed the story of the "Ghost Lights" as he had heard at the Hearst party, concluding: "The lights were from the people excavating the sets from Cecil B. DeMille's film, which he had buried in the sands of Nipomo Beach after shooting, so that other filmmakers couldn't make use of them."

Dickson studied the pylon, noting that the cartouche of Rameses the Great had been chiseled out, and replaced by another name. Fortunately, he'd picked up the skill to decipher hieroglyphs. The cartouche contained these icons: a twisted stalk of flax, a reed leaf, a load of bread, a serpent, a raised arm, and a mouth. He read aloud: "*H-I-T-L-E-R*."

"The ego…"

Dickson read more, picking out words chiseled here and there: *"Fuhrer For Life... National Socialist German Workers Party... Nazis... the Greatest of the Greats... Life... Health... Prosperity..."*

"All for the glory of a paper-hanger," Wentworth mused.

"You know, there's irony here," the detective said, sweeping his hand at the pylon, "Ramses, here, is smiting his enemies... the Asiatics... from what we refer today as the Middle East... that is, the Semites."

"I guess that fits. But didn't you say the Nazis believe their ancestors were Egyptians?"

"Yes," Dickson said. "But Egyptians, then, were not Semites."

"Well, enough of this journey down the Nile. I have to find Nita!"

"Okay, you go find her, and I'll see what more I can discover about what's happening here. It's surely more than just crazy Nazi-Pharaoh stuff. Especially if Georgette Cuvelier is involved."

"Keep alert."

"You, too."

Heading towards the valley, down through the pylon's gateway, Dickson waved a farewell to Wentworth heading towards the outskirts of town, in search of Nita Van Sloan.

Nita had found herself naked, in a strange place. That, in itself, was nothing unusual. What was unusual was that she was locked in an iron cage, hanging against a wall, in a cave dimly lit with flickering torches mounted in sconces. Again, this was not as frightening as the fact that she was only one of a score of naked men and women likewise suspended in cages. Stranger still: none of the captives appeared to be conscious. Beneath each was a wooden table, and upon each was a greenish-brown oblong object, some five-foot long, two wide and one high.

What is it? Nita pondered. *Some type of vegetation...*

Then: *Pop! Pop! Crackle! Snap!*

...as white sizzling, bubbling, foamy humanoid forms oozed out of these... *Giant Pea Pods?*

Nita had no more time to ponder this weirdness, or her own immediate predicament, when two burly Egyptian goons carried in another giant pod, vein-like vines wrapping around it, pulsating, nourishing it.

They set it on the table beneath her, and departed.

Then, the man appeared, grinning, his black eyes like coals in his handsome face. In his hand, he carried a branding iron. The blistering white-hot tip of was a five-inch long, stylized scorpion. He approached Nita. His grin widened. He raised the branding iron. He smiled more broadly.

Nita screamed.

At that moment, Richard Wentworth, a .45 in each hand, was searching for his girl-friend on the outskirts of town, creeping towards a neo-classic colonial manor: two-story with a four-pillared portico consisting of an upper porch supported by the house and four Doric columns.

Shadows cloaked his movements as he made way to the portico steps, mounting them. Light blazed from only one bottom floor room and he chanced a quick look inside. It was a study, empty of human occupation, though filled with wonders: cedar book shelves, glass showcases full of scarabs, figurines, amulets, and other *objets d'art*. Statues of Osiris, Isis, Horus, and Anubis dotted the room. Above an ornate throne of ebony and plated-gold hung a three-by-four foot, gilded framed painting of Adolph Hitler.

Wentworth slipped through the window, tipping, catching himself on the edge of an ornate wooden box. A sarcophagus. *Sans* mummy, he was pleased to discover.

Save for the painting of the former paper-hanger, Wentworth was impressed with the art collection, until he rubbed against the statue of Osiris and discovered that, like the sphinxes outside, it consisted of painted concrete.

Shrugging, he turned and then spotted, against the far wall, six steamer trunks, a couple opened, revealing the wardrobe from DeMille's *Ten Commandments*. No doubt, the source of attire for this city's goons. Rummaging through the other trunks, he found old playbills, costumes, props, and even an old make-up kit of Lon Chaney. A

It was then that something his half-brother Kent had told him once: *there is evil in the hearts of men... preying on superstitious beliefs... feeding on shadows and monsters... fears which are the masters of men.*

Wentworth grinned sardonically as he dived into trunks containing costumes from *The Hunchback of Notre-Dame, London After Midnight*, and other films: a hump, vampire fangs, fright wig, top hat...

Something had just snapped in Richard Wentworth's brain...

Dickson saw a set of headlights down in the valley, coming from the Tesla Tower, and ducked behind a stack of steel barrels labeled *Petro*. The tower was abuzz with flood-lit activity, though he could not determine exactly what was happening. All he could discern was a group of *faux*-Egyptian goons standing around, Tommy Guns relaxed in their arms, watching the townspeople moving like zombies, toting something out of a mine, loading objects into a garbage truck.

What are they mining?

As a garbage truck rolled slowly by the stack of gasoline barrels, Dickson creeped out of hiding, hopped on the tail gate and peeked into the carriage pit, wiping away a layer of straw to reveal:

"Pods... giant pea pods."

He dropped from the truck, stunned, wondering what fiendish plot for world domination was being hatched here...

"My darling Harry, I knew that a hick county jail couldn't contain you."

Slowly, Dickson turned to face Georgette Cuvelier, flipping back a lock of her hair which had fallen in her face. Her moist pouty lips went unnoticed by the detective. He was, at the moment, more interested in the two Tommy Gun-toting goons flanking her. They appeared to mean business.

"Have you found a new Daddy-Longlegs, my dear Spider?" Dickson smiled lop-sidedly as he watched her polish her glasses with a lavender silk kerchief.

She calmly replaced her glasses and stepped forward, then abruptly slapped him across the face.

"You know that I never kiss and *kill*." Then she leaned forward and kissed him on the mouth. "Well, that is: hardly ever."

The goons grabbed him, disarmed him as Georgette watched, an amused smile on her face. Dickson tried to struggle, but found the effort useless.

"Isn't that a shame," tut-tutted Georgette as she walked away, saying over her shoulder to the guards: "Take him to the cave... make him a *new man*."

Nita's blue eyes grew even wider as the Scorpion advanced toward her with the red-hot poker, grinning maniacally. He spit on the scorpion tip. It sizzled. He studied the delectable nude body of the socialite, checking her out as if she was a side of prime beef. Teasing her, terrifying her, he failed to provoke another scream from her. She wouldn't scream, or beg or even speak. She would *not* give him the satisfaction.

"This isn't for you, my dear," the Scorpion said with a grin. Then, he frowned, his eyebrows meeting, forming a continuous line. "Well, not yet anyway."

He approached a pod atop a table beneath a nearby cage. The pod had been completely transformed into the woman who had been in the cage above, yet still immobile, in a pre-sentient state of awareness. The caged woman—*the human*—was no more, having been transformed into grayish fluff, her vital essences now incorporated into the pod-creature.

The Scorpion laughed as he pressed the tip of the branding iron onto the doppelganger's buttock. The flesh sizzled. The scorpion brand burnt red. The pod-person did not react. At the edge of consciousness, though not humanity.

"No," he said, grinning at Nita, "you need not be branded."

"You mean..." she began.

"Not yet, my pretty, pretty," he said, producing a plastic bottle, squeezing a misty green spray into her face. She immediately became groggy. He reached in and stroked her hair: "It's time to sleep. Once you have been transformed, then you shall become my bride."

If she were conscious, Nita would have definitely screamed.

Now decked out in a hunchback-vampire costume, Wentworth creeped out of the den's window and was slipping away when he turned, noticing a light in the a second-floor room.

Scaling a trellis, he came to the window and snuck a peek. A bedroom: reds and pinks; canopy bed and fireless hearth. A girl—Natasha—sat behind an oak roll-top desk, concentrating, scribbling numbers on slips of paper, mumbling about alternative interior angles and inverse reciprocals.

Suddenly, in the hearth, a dry log burst into flames.

Wentworth noted this, then heard voices below him, from the den. He climbed back down the trellis. Flattening himself against the wall, he listened to the voices coming through the window.

Tang-Akhmut sat on the golden throne beneath the portrait of Hitler, while Georgette Cuvelier sat on a posh red settee, her legs crossed, flicking non-existent lint from her silk stocking.

"All goes well... as planned," she said.

"What about Harry Dickson?" the Pharaoh asked, absently scratching his neck with the end of his flail.

"He's been taken care of. He won't be a problem anymore."

"And the other man—Wentworth?"

"We're still searching for him. The Scorpion has the girl he was with. But he shouldn't be a problem. He's just a rich fool who has more money than he knows what to do with. Hell, he's probably half-way back to New York by now, girl or no girl."

"Typical capitalist," the Pharaoh mused. "How is the *merchandise*?"

"Being loaded on the trucks. They're set to roll at dawn. Soon, one-by-one, every politician in the nation will be replaced by an alien, all under our control."

"*My* control!" he interjected forcefully.

"Yes," she said with a hiss that the Pharaoh seemed not to detect. "Under your control, of course."

"Ha, Spencer in his *Eugenics* got it wrong. It's not the elimination of inferior beings with sterilization that matters, but their *substitution*. Not the creation of a Master Race, but of a race of *slaves*!"

"Yes. With my network—*my web*—I have control of a good chunk of the criminal activity, here, in the States. Just think of the power we'll have with even more judges, politicians, and cops in our collective pockets."

"*Our* pockets?" the Pharaoh asked, not letting the plural pass this time.

"*Your* pockets, Your Majesty," she replied between clenched teeth.

"And the child Natasha?"

"She will be processed once we have channeled her mutant abilities at the Tesla Tower, and attracted more pods from Outer Space. Her mother has already been processed."

Tang-Akhmut thought for a moment. "Still, even if the experiment suc-ceeds and we manage to contact more of these…"

"Pods."

"Yes, pods. It will take years for them to come here, to be harvested by us…"

"So what? By the time they arrive, the infrastructure will be in place, and the new arrivals will be easily integrated into the pool of pods held in reserve. Which, of course, is important as these doppelgangers have only a lifetime of five years due to the present of oxygen in our atmosphere which burns them out."

"Pod replicates of replicates will continue the Third Reich's domination of the United States… of Europe… of the *World*."

"Yes."

"Heil, Hitler!" Tang-Akhmut declared with a half-hearted salute to the painting as he stood.

He left the room. Georgette followed, refusing to lock-step.

Outside, Wentworth had heard enough. He had to find Nita and get the Hell out of this god-forsaken place.

The two machine gun-toting goons ushered Dickson, his hands over his head, toward a cave opening. Suddenly, one guard said: "What was that?

"What was what?" the other guard asked.

"That… *there*! Against the horizon!"

Illuminated by the full Moon, a strange creature lurched; then, dashed across the horizon. Only to stop and stare at them. In the glow of the lights illu-minating the Tesla Tower, the guards could discern the figure: long stringy hair, glistening fangs, and black wings floating, scintillating in the night's breeze.

"*A Nosferatu!*" a guard said in a thick German accent.

Dickson didn't know who—or what—the apparition was, but at the mo-ment, he didn't care. He threw himself backwards, slamming into the backs of the two goons, scrambling them and their machine guns.

The detective tried to grab one of the Tommy Guns, but it was booted away by the second guard who then kicked Dickson in the chin, driving him backwards, landing him flat on his buttocks. Groggily, the Detective shook his head, trying to get a beat on what was happening. He discovered with surprise that the mock Egyptian guards were no longer paying attention to him. Firing from their hips, the goons sprayed bullets at the abominable apparition on the horizon. But to no avail. The wraith moved as if the mist itself. After five seconds of continuous fire, the Tommy Guns' drums where depleted.

Dickson reacted, banging hard into the back of one of the guards, sending him crashing hard to the ground, then jumping on him and ham-fisting his face. The other guard threatened to join the fray, when three gun shots boomed through the air, striking him squarely in the chest. He didn't even have time to scream before his legs crumbled.

Having beaten his man into unconsciousness, Dickson rubbed his knuckles, then scooped up his .38s from the guard's waistband, kneeling, posing with both firearms aimed at the silhouetted figure, wondering: *friend or foe?* Then, he realized the truth:

"Is that you Wentworth?"

"It's not the Shadow!" came the booming reply, followed by an eerie, echoing crackle which morphed into a long shrill.

Richard Wentworth stood still. His .45s were still smoking. For the first time in his life, he felt really *alive*. The power... the kick of automatics in his hands, had invigorated him. This wasn't like skeet-shooting or target practice. This was something different, something more primal. The handguns erupting fury from his palms as he became one with them, forging a strange kinship between his mind and his trigger fingers... It was something he couldn't explain. Something he imagined his half-brother might also feel. Perhaps, it had something to do with the costume he now wore...

Or perhaps not.

Strangely, the gunfight had drawn no attention to the two men. And, even stranger, Dickson didn't question Wentworth's get-up as he approached him, other than to say: "Halloween, already?"

With a shrug, Wentworth replied: "I have to find Nita."

Dr. Fairchild had left his comatose brother in the cellar, and was making his way back towards the valley when a voice boomed out: "Hey, you!"

The old doctor stopped dead in his tracks and turned. A Tommy-Gun was leveled at him.

The faux-Egyptian guard dragged him to the town's doctor's office and, there, ordered him to tend to an unconscious colleague stretched out on the examination table.

But before Dr. Fairchild could even began the examination, gunfire erupted outside. The guard rushed to the window to see what was going down. He could see nothing and turned back, but had no time to react as the old doctor brought a plaster skull crashing down on his head.

The goon dropped like a fly. Tossing aside the remaining fragments of the skull, the old doctor sat on the edge of the desk, not really sure of what had just happened. His fingers fell upon a hand-stamp. Picking it up, he stared at it. Then, absently, he rolled the stamp across a pad of ink as he glazed down at the unconscious guard.

Without thought of his Hippocratic Oath, Dr. Fairchild brought the hand-stamp down hard on the guard's forehead, with force enough that the face of the stamp snapped, driving the ragged handle deep into the man's skull. Through the blood, the guard's forehead now read: *Canceled.*

Dr. Fairchild smiled.

I have to find Nita," Wentworth repeated.

"Yes, but I think we have a more immediate problem," said Dickson.

"Of course." Wentworth filled the Detective in on the conversation he had overheard between Tang-Akhmut and Georgette Cuvelier.

"Hmm," said Dickson thoughtfully, sorting out the data in his mind. "So, their plan is to take over the pols and cops in the U.S., and replace them with... what? Members of a collective? Communists?"

"No, more like zombies from Outer Space."

Then, they heard shuffling feet and turned in unison, guns leveled at the source, ready for action. They saw Dr. Fairchild approaching, cradling an unconscious, younger man in his arms.

"I come in peace," said the doctor. "This is my brother, Robert."

The old doctor didn't appear surprised or frightened by Wentworth's disguise—perhaps became of his own. After placing his brother into the protective arms of Dickson, the old doctor began rubbing his own face. The wrinkles disappeared from his jowls, cheeks and brow. Tearing the strip which secured his gray wig revealed his jet-black hair. Finally, the removal of the two padded-wire hooks from his lower jaw completed his transformation into a must younger, healthier, competent man.

"Now I recognize you," said Wentworth. "You're Dr. Jeffrey Fairchild, the head of Mid-City Hospital!"

Fairchild nodded. "I came here to rescue my brother, who'd managed to get himself mixed up in this Nazi crap."

"Why the old man disguise?" Dickson asked after a quick glance at Wentworth. *Hell, perhaps Halloween has indeed arrived and no one thought to inform me*, thought the Detective.

"I adopted the kindly old doctor disguise because people feel more comfortable, put more trust in a seasoned professional, than with a younger man. Also, an older man is considered a non-entity, making it easier to blend into the background. Thus, while searching for my brother, I used this disguise."

"What's wrong with your brother?" Dickson asked, glancing down at the unconscious man cradled in his arms.

"From what I can diagnose, some form of radio-metric poisoning." Fairchild noticed Dickson was becoming antsy with the "radioactive" man in his arms and took his brother back into his own arms. "The poisoning was from *Vrilium*. A low-yield beta producer. No more dangerous than an x-ray exam, if not prolonged. As in my brother's case."

"You have any idea what's going on here?" Wentworth asked.

"First, you two have been Heaven-sent. I've been trying to get out of town with my brother for a week, but have been forced to remain here by these Nazis. But I've learnt quite a bit about their plans."

"Do tell," Wentworth said with a haunting crackle.

"It has to do with the Tesla Tower, which the inventor abandoned in 1923," Fairchild began, pointing at the structure in the valley. "Some say he was trying to contact Mars or Venus, but was forced to call it quits when his finances fell through. Tang-Akhmut believes that Tesla succeeded in contacting aliens, but not from our neighboring planets, but from what astronomer Ernst Öpik believes is a section of space containing comets on the outskirts of our Solar System. These aliens—these *pods*—received Tesla's message and followed its electromagnetic pulse, taking eight years—that is, last year—to land here, on Earth.

"Tang-Akhmut and Miss Cuvelier also believe that a similar event occurred in relation to Tesla's experiments at Wardenclyff, New Jersey, which resulted in the Tunguska Event, in Siberia: an explosion which leveled thousands of forest acres, eight years after Tesla's Jersey demo."

"And," Wentworth said, recalling the discussion he overheard outside the Pharaoh's window, "these pods duplicate humans and take their place."

"More than that," Fairchild said, "they *replace* the human hosts, while he or she turns to dust. As does all their love, desire, dreams and ambition, their faith, leaving only a shell which is a mockery of humanity. They are truly soulless creatures—under the control of a mad-man!"

"Then how," Wentworth said, "do they differ from regular politicians?"

"I know what you mean," Dickson said, allowing himself a grin.

"From what I overheard," Wentworth said, using his mathematical skills honed from years of calculating odds at the race tracks, "these doppelgangers only have a shelf-life of five years. If this Tesla Tower is fired up and succeeds in contacting more pods, they won't get here until, er, 1940 or so."

"But it wouldn't matter," Dickson said. "The infrastructure would already be in place, with substitute pods already on hand, to be used before more zombies from space arrive."

"Then we have to stop them now!" Wentworth turned to Fairchild. "When is this all to take place?"

"Tonight. The Interocitor has been constructed. It is connected to an underground deposit of crystalline *vrilium*, and both are connected to the Tesla Tower, to charge the assimilator on top, to summon the pods. And now, they have a power source."

"A power source?" Dickson said, "I thought…"

"No. The vrilium crystals are not the power source, but merely a channeler. The true power source is the girl Natasha." He shifted his unconscious brother in his arm. "Einstein's granddaughter! They're going to harvest her mutagenic pyrokinetic abilities, just erupting due to her onset of puberty, as their power source."

"We must stop them!" Dickson exclaimed. To Fairchild, he said: "You take care of your brother. Wentworth and I will take care of the Nazis!"

"We will?" Wentworth said.

Suddenly, an ear-piercing scream echoed through the still night air.

"Yes, we *will* stop them," Wentworth hissed, his pearl white teeth clenched tight, with coldness in his soul.

Natasha was being dragged, screaming, struggling, towards the Interocitor's two copper poles, each ten feet tall, their ends dug deep into the ground, embedded in a vein of vrilium. From the poles ran thick wires, hooked to a polyphase generator, then to the tower's metallic ball cap: the assimilator from which the electromagnetic pulses will be projected. And Natasha *was* the polyphase generator!

Pharaoh Tang-Akhmut sat upon his Royal Litter, watching the proceeding with rapt interest. At his side, in the position of Fan-Bearer on the Right, stood Georgette Cuvelier, studying her fingernails, noting she had cracked one when she slapped Dickson. *Another point against the gumshoe.*

Seated next to Tang was Liserl, Natasha's mother, who showed no emotions while her daughter screamed as she was being tied to the polyphasic poles. Liserl had just completed pea pod conversion: *Zombification.* The Pharaoh's wish was now her command. At the moment, he commanded nothing of her save the use of her daughter. Liserl was therefore at peace, untroubled, emotionless, even as her still very much human daughter continued to scream.

Two goons bound the girl to the copper poles and placed a copper helmet on her head, its electrodes hooked to the poles. Then, they quickly departed the scene, fearful of the promised electrical show.

"Let my people come!" Tang-Akhmut declared, thrusting up his royal scepter, the gold shimmering in reflections of the flood-lights spotlighting the tower. With his other hand, he threw the master-switch.

The surge of electricity ran down the cable. Natasha stiffened as the electro-pulse surged through her. Her hair stood on end beneath the helmet. She wanted to scream again, but no longer could. Sparks began to fly. The dome of the Tesla Tower began to glow an eerie red as the electro-plated copper was energized, building towards a polyphasic potential which would project a coherent electromagnetic pulse into space.

"Concentrate on the Tower," a voice suddenly said behind Natasha as she felt herself being unbound. "Concentrate!"

"I... I... can't ..."

"Do it!" the voice demanded. "Aim your thoughts at the Tower. Concentrate. Calculate *pi* to its furthest digit!"

Natasha concentrated. "Three ... point... one... four... one... five... nine... two... six..."

"Good," the voice encouraged.

Suddenly—directed by the girl's thoughts, the wooden Tesla Tower burst into flames. The conflagration shot up the structure and danced about on the huge copper ball as Natasha continued concentrating, mumbling digits: "...three... nine... one... eight... seven..."

"Good girl," the voice whispered.

With her eyes wide shut in concentration, Natasha didn't see the whispering man leave and join up with Dickson, or hear him say: "Let's do it!"

"But what about the townspeople?" the Detective asked Wentworth.

"They are better off dead than zombies."

Dickson nodded.

The duo swung into action, their guns blazing as the Tesla Tower burnt, cutting down Nazi goons as they rushed them. Emptying their pistols. Tossing them aside. Scooping up fallen Tommy Guns. Emptying them. Also tossing them aside and retrieving others as the Nazis fell by the wayside.

The smell and the clouds of cordite threatened to suffocate the blazing heroes, but they battled on. Blood erupted, splattered, as bodies toppled all around.

The zombified townsfolk put up no resistance, yet they were caught in the crossfire, their life-force evaporating, the bodies dissolving into grayish fluff.

"Ashes to ashes," Wentworth said with a chilling laugh as he mowed down the former humans, "dust to dust..."

The entire valley was alight with flames of deafening violence as Wentworth continued pumping round after round into the cowardly yellow Nazi bellies. Tossing aside an empty Tommy, scooping up another, he continued the massacre.

Dickson skirted off after the Pharaoh and Georgette Cuvelier. But the cordite clouds were too dense and prevented him from finding the evil masterminds who had fled when the violence erupted. All he found was Liserl. Shot. Her podbody already dissolved into dust. In her last seconds of life, however, she retained a kernel of her humanity, muttering: "Tell Papa ...I'm sorry." And, with that epitaph, Albert Einstein's daughter was gone, literally, with the wind.

Ironically, Dickson's had found the scientist's daughter and completed his assignment complete. Yet, he found no joy in it.

Natasha was still reciting digits when Wentworth stopped her, telling her that she had saved the day, and possibly the world.

"Mother went to sleep, didn't she?" she asked Wentworth, ignoring his costume.

"Yes."

Natasha wept.

Wentworth tried to comfort her, but found it difficult. It wasn't in his character, and he was relieved to surrender her into Dickson's care. Then, with his .45s leveled, he took in the scope of the destruction: the entire valley and the city was ablaze, the Tesla Tower so much kindling.

Wentworth gritted his teeth. "I still have to find Nita."

Nita had fallen asleep. The pea-pod beneath her cage *hissed... popped... crackled...* as her doppelganger began to form. As her humanity siphoned away...

Against the cave wall, leaning back in his chair, the Scorpion applied a rasp to sharpen the emblem on his branding iron. Satisfied, he placed the iron into burning coal embers. He smiled, oblivious to the carnage taking place in the valley, dreaming only of the wealth that soon would be dropped in his lap when his trucks full of pods were delivered to the Crime Syndicate.

For now, he just waited for the original Nita Van Sloan to turn to dust and the *faux*-Nita to fully form, to become his love… his slave.

Then, chips of limestone erupted as bullets smashed into the cave walls, dust mixing with cordite, choking the oxygen in the tight confines, causing the caged humans—or what was left of them—to heave in coughing fits. Yet Wentworth's .45s continued to lash tongues of flame from their barrels. Consumed by his mission, he dealt out justice in a mock imitation of the old wild, wild West.

Lightning fast the Scorpion scooped up the red-hot poker and stabbed at Wentworth, who ducked, avoiding the madman's thrusts. He ejected spent clips from his .45s, ramming in replacements, turning back and firing.

Yet, through the dust and smoke, the Scorpion kept thrusting the poker straight at Wentworth's eye, who barely had time to duck and pivot on his left foot, sweeping his right out, and toppling his attacker. The sizzling poker flew through the air, tumbling, until its fiery end came straight down toward the Scorpion. The villain tried to duck, but froze. The blazing scorpion hit, searing the band into the left side of his face.

He screamed and ran from the cave.

Wentworth let the madman go. There would be other days. Another time for vengeance! Twirling his cape, whipping the smoke and dust and cordite away, he tried not to cough. Then he saw her…

"Nita…" he choked out.

She was unconscious in her cage, curled up fetally. Her nude body waxy, draining of blood. On the table beneath, her mirror-image—also waxy and bloodless in appearance—was forming, like the first impression of a coin being minted. It was all there—yet it wasn't!

Wentworth knew he had to act now or risk losing Nita …forever!

Reactively, he grabbed a machete hanging on the wall and hacked maniacally at the pod beneath Nita's cage. Pseudo-blood and guts erupted from the pod creature, but there were no screams, no reflexive jerks, as the hacked pieces of cellulose flesh flew away and began to dissolve into fine gray fluff, which soon drifted away.

Wentworth scooped up a set of brass keys from a table and swiftly unlocked Nita's cage, pulling her out, letting her down into his waiting arms.

Slowly, absently, Nita's eyelids flickered, then slowly opened, groggily coming into focus on the apparition before her. She began to react, to scream. But suddenly, she realized it was Wentworth, recognizing the strong, comforting which held her.

"Oh, Dick, you came... I knew you would. I tried to stay awake... I love you!"

That simple statement told Wentworth this Nita was real—not an alien facsimile.

"Hush," he said. "Let's get out of this hell-hole!"

He draped a blanket over her naked body and carried her out of the cave, and back towards town. There, he found Harry Dickson kneeling, talking to the 13-year old orphan, Natasha, who still had tears in her eyes.

"What now?" Wentworth asked.

"We did some good here," Dickson said, standing up, holding the girl's hand in his. "But the main parties have escaped."

"There will be other days, other places to deal with them."

"I will report the death of Einstein's daughter, but nothing about her being zombified. And, of course," Dickson said, looking down at Natasha, "introduce him to his granddaughter. However, this invasion is best kept a secret. Let the authorities sort it out."

"Agreed," Wentworth said, tossing Nita over his shoulder, calmly grabbing his holstered .45 and absently shooting, exploding, the skull of a pod-person approaching them. "This must be cleaned up. People seems to allow their humanity to be drawn away and don't seem to mind... Only when we have to fight for it do we realize how precious it is. Society must be protected from this organized anarchy at all costs!"

"I hope this isn't just the beginning of the end."

"We may look to the skies, but we have trouble right here. A vast criminal conspiracy, gangsters corrupting the police, the politicians, and other elected officials. Mad scientists! Nazis! Commies! Saboteurs! It's a crime wave and honest cops like Kirkpatrick can't tackle it alone. I'll have to take a page out of the Shadow's play-book and strike terror into the hearts of crooks and gangsters. Become a *Master of Men*..."

"...and women," Nita whispered as Wentworth shifted her back into his arms.

"And, Nita, we cannot marry," he said with a grin, "as long as the work of the *Vampire*... no, what did you say that Georgette dame is known as, Dickson? *The Spider?* Yes, a spider to tangle crime in my web. Wherever there is a criminal conspiracy, I will be there!"

Postscript: 1972

From: Billy Brown, Director, Consortium for Law-enforcement Action for the Security of Humanity.
To: The Shop

Our Psi Division has located a possible "Diamond File" subject who appears to be a direct descendant of Albert Einstein. His granddaughter, *Natasha,* according to reports, displayed pyrokinetic abilities and married a recessive carrier. Their daughter, *Margaret*, also a carrier, married the brother of astronaut Ted White. Margaret White gave birth to a girl: *Carrietta*, The girl, who prefers the name Carrie, is presently a teenager attending Ewen High School, in Chamberlain, Maine. Please check into her latent abilities and whether she might pose a threat to world security in the future.

Our regular contributor Rick Lai takes a break from narrating the secret history of the Black Coats in this tale, but does not entirely leave the literary world of Paul Féval. He chooses here to unveil the origins of The Vampire Countess, *whose unlife is chronicled in the eponymous Féval novel, as well as in Brian Stableford's* Empire of the Necromancers *saga, where she even meets the All-Father of the Black Coats. Rick's story has her meet an even more fearsome foe...*

Rick Lai: *Vampire Renaissance*

Hungary and Wallachia, 1470-1477

> *"Throughout Hungary and Serbia, the victims of the Undead litter the countryside. Most corpses are found solely drained of blood. Nevertheless, mutilated bodies of women have been discovered along the banks of the Sava. These unfortunates are hairless as well as bloodless. One vampire is scalping its prey."*
> Armand Tesla,
> *The Supernatural and its Manifestations* (1744)

"You have such lovely black hair, my darling," observed Count Marcian Gregoryi as his right hand brandished a knife. His left held a metal goblet filled with wine. "It's a pity that you must lose it."

"You intend to cut my hair!" shouted the Countess.

"No, my dear Addhema. I've been reading Herodotus. His account of the Scythian soldiers was most illuminating. The Scythians scalped their enemies."

"I'm not your enemy! I'm your wife!"

Marcian drained his goblet before throwing it on the ground.

"Harlot! Slut! I know that you've been cheating with Janos! That's why I invited him to our castle! The fool is sleeping peacefully in the guestroom! Once I finish with you, I shall take his scalp!"

Marcian advanced menacingly towards his wife. Addhema screamed.

Suddenly, the door of the noble couple's bedchamber was thrown open. Standing in front of the couple was a tall handsome man.

"Did Addhema's wails disturb your slumbers?" asked Marcian.

"Drop your weapon!" commanded Janos Szandor.

"Only after I have taken two scalps!"

The muscular Marcian leaped at his wife's lover. Seizing Szandor's throat with his left hand, Marcian raised his knife high in the air.

"Your hair is almost as pretty as my…"

Marcian never finished because the goblet smashed brutally into the back of his head. Retrieving the metal cup from the ground, Addhema had struck her husband from behind. Relinquishing his grip on Szandor, Marcian collapsed. He sprawled face downward on the ground as his wife pounded his skull repeatedly with the goblet.

"Count Gregoryi is dead," declared Addhema. "You must throw him out the window. Everyone will believe he fell to his death in a drunken stupor."

Countess Gregoryi's prediction proved to be accurate. Born Addhema Yorga, she was the granddaughter of a nobleman who fled to Hungary from Bulgaria after the Turkish conquest of 1396. When she was only 18, Addhema had married Marcian Gregoryi. At the age of 25, she was an eligible widow. After a period of suitable mourning for her first husband, she celebrated her nuptials with Count Janos Szandor in 1470. Szandor was in favor with Matthias Corvinus, King of Hungary. The sovereign even permitted him to gain dominion over the late Count Gregoryi's vast estates along the Sava River.

Five years later, Count Szandor was summoned to an audience with Matthias Corvinus.

"What do you know of Dracula?" asked the King.

"He is also called Vlad the Impaler," replied Szandor. "Dracula is the former ruler of Wallachia. When the Turks drove him from the throne, he fled to Hungary. Your Majesty imprisoned him for a dozen years. Recently, he was granted his freedom. Your Majesty even gave permission for Dracula to wed your cousin."

"How would you explain my change of heart towards Vlad Dracula?"

"When he was incarcerated, Hungary had just negotiated an armistice with the Ottoman Empire. Dracula was punished to appease the Turks. Our relations with the Turks have changed drastically with their invasion of Bosnia. Your Majesty released Dracula to fight in a new crusade against the Turks."

"Quite correct, Count Szandor. The man is a military genius as well as a depraved hedonist. Do you know why he has been christened the Impaler?"

"Dracula takes a perverted pleasure in impaling human beings on wooden stakes. This horrible fate has been bestowed on his Turkish enemies as well as any citizen of Wallachia who has earned his displeasure. Thousands have perished by impalement on his orders."

"While he was my prisoner, his jailer told me that he amused himself by impaling mice."

"Can such a maniac be trusted, Sire?"

"It is in Dracula's self-interest to be loyal to me. As a precaution, I must appoint one of my more reliable vassals to act as his aide-de-camp. Will you take this commission, Count Szandor?"

"You honor me, Sire. I shall be your eyes and ears in Dracula's entourage."

"My only regret is that the military campaign will force a long absence from your charming wife."

"Addhema has an adventurous soul. She will insist on accompanying me."

"But surely she must remain behind to take care of your heir?"

"Our young son will be entrusted to the care of my brother-in-law, Count Yorga."

In the winter of 1475-1476, Dracula helped King Matthias recover Bosnia. During the summer, he was given command of an army to restore his rule over Wallachia. By the end of November, the forces of the Impaler were triumphant. With Count Szandor at his side, Dracula was once more invested as the reigning Voivode of Wallachia

In early December, a private dinner was held in a mansion in Bucharest, the capital of Wallachia. The host was Vlad Dracula. The guests were Count and Countess Szandor. The festivities lasted long into the night.

Seated in his chair, Szandor was slumped apparently unconscious across the banquet table.

"Your spouse does not drink wine well," pronounced Dracula.

"You must forgive my husband, my Lord," beseeched Addhema.

"I shall if you do me a small favor, Countess."

"What do you wish of me?"

"Merely to answer a question. Do you know the significance of my name?"

"Your father belonged to the Order of the Dragon, a society of nobles dedicated to crusades against the enemies of Christianity. He was known as Dracul, which means 'Dragon.' Dracula signifies the Son of the Dragon."

"My detractors often comment that my name can also be translated as Son of the Devil. My father joined the Order of the Dragon for an ironic reason. My family has a very ancient lineage."

"I know of what you speak, my Lord. The Szandors are descended from Attila the Hun. My husband told me that the great warrior was also your ancestor."

"That is true, but I refer to even more remote forebears. Come with me, Addhema. There is something that you must see."

Dracula's green eyes gazed into Addhema's. The Voivode had a commanding appearance, even though he was not a tall man. Long black hair fell on his shoulders. A bushy black mustache hung beneath an aquiline nose. While his face was gaunt, his body was stocky and strong.

The Voivode escorted Addhema out of the banquet chamber. After traversing corridors lit by torches, the duo reached a locked doorway guarded by two sentries. They were members of Dracula's bodyguard of 200 Moldavians. Fiercely loyal to the Voivode, the Moldavians cultivated their hair and mustaches in the style of their master.

Opening the door with a key, Dracula ushered Addhema inside. She saw a pillar on which rested an object covered by a black shroud. Dracula closed and secured the door. He removed the shroud.

"Behold the Draconic Adder!"

An ivory statue of a winged dragon was revealed. Its worm-like body was coiled thrice. Three horns made from rubies sprouted from its head.

"Is this some talisman of the Order of the Dragon?" asked Addhema. "It smacks of paganism rather than our Christian faith."

Dracula laughed. "The Order is composed of pious hypocrites! If they were true Christians, they would turn the other cheek to our enemies. Instead, they condone their slaughter. It amused my father to join the Order because their symbol invoked the god of our forefathers."

"I don't understand, my Lord."

"The Draconic Adder, also dubbed the Drac, roamed the Earth with the Great Old Ones before the Age of Man. His parents were Yiggurath, Father of Serpents, and Tiamit, the Dragon of Arabu. The ancient civilization of Lemuria revered the Adder under the name of Slidith. Our early ancestors were preyed upon by minions of the other Old Ones. Yiggurath had also mated with Adana the Snake Mother. Their progeny was Set, the Great Serpent. Set spawned the Serpent Men of Hyperborea. Together with the Werewolf Folk, the winged Akaana and other monsters, the Serpent Men warred on humanity. Taking pity on mankind, Slidith empowered an elite group of mortals, the Red Brotherhood, to lead a crusade against the Serpent Men and their allies. Assisting the Brotherhood were the children of Slidith, the Dragon Kings. After a brutal conflict that spanned centuries, the Serpent Alliance was defeated. However, some Serpent Men survived. Disguising themselves as humans, the Serpent Men poisoned the minds of the Lemurians against the Red Brotherhood and the Dragon Kings. The adherents of the Draconic Adder were persecuted. All worship of Slidith disappeared from our world.

"In Stygia, the civilization preceding Egypt, a scholar named Rammon unearthed records of Slidith. Recognizing the Draconic Adder as mankind's true benefactor, Rammon performed a ritual to invoke the god's assistance. Slidith rewarded the scholar by making him his Viceroy on Earth. Rammon inducted other Stygians into the religion of the Adder. His greatest convert was Princess Akivasha of the ruling dynasty. Unfortunately, human allies of the Serpent Men had also established the cult of Set in Stygia. Gaining the support of the Stygian monarch, the priests of Set murdered Rammon and entombed Akivasha alive. The adherents of Slidith were forced into hiding. The post of the Viceroy of Slidith remained vacant until the emergence of the Roman Empire. There was a certain governor of Judea during the reign of Tiberius."

"Enough of your half-truths!" interrupted Addhema. "I know the legends of the Undead! The governor was Pontius Pilate! When he died, he became a vampire!"

Dracula smiled. "You are very perceptive. Yes, Slidith is the Lord of Blood. He transformed the Red Brotherhood into immortals feasting on human blood. The Viceroy of Slidith is also called the Great Vampire."

"You talk of these vampires with admiration."

"My family has secretly venerated Slidith for centuries. We have sought to learn the details of the Ritual of the Viceroy. I studied at the Scholomance, a school of occult knowledge in the mountains over Lake Hermanstadt. There, I discovered *The Book of Simon the Mage*. The Samaritan author had extinguished the Undead existence of Pontius Pilate. The tome unmasked the method by which Pilate was elevated into the Great Vampire. Slidith requires that a candidate to be his Viceroy perform acts of extreme brutality to prove his worthiness. Pilate attempted to gain Slidith's favor by massacring scores of Jews. Eventually, it dawned on Pilate that sacrificing a single individual of great uniqueness would pacify Slidith. Pilate ordered the crucifixion of Jesus."

"Pilate became the Great Vampire by murdering the Son of God?"

"I don't know whether Jesus was truly the Messiah, but he was clearly a being of unimaginable power. Pilate then slaughtered Samaritans to further placate Slidith. This action caused Tiberius to summon Pilate to Rome. By the time Pilate reached Rome, Tiberius had died. The disgraced governor was forced to explain his conduct before the new Emperor, Caligula. Chanting the name of Slidith, Pilate swallowed poison in front of Caligula. The soul of Pilate was sent to the Pit of the Draconic Adder. Pilate presented his petition to be resurrected as the Great Vampire. If Slidith had refused his candidacy, Pilate's fate would be eternal damnation. But his request was granted by Slidith."

"But vampires fear the cross! They are servants of Satan! Not some pagan deity!"

"There were consequences to Pilate's murder of Jesus. Vampires became vulnerable to the crucifix and other Christian symbols. Simon the Mage ended Pilate's reign as Lord of the Undead. My ultimate goal is to succeed Pilate as the Great Vampire. The impalement of countless victims has been my road to a great destiny! Unlike Pilate, there shall be no unintended results from my atrocities! Vampires are already susceptible to the dangers of the stake!"

"Fiend! Blasphemer! You mock the Christian faith that you swore to protect!"

"I'm no more a hypocrite than the self-styled Christian King of Hungary! My actions as Voivode are clearly horrid crimes, buy they have been excused because many of my victims are Moslems! You are in no position to condemn me! You're as much a dissembler as Matthias Corvinus! I have heard the rumors! You murdered your first husband to marry your lover!"

"My sins pale before yours!"

Dracula grabbed a knife that rested on the pedestal near the idol. "This blade is sacred to Slidith. A French warlock, Gilles Grenier, sold it to me. He found this weapon in the ruins of the Cathar fortress at Montségur. I have only used this knife on one other occasion. I had a mistress who claimed to be carrying my child. I carved open her belly to test her veracity."

Addhema shuddered in horror.

"Don't fret, my dear," stated Dracula in a soothing voice. "I must take insurance before I arrange my audience with Slidith. If only I could conceive one great sin to climax my career... Fortunately, Slidith is amused by pretty acts of cruelty. Raping the wife of a loyal subordinate should suffice to divert the Draconic Adder. I will only use the knife if you resist me. *Ia! Draco im Bab-el! Yiggurath im Ngoth!*"

Hours later, Addhema and her slumbering husband were escorted back to their Bucharest residence by Dracula's Moldavian bodyguards. When Janos Szandor awoke in the morning, Addhema tearfully apprised him of her ordeal.

"That monster shall die by my hand!" swore Janos.

"He's married to the King's cousin," noted Addhema. "You must use guile to assassinate him."

"What do you suggest?"

"Kill him during a battle with the Turks."

"His Moldavian bodyguards would never allow me to slay him."

"You must betray Dracula and his Moldavians to the Turks."

"That would be committing treason!"

"Avenging my honor is worth any price!"

In late December, the corpses of 190 Moldavian bodyguards sprawled on the battlefield outside Bucharest. The surviving 10 bodyguards had fled on their horses from the carnage. The commander of the triumphant Turkish soldiers rode up to the Hungarian who had betrayed Dracula's battle plans.

"Where's the Impaler?" asked the Turkish leader.

Count Szandor extended a sack towards the commander. Grasping the bag, the Turk reached inside. He pulled out a human head with long hair and a mustache.

"I commend you, Szandor. You slew Dracula without our assistance."

"I had a personal score to settle. What do you want me to do with the body?"

"Throw it in a ditch!"

The Turkish commander rewarded Szandor with a chest filled with gold.

The Turks conquered Wallachia. Masking their treachery, Janos and Addhema sought refuge at the monastery of Snagov. The monastery was located on an island in a lake near Bucharest. One morning in January 1477, Janos had starling news for his wife.

"The monks found Dracula's body. They are going to give it a decent burial."

The mortal remains of the Impaler were interred in a sealed coffin. The burial occurred in the monastery's southern chapel. Three nights after the funeral, Addhema had a sudden urge.

"Come with me, Janos, to Dracula's grave. I want to spit on his headless carcass."

The Szandors surreptitiously approached the chapel in the corner of the monastery's main courtyard. Janos pushed open the heavy oak door. The couple entered a chamber with a length of 20 feet and a width of 10 feet. There was an altar at the back of the chamber. Two candles on the altar provided a dim light. At the foot of the altar was a grave. It was covered by a stone slab bearing a simple inscription: *DRACULA*.

After Janos removed the slab and the lid of the coffin beneath, Addhema peered inside. In the faint light, she could barely discern the corpse within. She bent downwards to spit on the prostrate Impaler. Suddenly, the figure in the grave rose to its full height. Its right hand seized Addhema's throat.

"Slidith has blessed my candidacy," hissed Dracula. "I am the Great Vampire now!"

The physical form of the Impaler had been altered by his transformation in the Lord of the Undead. His frame was taller and leaner. His ears were pointed. Fangs sprouted from his mouth. Hair grew from the center of his palms. Dracula was dressed in a long scarlet robe. A ring bearing an effigy of the Draconic Adder adorned each of his ten fingers.

"You were foolish to trust your husband. Months ago, he swore fidelity to me. His drunkenness was feigned on the night of the banquet. He willingly surrendered you to my carnal lust. I am indebted to you, Addhema. You provided the inspiration for my final act of earthly evil. With your husband's help, I betrayed my loyal followers to the Turks. This ultimate treachery sealed my bargain with the Draconic Adder."

Dracula released his grip on Addhema. She fell gasping to the ground.

"As I watched from a safe distance, the Turks butchered my soldiers," explained Dracula. "Beheading one of my bodyguards, Janos tricked the Turks into believing that he had murdered me. Invoking Slidith in the Ritual of the Viceroy, I consumed poison."

Dracula extended his right hand towards Janos.

"Count Szandor, remove one of the rings from my fingers. It's my gift to you."

Janos complied with Dracula's command. The Hungarian placed the ring on his own finger.

"This ring shall link your thoughts to mine," said Dracula. "I shall summon my three sons. They will transport my coffin to a suitable fortress in either Wallachia or neighboring Transylvania. As I establish a base here, you shall be the first of my emissaries to the outside world. You and your future comrades shall be known as the Stepsons of the Dragon."

"Command me, Master."

"You shall return to your domain on the Sava River. King Matthias must suffer for my 12 years of imprisonment. You shall launch a rebellion against him. With the powers that I will bestow, you shall be able to resist his forces."

"My family will adopt a new motto: *In vita mors, in mors vita!*"

" 'In life, death; in death, life!' An excellent choice, Janos."

"When will you induct me into the immortal ranks of the Undead?"

"As soon as I am finished with your wife. You will need her advice in the coming insurrection."

From a sheath on his belt, Dracula removed the knife from Montségur. Holding the blade in his right hand, Dracula's left hand locked itself into the moaning Addhema's raven tresses. Yanking the Countess by the hair to her knees, Dracula placed the knife against her forehead.

"You shall be punished for your impertinence, Addhema. Janos has told me of your first husband. His idea of punishment was very original. I'm going to scalp you!"

As Dracula's blade bit into her flesh, the shrieks of Addhema resounded through the chapel.

"Poor Addhema has fainted from her pain," observed Dracula sheathing his knife. "I must console her."

Casting aside the bloody scalp, Dracula bent down towards the prone Addhema. His fangs bit into her neck. Once he had finished dining on her blood, Dracula pulled open his robe. One of the vampire's long fingernails cut into his own chest. Dracula's blood dripped slowly. Raising the head of the comatose Countess, Dracula pressed her face against his breast.

"Feast, Addhema, feast on my blood! You're the first of my Undead brides. You shall be a unique predator. You will do more than drain the blood of your victims. You will steal their hair to adorn your mutilated skull. The stolen hair will only last a few nights. You will be forced to constantly replenish it. In the centuries that follow, sweet Addhema, you and Janos shall wash Europe in blood!"

Dracula's reign as the Great Vampire had begun.

From the vampires described by Rick Lai in the previous tale to other types of monsters, the age of the Man-Beast as fictional hero (or villain) truly began in the 19th century, although, as our new contributor Joseph Lamere points out in his story, there were some truly remarkable precedents in earlier times...

Joseph Lamere: *Satan's Signature*

The Pyrenees and England, 1881

> "If ever I read Satan's signature upon a face,
> it is on that of your new friend."
> Robert Louis Stevenson,
> *Dr. Jekyll and Mr. Hyde*, Chapter 2

Dupin, huffing slightly, mused on the mutability of the Basques as he trudged his way up into the foothills, the spires of the distant castle visible through the trees. The first Marquis and occupant of the castle, an adjutant of Charlemagne who had earned his barony as a result of battlefield distinction, had built the place to be inaccessible to the Basques in the region. A narrow foot path led its way deeper into the forest. The august French ratiocinator had brought with him provisions from Paris, a skin-full of wine and some fresh cheese.

The aging Chevalier paused to take a breath. He thought about dipping into the wine but decided against it. He would need his strength for the walk back. According to what he'd read, the mausoleum lay just beyond the back side of the family seat, a Gothic expanse built at the height of the family's wealth, a time long since past. The current marquis, living in Paris now, had fallen into debauchery and was often criticized in the press for siding with the Basques in the region who no longer wished to pay fealty to Paris. Mutability: fortunes reversed; governments toppled; people evolved.

Another two hours along the foot path and he'd be there, so long as he wasn't accosted along the way by Basque bandits, their faces hidden by masks and jabbering away at him in their bastardized tongue so discordant to his ears. But Dupin had brought along a small pepperbox Derringer for just such an exigency.

Along with it, he carried an almost inchoate prejudice against the Basques. They weren't French; they weren't Spanish. They stood apart, speaking some bastard patois he couldn't fathom. Fiercely independent, murderously self-reliant, they couldn't bring themselves to oblige the Chevalier who had come

154

here from Paris to pry into their affairs. He had made inquiries in town about the crimes of which he had read in the newspapers. He had been met only with a stone-faced silence. But he had somehow managed to stumble on the foot path on his own.

Long retired, Dupin had come here because of a story he'd read in *L'Echo de France* about a series of grave robberies, at first thought to be the work of local vandals. When the old man learned that most of the robberies had been localized around the area of the castle, he had made the decision to take the train here, despite his feelings about the Basques.

The Chevalier carried a copy of Grimm's *Fairy Tales* under his arm, the pertinent passages underlined. Grimm, carried along by the insistent need of the fairy tale, had been vague about details, and Dupin had had to put his ratiocination skills to work on literary matters rather than crimes, a pastime which had whiled away the dreary winter just past. It had been difficult, using those long-unused muscles after all these years, but it had given him a purpose lacking in recent years.

He had long harbored suspicions about a much-celebrated case of his which had taken place in the Rue Morgue years before, and these suspicions had led him here to the Pyrenees.

Before long, the detective found himself passing through the gates marking the marquis' territory, their ornate craftsmanship fallen into disrepair due to neglect and the elements. The portal itself was hanging off its moorings and squeaking as he made his way through. He skirted the darkened, tumble-down castle and found himself in the family mausoleum, overgrown with weeds. The local youth made the arduous trek, no doubt to read poetry and philosophize, and the ground bore the marks of their boots, five different pairs by Dupin's calculations.

One of the boot marks stood out. The old man bent with some effort and saw the markings of a London boot-maker. In his leather notebook, he took note of the dimensions of the boot, as well as the tell-tale markings stamped *MW&S*.

Dupin leaned against the dank mausoleum wall, in the shadow of a wry gargoyle, and carefully set out the makings of a late lunch, taking his time about it. His age had weaned him of the passions of youth, the need for completion to the exclusion of all else. He had given his life over to intellectual pursuits and had never found much time for the voluptuary tendencies clichéd in his people. As a result, his limbs were still limber enough for peregrination and the effort which this, no doubt final, case would require.

The food helped nourish not just his body, but his mind, in which he saw the still-shadowy Englishman enter the mausoleum, doctor bag in hand. For there remained no doubt in Dupin's mind that his quarry was a medical man. He would have to be in order to carry out the labors necessary to his cause, the particulars of which the French detective only just now brought into focus. The doctor had gone about his work nocturnally. He would have felt that innate shame indigenous to all Englishman when it concerned the dead.

In addition, the Englishman wouldn't have wanted to risk hiring locals. Despite his public school background, he would have insisted on taking care of the manual labor himself. To this end, he would have brought digging tools with him. To the medical bag, the Frenchman mentally added a heavier duffle across the shadowy Englishman's shoulders. Indeed, the mausoleum doors bore scratch marks consistent with digging tools. No subtle effort this. The detective ran his hands along the rough surface, his ratiocination skills allowing him to see the shadowy Englishman intent on his labors, his pallid face wracked with effort and dark purpose.

Dupin finished his meager lunch, folded the wax paper and stuffed it into his pocket. He set the remains of the wine beside the mausoleum door, careful not to spill any. It occurred to him then that, perhaps, he was delaying the inevitable trip inside the mausoleum proper, though he long ago had foresworn any superstitious notions.

Crossing himself, he pushed at the mausoleum door and entered the darkened cloister, brushing aside the cobwebs that had grown up since the Englishman's visit. He breathed in the dank air which brought to mind his mother's root cellar and, with it, the inevitable smell of ancient corruption. Seven generations of the marquis' family had been buried here since the 16th century; it was the tomb of the fourth marquis, Eric, which concerned him today. With some effort, the Chevalier kept his keen mind from dwelling on the certainty of his own impending mortality.

The local gendarmes, making their monthly rounds, had found signs of the break-in, and the Paris papers, always searching for grim or ghoulish tales, had trumpeted, and no doubt hyperbolized, their report, one of many which Dupin had cut from the newspaper and pasted into his case files concerning the arcane detritus which fell through the cracks of the Law.

The old man frowned and lit a match against the gloom. Brass plates, dulled with age, bore the remembrances of the faded family glory, their family crest and epigram, *Quod Dubitas Ne Feceris,* embossed under each name. The first marquis, Charlemagne's adjutant, possessed a simple wooden cask, but the second marquis, Alain, had had wrought for himself a gold-inlaid box with obtuse Egyptian markings. The third marquis, Eric, whose dark, brooding portrait hung in the Louvre, had been the first of the titled gentry to embolden the family fortune with speculation in the foreign markets. His son, also named Eric and the subject of Dupin's investigation, had been, by all accounts, a rash young man with impetuous gifts. According to what the Chevalier had managed to find out, the second Eric had been interred next to his lady fair, a beautiful girl of uncertain birth whose tale, arguably bastardized, had been told, first by a woman named Le Prince de Beaumont, then more famously by the brothers Grimm.

The second Eric had chosen for himself a simple, if utilitarian, casket made of a burnished amber-colored stone. A small carving showed two hearts intertwined with a rose. According to local legends, he had been buried with his base-born lady love.

Needing light for what he was about to do, the Chevalier gathered some scraps and rags into a torch and lit it. Dupin had had cause to question his faith in the past, but it was to his faith he returned now, sending up a prayer in bad, half-remembered schoolboy Latin, a prayer which died in the unholy echoes of the mausoleum.

Grunting with the effort—and seeing in his mind's eye the still-shadowy Englishman doing the same—Dupin managed to move aside the stone coffin lid. He peered within the darkness. He needed more light for the task. Heart pounding from the effort, he brought the torch over and leaned further into the casket, the flickering light throwing uncertain shadows on the stone walls.

He gasped at what he found there, backing up almost to the mausoleum door. The gathered gloom of the gargoyle seemed to reach for him. Collecting himself, he sent up another prayer, waited for his heartbeat to resume its normal rhythm and, grim-faced, reentered the mausoleum on unsteady feet.

Dupin had thought himself incapable of shock after all these years, but what he had seen had truly shocked him to the core: the Marquis Eric de Drummondville's beastly, cursed, uncorrupted features staring at him out of that unspeakable array, his mouth twisted in a feral grin, his arms wrapped tightly around the young woman who had been his bride.

Following his incomparable instinct, the Chevalier took note of the rust-colored flakes around the Marquis' head, barely visible against the faded satin interior. Licking the tip of his index finger, he dabbed at the satin lining and retrieved a flake, placing the smear carefully inside the wax paper he'd used for the lunch he'd brought. He sniffed the tip of his finger; the charnel-house taint of blood was unmistakable.

If Dupin hadn't known what he was looking for, he never would have noticed the flakes on the pillow, or else would have taken them for something which had fallen from the body. But he had come here, to this place, on just such a supposition. Now, all that remained was to find the Englishman before the damage had become irreversible.

Sighing with the effort, the Frenchman brought himself to his full height, his back creaking with the effort. It would be dark soon. He had taken rooms at the local inn. Tomorrow, he would take the train back to Paris and put together what he had found with the tattered edges of the most notorious of his cases, immortalized in the penny dreadfuls as "Murder in the Rue Morgue."

A week later, Chevalier Dupin stepped off the train at Paddington Station, his cane with a death's head and obsidian core in one hand, a battered valise in the other. Sherlock Holmes had sent a cable which he had been handed at the Dover crossing, reading:

MY YOUNG PROTÉGÉ WILL MEET YOU AT THE STATION. STOP. AN INDEFATIGABLE MEMBER OF MY "IRREGULARS." STOP. TRUSTED MEMBER OF MY STAFF. NAME OF SUNNY. REGARDS. S.H.

Using his cane as a metronome, the Chevalier found his way outside the station. He had expected this London to be the London of fiction, fog-draped and forlorn, the people dour and grey-featured, but the teeming metropolis he found bore none of the markings of fiction on this rather sunny day. He and Holmes, had been corresponding for three years, the Englishman writing to an old address of the French detective which he still used as a sometime necessary hideaway.

"You're Dupin," said a voice at his elbow. A pinched-looking young boy grinned vaguely up at him. "I recognize you from your descriptions."

Dupin felt a greasy sort of discomfort about the fictional accounts of his exploits. "You're the young man I was told to expect."

"Call me Sunny," the young boy said, tipping a ragged cap. Though there was a tattered grandeur about the boy, he seemed dispossessed of it at present. He offered to take the Frenchman's valise, but Dupin shook his head. The samples he'd taken from the Marquis were inside.

The Chevalier managed to find his equilibrium after the clackety-clack of the train, leaning his insubstantial weight uncertainly against his sturdy obsidian cane. "'Sunny' because of your disposition?" the old man asked with his crisp, precise diction, his French accent almost non-existent.

The young boy frowned with disdain. "Sunny," he said, "on account of me name—Solar. Me mum couldn't remember if 'Apollo' were spelled with one L or two."

Dupin nodded. "You're just as your boss described you."

"He's not me boss," the young boy said. "He's me mentor." The Chevalier detected the slightest whimsy of an Irish accent in his undertones. "There's a difference."

"I see."

"If there's an easy way to do things and a hard way to do them," the young boy said smiling, "be assured your pen pal will do them the difficult way."

The Chevalier chuckled at the thought of the English consulting detective being his "pen pal." "And that includes your being his protégé?" he asked.

"That's right."

"Why couldn't Holmes meet me in person?"

Sunny said, "He's nervous, he is."

"Nervous?" Dupin asked. "But why?"

"About meeting your eminence, of course. That's what he calls you in private: your eminence. I wasn't supposed to tell yer that. I'm given to unner-stan' you're a Chevalier," he said. He pronounced it *shay-val-year*. "But then, as Mister Holmes likes to say, the French are prone to giving out honors for the merest trifle, so..."

"Is that what your Master says?" Dupin asked, smiling despite himself. Dupin found he enjoyed the young man's company immensely. He didn't possess any of Holmes' tendencies toward the pedantic, a marked theme common to the English consulting detective's missives.

They fell into silence for a time, the Chevalier enjoying the bustle of the city, not enough however to drown out the tick of his own thoughts. When they next spoke, their words tumbled over each other.

Sunny started to speak, but thought better of it.

Dupin sighed and asked the question the young man had been about to ask. "In what way are your Master's habits irregular?" Dupin asked absently, his voice quiet, thoughtful.

Sunny stopped short; a street vendor barked at him and threatened to cuff him on the back of the neck. Sunny, an expert at such dodging, skirted the fray. Brow knitted in consternation, he asked, "How could you know what I was about to ask you?"

The old man tapped his temple. "Pure logic, of course, applied to the circumstances and the principles involved. The line of our conversation was headed logically toward that question I asked, and which you were about to ask. How did I know? Because you'd just told me your Master's opinion of me, which devolves upon you to tell me what you think of him, first impressions being what they are, a matter best expressed through his habits which, if you are my primary example, are extraordinary and a matter for comment, the suitable adjective used to describe these habits being 'irregular,' which, it should be noted, he applied to you, Sunny."

"You really are him," Sunny said, his voice touched with the kind of awe reserved for boys his age.

"I suppose so."

"You'll find Mister Holmes to be… irregular in 'is habits," Sunny said uncertainly, touching at the top of his head as though looking for the skylight through which the old Chevalier could see into his thoughts.

"How so?" The Frenchman was distant, having already had a version of this conversation in his head though the application of his ratiocination skills.

"He's a mind to take 'is target practice indoors, and to smoke this absolutely dreadful shag, and when he's in a particularly pensive mood, he'll shut the blinds and not see anyone for days at a time." The pinched-featured young man frowned at the thought. "I'm not too fond of 'im on these occasions."

"How old are you?" the Chevalier asked. The ancient metropolis thrummed with purpose, and the two were carried along toward the boot-maker's whose markings matched those of the footprints found inside the Marquis' mausoleum.

"Fourteen in March," Sunny said, tugging at his earlobe. "Why do you ask?"

"You seem… older than that."

"Mister Holmes says I'm an old soul. Pays me right regular, he does. Never shirks me an' so I never shirk 'im. I tell 'im the education he gives me's enough, but…" With a rapscallion grin, the young man rubbed his thumb and forefinger together, the old man struggling to keep up with Sunny's train of thought. "I does me part. For odds 'n ends mostly, a bit o' this 'n that: following this one, standing at a certain corner for hours at a time, running down to the apothecary's to pick up his solutions… it never gets dull, I'll tell you, working for Mister Holmes." Sunny stopped short. "We're here." He pointed to a chipped wooden sign dangling above their heads: *M. WILSON & SONS, COBBLER*. "Mister Holmes' apothecary is next door. If you don't mind, Chevalier, I'll pop in and pick up 'is solutions while you do your business, eh?"

The Chevalier extended his hand. The young man shook it warmly. "I'll see you later then?"

"Later," Dupin said. "Certainly."

A tiny bell above the door tinkled when Dupin entered the shop, dimly lit and thus restoring the image of London he had anticipated, small, cramped and quiet save for the tapping of hammers against shoe soles.

"Mr. Bunbury, is it?"

A well-dressed young man held his claim ticket aloft. Something about his face bespoke sly sin and opportunity. He wore a green carnation in his buttonhole. "That would be me."

"Your shoes are ready, sir."

"Splendid, just… splendid." The well-dressed young man wore a straw boater at a rakish angle and seemed unconcerned that his fly was undone. "You do take a check, don't you?"

The proprietor nodded and frowned past the well-dressed young Mr. Bunbury, picking daintily at his pockets, to where the Chevalier stood waiting, his hand in his pocket, grasping the paper he'd come here to confirm.

The proprietor, wearing a smudged white apron, came from around the counter to attend his, his face creased with concern. "Can I help you, sir? Have you come to pick up a pair of shoes?"

The Chevalier handed the proprietor the piece of paper he'd brought with him from the Pyrenees, crumpled now from much handling.

The proprietor frowned at the piece of paper he'd been given. "I'm sorry, sir, but I don't understand."

"Those are the markings of your shop, are they not?" Dupin asked.

"Yes, they are."

"Can you tell me anything about the owner of those shoes?"

The proprietor frowned first at Dupin, and then back at the piece of paper in his hand. "You're an officer of the law, aren't you?"

"Yes," Dupin said, comfortable with the half-truth that his mother, a devout Catholic, would have called a sin of omission.

"These markings are my own handiwork," the proprietor said with some pride. "They're a sort of reference, each marking individualized to the customer. See this here, the curlicue?"

"And they denote whom?"

"They belong to the apothecary next door, Dr. Henry Jekyll. See the reversed H and J? I try not to make it too obvious."

Sherlock Holmes, sleek, ascetic, swung a rapier through the air, making *snick-snick* sounds which he claimed helped his thought processes. Sunny and Dupin ducked out of the way of the rapier's trajectory.

"My apothecary," the English detective said.

"The very same," Dupin replied.

"Did the boy tell you... he... he prepares my solutions, for when I need relief from my mental fatigue?" he asked, leaning against the rapier. "Do you find that to be true of yourself, Chevalier?" There was a persistent quality to Holmes' question which the old Frenchman found discomforting. "Do you find sometimes the vagaries of the world too much to bear?"

Dupin ignored the question. "May I ask," he began tentatively, "what kind of solutions are these?"

"A cocaine solution," replied Holmes. "Never more than a seven-percent solution at the very most. Anymore would... rob me of my senses."

"Seven, at the very most," Sunny echoed, tugging at his ear lobe.

"It helps me subdue my overreaching mind," Holmes explained, eager to return the conversation to the subject they shared in common: ratiocination. "I go for days on end, usually when I'm working on a case, without sleeping. The cocaine helps to soothe the beast within."

Dupin nodded. He understood completely about *the beast within*, that voracious leviathan eating at him from the inside out, the beast that kept him at his labors.

"He wasn't there this afternoon when I picked up your solution," Sunny said, tipping a wink at the old man, showing that he, too, could apply the skills of ratiocination. "His apprentice was behind the counter, and when I remarked upon the absence of the doctor, he told me that Dr. Jekyll was teaching a night course at the University of London. So if you two gentlemen were of a mind to take a ride out there this fine evening..."

They caught the young apothecary just as he dismissed his night course, young feral-featured students gathering their books and discussing the pubs where they would gather later. The two men and the scrubby boy sat in a carriage; Holmes' whimsy had made them take the second one offered outside his lodgings near the British Museum.

"That's him," Sunny said, pointing. Holmes had been against bringing the boy because of the possibility that they would encounter trouble, but Sunny had insisted, offering his services as a trail hound.

"He teaches a Chemistry course," the boy said, consulting his notes. "According to what his apprentice told me, he has to teach the night course in order to make up for outstanding University fees and some gambling debts he's incurred."

The young apothecary, small and wiry and hollow-eyed, much as Dupin had pictured him in his imaginings, hustled away from the University on foot.

"You follow him on foot," Holmes said to Sunny, pressing some coins into the young man's hand. "The carriage will be too noticeable. See where he goes, but under no circumstances engage him." The young man nodded and started off, but Holmes held him back with a gloved hand. "You'll meet us back at my lodgings and we'll decide what to do next."

"Yes, sir." With a final nod and a tug of his ear lobe, Sunny left them, following their quarry into the gathering gloom.

"I've made some inquiries as well," Holmes said to Dupin. "Among some of my more disreputable acquaintances, our apothecary has acquired a reputation for dispensing mind-altering drugs."

"But is not cocaine of that designation?" the Chevalier asked.

The Englishman smiled in the shadows thrown by the gas lamplight, his aquiline features alight with glee. "Cocaine is a stimulant, no different from tea or coffee, or even wine." Smiling wryly, knowing the Chevalier's affinity for cognac, he added, "or Amontillado, for that matter."

Dupin bowed =, acknowledging his fondness for that most rare of liquors.

Holmes continued. "I find cocaine to be... freeing, if I may use such an ambiguous term with such an august personage." Holmes returned Dupin's bow. "Our young apothecary has been supplementing his income providing the types of mind-altering drugs said to be beneficial to, ah, the aesthetes who frequent the homosexual brothels, like that young Mr. Bunbury you met before."

"How did you know about Mr. Bunbury?"

"I was following you," Holmes said with a laugh which could have been described as cruel. "I have an affinity for disguising myself. I spent some time upon the stage in my younger days."

"Cambridge?" Dupin asked, his gimlet eyes twinkling. "And Eton before that?"

"Hmm," Holmes said. "Yes. Well." They sat in silence for a time, each listening to the clop of the horses' hooves on the cobbles. "I was given to understand you were retired."

"Something about the case drew me," the Chevalier answered, still half-listening to his own thoughts, wondering if he had read the apothecary correctly. A simple man trying to complicate his life. A simple man reaching beyond himself.

162

"*Cherchez la femme?*" Holmes enquired.

"You might say that."

Holmes nodded in that curt, pedantic way he had. "This is about that Rue Morgue business, is it not?"

Dupin stopped short, his full attention now on the man sitting beside him. Outside, the horses snorted and pawed at the cobbles.

Holmes continued. "If I recall the details correctly, you identified the murderer as an orangutan, one who had escaped from…"

"Yes." The Chevalier felt uncomfortable in the glare of the Englishman's intellect. *So this is what it is like to be in my presence,* the old man thought. He felt a pang of guilt, short, sharp, localized, for the people he had loved over the course of his life, especially the fair B***, the woman who had taken the brunt of his cruelty.

More disturbing than his own self-evaluation was this nagging thought, the competitive instinct which had sustained him all these years: Holmes had anticipated him. Somehow, the Englishman had anticipated him. Holmes possessed gifts far exceeding what Dupin had first thought. The supercilious tenor of his correspondence was, upon further inspection, a ruse which Dupin had used himself on occasion. If one presents a bumbling fool to the populace, one gains the advantage of being underestimated.

Holmes favored the shadows. "The orangutan wasn't just an orangutan, was he?"

"No, he was not."

"This is not about mind-altering drugs," the English detective said. "This is about altering a different kind of consciousness."

Dupin had spent his younger years in divesting himself of any characteristics which would have made him remarkable. He had attained what his gambling cronies would have called a "perfect poker face." He had smoothed his personality such that the image he presented to the world was that of a weary old man. He allowed himself now, in the presence of the Englishman, to relax the façade he'd been carrying around with him all these years.

"The orangutan had been trained," Dupin said, his voice finding a rhythm. Holmes settled in for the tale, his face still half-caught in shadow. "Or so I thought at the time." He struggled with the English words, gamesmanship no longer an issue between them, his mask foresworn but still not at ease. "I was younger then… I was concerned mainly with intellectual matters. I concerned myself with the problem which presented itself and less so the morality. I could see, with perfect clarity, the hands which had left their imprint behind at the crime scene, and I found myself inarticulate in the face of others' inability to see the world as I did. They emotionalized the crime. I, desensitized to such matters, was able to divorce myself from emotion and focus solely on the facts."

"Yes," Holmes whispered, enraptured.

"I was too rigid in my thinking," Dupin said. "I thought—ah—that I alone knew the answers, because I was so far advanced. I had trained myself in the fine art of ratiocination, of syllogism, of the need to have centered my life on the belief in logical conclusions based on observation. I had boiled deduction down to a casual truth of observance—what we see is what we get."

"Yes," Holmes said, understanding completely, the first human being in Dupin's life of which this could be said.

"But I began to turn the case over and over in my mind. The years passed. I retired. In my quieter moments, I returned to the scene of the crime. Still, the case haunted me. I revisited certain details about the man who had, I was becoming certain, trained the orangutan to kill. A sailor he was, who had found the orangutan in Borneo, or so he said.

"I found he had a brother, and that the brother had been an apothecary, like our young doctor. Certain uncomfortable truths began to reveal themselves. Certain uncomfortable conclusions could no longer be avoided. It slowly began to dawn on me that, as you said, the orangutan wasn't just an orangutan, though his brother, the sailor, cleverly maneuvered that particular conclusion."

Holmes smiled thinly. "I am given to understand our apothecary has been obsessed with... metamorphoses since his university days. I spoke with his former roommate. Were you aware that our young apothecary studied abroad?"

"Yes," Dupin said, recalling the trail of his thoughts as he'd made the trek to the Marquis' castle in the foothills of the Pyrenees. "And I am aware just where. You see, the sailor had traveled to America, where he had deposited his younger brother with a professor who has gained a rather, er, curious reputation at a New England university. The sailor arranged for his brother to study with the professor there, as a personal favor. His brother, you see, had been mangled in an industrial accident, his face rent with ghastly scars. This professor began a radical series of medicinal cures rather than surgery."

"These cures..."

"Changed him into a beast," Dupin said. "Which I, at the time, mistakenly took for an orangutan."

"Our young apothecary also studied with this professor," Holmes said, "at Miskatonic University," he added as an afterthought.

"Yes," Dupin said. "The Rue Morgue murderer and our apothecary both attended Miskatonic University, where they dabbled in certain unhallowed arts."

Holmes ignored this last bit, choosing instead to focus on the Chevalier's feet. "Tell me about the Pyrenees," he said with a smug tone Dupin found increasingly irritating.

Dupin frowned down at the cuffs of his pants, where telltale splotches of mud indigenous to the Pyrenean region gave away his recent sojourn. Weariness aching at the edges of his voice the old man related the tale of the Marquis de Drummondville, the Beast of Legend.

Holmes sighed and settled himself further in his seat. "Positively Ovidian. What you've told me fits with what I've managed to find out on my end. The young aesthetes who comprise the bulk of our apothecary's customer base are ashamed of their behavior, you see, and they need to step outside themselves. They find our apothecary's concoctions to heighten the experience, imagining themselves to be gods or monsters or... vampires, giving their encounters an almost mythical quality."

"Vampires?"

"Lord Ruthven—you've heard of him?"

Dupin nodded. "In my younger days, I saw a reenactment of some of his crimes at the Grand Guignol. As I recall, he had a fondness for the blood of virgins. Never caught, or so I heard"

The carriage driver tapped on the door and begged pardon for interrupting, but there were local ordinances against such loitering. Holmes laughed as he handed the carriage driver some coins. The carriage driver, pleased with that, tipped his hat and hushed the horses.

"Lord Ruthven? He was a sadist who happened to be a peer of the realm. To some of these aesthetes, he has become a sort of heroic ideal." Holmes frowned and felt in his pocket for his pipe, tapping out the remains of his earlier shag. "He wrote poetry—dreadful poetry—and there were rumors that he died in Greece, aiding in their cause against the Turks, though there exists contradictory evidence to this. Some say he is still alive and living—if you could call it that—in Paris. There were those who petitioned for his body to be buried at Westminster Abbey, but Lord Ruthven was as a precaution buried in unhallowed ground, in this case an annex to a French cemetery called..."

"Père Lachaise," Dupin said.

Holmes registered only the slightest twinge of surprise. "You know it?"

"I recall it was robbed three weeks ago—specifically the area of the annex where Lord Ruthven is said to keep his...home."

"Ah," Holmes said. "You collect crimes, as I do."

Dupin demurred. "Our apothecary traveled to France three weeks ago. He made three stops, two in the Pyrenees. He went first to Père Lachaise, where Lord Ruthven keeps his home, and then to the Château de R*** not far from Toulouse, where he..."

"Alinska," Holmes mused. "The Hungarian girl."

"You know the tale?"

"I sense the thread of a theory." Holmes lit his pipe and puffed contemplatively. "Lord Ruthven—a man who managed to convince himself he was a vampire, a more than aesthetic metamorphosis which resulted in the death of at least one young woman. And then there's Alinska, the so-called Virgin Vampire. And then we have your Marquis—a man cursed to...what was it? I'm afraid I'm rather lacking in familiarity with fairy tales."

165

"He was cursed by a witch who felt he put too much stock in appearances. He was thus changed by this curse into a beast." A couple passed then, arm in arm, out for a night on the town. The woman gasped at the tenor of their conversation. Dupin continued in a harsh whisper, retreating into the shadows of the carriage. "It was only through the intercession of a young woman that reversed the effects of the curse."

"We may conclude from this that the robbery at Père Lachaise was passed off by the local constabulary as a simple case of trespassing and vandalism, and that our apothecary drew blood from what remained of Lord Ruthven."

"Ironic," the old man mused.

Holmes acknowledged Dupin's observation with a vague nod. Sunny's assessment of the Englishman's taste in tobacco—cheap shag—was accurate; the interior fairly reeked with the ragged scent. "We conclude from this that our apothecary is creating some sort of concoction out of the blood of beings which evinced signs of mutation, in the hopes of, what?"

"In the hopes of creating a concoction," Dupin said, the unfamiliar word like rust in his mouth, "which would allow one to mutate oneself."

"Ah," Holmes said. "Our apothecary is a mercenary selling his concoction for…"

"Perhaps," the old man said. "Perhaps not."

"To what end then?"

"He hopes to mutate himself."

This stopped Holmes short. He tilted his patrician nose and seemed to sniff the air like a wolfhound. "He's a young man."

"Lonely."

"He hates himself."

"Hates his lot in life."

The two men faced separate directions, a duel in reverse; to a passerby they would have seemed strangers passing the time by talking about the weather.

"He reads," Holmes said.

"Voluminously."

"He has theories."

"He wants others to admire him for his erudition. He wants to be considered learned. He wishes to outrun his meager beginnings."

"And we conclude from this that our apothecary is familiar with lesser literature: fairy tales and shilling shockers." Holmes seemed to pace while seated, stopping theatrically in a criss-cross of shadow. "He has a tendency toward the romantic. He is doing this because…"

"He doesn't think he can change his life in any other way. He wants control of his life. Both of the men from whom he chose to draw blood were of the nobility."

"Noble blood," Holmes mused. "And the woman?"

"A romantic tale: love and loss. It fits the pattern, fits his sense of his cause being a worthy one, a moment of grace, of Chivalry."

"He wishes to rise above his station. He has dreams. He has ambitions."

Dupin nodded admiringly; the young man had come far in his ratiocination skills, honing them, refining them. The Englishman would need to learn to divorce himself from the process. Dupin sensed some autobiography in Holmes' assessment of the young Dr. Jekyll.

Holmes shifted the pipe from one side of his mouth to the other, a sort of declaration. "What's his next move?"

"He's not finished," Dupin said. "Before he tries it on himself, he will have wanted to perform a trial. When he takes the concoction, he wants it be in its purest form."

"No. If he were finished he would have tried the concoction himself by now. Our observation of him earlier bears this out. His mien outside the University tonight bespoke a man anxious to be finished with a chore. He's become obsessed. He's been trying the concoction out on his aesthete customers. Different doses. Different mixtures."

"He wants to refine it."

"The question remains: what's his next move?"

Dupin sighed. "I think I know."

A constable's whistle interrupted their discourse. Footsteps clattered over the ancient cobblestones. They overheard the word "Soho." They overheard the word "orangutan."

"Soho!" Holmes bellowed to the driver. Then, to Dupin: "Tell me what you know and I'll tell you what I know."

"There is in France an old tale, an old wives' tale dating back to the time of Chivalry, about a baron named Bisclavret."

"I recall the story from Malory," Holmes nodded. Though the consulting detective had claimed in the epistles they'd exchanged to know very little of literature, this claim appeared to be yet another of the sly gambits with which he plied his trade. "Something about a wolf, as I recall."

"Yes," Dupin said. "It is my habit to obtain from the French government, which still allows me certain... boons... certain official papers. I took the liberty of looking over the passenger logs of any trips abroad which I make. I noticed the name Bisclavret on the Dover packet's manifest." The old man's wizened face looked gray in the shivering shadows. He buttoned his jacket against the chill.

"My brother," Holmes said, "works for the Government. There are those who say he *is* the Government. Great minds think alike, as they say. Our apothecary needs one last bit for his potion it seems. Earlier today, I too got a glimpse of the passenger log at my brother's club. Bisclavret, the descendant of the infamous Bisclavret of legend, has fallen on hard times, like much of the French aristocracy. He works in a Chinese restaurant in Soho, a place called Le Ho..."

"Soho!" their driver called out, the carriage rattling to a stop amidst the screams and gasps of passerby.

Sunny greeted them grimly as soon as they exited the carriage. Holmes tossing some coins at the driver, his free hand on the grip of Dupin's pepperbox Derringer. Dupin leaned against his cane, struggling to keep up.

Chunks of masonry fell from the buildings above, some of them the size of footballs. They ducked out of the way. A man in evening dress stood bleeding from a wound in his head, a medical man attending him. Several well-dressed pedestrians had taken shelter under awnings and in the doorways of shops now shuttered for the evening. Sunny ignored the chaos; he possessed a battlefield calm Dupin found disquieting.

They stood outside a Chinese restaurant, its name rendered in unfamiliar characters, the sign swaying despite the lack of a breeze.

"He's up there!" a constable yelled, pointing to the sky. "Is Colonel Moran still with the…?"

Dupin, Holmes and Sunny stepped under an awning. "I followed the apothecary to a Chinese restaurant," the boy said. "I stayed outside, watching the doctor from the curb. He took a seat at the window."

"Where is he now?"

"Gone," the boy said. "He left as soon as the waiter…changed." Something in the boy's dark eyes gave away the dread he felt. "Doctor Jekyll scratched the waiter with a sort of knife. He pretended it was an accident, but…as soon as he had the blood, he disappeared."

"And you let him get away?" Holmes asked. "How could you?"

"Holmes," Dupin began. "I don't think now is the time to…"

The boy pointed skyward. "I'm sorry, Mister Holmes. A melee ensued when the waiter made his metamorphosis and escaped. I don't think he trucked much with what Jekyll did to 'im. I lost him in the fray."

"Think nothing of it, young man," interrupted a corpulent pedant with an orchid in his buttonhole. Despite the differences in their size, Dupin knew immediately the larger man was Holmes' brother, elder by perhaps as much as eight years. He was attended by an officious-looking acolyte almost as corpulent as he. "We'll take care of the rest."

"Mycroft," Holmes said. Then, with a sigh of recognition: "And your amanuensis…"

"Bancroft?" Sunny gasped; his features aghast with surprise. "What're yew…"

"My brother needed a secretary," Holmes said, disappointment creasing his weary face. "I recommended your brother. I hope you don't mind. He's a good worker, Sunny, like you are. He learns quickly. He'll rise quite high in the ranks I would suppose, given my brother's tutelage."

"Hello, Sunny," Bancroft Pons said. The boy ignored him. A government carriage stood waiting, its interior shadowy, and its driver taking great pains to disguise himself from the gawking crowd.

"We'll take over from here," Mycroft Holmes said. "We have a man on the way who is supposed to be the best shot in the United Kingdom. A crack shot with an air rifle supposedly. He'll take care of Monsieur Bisclavret, an unfortunate French citizen with ties to the Bolsheviks."

"Officially," Dupin said.

Mycroft Holmes didn't answer.

Sherlock Holmes chuckled, his thin, pale fingers working out some complicated violin passage while he resolved this unsatisfactory end. "And when you say *we,* you mean…"

"The British Government, of course," Mycroft said. "As always, we are thankful for your timely intercession, brother, you and your Gallic *bête noire.*" The elder Holmes bowed and said, "Chevalier" with a flawless inflection. Dupin nodded back, still uncertain about what was transpiring.

"You roused yourself from dinner at the Diogenes Club for this?" Holmes asked not without more than a hint of irony. "What does the British Government see in the apothecary?"

"I was importuned," Mycroft said amiably. "Doctor Jekyll will be of some use to us, I suppose," he continued, his secretary Bancroft dutifully taking notes literally in his not-insubstantial shadow. "His experiments, though officially unacknowledged, might prove useful in the future."

Debris rained down on them from the upper floors of the buildings opposite them. Mycroft Holmes seemed amused, mumbling something under his breath about "bread and circuses."

Sunny glared at his older brother Bancroft, who seemed to wilt in the face of his younger brother's disdain though he managed an official position of supercilious antipathy. The medical man who had earlier been attending to the wounded sensed Mycroft Holmes' official status and approached angrily, his moustache wax catching the dim gaslight. "And what are you going to do about this then?" he asked. "My wife and I were having a perfectly pleasant meal before this…this…beast showed up and began his ghastly business."

Before Mycroft Holmes could answer, another darkened government carriage pulled up to the curb behind his. A bulky, red-faced Irishman, looking as though he'd be more at home on the moors, stepped out of the carriage carrying what looked to be a case for a billiard cue under his arm.

"Ah, Colonel Moran, I assume," Mycroft Holmes said with a nod. "Have you met my brother Sherlock?" The two men warily shook hands. Mycroft Holmes addressed the sharpshooter. "Your quarry tonight is a… orangutan," he said with a wry nod to Dupin.

"An orangutan?" Moran asked, wielding his rough-hewn Irish brogue like a backup weapon behind the air rifle he now removed from the case and pieced together while he talked. "You mean like that Rue Morgue business I read of a few years back?"

This was met with an agonized cry from the parapets of the building directly opposite where they stood. The medical man slunk away and into the arms of his waiting wife. An arm, its sinews dangling, fell at their feet. The medical man's wife fainted dead away.

Mycroft Holmes smiled broadly and addressed the latecomer. "See to this business, will you, Colonel?"

"Aye."

The Colonel, spotter in tow, headed into the Chinese restaurant, shrugging off the protestations of what Dupin assumed was the proprietor, a tall, distinguished Chinese with longish fingernails and a well-manicured moustache.

Mycroft Holmes addressed his brother, Dupin and Sunny, a conquering general conferring favors upon underlings. "Bravo to all of you for a job well done. You have led us to a man we have been keeping a weather eye on for quite some time. The Queen thanks you and it need not be said that I echo her thanks."

"And Doctor Jekyll?" Holmes asked. "What of him?"

"That remains to be seen," Mycroft Holmes answered, smiling at the empty case Colonel Moran had left behind. "We'll continue to monitor the situation."

Olivier Legrand's contribution to this volume of Tales of the Shadowmen *is a prequel to his more ambitious tale, "Castle Atlante," recently published in* Doctor Omega and The Shadowmen, *in which Catherine L. Moore's fiery swordswoman, Jirel of Joiry, teams up with the mysterious Doctor Omega to defeat the evil of the Dark Tower. In that story, it was hinted that Jirel had previously had a romantic relationship with the French scholar and Occult detective Jules de Grandin. This is how they met...*

Olivier Legrand: *Lost in Averoigne*

Averoigne, 1925

"*Nom d'un petit bouc vert!*" exclaimed Jules de Grandin. "Do you realize what stands before our very eyes, Professor Jones? The crypt of Azedarac!"

Henry Jones, Sr. suppressed a sigh. After more than four weeks spent exploring the secret tunnels of Averoigne with the eccentric little Frenchman, he still wasn't used to his exuberance, not to his unusual creativity in matters of colorful swearing.

"My theory was correct!" de Grandin went on with growing excitement. It is here, in this very chamber, that Azedarac resumed his sinister dealings in necromancy after he faked his own death at the end of the 12th century... And those fools canonized him! Saint Azedarac, really! Azedarac the Demon, more like! And here we are, at the very heart of his infernal lair...

"I understand your enthusiasm, Jules, but archaeology is a scientific discipline, which is based on proven facts and not on vague legends... Indeed, this site does seem most interesting but you have no proof whatsoever of...

"Proof?" de Grandin bellowed. "You ask for proof, my American friend? Just open your eyes! See! It is here, on this abominable altar of black stone that the sorcerer of Averoigne sacrificed young maidens of France to the unspeakable powers of the Outer Dark! What? Still in doubt? Get your flashlight closer and take a look at these blasphemous bas-reliefs! I think you'll find them revealing enough!"

Striving to ignore the Frenchman's gesticulations, Henry Jones moved closer to the walls of the crypt to take a closer look at the strange images engraved in stone, a succession of ominous and grotesque figures which, in the beam of his flashlight, suddenly seemed to animate in some obscene and hellish serpentine dance.

"Interesting," he whispered. "It looks like some kind of *danse macabre...*"

"A *danse macabre*, indeed!" shouted an overexcited de Grandin. "I'd rather say an unholy parade, a stygian and demonic pavane! Behold this loathsome toad-faced Leviathan! It is the monstrous idol of Saddoqua, the pre-human god of Hyberporea! And here! This grinning ghoul dressed in druidic rags: it is none other than Azedarac himself!"

There is something wrong with the pictures, Henry Jones thought. Behind him, de Grandin, whose voice seemed oddly distant, was raving about the pre-Adamite lubriciousness of Lilith, a thing called Iogsotott and a mysterious Book of Eibon.

Suddenly, Henry became aware of another presence, at the edge of his field of vision.

"*Mort d'un démon!*" swore de Grandin. "*Qu'est-ce que c'est que ça?*"

Averoigne, 1225

"By the Black Goat with a Thousand Young!" cursed Azedarac. "So there really *is* no rest for the wicked..."

Muttering another curse, he diverted his attention from the naked, terrified virgin his acolytes had just bound on the black stone altar and listened to the confused yet ominous noises emanating from the corridors of his underground lair—footsteps, metallic clanks, muffled voices...

Sensing an imminent intrusion, the necromancer grabbed one of the small vials he was always carrying with him; at the very same moment, the door was smashed down and the room was invaded by half-a-dozen men-at-arms, led by one the most spectacular apparitions he had ever seen in his existence, although he had lived for many centuries: a woman with flamboyant red hair, clad in a black suit of armor and swinging a broad-bladed sword with only one hand.

"Azedarac!" screamed the Amazon in the voice of a Fury. "Accursed spawn of the Abyss! The time has come for you to pay for your damnable crimes... and it is Jirel of Joiry who shall have the pleasure of sending your soul to Hell!"

By Lilith, what passion! mused Azedarac in the span of a heartbeat, fascinated despite himself by the savage damsel. Gathering his wits, he drank from one of the vials and vanished before the furious eyes of red-haired Jirel.

Averoigne, 1925

Azedarac knew instantly where he was: in the same place, inside his dark sanctum, deep in the secret tunnels of Averoigne, but 700 years later, thanks to the properties of this invaluable temporal potion which had already saved his life on numerous occasions.

Of course, in his hurry, he had had to abandon his most prized possession: his library, which held many infernal tomes, including the priceless Book of Eibon which had given him the key to the dark lore of a forgotten era... but still, he had saved his skin—*again*—and that was all that mattered. There would always be time in the future to go back further in time, retrieve the precious grimoire, and perhaps even get rid of this arrogant redhead before she started meddling in his affairs.

He had reached this point in his meditations, when he noticed the two men who, since he had emerged from the abyss of time, had been staring at him in the light of their weird luminescent wands, a bewildered look on their inept faces.

Damn! thought Azedarac. *This is supposed to be a hidden lair, not an open house! That being said, these two men from the future do not look very dangerous—far less, in any case, than this damned Jirel of Joiry with her sword and her ruffians. And they do not seem to be carrying any sort of weapons—ah yes, the tall one has a whip attached to his belt. A whip? Seven hundred years in the future? These mortals are decidedly dreadful.*

"Azedarac!" cried the other denizen of the future, a short man with a blond moustache and a singularly piercing gaze. "That's him, Henry! The abhorred necromancer of Averoigne!"

"So you actually know who I am?" asked Azedarac, sincerely surprised and secretly flattered to hear that his notoriety had crossed so many centuries.

"Hold on, Jules!" called out the man with the whip in a strange accent. "I'm sure there is a perfectly rational expla…"

Henry Jones Jr did not have time to finish his sentence. Before his bewildered eyes, another character had just appeared from the surrounding shadows—and what a character! A woman with fiery hair, wearing a black medieval armor and brandishing a sword, just like on the cover of that pulp magazine he had confiscated from a student during his last lecture back home.

"You thought you could escape Jirel of Joiry, you minion of Satan?" roared the red-haired warrior-woman. "Unfortunately for you, you dropped something in your cowardly flight!"

Searching frantically through the folds of his robes, Azedarac could only find one of the two vials…

By the horns of Shub-Niggurath! Azedarac realized that he must have dropped the missing vial earlier, whilst grabbing the one he had drunk… Not only did this damned red-haired trollop had found it, but she had actually had the presence of mind (or foolhardiness?) of emptying it to track him down beyond the abyss of time. Never mind! He still had one vial left.

"*Par l'enfer!*" roared Jirel of Joiry, rushing toward the necromancer as he was lifting the vial to his lips. Azedarac was only a few yards from her, but she knew it was too late—the accursed wizard was going to escape her once again, and, this time, she would be unable to chase him!

"No!" shouted Jules de Grandin. "Henry, stop him!"

Fast as lightning, the whip of Henry Jones, Sr. struck the hand of the sorcerer, who dropped the vial. It shattered on the floor in a burst of crystal and green drops.

Azedarac then uttered a terrible scream, an inhuman cry, full of the darkest fury, a cry which was abruptly cut when the sword of Jirel of Joiry fell down on his neck, beheading him in a single blow. The necromancer's head rolled a little farther and quickly crumbled to dust, along with the rest of the body.

Azedarac, who had extended his unhallowed life far beyond the limits set by nature and fate, had finally been caught up by death.

Jirel was unable to suppress a wide grin while thinking about the torments that awaited the sorcerer's soul in the black fires of Hell.

She then turned around to face the two men from the future she had first mistaken for acolytes of the necromancer.

The tall, young and rather handsome man with the whip stared in amazement at the dusty remains of the necromancer, which finished disintegrating. His companion, a short, blond man with a bright gaze but a slightly ridiculous moustache, seemed, on the contrary, to have all his wits about him.

"You have my thanks, good sirs," said the Lady of Joiry. "You have helped me rid the world of one of mankind's worst enemies…"

The young man with the whip blurted out something Jirel could not understand and, with an even stride, headed for the entrance of the crypt.

"Henry! Where on Earth are you going, *mon ami*?" yelled the other.

"Everything is fine, Jules," replied the man with the whip in a strangely detached voice. "I shall soon wake up and then, I will tell you of this strange dream I'm having right now. Please remind me not to mix oysters and Sauternes again—ever!"

The small blond man turned back his attention to Jirel.

"*Mademoiselle de Joiry*, I presume?" he said with a slight bow. "It is a great honor to meet you in person. My name is Jules de Grandin."

"De Grandin? Are you perchance related to one sire Amaury de Grandin, with whom I had the honor to battle the demonic Hunt of Hellequin?"

"Indeed, *mademoiselle*. I am proud to count this valiant paladin among my remote ancestors… which brings me to the next point. I cannot tell whether you are aware of this or not but… we are in 1925."

"I know," sighed Jirel. "And here I am, stuck in this alien time, with no way back… Tell me, sire Jules, you wouldn't happen to have some knowledge of temporal magic, by any chance?"

Nom d'une louve rouge, what a woman! thought Jules de Grandin while smoothing his moustache.

"I'm afraid my knowledge of this field is rather limited… but I do possess some rudimentary notions of alchemy, as well as a copy of the *Liber Ivonis*, also known as the Book of Eibon. Would you agree to conduct some little experiments with me?

"All in good faith, of course!" he hastened to add at the sight of Jirel's frowning eyebrows over her icy eyes. "You have the word of Jules de Grandin!"

Paris, 1925

"*Voilà!*" declared Jules de Grandin with a rather dramatic solemnity, while holding the test tube containing the weird red glowing liquid. "I have precisely followed the quantities... This should transport you seven centuries back... give or take a few years, perhaps."

"The time has come to bid farewell, sir!" replied Jirel while donning her armor with obvious pleasure, after more than two weeks spent in these outlandish clothes from the future, created by the mysterious enchantress Cocochanel—dresses which were most alluring and comfortable but which definitely did not suit a Lady of Joiry.

This was such a strange time: magic ruled supreme under the name of science, horseless carriages moved as fast as the wind and machines with barbaric names captured the sound of human voice as well as the moving image of life. This world was definitely not hers. How she longed to get back to her own time and life—the clash of arms, the frenzy of battle, the infernal rides through demon-infested lands...

Yet, at the moment of leaving this strangest time—and sir Jules—forever, she felt a singular emotion... What on Earth was happening to her? Had a fortnight in the future been enough to turn the Lady of Joiry into an enamored damsel? And enamored of whom, anyway? Swallowing a curse, Jirel banished those distracting thoughts from her mind; without further hesitation, she took the glass tube Jules was holding out to her, pretending not to notice the gleam of a tear in the little man's blue eyes.

"*Adieu, mon ami,*" she said in her forthright voice, before emptying the vial in one gulp.

"*Adieu, ma dame,*" whispered Jules de Grandin, closing his eyes.

When he opened them again, the living room was empty.

With a sigh, Jules de Grandin lit a cigarette and pulled the telegram he had received earlier this morning out of his pocket:

NEED YOUR ADVICE ON PRECOLUMBIAN ARTIFACT. STOP. POSSIBLE HYPERBOREAN CONNECTION. STOP. CAN YOU COME TO CHICAGO BEFORE END OF MONTH? STOP. REGARDS. STOP. HENRY JONES JR.

(English adaptation by Olivier Legrand)

175

The first "Affair of the Necklace" is, of course, the historical case from the 1780s involving Queen Marie-Antoinette and Cardinal de Rohan, which contributed to discredit the French Monarchy before the Revolution. Alexandre Dumas used the story as the basis for his novel The Queen's Necklace *(1849-50), a sequel to* Joseph Balsamo, *in which his version of Cagliostro plays a much greater and more romanticized part. In 1906, Maurice Leblanc used the same necklace as a springboard for a short-story (included in Black Coat Press' edition of* Arsène Lupin vs. Countess Cagliostro*) in which young Arsène steals it from the wealthy Dreux-Soubize family. This is the third, and heretofore untold, Affair of the Necklace...*

J.-M. & Randy Lofficier: *The Affair of the Necklace Revisited*

Paris, 1939

It was the smells that Richard Benson remembered the most. The smells of wood smoke and chestnuts that heralded the early days of winter in Paris.

War had been declared, but other than the bellicose and chauvinistic articles in *L'Echo de France* and *Le Matin*, one never would have guessed it. There were no military operations, the Germans being occupied in the demolition of Poland, while the French felt totally safe behind their impregnable Maginot line.

The journalists had coined a name for it: the "*drôle de guerre*" or "Phoney War," but to someone like Benson, attuned to even the tiniest shift in the zeitgeist, it was but the ominous calm that precedes the furious storm.

The American still remembered the intoxicating smells of freedom and futures unbound that had filled the French capital two years before, during the *Années Folles*, when he had taken his wife, Alice, to a Picasso exhibit at the World's Fair. They had met the famous painter's paramour, the photographer and poet Dora Maar, who had tried to teach Alice the knife game.

But all that was in the past now. Alice, and their daughter Victoria, were no longer of this world; they existed only as memories, just as tragic to him as Picasso's *Guernica* had been that night, when it had been unveiled.

So much death, so much blood.

And what of him, the survivor? Like the dead soldier in Picasso's painting, he wore the stigma of his martyrdom on his face. He had become a mockery of a man who found succor not in painting bloody visions of a dead horse and a bull, but in the purging of the world's vilest elements.

But it didn't stop the nightmares. Nothing did.

And now, the melancholy smells of Paris had contributed to the loss of another chunk of his past which, like a giant iceberg breaking away from the shelf, would disappear slowly in the impenetrable, murky waters of the past.

Benson chased away the memories and turned into a small street two blocks south of the Luxembourg Gardens. It ended in a cul-de-sac with an imposing building that had known better days. It was an austere bourgeois house that belonged to his friend and business associate, Pierre Duchêne.

Benson had last met the tall, bearded Frenchman in the Congo, where he had been trying to launch an oil company that he wanted Benson to invest in. In the American's opinion, Duchêne was an unusual Frenchman in that he treated the natives with remarkable grace and generosity. This, more than anything else, had convinced him to invest in the venture, and he had never regretted it; since then business had boomed.

Now, Duchêne, unaware of the profound changes that had transformed Benson's life forever, had asked his partner to come to Paris to discuss a "pressing business matter." Filled with curiosity, Benson had cabled his acceptance and date of arrival.

In the declining light of the day, the façade of Duchêne's house exuded a quiet air of finality, as if it was trying to repel an intruder, or at least warn him away. Benson shrugged off the feeling, climbed the five steps of the *perron*, and rang the bell.

A butler appeared and invited the American inside. Monsieur Duchêne, he said, was in the library. Would Monsieur Benson please follow him? Monsieur Benson had no objection.

Guided by the manservant, the American climbed a great marble stairway lined with old-fashioned, dusty oil paintings, which he presumed were a gallery of Duchêne's ancestors. He was then introduced in the library, after which the butler discreetly shut the door behind him. The long room smelled of leather and old books, and was lit only by a desk lamp.

Duchêne, who had been at work sitting behind a large and beautifully carved mahogany desk, rushed to greet his friend.

"Richard. You have come. I am so glad to see you," he declared effusively.

"The same here, Pierre."

"How long has it been? Five years, *non*? Much too long anyway. I've been meaning to come to New York, but you know how it is with business. It is the most demanding of mistresses."

"I wouldn't know."

"*Bien sûr*! I forget. You are married now…"

"Alice and Victoria were killed six months ago…"

Benson generally felt no desire to tell the world the details of the tragedy that had cost Alice and Victoria their lives. So he normally used the white lie of a "tragic plane accident" to ward off even well-meaning inquiries.

The Frenchman's face at once became crestfallen.

"*Mon Dieu*! I didn't know. I am so sorry…"

"But the people who did it paid for their crimes. Their death was avenged."

"That is good," said Duchêne, shaking his head. "That is good indeed."

"Life must go on, as they say. Why did you call me, Pierre?"

"I have the most wonderful business opportunity to present to you Richard. One must act quickly—not too quickly however. It will be best to discuss this in the morning, when our spirits are fresh. Besides, tonight, I have been invited to a most interesting soirée… I thought you might like to join me?"

Benson sighed internally. A Parisian function was just about the last thing he wished to attend. But he perked up when he heard Pierre say:

"…The unveiling of the Queen's Necklace."

The gala was held at the *hôtel particulier* of the Comte and Comtesse de Dreux-Soubise, a stately mansion located in the posh Faubourg Saint-Germain.

The evening was already in full bloom when Duchêne and Benson arrived, dressed in the best of tuxedos. All of Paris' high society was in attendance: businessmen and politicians, archbishops and dons, bankers and generals. Duchêne quickly left Benson to his own devices to go and shake hands with various friends and acquaintances.

Alone and not feeling very social, the American drifted towards the dais where the Necklace was being exhibited, resting on a bed of dark purple velvet in a glass case carefully guarded by two policemen. It was a resplendent piece of jewelry with four heavy tassels, festooned with diamonds, and a smaller piece comprised of even more beautiful, glittering stones arranged in pendants.

"It is a marvelous, *n'est-ce pas*?"

Benson turned and saw a beautiful young woman, with luscious black hair and sapphire blue eyes, dressed in a stunning Schiaparelli gown, standing there, holding a glass of champagne.

"I am your hostess, the Comtesse de Dreux-Soubise," she introduced herself. "And this is my husband, Comte Renaud."

"Richard Benson," the American introduced himself, offering a light *baisemain* to the Comtesse and a slight nod of the head to the older man with a square and rubicund face who had just joined them.

"Glad to meet you, Mister Benson," said the Comte, smiling. "We have already received several offers from your country to exhibit the Necklace. I'm always delighted to do business with Americans. Your people are so, er, straightforward."

"I'm quite sure folks will be lining up for blocks to see it, Monsieur le Comte. So it is Queen Marie-Antoinette's legendary necklace?"

"Only a reconstruction, I'm afraid, but the best we could do under the circumstances. The original was stolen by Jeanne de La Motte in 1785, who dismantled it and sold the stones to British jewelers. I, myself, am descended from the unfortunate Cardinal de Rohan, who had thought to gain the Queen's favor by offering her such a magnificent gift. It's taken my family several generations to put it back together..."

"I had heard it had been stolen again—by the notorious Arsène Lupin?"

The Comte raised an eyebrow at the evocation of what was obviously a painful memory.

"You are well informed, Mister Benson, Yes, that scoundrel Lupin stole it from my late uncle in 1880, but even he eventually felt compelled to return the mounting to us, its rightful owners—a publicity coup, if you ask me. It has taken the Dreux-Soubise another generation and over 30 years to locate and acquire the right kind of stones to restore the Necklace to its original glory."

"I am impressed, Monsieur le Comte," said Benson, truthfully. "I hope you are well insured."

"Such a jewel is more than an heirloom," said the Comte, somewhat haughtily. "It is part and parcel of French History. You cannot put a price on it."

Benson thought that he knew several people in the less savory diamond districts of Antwerp and New York's Nassau Street who would be eager to do just that, but he decided it was wiser to remain silent.

The Comtesse saw that the Comte had intended his remark to be a light rebuff of the American's honest intentions and stepped in.

"Don't be offended by my husband, Mister Benson," she said in a sweet and compassionate tone. "He is very sensitive when it comes to the Necklace. His uncle was shot by Zigomar when he tried to steal it many years ago. He'd give his life to protect it. I'm sure that, with what happened to your wife, you can understand his feelings?"

Benson nodded. "Of course, it is I who must apologize if I unintentionally gave any offense."

"We shall talk no more of it," said the Comte, back to his jovial self. "I am, in fact, interested in hearing your opinion about the Winstons, Mister Benson..."

QUEEN'S NECKLACE STOLEN!

The *Paris Herald Tribune*'s headline immediately caught Benson's eye as he exited his hotel near the Rue Monge the next morning at around 11 a.m.

He had left the soirée at an appropriately late hour. He had lost sight of Duchêne in the growing excitement of the night, and decided to walk back to his hotel alone. His friend was probably busy gathering more investors for his new business venture—whatever it might be. It was around 2 a.m. when the American had stepped inside his hotel, having enjoyed the long stroll down the Boulevard Saint-Germain.

At once, Benson bought a paper and sat at a café to read the article. Past the usual hyperbole, the facts were as follows: the two policemen making up the daytime watch had come on duty at 6 a.m. and had found the body of one of their colleagues strangled in the tiny bathroom adjacent to the exhibit room, and that of the other guard stabbed near the display case which was, needless to say, empty. The doors of the exhibit room were supposed to have been locked at all times, and since the two policemen could not have killed each other, the only logical conclusion was that someone had come into the room and done the deed.

According to the article, the two policemen were above suspicion, so the notion of them being bribed by an outsider had been quickly dismissed by the police. The thief and murderer had to be someone whom they trusted. The Commissioner in charge of the investigation, Monsieur Gilles, had immediately insisted on talking to the Dreux-Soubise and their staff. But he had met with yet another unexpected discovery: the Comte had disappeared!

The Dreux-Soubise slept in separate bedrooms and the Comtesse reported having said good night to her husband when they had retired for the night at around 3:30 a.m. However, the Comte's bed had not been slept in. Could he have murdered the two policemen and scampered away with his own property? As illogical and insane as it was, it seemed the only possibility.

Benson shook his head in an almost instinctive gesture of denial. He couldn't accept that version of events. Everything in him screamed that there was more to it than what he had just read; there was a darker and more sinister plan at work... But he couldn't figure what it was. He finally decided to let the matter rest for the time being and, since the weather was unusually sunny for the season, walk up to the Luxembourg gardens and his friend Duchêne's house.

The *Paris Herald Tribune* was only a morning paper with a single edition. By the time Benson reached the Luxembourg, the *Matin* had come up with a new edition which shouted (literally in this case, as it was being advertised by a young street vendor): "*COMTE DREUX-SOUBISE ASSASSINÉ!*"

Benson's French was more than adequate for reading a newspaper and, a quick purchase and several minutes later, he learned that Commissaire Gilles had been anything but idle. The body of the Comte had been discovered, stuffed in a trunk in a baggage room rarely visited by anyone. What was even more amazing, however, was that all medical signs indicated that Monsieur Dreux-Soubise had been murdered—stabbed, no doubt by the same dagger as the policeman—*no later than 1 a.m!* So it couldn't have been the Comte who had killed the two policemen and stolen the Necklace. More disturbing—*to whom, then, had the Comtesse said good night?*

The writer for *Le Matin* was hysterically blaming, *en masse*, the legendary Fantômas (presumed dead), Belphégor (ditto), Ténébras (ditto) and a host of other criminal masterminds of the past, or their ghosts, but in truth knew nothing for certain, and wrote even less.

One line, however, caught Benson's eye. It was a quote attributed to Commissaire Gilles, a simple statement that said: "It is as if the murderer *had the ability to change faces.*"

Benson thought long and hard about this. He was lucky that no one in the French police knew of his presence in the City of Lights. His visible interest in the Necklace the night before and his unusual abilities might have easily branded him as their number one suspect.

What Benson didn't know was that there were other, more sagacious, guardians of the Law in Paris than the police...

Benson took a shortcut through the Luxembourg Gardens. The trees were devoid of leaves, and only the evergreen bushes and the lawns reminded him of past springs in Paris. He saw a white dove flutter by and land gracefully on a skeletal branch. He sighed when he stopped briefly to admire the view of the Pantheon. That, too, evoked other painful memories of Alice. Victoria had played here, launching her small boats in the basin, watching them float slowly away, waiting for her daddy to go recover them in his bare feet...

Shutting the windows of the past, Benson hurried toward Duchêne's house. Something he now remembered from the previous night was puzzling him. A theory of the crime was forming in his mind. His friend might hold the key to the mystery, he thought.

The cul-de-sac was empty, except for a black mastiff rummaging through a trash can, looking for scraps of food.

Once at the house, the American knocked at the door. Twice. Three times. Strangely, no one came to answer.

He tried the handle. The door wasn't locked.

Benson entered the house, which appeared to be deserted. He yelled a couple of times, but got no reply.

Worried, he climbed the stairs with the grace of a jungle cat and proceeded toward the library, where he thought he might find Duchêne.

Stealthily, he opened the door and took a step inside the room.

At that moment, he felt a blow on his skull which was like the explosion of a thousand lights inside his head.

Benson dropped the floor, unconscious.

When he awoke, he was no longer in the library, but inside a small, damp cellar, solidly tied by a rope to an iron ring embedded into the masonry. The ground was wet. Water was seeping from under a square metal gate located at ground level on the wall to his right. Benson easily guessed that if it was raised, water—from the sewers, judging by the smell—would quickly fill the tiny cell and drown its occupant. As it had, in fact, killed the previous occupant, whose foul-smelling and putrefying body, half-eaten by rats, lay discarded on the soil.

Despite the sorry state of the corpse, the American could still identify the unfortunate victim.

Pierre Duchêne.

But if Duchêne had been dead for what looked like at least ten days, who, then, had he met and talked to the day before?

The murderer, of course. The man whom Commissaire Gilles had said, *had the ability to change faces*. The man whom the Comtesse de Dreux-Soubise had said good night to, instead of her husband, who already lay dead in the baggage room. The man who, looking just like the Comte, had had no problem getting the two guards to open the door to let him in—and then, had killed them both savagely.

The door, which was situated on the opposite wall, made of ancient oak and reinforced with iron, suddenly opened with a groan.

Pierre Duchêne walked in, holding a torch—except it wasn't Duchêne, but a ghastly imitation with an unspeakably evil grin on his stolen face.

"I see that you're awake, Mister Benson. Good. It is fitting that you die slowly and painfully," said the murderer.

"Have you come to gloat?" asked the American.

"Actually, no. I'm here to collect samples."

"Samples?"

The man began touching Benson's malleable face, rubbing away the makeup, revealing the pallid complexion beneath.

"Amazing," he muttered. "And this is entirely natural? A consequence of your tragedy? You didn't take any drugs? Undergo any operation?"

"Not as far as I know," said Benson, acidly. "What about you? Because, if I guessed correctly, you and I have the same power. You used yours to impersonate Duchêne, then at the soirée, you murdered the Comte and took his place. From that point on, it was child's play to kill the guards and steal the Necklace."

"Fine detective work. I'm sure you'll be greatly missed," said the man, who had begun to carefully remove skin cells and hairs with small metal instruments and put them into tiny glass vials. "As you surmised, my own condition is entirely artificial…" His face began to shift and change into that of a man in his fifties with almost no chin and a thin, aristocratic nose.

"My real name is Baruch Jorgell," he said, while continuing his macabre task. "I belong to a criminal society called the Red Hand. My abilities are, indeed, the result of a series of operations performed by our master, Dr. Cornelius Kramm, who has rightfully been nicknamed the 'Sculptor of Human Flesh.' We make a point of keeping tabs of new crime fighters, and when we heard about you and your, er, talent, we decided to kill and impersonate your friend Duchêne in order to lure you to Paris. First, my masters thought you would make an excellent culprit for the Necklace Affair. After all, one of the oldest mottos of our organization is to always *pay the law*. But also, Dr. Cornelius wanted to study you—I mean, your body—to see if we couldn't manufacture more people like you and me. You see, my creation, too, was something of an accident, a successful but wholly unintended side-effect of the operations. But think what a criminal army of faceshifters could achieve… The mind boggles!"

Having finished his grisly task, Jorgell got up and walked to the door.

"I will come and recover your body later. Good-bye, Mister Benson. I hope you're not afraid of rats."

The door shut. Two minutes later, Benson saw the grate slowly being lifted by a cable buried within the wall. The foul smelling waters of the Paris sewers began to invade his cell.

And the rats, too.

Try as he might, Benson could neither break his bonds, nor pull the ring out of the wall. The death trap was centuries old, and had often served its grisly purpose, without fail. Duchêne's body was there to attest it. The American reflected that his crime-fighting career had come to an abrupt end, far sooner than he had anticipated. He knew that he had now fully solved the mystery of the Queen's Necklace robbery, but it was unlikely that he would ever share the truth with anyone.

A more aggressive rodent made a move toward him and Benson used his feet to stomp on it, keeping the others at bay—for the time being.

Suddenly, a massive black form swam through the opening, pushing its way through several rats, the necks of which the creature broke with its powerful jaws. Benson thought he recognized the mastiff he had seen earlier wandering about the cul-de-sac. But what was it doing here...?

Having disposed of the vermin, the dog paddled quickly towards the American and started to chew on his bonds. In seconds, Benson was free. The dog then delivered a powerful lick to his face, creating light ripples in his malleable skin. The Avenger didn't know what say.

"Er, *bon chien*," he finally muttered, petting the animal on the head.

The animal nodded, as if he acknowledged the compliment, and ran to the door. Benson followed him. Jorgell had been so certain of his victim's fate that he hadn't bothered locking it.

In the corridor outside, Benson first turned the metal wheel that controlled the raising and lowering of the gate, then ran swiftly and silently up an ancient flight of stone steps, the black mastiff on his heels.

He arrived in a wine cellar, stepping out of a secret passage hidden behind a movable bottle rack, and, running up another flight of stairs, came out of a small door located on the ground floor under the main marble stairway.

His timing could not have been better, for Jorgell stood on the threshold, with a small suitcase standing next to him, preparing to lock the main door behind him.

When he saw Benson and the dog running towards him, the murderer muttered a curse and swiftly pulled a gun from his pocket. Benson knew that it is only in Hollywood serials that villains missed the hero. He was too far to stop Jorgell, and there was no place to hide in the straight and narrow corridor. The man from the Red Hand would probably hit him with the first shot. He could only hope that it wouldn't be fatal. And that the dog would get him.

Suddenly, just as Jorgell prepared to shoot, a white dove flew in and scratched his face, pecking at his eyes, hurting him, forcing him to instinctively raise his arms to chase the bird away. Several shot were fired. In the air. Harmlessly. Then Jorgell fell with a thud.

Benson had been right.

The dog had gotten him.

The American took the suitcase and opened it. It contained some papers and makeup products, but no necklace, no jewels. He wasn't surprised, because he had a good idea where the Necklace was.

Then, he heard the bells of the neighboring Saint-Sulpice church toll 10 p.m.

"If I hurry, I'll be just in time," said the Avenger.

The night train to Antwerp was scheduled to leave the Gare du Nord at 10:28 p.m. At exactly 10:25 p.m., a man who looked exactly like Pierre Duchêne stepped aboard. He strolled through the first class sleeping car, spoke in whispers to a steward, then proceeded toward a numbered compartment.

He slid the door open and said:

"I'm afraid your trip to Antwerp will have to wait, Madame la Comtesse."

The Comtesse de Dreux-Soubise appeared surprised to see him.

"Jorgell? What are you doing here? You were supposed to take care of the American..."

"I thought it was you, but I needed to be sure," said the Avenger, erasing Duchêne's features from his face and remolding it into his usual likeness.

The Comtesse's eyes grew wide and her jaw dropped slightly as she heard the whistles in the station outside. The train didn't move.

"Yes," confirmed Benson. "Commissaire Gilles' men are already here. Tonight, you will sleep at La Santé. After that..." and he slowly drew his hand across his neck.

The Comtesse fainted.

Benson took a hat box from the baggage rack and opened it. Even under the feeble lights of the train compartment, a myriad sparkles filled the air.

"The Queen's Necklace has been found," murmured the Avenger.

The day after, Benson sat at a café overlooking Notre-Dame, sharing a glass of wine with the mysterious, dark-clad avenger known as Judex. He was a tall man, with dark hair and steel grey eyes, which could become very soft when he felt compassion. He also looked much younger than he ought to have been, but Benson didn't feel it was any of his business to inquire about that.

"Thank you for all the help," he said, pointing at the dove perched on a nearby Colonne Morriss and the black mastiff sleeping peacefully at his master's feet, "and also thank you for trusting in my innocence and letting me finish with my investigation."

"It was quite natural," said Judex. "I never believed for a minute that you could be guilty. I am, however, interested in learning how you exposed the Comtesse so quickly?"

"Easy. When we met, she made a mention of my wife being shot by a gangster. The only person I had told was Duchêne—I mean, Baruch Jorgell. So it came to reason that he must have told her, and she inadvertently let it slip. That proved they were in it together."

"I see," said Judex, nodding slowly. "I predict a bright future for you in our common field of endeavor, Monsieur Benson. Shall we toast to it?"

Judex raised his glass. "To Justice," he said.

"To Justice," replied the Avenger.

The glasses shone briefly in the Parisian sunlight and clinked. Somewhere in Heaven, Alice's spirit smiled.

As Tales of the Shadowmen *reaches its eighth volume, our overall tapestry of heroes and villains has grown more complex, and sometimes threads cross and lives intersect. This story, by our new Australian contributor, David McDonald, could be read as a sequel to Joseph Lamere's earlier tale, in which a new generation of heroes must deal with the sinister experiments of the previous generation. Curiously, its exotic locale also echoes Travis Hiltz's story in this volume...*

DavidMcDonald: *Catspaw*

Afghanistan, 1893

Harnesses jangled as they rode down the dusty street, sweating under the harsh glare of the Sun. A few old men lounged indolently on the verandas of the larger buildings, and a gaggle of young children played the same games young children might have been playing in the alleys of London, a thousand and more miles away, but little else disturbed the sleepy heat of the early afternoon. The thought of London, and what he could be doing instead, only increased Harry's irritation. He swatted irritably at a fly, and turned to the man next to him.

"Ballantine, how much further do we have to ride today?"

"Not much further, sir." The words still carried the hints of heath and whiskey that 20 years in the Queen's service hadn't been able to take away. "The fort is on top of yonder hill."

The big Scotsman didn't stop scanning the streets for possible threats as he spoke. Harry had often wondered what the sergeant could possibly be worried about in a place like this. He couldn't imagine anything short of a cannon having an effect on Ballantine. Harry grinned, perhaps Ballantine thought one of the urchins might try and stab him with the stick they were pretending were swords.

"So, what is the purpose of this visit, Sergeant?"

"Karram Khan knows the movements of every bandit, slaver or opium smuggler who moves through the hills here for 30 miles in any direction. A useful man to know, sir."

"If you say so, Ballantine. I haven't met a single man I would want to know so far." He sighed. "It wouldn't matter how boring they are if any of 'em had any booze handy, or let their daughters out for even a moment. I haven't seen a woman for weeks."

"They do keep their lasses locked up tight, sir." The sergeant's tone was carefully bland.

"What is it you aren't saying, Sergeant? Speak your mind, I am getting sick of your hints," Harry snapped. The heat really was getting to him.

"Well, sir, it seems to me that you weren't sent here for the ladies or the drink but to learn the ropes."

"For such a big man, you can be an old woman, Ballantine."

Now there were red spots burning on the Scotsman's cheeks. "Yes, sir."

Harry was suddenly sick of the squabbling. He dug his feet into his horse's flanks, and urged it into a gallop. Ignoring the Sergeant's shouts behind him, he followed the winding path up the hill towards the fort, relishing the feel of the wind in his sweat soaked hair. He could see the fort, a squat ugly building like most of the others he had seen, in the distance but perhaps halfway he could make out another rider. His curiosity piqued he decided to introduce himself.

As he approached, he realized that this was no native, but another European. Harry grinned, perhaps they would provide some civilized conversation and some entertainment. The man stopped what he was doing and looked up at Harry, a ready smile already on his face. He was perhaps 40, but had the well preserved look of a man aging gracefully. Black hair was parted neatly to the side, and underneath a high brow intelligent brown eyes met Harry's. His upper lip sported a neat, thin moustache. Harry unconsciously stroked his thick and luxuriant cavalryman's whiskers; now that was a real moustache.

"Bonjour, Monsieur!" The man walked towards Harry, a cane tucked under his left arm. His right hand extended in greeting. "I am Jean Saint-Clair. I'm glad to find another European in this strange land. Whom do I have the pleasure...?"

A Frenchman? That wouldn't have been one of Harry's preferences in a companion, but the last few weeks had been so dull that he wasn't going to complain. There was something about this man that he liked immediately, and Harry trusted his judgment of people; it was one of the gifts he had inherited from his father, along with a natural aptitude for languages and horse flesh. He took Jean's hand and shook it heartily; the grip was surprisingly firm, and stronger than he expected. He gave his name, and winced as he waited for the usual reaction.

The Frenchman's eyes widened slightly. "That name is a familiar one. Your father, is he not..?"

"Yes." Harry cut him off, his voice harsher than he intended. "He is indeed my father."

"Interesting." Perhaps sensing that Harry didn't want to pursue the subject any further, Jean left it at that. "Well, Monsieur Harry, it is a pleasure to meet you. It seems we are heading in the same direction. Do you mind if I join you and your companion?"

Harry looked around to see Ballantine reining in his horse, his face flushed with anger and perhaps the heat. He hesitated, not sure whether the Scotsman would welcome a travelling companion.

Jean opened one of his saddlebags, revealing a number of dark brown bottles sealed with gold foil. "This is far too good a brandy to drink alone, *n'est-ce-pas?*"

Harry grinned. "Welcome to our little caravan, *mon ami!*"

"So, this is the son of the great Bloody Lance!"

Karram Khan perched on his throne like a benign vulture, eyes glittering above a vast, hooked nose as he looked down upon the travelers. His wizened body shook as he began to emit a hideous rattling noise. Harry felt a jolt of alarm; was the old buzzard about to die? He was sure that would not look good in his first report, but moments later, he relaxed as he realized that the old man was merely laughing.

"You are as welcome here as my own son! Your father and I, oh the adventures we had!" Karram Khan cackled again, a slightly obscene sound, and licked his lips. "And the women! Does your father tell stories of his time in our land?"

Harry had long since learnt to tune out his father interminable stories; after a while they began to blend into one another. Of course, he didn't want to tell his host that.

"With great fondness. I think they were the best times of his life."

That seemed to please the old man. He gestured irritably at his attendants, who rushed to his side and began to fuss with his clothing. "We will feast tonight! I will tell you many stories of your father's adventures."

"Oh joy."

Harry was drunk. True to his word, Karram Khan had rambled on about the exploits of Harry's father, and at great length. Harry had nodded at all the right times, and made appreciative comments when it seemed warranted, but his attention had been fixed on the truly excellent brandy his new companion had supplied, and a young woman who seemed to spend the whole meal staring at him. All that was visible of her was a pair of gorgeous eyes above her veil, but they were worth looking at for themselves and they had been a very pleasant distraction. Finally, the last dish had been cleared away and he made his excuses and left for bed.

Harry walked towards the exit of the great hall, thinking only of sleep. He was watching his feet, when he walked into what felt like a brick wall. He looked up, and met a pair of furious eyes.

The man standing before him was almost a hand taller than Harry, who was tall himself, and almost twice as wide across the shoulders. From the beak of his nose, he was obviously related to the old emir in some way.

"Watch where you are going, *fereenghi!*" He spat on the floor, narrowly missing Harry's boot.

Harry felt himself flush with equal parts anger and fear, reflexively reached for the hilt of his sword before forcing himself to relax. Shedding blood, especially of a son or nephew or whatever this man was, would not endear him to his host, but there was a more practical objection. The man was huge and looked like he could handle his blade. No one but Harry knew this, but he had never relished combat. In fact, it was Harry's deepest, darkest secret that he was actually something of a coward. He had managed to hide it from those around him by a convincing facade of bravado, but deep down, he knew there was something wrong with him. He remembered the one time he had tried to ask his father about it, about where he had gotten his famous courage from. A strange expression had come across his father's face, and, for the first time, the old man hadn't had some rambling story, only silence.

Harry thought quickly, desperately trying to find a way to extricate himself from the situation. "I am a guest here. I would hate to have to shed blood in my host's hall."

"The insolent dog needs to learn not to yap at his betters! You have my permission to teach him a lesson." There was an eager note in Karram Khan's voice. "I know my old friend's son will be more than capable of leaving Yusuf chastened...but alive."

Harry cursed silently. Again, his father's reputation had preceded him. Looking at the glowering figure in front of him, Harry thought he would struggle to prevent harm to himself, let alone his opponent.

Further thought became a luxury he couldn't well afford as Yusuf drew his tulwar in a fluid motion that send it hurtling for Harry's face, who just managed to pull his head back far enough that the razor sharp blade left only a shallow gash across his cheek. Stumbling back, Harry yanked his saber free and settled into a guard position. Adrenalin coursed through his veins, bringing his surroundings into sharp focus, every sense heightened to almost painful acuity. His heart hammered in his ears and the light glimmered off the edge of Yusuf's curved blade, Harry could even make out the dark stain of his blood and watched as a drop beaded on the lowered tip, before falling to the dusty floor.

"I saw you watching my sister, dog," Yusuf hissed.

And then Yusuf was upon him and every ounce of Harry's skill and training and luck went towards holding him off.

Yusuf was not much of a swordsman, but he was incredibly strong and knew it, bringing his sword down again and again as if he was hewing wood, hoping to wear down Harry's defenses. Harry could feel the jolt of each blow running down his blade, and the muscles beginning to burn. In desperation, he searched his memories for something, anything, that he might be able to use. Then it came to him, a sword move his father had often described in his stories. If he weren't so terrified, Harry would have grinned. Who would have thought one of the stories might have some real world application?

Advancing on Yusuf, Harry began to move his sword in rapid cruciform pattern, the tip moving up and down, then from side to side, weaving a mesmerizing pattern in the glow of the torches. It formed an impenetrable barrier of steel, leaving no opening for Yusuf to exploit, but Harry could feel his arm protesting against the strain, and knew that he would not be able to keep it up for much longer.

He tried pushing Yusuf back, but as he put his foot forward to advance, one of the rough stones turned beneath it. Twisting desperately, Harry just avoided skewering himself on his opponent's blade, feeling the flat of the tulwar slide along his side. As he fell, he felt the guard of his sword slam into Yusuf's temple with a dull clunk. The big man's eyes rolled back in his head, and he slid to the ground bonelessly.

"Shabash, bahadur, shabash!"

Slow applause echoed through the chamber and Harry turned, limbs heavy and sluggish as the adrenalin left him, to see Karram Khan coming towards him. He was grinning from ear to ear, yellowing teeth exposed. Ballantine and Jean Saint-Clair were to either side, discreetly supporting the old man. The big Scotsman wore an expression of surprise and...—was that respect? The appraising look the Frenchman wore was a far cry from his earlier good-natured smile and, weary though he was, Harry knew that he would need to keep an eye on him. It was the same look the head boys at Rugby had given him when they had suspected Harry was hiding something, and had usually presaged a few strokes of the cane.

"Well, it is true what you Englishman say! The apple does not fall far from the tree! What swordsmanship! Even your father could not have done better and he was the finest man with a blade I have ever seen." The old man was positively capering with delight. "I bet he learnt that trick from one of our men and taught it to you. What cunning! To lure him in like that and then to end it without killing him!"

"Indeed, marvelous was it not?" The Frenchman's voice was thoughtful.

Harry swayed as the lights seemed to dim around him. All of a sudden, he felt very tired, and very drunk. "I think I should go to bed"

The old man clapped him on the shoulder. "I will see you at breakfast. We have much to talk about."

Ballantine walked Harry to his quarters, which were fairly luxurious given where they were. A magnificent four poster bed dominated the room, festooned with velvet drapes and match red coverings. Harry was sure that there was a story behind such a opulent furnishing being in the middle of the Afghani desert, but frankly he was more interested in how comfortable it looked.

Ballantine was surprisingly gentle as he removed Harry's boots and belt, and eased under the coverlet.

"That was a good thing you did, sir. It would have done us no good if you had killed him, but if there is one thing the Afghans respect it is a strong man and by showing that you were so much better than him that you didn't need to kill him...well, you've gone up a lot in their estimation." He paused, then said softly, "And in mine, sir."

If there was more Harry missed it, as he finally lost the battle with sleep and drifted into its comforting embrace.

Harry was in a foul mood. His head pounded like a drum sergeant major was running a drill session in it, his mouth tasted like a latrine pit and he was starting to wish that Yusuf had managed to kill him. It didn't help that the Khan would not leave him alone, exclaiming over his prowess and pushing delicacy after delicacy on him. Harry's idea of a good breakfast was a kipper and some strong tea, not pungent dishes of goat or even less savory ingredients. His stomach roiled as he examined the latest offering, it appeared to be still moving. Harry hoped he was imagining it.

He was jerked from his unpleasant reverie by a hard elbow digging into his ribs.

"Sir!" Ballantine whispered loudly.

Harry realized that the Khan was looking at him expectantly, as if waiting for a response.

"I'm sorry, Karram Khan, I was so enjoying my meal that I must have missed that."

The old man beamed at the compliment to his hospitality. "I was saying that these are strange times we live in. This week, I have had dozen of reports of a village to the east of here that is infested with djinns!"

Harry was confused. "Djinns? What the deuce are they?"

"Allah created all the world, including men and angels. It is said that He also created the djinn, who have powers like angels, but who, like men, can choose to be good or evil." The old man's eyes were wide, like a child's. "There are many types of djinn, but dealings with them never end well."

"And, these djinns, you believe they are real?" The old man nodded. "And you are being told this village is full of them?"

The old man did not sense the mockery in Harry's voice. "Yes, O son of my friend! Many men, some of whom I would trust with my life, have told me this. They speak of men, huge men, with the face of tigers who fight like demons and eat the flesh of those they defeat in battle!"

Harry began to laugh. "You are joking, of course! You can't expect me to take this seriously, can you, old chap?" His laughter tailed off as he noticed the anger rising in the old man's eyes.

"Bah! You think I am some credulous old fool?" Karram Khan shouted over Harry's attempt to deny it. "The first man, I had flogged for his lies. The second, I burnt out his tongue with a red hot poker to make an example of him."

The doddering old man was gone now, and Harry could see the tyrant who had ruled this region for half a century with an iron fist. He felt the cold fingers of fear clutching his heart.

Karram Khan was still speaking. "Do you think anyone would come before me with lies after that? I have seen the injuries with my own eyes, huge claw marks in the flesh of men dying a slow painful death from suppurating wounds."

Jean broke in. "I am sure that Monsieur Harry was not casting doubts on your discernment. It is merely that, for those of us who are not familiar with such things, well, it is a bit of a shock, *n'est*-ce *pas*?" He shot a look at Harry, who was quick to take the hint.

"Of course, Karram Khan, that's right. We just don't see much of that sort of carry on in England, you know?" He shook his head, and tutted. "Terrible business."

Karram Khan seemed mollified, and his voice went down in volume, if only slightly. "It is terrible. My people look to me for protection, but time has caught up with me." He held up hands that, while still large and powerful, were covered in liver spots and shook with a mild palsy. "Even ten years ago, I would have taken a troop out and dealt with such abominations myself, but now? Who am I meant to send? Yusuf?"

He spat, a large wad of green phlegm landing next to Harry's bowl. Surprisingly, it didn't make it appear less appetizing.

All through the Khan's rant, Ballantine had remained silent, which was why Harry was too surprised by what followed to act until it was too late.

"Well, sir, perhaps we could take a group of men there. It is not too far off the path we had planned." Harry noticed that Ballantine was very careful not to make eye contact with him.

Harry did not even have a chance to protest before Karram Khan had leaned over the table and grabbed his hand.

"Ah, I see that the son is as loyal a friend as the father! You will have my undying gratitude."

As the Sergeant and the Khan began to plan their expedition, Ballantine quietly and methodically, the Amir with much waving of hands and imprecations of Allah, Harry slumped back in his chair. He wasn't sure how he had gotten into this, but he desperately wanted a drink.

"So, what brings you to this part of the world, Monsieur?"

The Frenchman had surprised Harry when he had offered to accompany them, but after days of riding through the same featureless, ugly country, Harry was glad of the companionship. Despite being nominally in charge, he had little to do, Ballantine had taken to the task of instilling some discipline into the ragged bunch of cutthroats that Karram Khan had put under their command with a great deal of gusto.

Harry had spent many idle hours playing cards and wenching amongst the lowest elements of the London underworld--any nobles shared a taste for slumming—and he thought he was familiar with foul language. But the Sergeant had a talent for it, and Harry had learned much simply from listening as Ballantine had reduced the Afghans to quivering and obedient soldiers with inventive and profane explorations of at least three different tongues. Even that had grown boring after a while, though, and civilized conversation appealed.

"I serve France as a very minor functionary in her diplomatic service. My government has seen fit to post me to Russia to help keep an eye on our mutual friends, though I have found little excitement."

The Frenchman had an easy, self-deprecating way of speaking that Harry had warmed to, and he handled his horse with ease and a seat that the cavalry man in Harry admired.

"My wife pines for Paris, who can blame her, so she is with her mother for a few weeks while I spend my time collecting illustrations for my book."

Despite himself Harry was intrigued. "Your book?"

"*Oui*, Monsieur Harry, I am something of a botanist, an amateur only, and I heard that there are some unique plants in this region. I could not stand St Petersburg without the company of my wife, so I thought that I would spend some time collecting samples."

Harry made a polite noise in the back of his throat. He could not think of anything more boring; unless he could smoke a plant or eat it, he considered it beneath his notice. However, he liked the Frenchman so he continued to give the appearance of an attentive listener. Anyway, what were his options? To try and converse with the still glowering Yusuf about the price of horseflesh and best way to cook goat to preserve its delicate flavors? He'd stick with Jean and his refined conversation, thank you very much.

And so, the day passed and the Sun sank lower into the sky. While the layout of the countryside had not altered much, rocks and the occasional scrubby tree with towering mountains forming an awe-inspiring backdrop, but a darkness of the soul began to settle across the party. Harry did not know whether it was the rumors playing on the superstitious locals, but even the three Europeans felt the creeping miasma that seemed to sap the vitality of the riders. Conversations died to the odd mutter and curse, and shoulders slumped as energy drained from them all. Harry was born in the saddle and normally could ride all day, but even the hardy Afghanis breathed a sigh of relief as they slid from the saddle and began to make camp. No one had much of an appetite and as darkness fell, silence enveloped the camp, punctuated only by the occasional faint snore or burst of flatulence.

"Sir! Wake up!"

Harry blinked away sleep and struggled awake. The watch fire had died down to embers and the Moon was behind clouds, the darkness not helping Harry get his bearings.

"Sir, something is out there. And, I am not sure, but I think one of the sentries is gone."

"Gone?" Harry kept his voice soft. "What do you mean gone?"

"I haven't seen him walk past that ridge there for a while, and before it was every fifteen minutes, like clockwork. He might have just had a kip, sir, but whatever we might say about your lad Yusuf, he runs a tight ship and I think they would be too a feared to sleep on the job."

Harry could see Jean to his left, staring out into the darkness. There was a muffled shout just past the ridge, and then chaos erupted. At least a dozen huge figures swarmed into the camp, strangely hunched, yet still taller than even Yusuf.

Jean and Ballantine were already on their feet, weapons to hand, but their Afghani companions were slow to react and were still drawing their swords when the figures hit them. Harry was surprised to find that he had been as quick to action as his two companions, and he had a brief moment to wonder whether perhaps Ballantine's lessons were rubbing off after all. Then he had no time for any thought but self-preservation.

It was too dark to make out the assailant's faces, but Harry didn't need to see any more than their body to aim his sword. He did his best to hide behind Jean and Ballantine, but, from time to time, he was forced to defend himself. The attackers were armed with stout cudgels rather than blades, and used them to good effect.

Soon, the three westerners were standing alone back to back, desperately trying to hold off multiple foes. Harry lashed out in fear and rage and sent one of them reeling back into the campfire. There was what he could only describe as a yowl of pain and the smell of burning fur. The flames rose up, throwing light over the shambolic scene, bodies scattered everywhere like wheat in the field after the thresher. Another figure threw itself at Harry and, in the light, he could make out bestial features, a fanged mouth splitting a striped face. He was unable to stop himself from flinching from the hatred and hunger burning in the cat-like eyes, and that hesitation was his undoing.

There was a red flare as the cudgel struck the side of his head, then darkness.

For the second time in as many days Harry awoke with a pounding headache, but this time it was no hangover. His eyes were gummed shut with a sticky substance that took a few minutes to blink away, and even longer for him to realize it was his blood. Once he had recovered enough to look around, he quickly decided that he might have been better off leaving his eyes sealed shut.

Out of the corners of his eyes he could make out Jean Saint-Clair and Ballantine to either side of him, like him restrained with metal clamps screwed into thick oaken chairs. But it was not that which held him mesmerized with horror. They were in a large room dotted with scientific apparatus, from bubbling test tubes to copper balls spouting electrical arcs, dominated by tall, glass cylinders filled with an almost clear, yet slightly green-tinged, fluid. Inside were suspended naked human forms, floating in the solution and secured with tubing that pierced their sides.

As his vision cleared, Harry could see there was something wrong with each of them. There was one where the left forearm had been stripped down to bare bone, and the rest of the arm flayed free of skin all the way to the shoulder muscles, glistening raw and wet. Another had the top of the skull missing, the coral-like folds and intricacies of the brain pulsating gently in the liquid surrounding it. Almost directly in front of him, one rotated gently in its enclosure, coming to rest facing Harry. He could see that the rib cage had been peeled back to reveal the internal organs, the heart still beating and the lungs expanding and retracting as if breathing the green liquid instead of air.

Harry looked up, and into eyes driven insane with terror or pain, or both, and realized that it was Yusuf. Harry was not sure whether the agitating rolling of the eyes as they locked his gaze was born of recognition or merely animal reflex, but he felt his gorge rise all the same.

"*Mon Dieu!*" Obviously, Jean had awoken as well. "Well, Monsieur Harry, it seems as if we have found what we were both looking for, no?"

Harry could not tear his eyes away from the hideous sight in front, but something in Jean's words caught what remained of his attention.

"What we've been looking for? What the deuces do you mean, man?" Harry exclaimed. "I can tell you I would have been happy to never see anything like this as long as I lived!"

The Frenchman laughed softly. "I appreciate your professionalism, especially in the face of such dire straits, but surely the time for acting has passed? Both our governments sent us to find a nest of vipers; sadly, it seems we have fallen straight into it."

Baffled, Harry sought to find a reply to Jean's words, but his reply was cut off by the sound of a door opening. Three figures marched into the room and stopped, standing directly in front of the captives. In the middle was a severe looking man of perhaps middle age, dark hair swept back from a high brow and cold eyes that made Harry feel as if he was being dissected and weighed and reduced to mere spare parts. It was a measure of his presence that Harry did not immediately notice the hulking figures flanking him, bizarre as they were.

When he did, though, he sucked in a shocked breath. They towered over the middle-aged man, despite the fact that their massive shoulders were hunched and slumping forward. Their faces were bestial, with whiskered muzzles and fang-filled mouths, their skin covered with a fine orange fur slashed with black stripes, a coloration repeated over every patch of exposed flesh. Viciously taloned hands gripped crude cudgels, but Harry thought that even had they been unarmed, he would have thought twice if not more before taking one on, such was their air of barely leashed menace.

"So, it seems that Karram Khan was a worthwhile investment. Not only has he sent me the test subjects I requested, but he has also delivered into a trap those who would interfere with my work."

Harry could hear a stream of vicious cursing coming from Ballantine, quiet enough that he could only make out the occasional phrase, like "treacherous son of a lecherous camel," which reflected how Harry was feeling. So much for friendship and loyalty.

The man was now speaking to Jean. "So, Monsieur Saint-Clair, it has been a long time since we last met. I should have known that the French government would send you."

"Not long enough for my tastes, Moreau."

Moreau darted forward, sinuous as a snake, and there was a sharp crack as he brought the back of his hand smashing into the Frenchman's face.

"That is *Doctor* Moreau to you."

Blood trickled from the corner of Jean's mouth, but he stared at Moreau uncowed.

"I see that you have continued on where your illustrious mentor Oxus and that mad monk Fulbert left off. Corruption breeds corruption, it seems." He paused to spit blood at the doctor's feet. "No matter, I will deal with you as I dealt with them."

Moreau laughed. "Brave words for a man in your position! And who are your companions?" His gaze slid over Ballantine and fixed on Harry, eyes widening slightly. "The big one is a nobody, but you! Your fame, or should I say your father's fame, precedes you! No wonder Karram Khan thought it worth the risk of sending you my way. I should feel flattered. Her Majesty's Government has sent her best and brightest."

Harry was almost speechless, and he wondered what exactly he had become entangled in. "I think there has been some sort of mistake!" he said.

The doctor's lip curled contemptuously. "Spare me your British bluster. I know why you are here. It's a shame; in a week, I would have finished the last of my experiments." He paused, thinking, then continued. "Still, delivering you to my Russian sponsors may cause them to be a bit more generous with their finances."

He turned and walked towards the door, and paused for a parting shot.

"You must forgive me for the quality of your accommodations. Don't worry, I am expecting my Russian friends tomorrow so you will not be here for long." He smiled humorlessly. "Of course, I can make no promises that what they have in store for you will be preferable."

"Well, Monsieur Harry, it looks like we are on what you Englishmen call a sticky wicket."

"Yes, we are, Jean! But, what were you talking about earlier, you made it sound as if you were looking for this place?"

Saint-Clair sighed. "I was involved in foiling the plots of Moreau's predecessor, who was experimenting with grafting animal tissue onto humans to create super powered hybrids. Oxus' first attempt was some sort of man-shark called the *Hictaner*. It was a very nasty business."

Normally Harry would have laughed at such errant nonsense, but it was hard to argue with the evidence before his eyes. It was as good as explanation as any for the tiger-men. Two of them stood either side of the door, putting paid to any chance of Harry being able to pretend it had all been a dream.

Jean continued. "So, when my superiors heard that Moreau was continuing on with Oxus' research somewhere in the hills of Afghanistan, I was the natural choice to find out was happening. This part of the world is volatile enough without a horde of super-soldiers pouring down into the British Raj." He laughed. "And, of course, my government wouldn't say no to getting its hands on the research for ourselves. Aside from the military applications, think about how it could improve the way we do medicine! Imagine a man who might otherwise be cut down in his prime given a new heart, or a man able to see in the dark like a cat!"

Harry could see this was a subject Jean was passionate about, and cut him off before he could launch into a lecture.

"Well, strange to say, but that all makes sense to me. It explains why you were here in Afghanistan, but why were you so keen to attach yourself to us?"

"It's obvious, *n'est-ce pas*? When we heard you were making your way around here, we assumed that your government was as concerned as mine about what Moreau was up to. And, well, forgive me, but your father had a talent for causing excitement wherever he went. So, I felt that you had a good chance of finding what you, and I, were after."

Harry was rather sick of references to his father, and a tad hurt that the Frenchman had simply been using him.

"But that's the thing! I was simply on a training mission and knew nothing about Moreau or these bizarre experiments, and neither did my superiors"

There was a slight cough to his left.

"What, Ballantine? Have you got something to say?" Harry snapped.

"Well, sir, I don't see any reason to keep it from you now. Part of my orders was to try and discover the location of this facility, if it existed, and try and infiltrate it."

Harry was nearly apoplectic with rage, and he could barely sputter out his next question.

"What?! Why wasn't I told about this? This is outrageous!"

"It was felt that, with your name, the Russians would take you seriously, and try to eliminate you—hopefully, leading us right to them."

"So I was bait?"

"God's truth, sir?"

"Out with it, Sergeant Ballantine." Harry's tone was icy.

"There were those amongst our superiors who saw you simply as another noble dandy, who wouldn't be much use for any real work, and that, this way at least, England would get something of worth from you." The big man paused. "I have to admit, sir, that when I first met you, I didn't think they were far wrong. But, after the things I have seen from you, I think they made a mistake. I think you are the real thing. I made a mistake, sir, and I am sorry. You didn't deserve to be deceived like that, and I apologize."

Harry wasn't sure what surprised him more, the revelations or the praise from the Sergeant. As furious as he was, he had to admit that it was a good feeling knowing that a man like Ballantine held him in such regard, deserved or not. Slightly mollified, he sat silent for few minutes before another question occurred a minute.

"It's all very well, instructing you to infiltrate, but what were you meant to do if you were successful?" Hope bloomed. "Is there a regiment of cavalry waiting for your signal to ride in and rescue us?"

"Not exactly, sir."

"Then what, Ballantine?"

"I am the cavalry, sir."

Harry was getting sick of riddles. "And what the blazes does that mean, Sergeant?"

"Well, sir, what Monsieur Saint-Clair didn't exactly spell out, begging your pardon Monsieur, is that the French have been working on their own super-soldier project, as have most of the Great Powers. The Turks have their Golden Janissaries, the Nipponese have their Tengu Project... Of course, Her Majesty's Government can't allow any other nation to gain an edge, so we have been working on our own."

Harry was shocked. "You can't tell me we have been doing things like..." he tried to gesture at the abominations all around them, forgetting in his horror that he was still restrained, "...that?"

"No, sir! Our scientists always considered vivisection a dead end, anyway. We took a pharmaceutical route."

"Pharmaceutical?"

"Chemicals and formulas to enhance the human body, sir. Do you remember about ten years ago the fuss in the papers about a rampage in London by the so-called Mr. Hyde? Or were you too young?"

Harry remembered it well, he and his schoolmates had been transfixed by the stories of the brutal Mr. Hyde and how he had flaunted every social more imaginable, committing crimes of terrible violence and debauchery before mysteriously disappearing. "Yes, I do."

"Well, sir, it turned out that Mr. Hyde was, in fact, a noted chemist named Dr. Jekyll who had discovered a potion which transformed him into a brute. He was eventually imprisoned, but instead of execution, he was put to work by the government. Eventually, we ended up with a chemical which produced all the desirable effects of his earlier potion, like extreme physical strength and lack of fear, but without any of the nastier emotional effects. Any soldier who took it would be almost invincible for a brief span of time. Unfortunately, we can't mass produce it, but it comes in handy."

Harry snorted. "I am sure it does, but it isn't much good to us here, is it now?"

"Oh, I think it might be, sir."

His voice was strangely muffled. By craning his neck, Harry could see that Ballantine was working his tongue around in his mouth, pressing it against his teeth. There was a sharp crack, and one of his molars snapped off at the gum, and the Sergeant bit down with a grotesque crunching noise. He began to convulse, the tendons in his neck standing out in cords, his eyes bulging as his feet began to hammer on the floor.

Silent until now, Jean broke in. "What is happening, Monsieur Harry?"

"I don't know! I think he has taken something, some sort of poison."

As Harry watched, Ballantine began to change, muscles swelling, his features coarsening as his brow lowered and his jaw thickened. There was a rending sound as his clothes began to tear along the seams, trying to make room for his massive new frame. The Sergeant looked down at his broad spatulate fingers and flexed them, then bunched them into ham-sized fists. Slowly, he curled his arms, metal screeching as the bolts holding the restraints bent and then popped, pieces of metal shooting across the room and hitting the walls. Ballantine looked up, the grin on his face enough to make Harry recoil.

"Oh yes, that feels mighty fine, sir. Now, listen carefully before I get too carried away. This isn't perfect, it will only last about quarter hour, and when it runs out, I will be as weak as a wee bairn." He stood, and the chair came with him, his body now filling it to overflowing, but Ballantine simply flexed and pieces of wood fell to the floor in a shower of splinters. "Now, to get you both free before our friends return with company."

Harry hadn't even noticed their guards disappearing through the door, all his attention had been focused on the incredible transformation. As Ballantine approached, Harry couldn't help but slightly flinch away but the Sergeant merely leant forward and, with a sharp twist, wrenched the restraints away, then did the same for Jean.

The Frenchman looked the Scotsman up and down; he was easily a foot taller than he had been and twice as wide.

"*C'est incroyable*," he said softly, then visibly gathered himself. "Monsieur Harry, I hope that you are as good with your hands as you are with your blade, we have company.

Harry grinned. "Oh, I think I can do better than that, old chap." He picked a hunk of wood from the remains of Ballantine's chair, and whacked his palm with it, enjoying the heft of the solid oak. "I was in Rugby's First XI, you know."

Harry leaned against the wall, surveying the wreckage of the laboratory as he tried to catch his breath. Puddles of noisome green fluid mingled with shards of broken glass, and bodies were scattered the length of the chamber. Some were the twisted remnants of Moreau's vile experiments, but most were the tiger-men who had been unfortunate enough to be sent to deal with the prisoners.

As the first wave had poured through the door, roaring and snarling, Ballantine had thrown back his head and howled, then charged into the fray. The first tiger-man to reach him had simply been grabbed and hurled into the wall with a sickening crunch, sliding limply to the ground. Ballantine grabbed the second and twisted its head with such force that it actually popped off, a geyser of blood spurting into the air. Laughing wildly, an unholy note of joy amongst the carnage, he had waded in, throwing blows left and right that splintered bone each time they connected. But, such were the numbers that some spilled past to either side and moved swiftly to where Jean and Harry waited.

The Frenchman had seemed oddly relaxed, balanced lightly on the balls of his feet. His calm has been in stark contrast to Harry, who had been clutching the length of oak with such force his knuckles were bone white. Jean had fought with a calm precision, almost dancing amongst the enemy, feet lashing out to hit vulnerable points, joints snapping and cartilage wrenching. Harry had fought with all the brute force of sheer terror, hunk of wood landing with terrible potency, bones breaking and teeth flying with every blow. Their contrasting styles had seemed to confuse the tiger-men and they had begun to fall back cautiously, until Ballantine had come crashing into their rear, almost ululating in his frenzy. From there, it had been rout, with only the three Europeans left standing, virtually unscathed bar a few cuts and grazes.

"What do you call that?"

"Pardon, Monsieur Harry?"

"That fighting with your feet and hands. I have never seen anything like it. It was like ballet mixed with boxing!" Harry smiled to show it wasn't an insult. "Deuced effective, what?"

"Ah, *la savate*! It is a martial discipline developed in France. Very useful."

"Very!"

"But, your methods, Monsieur Harry, were very effective too." The Frenchman bowed, then straightened to his full height. "It was an honor to fight at your side."

It should have been ridiculous, but instead, it was absurdly touching, and Harry returned the gesture.

"The honor was all mine." He wiped away some blood from his eyes and looked over to the corner. "Do you think the Sergeant will be okay?"

Only a few minutes after the last tiger-man had fallen, Ballantine had staggered and dropped to his knees. Harry had rushed to his side, fearing that the Sergeant had sustained a serious injury in the fight, but the big man had pushed him away. "I will be fine," he had whispered, and crawled into the corner. Then he had begun to shrink, gradually returning to his former self.

"I am sure he will be, but we must get him, and ourselves, out of here. But, first…"

Jean darted over to a large cylinder, painted a glaring red, and turned a dial. There was an ominous hissing sound and an acrid smell. "Quickly now, Monsieur Harry!"

Harry grunted as he hoisted the Sergeant over his shoulders, and began to half-run, half-stumble after the Frenchman. Later in life, he would wake screaming from dreams of their escape through a winding labyrinth of tunnels and passages ways that seemed to stretch on forever. But finally, they broke free and burst panting into the cold night air of the desert.

"Do not stop now!" The Frenchman dragged Harry on until they collapsed in the shelter of a large cluster of rocks.

Harry opened his mouth to speak, but was cut off by a tremendous roar as the night flashed red and a wall of heat rolled over them. He clambered back over the rocks, and gazed over the blazing inferno that was the wreckage of the laboratory. As he watched it burn, he felt Jean settle in beside in him.

"Do you think Moreau is still in there, Jean?"

"*Je ne sais pas*, Monsieur Harry. But if he is, he is undoubtedly dead." Jean sighed. "We can only hope he has gotten what he deserved, and those poor souls he tortured have gotten some sort of justice."

Privately, Harry doubted it. Moreau seemed like the sort of bad penny who would turn up again, somewhere. But, that was a problem for another day and so he kept his thoughts to himself. Something else struck him and he began to laugh. Jean looked at him quizzically.

"I can tell you one thing, though, Jean."

"What is that?"

"At least, I now have a story of my own that might shut up my father for five minutes!"

Jean stared blankly, then began to laugh with him, the sound of their relief echoing under the starry sky.

Like the previous tale, Chris Nigro's contribution also builds on previous stories published in Tales of the Shadowmen, *in this case, Matthew Baugh's "Mask of the Monster" from Volume 1, and Kim Newman's "Angels of Music" from Volumes 2 and 4. Readers may also want to refer to our short story "His Father's Eyes" contained in the Black Coat Press edition of* Phantom of the Opera. *Finally, the name of "Gouroull," attributed here to the Frankenstein Monster, comes from a series of original Frankenstein novels written in France by renowned screen writer Jean-Claude Carrière, and published in the early 1950s by the same horror imprint of Editions Fleuve Noir which also released the Madame Atomos books...*

Chris Nigro: *Patricide*

Paris, Early 1914

Gerard Leblanc wasn't a weak man. He had been a feared enforcer of the Red Hand for 12 years. But at this precise moment, he could barely move his battered head upwards, and he succeeded in doing so only after considerable effort. He could feel streams of blood flowing freely from both nostrils and his mouth, and the pain of several broken teeth. His left eye was swollen shut, so he proceeded to look about the room with his one good eye, straining to remember where he was and why he was brought here.

It was quite clear to him that he was standing in an upward position, his arms chained to the wall. The limited visual acuity he now possessed strained to make out the features of the musty-scented room. It was then that he began to see a dark figure coming into focus. He could vaguely discern a mask covering the visage of the dark-clad man standing before him. In the figure's right hand was an implement that Leblanc couldn't see clearly.

"I see you are awake again, Monsieur Leblanc," an icy voice said. "That is good. Now we can start again, and we will continue until you tell me what it is I wish to know."

Leblanc struggled to utter a single syllable. As he was desperate to avoid another round of the vicious torture that had already been heaped upon him for hours, he successfully forced himself to speak.

"I... I do not know what you asked," he said. "Please... no more... I don't know anything about..."

"*Au contraire*," the cold but mellifluous voice of the masked man firmly stated. "I trust my sources implicitly, as they dare not fail me, lest they end up in the unfortunate position in which you presently find yourself. Now, be so kind as to tell me the information I have been requesting and I will end your torment."

Hacking forth a mixture of blood and phlegm, Leblanc did his best to assuage his tormentor while simultaneously keeping his oath of secrecy in mind.

"I... never worked for Dr. Cornelius... I know nothing of his work or his..."

The figure before Leblanc frowned under his mask, then felt an intense wave of anger. He raised the implement he wielded until its edge touched his prisoner's face. Thus, the emaciated victim could now clearly discern that it was the sharpest razor he had likely ever seen.

"Monsieur Leblanc, I am going to explain something to you, and you had better listen if you wish to avoid having the lens of your eye punctured," the masked man said with the utmost seriousness. "The information from Dr. Cornelius' office that I know you possess is something that I have sought for the better part of my long, agonizing life. You grew up handsome, easily able to obtain the admiration of others and the sensuous touch of a woman, if you so desired them. Do you know what my lot has been in contrast to yours?"

Stepping forward and violently pulling Leblanc's head upwards to insure that his one functional eye could see precisely what his tormentor wanted him to see, the dark clad man pulled his mask off his face, revealing a nightmarish visage that resembled a skull with nothing more than a thin layer of yellowed skin, displaying the barest hint of a nose.

"I have been known as Erik all my life, but my true lineage is unknown to me. I am well aware that my mother perished whilst giving birth to me, but I have always been uncertain as to the identity of my father. Who was he that his loins could produce one such as I? Considering some of my physical attributes, particularly what appears to be my preternatural longevity, my sire must have been something more than human. He needs to pay for what he brought forth into this world, which is the life of loneliness that I have lived. My agents have informed me that Dr. Cornelius made an interesting discovery before the destruction of his laboratory two years ago.[2] I know you are among the few who are privy to that precious information as a result of having ransacked what was left of his laboratory. Those papers were sealed in a small safe that survived the explosion, and they ended up in your hands. You will give me that information now. If you do not, you will find out precisely why I am feared throughout the underworld of Paris as the most skilled practitioner of the art of torture—bar none."

Erik moved the razor-shaped implement closer to Leblanc's face, stopping the sharp point of the object less than half an inch before his one good eye.

"Please... stop... I will tell you. I will tell you everything. Please..."

---

[2] See "Mask of the Monster" in *Tales of the Shadowmen*, Volume 1.

What Leblanc told Erik astounded the Phantom of the Opera. His eyes appeared to bolt from their sunken sockets, so startled was he by what he heard. He quickly felt, deep within his tainted soul, that this information could be nothing less than the truth. He was now satisfied.

"*Merci beaucoup*, Monsieur Leblanc," Erik thanked his victim. "As promised, your torment is now ended."

The Phantom grabbed a hatchet and, with an apparent sense of complete calmness, struck Leblanc on the crown of his head, instantly shattering the man's skull. As promised, the man's horrific torment was now ended.

Roughly one month later, a gang comprised of five young ruffians sat on the stairs of a decrepit tenement bordering the Seine. Their leader, a lad named Alain, already bore a scar above his left eye that he wore as a proud souvenir from the battle that had won him control over the neighborhood.

Suddenly, without warning, a huge hand the color of chalk, seemingly stitched to the wrist by surgical means, slowly emerged from the surface of the water. Within seconds, the being to which the hand belonged pulled himself up from the murky waters of the river, exposing himself in his full horrifying glory to the startled young men sitting but a few feet away.

The being was clearly an adult male, but unlike any man the boys had ever seen before: his hideous face was covered with stitches and scars; it was further distinguished by a pair of horrid, yellow eyes and a long mane of black, lustrous hair. The creature was dressed in tattered clothing and massive boots that appeared tailor-made for him. Gouroull, known to some as the Frankenstein Monster, had again returned to the world of the living!

"Alain, look at that!" exclaimed Benoit, Alain's second-in-command. "Have you ever seen a man like that before? What was he doing in the river?"

"I don't know," replied Alain. "But whoever he is, I don't want him in my neighborhood. He looks like trouble. I think we should send him back to the bottom of the river, *non*?"

With that settled, Alain lifted a heavy metal pipe he always kept handy, motioned for his fellow gang members to likewise brandish whatever weapons they may have been carrying, and approached the dazed Gouroull. Benoit grabbed a razor-sharp stiletto and joined his leader.

"I have no idea what in God's name you are," Alain stated, "but you're not welcome in this neighborhood. It belongs to the Red Hand."

Without a second of hesitation, Alain struck Gouroull on the head with his metal pipe. The monster reeled slightly, but remained on his feet, still looking confused. Frustrated that the beast had not fallen to the first blow, Alain struck twice more, this time succeeding in breaking the creature's skin. A stream of dark ichor leaked from the gaping wound. But still, Gouroull remained on his feet. However, Alain's second assault did have an effect on the creature, albeit not the one the hooligan was looking for.

Gouroull suddenly appeared to come to his senses. He vaguely recalled a battle with some armed men in the sewers of Paris, and being drawn away by a cascade of water. Most importantly, he was now aware of his surroundings. And with that came the realization that some foolish humans had dared to attack him...

Alain tried to swing his pipe at Gouroull's head a third time, but the creature intercepted the strike by catching the weapon in his massive hand. Easily wrenching the bludgeon from the thug's grasp, the monster then proceeded to crush the youth's skull with a single blow.

Aghast at the sight of his leader's brain splattering on the ground, Benoit quickly thrust his stiletto into Gouroull's kidney. The monster grumbled in pain and turned to meet his second attacker. Realizing that his assault hadn't disabled his opponent—as it should have—Benoit pulled the knife out and prepared for a second strike, but this was thwarted when the monster grasped the youth by his collar, lifted him with no apparent effort, and sunk his razor-sharp teeth into his neck. With a quick shake of his head, Gouroull ripped out Benoit's throat and spat out the youth's larynx. He then dropped the boy's lifeless body to the ground and turned to face the three remaining gang members.

Their jaws agape in unremitting horror, the trio turned and ran. Gouroull quietly laughed as he saw the boys flee. He was disappointed that they didn't try their hand, as he would have enjoyed killing them, too. But now that his memory had fully returned to him, a single name came to the fore of his consciousness: Dr. Cornelius Kramm. He would locate him and make him pay for his betrayal. Gouroull always expected treachery from the human race which he despised, but that didn't mean he would ever fail to exact revenge on those who dared perpetrate such a perfidy.

Determined to find out how much time had elapsed since he was insensate, and Dr. Cornelius' present whereabouts, Gouroull strode off into the night.

Little did the monster know that his return had been observed by Bouzille, a tramp in ragged clothing standing at the other end of the pier. *The Phantom will find this interesting,* thought Bouzille. *He will give me a few francs for bringing it to his attention...*

Two days later, in the wealthy 16th Arrondissement of Paris, Dr. Cornelius Kramm paced along in the new laboratory he had built for himself in the space of a large building overlooking the Seine.

The funding, as always, had come courtesy of his brother Fritz, who handled the business affairs of the Red Hand, the much-feared criminal organization they both led. The scientist was proudly studying a miniature, human-shaped figure floating suspended in a large glass flask filled with an unidentified liquid. Also present were Fritz and three armed bodyguards, each paid handsomely to protect their employers' lives.

"Cornelius, I am not sure how this latest project of yours is going to benefit the Red Hand," Fritz lamented. "How in the name of God are these... 'little people' you're cultivating going to be of any use to us? I've already given you over 100,000 francs, yet you're using that money to create something like this?"

"You must have vision, my dear brother," replied Cornelius. "Just think what this breakthrough will mean. If I manage to duplicate the exact procedure developed by Dr. Pretorius to create homunculi with the same advanced characteristics as his own, the possibilities are endless. They could be indispensable for stealth missions, they could gain access to locales that not even a midget could enter undetected, and the boon to science alone would be..."

"OK, I understand you've put a lot of thought into this, Cornelius," Fritz interjected, "but still, you have to consider the business end of things. I'm going to have to explain to the Council precisely why you're using our money to grow little people in a bottle. I'm not sure all of them will..."

Just then, one of the three bodyguards turned to the siblings.

"Er, boss, I don't want to alarm you, but I think I just heard something outside the door."

"What, exactly, did you hear, Marcel?" Fritz queried.

"I am not sure," the henchman replied, "but don't worry, we'll take care of it." He turned towards one of the other two guards. "Pierre, go to the door and take a quick look. It may be nothing, but we should be careful nonetheless."

"*Bien sûr*," said Pierre.

After pulling his firearm, he furtively proceeded towards the door, opened it, and cautiously extended his head into the hallway, looking in all directions to see if any unauthorized individuals had gained entry to the building.

Suddenly, he was struck a clear blow to the face. A fountain of blood spurted from the shattered cartilage of his nose and he fell on his back.

"*Sacrebleu!*" bellowed Eugène, the third guard, quickly drawing his own firearm. "What is...?"

But Eugène found himself disarmed in an even faster blur as a shapely and clearly female leg executed a side kick in just the right place to cause the guard's gun arm to go numb.

Now seeing himself confronted by an attractive young woman with long, dark hair, wearing a close-fitting garment that showed off her lithe body, Eugène swung at her—a quick move that the girl deftly evaded, trapping and fracturing the guard's arm between the wrist and elbow. Eugène screamed in agony and fell to the ground, looking in horror at the splintered bone protruding through a large tear on his arm.

The young woman, who couldn't have been older than her late teens, waved a finger at Eugene and sardonically advised him, "Please stay down, Monsieur, for you do not want to experience what I will do to you if you refuse to comply with my advice."

During that brief, but decisive battle, Marcel, too, had drawn his own firearm, only to find himself opposed by a second, similarly-clad young girl, this one with shoulder-length auburn hair.

In response to the guard raising his gun, the girl smiled, extended her palm and projected some kind of invisible force that caused the bemused man's weapon to fly out of his grip and across the room. Marcel then rushed towards his nemesis, determined to break her fragile body in his massive arms, but she again extended her hand and, this time, it was the guard himself who was sent flying through the air!

Marcel landed with great force on a table on the far side of the laboratory, smashing the glass vials and test tubes on its surface, and yelling in pain as the volatile liquids singed his flesh.

The second girl smiled to herself muttering, "So much for that bear of a man. A shame I don't have more time to play with him. I could use the practice. Ah well, *c'est la vie*."

As the fallen Pierre attempted to stand again, determined to do his job despite his shattered septum, he was dealt another bout of excruciating pain by a third female assailant—a girl with medium-length, dirty blonde hair who couldn't have been older than 14. She pummeled down on his groin, causing him to recoil amidst loud moans of agony, his hands clasped over his testicles.

"Pardon me, Monsieur, but if you try to play, your family jewels will pay," his youthful attacker quipped with a playful giggle.

After watching the entire scene in abject astonishment, Fritz Kramm began to reach for the gun he always kept in the top drawer of his desk—only to see the drawer seemingly close of its own accord so tightly that it squeezed his fingers. The criminal yelped in anguish, unable to extricate his hand from the desk. He then noticed that the same auburn-haired girl who had neutralized Marcel was smiling at him, her hand extended.

"Excuse me, Monsieur Kramm, but you can't do that," she said with a squeaky voice. "Now please be calm and I will allow you to keep those fingers, however broken they may now be."

Dr. Cornelius had looked at the amazing tableau before him and had wisely decided not to take any action against the trio of femme fatales who had so effortlessly thrashed his three bodyguards and his brother. Nevertheless, taking no chances, while making it known that she and her cohorts meant business, the second girl—clearly the leader of the trio—leapt atop a table with the nimble grace of a panther, landing on her knees, holding two blades close to the scientist's throat.

"Bonjour, Dr. Cornelius," she said courteously. "My name is Hélène Gurn. It's an honor to make your acquaintance."

"Well, yes, the pleasure is all mine," Cornelius replied, remaining as cool and resolute as ever.

Hélène smiled at the scientist's polite response. Her instincts told her that he may not be as unarmed as he looked, that, and in fact, Cornelius may well be the most dangerous man in the room. But since he appeared eager to talk, she was happy to oblige.

"Where are my manners?" she continued. "Allow me to likewise introduce my two angelic accomplices." Hélène then pointed to the youngest girl. "This fellow lass of angelic grace is Florence Drummond, whose talent our master has stoked to a Flame." Then pointing to the girl with auburn locks, she said, "And this truly Charmed young warrior is Bri Warren."

Florence boasted, "I share blood with none other than the notorious slave trader Heinrich Van Drummond, who proudly sailed his ship the *Mary Stewart...*"

"If that is the best you can do to impress the esteemed Dr. Cornelius," snickered Bri, "then need I remind you how much *more* impressive my own ancestry happens to be?"

"Are you disparaging my family history, when yours consists of..."

Hélène promptly pulled a pistol from a holster and fired a bullet into the ceiling, instantly silencing her two companions.

"My fellow Angels, you can impress Dr. Cornelius later," she admonished. "Right now, the matter at hand must take precedence." She turned back to Cornelius and smiled again.

"What exactly is your purpose for invading my laboratory?" Cornelius asked in a dangerously low voice. "Obviously, it's not to kill me."

"Very true," Hélène replied. "We work for Erik, better known as the Phantom of the Opera."

"Ah—the legendary Opera Ghost. Word among the Red Hand is that he is an elusive, but formidable, being who runs a trio of female mercenaries."

"Those rumors are true," Hélène replied, lowering the blades from the scientist's neck, "although we prefer the term 'Angels.' Erik has sent us here to offer you a proposition—one that will likely save your life, which is now in great peril... in exchange for two small favors."

"Couldn't he have simply sent me a telegram?" Cornelius asked.

"I'm afraid not, doctor," Hélène lamented. "If he had contacted you through such mundane means, then you may not have believed the message really came from him. Also, this demonstration of our abilities should make it clear that he is quite capable of protecting you from the danger now heading your way—whereas these pathetic bodyguards of yours obviously cannot."

"Understood, I suppose," Cornelius answered. "Now, what does he want from me, and what exactly is the danger that you claim is looming over me?"

"I'm afraid you must hear both from the master in person, my dear doctor. Are you willing to come with us, or would you prefer to take your chances without the help of our employer?"

After looking at his three fallen bodyguards, and seeing his brother Fritz with his fingers still stuck in the top drawer of his desk, Dr. Cornelius decided that he should accept the Phantom's offer. Besides, the opportunity to meet the awesome Erik was not one a scientist of his caliber could lightly ignore.

"I will meet with your employer, but before I do, would you be so kind as to release my brother's fingers? I promise you, he will behave himself."

"Certainly," Hélène replied. "Bri, if you would...?"

Bri grinned. "But of course."

With a simple wave of her hand, the tightly closed drawer came loose and Fritz fell backwards, his broken fingers throbbing with pain.

"By the Lord's mercy..." the crime lord muttered, as he glared at his damaged fingers.

Within the hour, Dr. Cornelius was guided by his trio of lovely but lethal hosts through a hidden passageway located in a rarely used section of the Paris Opera. It led them into a dank underground labyrinth of tunnels that appeared to extend for miles, the sound of running water reverberating off the cavernous walls.

During their lengthy walk, Cornelius never attempted to engage his three hosts in conversation. Instead, he was pondering the rumors that circulated about this mysterious "master of death" throughout the European underground.

Upon approaching what a hallway leading to an ornately designed living chamber, Cornelius was struck by the sound of a beautifully compelling aria emanating from the main quarters. Though the scientist was by no means a connoisseur of opera, he was familiar enough with this genre of music to recognize Jacques Offenbach's *Ba-ta-clan* when he heard it—and never before had he heard it performed with such skilled gusto. It was clear that, had things gone differently, the Phantom of the Opera could have become a composer to rival Offenbach and Charles Lecocq. The composition reached a thrilling crescendo as Cornelius and the Angels entered the main chamber, finally beholding the artisan behind this amazing rendition of France's greatest operetta.

The first thing Cornelius saw was a large piano of a most expensive design. Seated in front of it was a man of impressive physical stature, clad entirely in black, wrapped in a long cloak. His facial features were entirely obscured by a mask reminiscent of the style worn by many opera performers. Upon completing his concerto, the Phantom turned towards his guest.

"*Bonsoir*, Dr. Cornelius," he said. "*Comment allez-vous ce soir?*"

Cornelius sardonically replied, "I was assaulted by your three agents in my laboratory, my brother was injured, and my three bodyguards will now be collecting a large amount of hazard pay from my organization, Monsieur Erik. Moreover, I was brought here under duress. I am certain a brilliant man such as yourself can consider your question rhetorical."

The three Angels giggled amongst themselves.

"I love this gentleman's moxie," Florence quietly stated with the churlish wink of an eye. "He is soooo *je ne sais quoi*, and would doubtless be lots of fun to... play with. I so hope the master doesn't hurt him."

Bri sniggered in response. "Always the scheming tart, eh, Florence? Didn't your mother raise you better than that?"

"Believe me, my dear Bri, my mother taught me quite well, thank you," Florence replied with a giggle.

Hélène elbowed her two fellow agents. "Now is not the time, ladies. Let the master speak."

The Phantom stood up from his seat and approached Cornelius. Remarkably, the scientist kept his composure despite Erik's awe-inspiring presence.

"I am most sincerely sorry," said the Phantom as he extended his hand to the scientist, "about the circumstances that preceded your visit, but I am certain that my Angels explained to you why it was necessary. You are doubtless aware of my reputation, as I am of yours. You are said by many to have one of the most brilliant scientific minds in the world—and to be totally without scruples."

"I have worked hard to earn my reputation, as you certainly have yours, Monsieur Erik," Dr. Cornelius replied after shaking the Phantom's hand. "Now, all niceties aside, can we get on with whatever business it is that your three agents said you have with me?"

Erik looked at Cornelius for several seconds without responding. Even though he did not show it, the scientist couldn't help but feel a little unnerved by the eerie mask that made it impossible to read the Phantom's facial expressions.

"Very well, Doctor," Erik finally said. "After all, my time is every bit as precious as your own. Let us therefore get right down to the matter at hand. Your life is in extreme danger because the monster known as Gouroull has emerged from whatever cesspool he was trapped within, and he is now believed to be looking for you to exact vengeance for your betrayal of him when he was working for you."

For the first time, Dr. Cornelius appeared stunned. "Are you certain of this?"

"Very certain, Doctor. He was seen by one of my agents, and they would know better than to make a *faux pas* of such magnitude. That leads to my generous offer to guarantee your safety, in exchange for two small favors."

"And what might that be?"

"I am well aware that you studied samples of what passes for Gouroull's blood when he was in your employ. I want you to make a comparison with my own blood."

Cornelius glared at Erik in frank astonishment. "You suspect that you may be related to that... thing?"

"That is the first favor I'm asking for," Erik continued, ignoring the question. "I will now mention the second. If your comparison of the two blood samples confirms my beliefs, I want you to help me lead that monster into a trap I have designed for him. Then I will kill Gouroull. That creature will walk the Earth no more, and will never succeed in taking the bloody vengeance upon you that he is now doubtlessly planning."

Cornelius promptly responded, "Very well, Erik. I will do both of these things. But do you truly believe you can kill this creature when so many others have tried and failed?"

Erik jumped to his feet. "Do you really doubt me?" he asked Cornelius with barely controlled rage. "Did you not say that you are familiar with my reputation?"

"I seem to have underestimated your, er, motivation," Cornelius said. "I didn't mean any offense, nor do I doubt your formidable reputation as an assassin, but I was simply pointing out that this monster is surely unlike anyone or anything you have ever tried to kill before."

Erik slowly sat down, struggling to calm his temper and firmly reminding himself how much he needed Dr. Cornelius alive. "I will keep my end of the bargain," he said finally. "Nothing lives that cannot be killed. I have proven that many times in the past. Right now, just get me that blood sample I require. In the meantime, I shall order the equipment that you will need to do the comparative analysis, and you can expect it to arrive within the hour."

Cornelius nodded. "Very well. It will be done."

A week later, Gouroull had located the address of Dr. Cornelius' house on the Avenue de Passy in the 16th Arrondissement. He only had to "lean on" a single tramp, Bouzille, whom he remembered from his days employed by the Red Hand, to acquire information about the doctor's whereabouts.

The monster utilized every iota of his stealth to sneak up on Cornelius unaware, though it somehow seemed *too* easy. Having quietly followed Cornelius out of the building and into an abandoned warehouse nearby, the creation of Frankenstein was looking forward to pouncing on his on his target to exact a bloody act of dismemberment. But the fiend was unaware that he had just entered a maze especially designed by the Phantom of the Opera, and that Erik himself was watching his every movement through a series of hidden mirrors.

Now it begins, Erik thought as he sat sequestered in the main chamber of the underground tunnel system.

Gouroull tried to catch up with Cornelius as the scientist entered what seemed to be an ordinary tunnel, perhaps abandoned since the construction of the Paris Metro. But he was suddenly cut off from his quarry when a steel door slid down in front of him. Another immediately slid down behind him, effectively trapping him. The creature approached the steel door barring the path that Cornelius had taken and began to tear it from its hinges.

Just then, a small door-like opening in the side of the wall slid upwards, and out of it rolled what appeared to be a gnome-like man with oddly artificial looking features, attired in a one-piece garment. Gouroull glowered at this unexpected intruder with a look of mild amusement on his face. The little entity rolled about two meters in front of the creature while awkwardly pulling himself into a standing position.

"Bonsoir, Monsieur Gouroull," the little man said with a tone that was a hybrid of politeness and malevolence. "My name is Cochinelle, and I work for the gentleman who's led you into this trap. I came to give you a little welcome gift before other agents proceed to kill you in a most painful fashion."

Cochinelle then drew what appeared to be a children's squirt gun and doused Gouroull with a viscous liquid that had an irritating sensation on the monster's skin.

Cochinelle then yelled, "Gentlemen! He is drenched with the fluid! Hurry up and perform your assigned task!"

No sooner had Cochinelle issued that command than two normal-sized men wearing gray full body outfits exited a larger hidden opening on the side of the door. They each carried a bulky metal tube-shaped object strapped to their backs, with hose-like objects extending from it, which they aimed at the monster.

Cochinelle hastily shouted another command. "Do it! Let our guest feel the heat!"

The two men squeezed a hidden control on the hose-like extensions, and each metallic nozzle fired a stream of intense flame at Gouroull, causing him to burst into a blazing inferno when the fire came in contact with the highly flammable liquid Cochinelle had shot at him.

"Don't stop!" Cochinelle hollered maniacally. "Keep the flames coming until those damned tubes are empty!"

Following these orders, the two men kept the flames spewing forth from the nozzles until the metal tubes on their backs were finally depleted. Cochinelle walked closer to the raging torrents of flame in front of him, expecting to see the charred remains of Gouroull within.

Instead, he was treated to a most unwelcome sight as the monster walked out of the flames, virtually unscathed save for his clothing. He wore a look of extreme anger on his face.

"Gah! I guess I had best heed the better side of valor!"

Cochinelle fled under the legs of the two men who stood almost in shock at the sight of the monster bearing down upon them. Grabbing the men by the side of their faces, Gouroull slammed their heads together with such force that their skulls jointly burst like blood-filled melons under a sledgehammer. The creation of Frankenstein's genius then turned back to his original task and completed tearing off the steel door barring his way further into the tunnels.

Soon, the creature found himself in a new chamber, furnished with a variety of household items, and a collection of daggers from all over the world hanging on a wall. Gouroull looked around in an attempt to get his bearings and decide on his next move. Suddenly, a door on the far end of the room slid open.

Into the room emerged the three lovely warriors known as the Phantom's current Angels of Music.

Gouroull would ordinarily have found the sight pleasing, but he correctly surmised that these three young women were certainly more than what they appeared to be.

Standing a foot in front of her two comrades, Hélène smiled and said, "Let's get down to business, shall we?"

After Gouroull raised his massive arms and began advancing towards the trio, Hélène and Florence both swiftly drew their pistols and opened fire. Hélène's bullet struck the monster directly in his chest, whereas Florence's hit him clear between the eyes. The creature appeared to stumble for a second, as a stream of blackish ichor poured down from the hole now embedded just above his nose; then, he shook his head a bit and continued to face his adversaries as if none the worse for wear.

"Very impressive," said Florence as she cocked her pistol.

"Stifle the compliments and shoot again!" Hélène ordered. "Aim directly for his eyes!"

Since he didn't want to find out how long it would take for his eyes to regenerate from a bullet wound, Gouroull snatched up a heavy armchair and hurled it at the two girls, managing to strike a glancing blow that simultaneously disarmed them and knocked them to the ground. Before he could advance upon them, however, he was suddenly skewered in the torso by four daggers that had been telekinetically launched from their mounts on the wall at Bri's behest. Startled by the sudden pain, the monster was then hit from behind by a wide array of heavy furniture items that Bri magically levitated and hurled at her opponent.

Gouroull was summarily knocked to the ground by the repeated impacts and momentarily stunned. Acting with great speed, Florence unsheathed a dagger from her belt and somersaulted towards the monster before he could recover his senses. Upon landing in front of the brute, the gladiatrix brutally slashed his throat with the blade, causing streams of the creature's blackish blood to pour out of the wound.

Choking, Gouroull nevertheless managed to grab Florence's arm, forcing her to the ground. Seconds before the monster could rip the limb from the Angel's body, Bri turned her power directly upon him. She propelled the creature clear across the room and caused him to slam into upon the far wall. After Gouroull slid to the floor, stunned, Bri pressed her advantage by telekinetically lifting him again and repeatedly smashing him against each of the walls with as much force as she could muster. Finally, approaching the limits of her endurance, she stopped and dropped him to the ground.

"*Merci*, but I can't keep that up any longer!" she gasped.

"That may be enough," Hélène remarked. "There is no way that even that creature could possibly…"

However, no sooner did Hélène utter those words than Gouroull was back on his feet, blackish blood pouring from his wounds, but clearly ready to re-enter the fray.

Exasperated but still undaunted, Hélène decided to go for broke.

"It's time to hit him with our *coup-de-grace*! We must sing until we cause that creature's brains to liquefy and pour out of his ears! We will sing *The Damnation of Faust*. Appropriate, *n'est-ce-pas*?"

The three girls stood beside each other, and, after taking a quick breath, began singing in unison: "*Le Roi de Thulé...*"

At first, the enchanting melody was almost charming, even to a soul as dark as Gouroull's, but it quickly began escalating in vibratory force until the monster began to feel biting sensations of pain throughout his body. Within moments, he could feel his internal organs being ripped asunder. Unable to remain on his feet, Gouroull fell to his knees, blood streaming out of every bodily orifice. Realizing that he was facing a force that could prove fatal, even to him, the monster struggled against the piercing pain, gathering every ounce of willpower and crawled across the floor towards a particularly heavy piece of furniture. Despite the massive pain he felt, and the torrents of black ichor gushing out of his mouth and ears, Gouroull exerted a Herculean effort of will and grabbed the leg of the chaise-longue.

Observing what the monster was doing, the three Angels redoubled their efforts, determined to crush every organ within their foe's body before he could achieve his goal. Despite each feeling their larynx about to burst, they continued singing. However, Gouroull, howling in agony like never before, managed to hurl the furniture with as much force as his muscles could muster.

Unable to evade the several hundred pound chaise-longue, all three Angels were smashed to the ground, their deadly song prematurely interrupted.

Slowly standing again, Gouroull stood victorious, if not unscathed. The monster was now aware that the unseen master of these "Angels" was a force to be reckoned with. He needed to find him, and kill him, as quickly as possible.

Suddenly, he heard a commanding voice booming from a hidden speaker.

"Do you want to meet he who was behind all of this, creature? Would you enjoy a chance of getting your hands on both Dr. Cornelius and myself? If such is the case, you had best walk through the sliding panel I am now opening for you."

Seething with rage, Gouroull ran through the new panel that had just slid open, intent on locating and destroying his intended targets.

The next room was featureless, with several large spigots layered across its walls. Heading towards a reinforced steel door on the other side, the monster was then besieged by torrents of a vile-smelling liquid that poured out of the spigots. His nasal passages stinging, the monster glanced down to find the room rapidly filling with the acrid fluid. Gouroull noticed a severe burning sensation as what was left of his clothing was becoming soaked with the corrosive juice.

He then realized exactly that the liquid was a kind of potent acid. He hastened to break down the steel door as quickly as he could, uncertain of how long his body could withstand the caustic power of the acid if fully immersed in it.

On the other side of the door, Erik sat in a state of apparent calmness. He watched Gouroull's knuckle prints form on the steel door he had himself designed with every blow delivered to it by the monster. He realized that the creature would break the door down before the acid could destroy him. Not wanting his lair ravaged by the acid, Erik had no choice but to close the spigots and open drains to empty the other room of the fluid. He then grabbed an exotic-looking weapon while patiently awaiting Gouroull's entrance.

Within moments, the door came flying off of its hinges, and in walked a battered, enraged Gouroull. The monster looked upon the masked man sitting across from him and realized that he was at last confronting the mastermind behind all the death traps he had just encountered in the tunnels.

Erik stood up and pointed his weapon at the monster. *My god*, the Phantom thought, gazing into Gouroull's features. *I have his eyes!*

"At last, I meet the one responsible for the decades of misery that I have called my life," Erik said with a venomous mien.

Gouroull was puzzled by this man's strange statements. He stepped forward, but hesitated when he saw the peculiar-looking weapon wielded by his enemy—a man whom he now understood to be extremely dangerous. He decided to proceed with caution and stopped.

"You are right to keep your distance, creature," Erik said. "This weapon fires special projectiles that can cause lethal damage, even to one such as you. If forced to fire, I will make sure I aim at your brain first—and my aim is without peer. First, I think it's only appropriate that I tell you who I am and why I hate you as I do. Not that any other emotion would be suitable for the likes of you..."

Gouroull cocked his head, genuinely intrigued as to what revelation this strange man was about to share with him.

Erik then pulled the mask from his face, revealing his own hideous countenance. "Do you see what we have in common, creature? Look at my eyes. Look at them! They're identical to yours."

Gouroull continued to gaze at Erik with rapt curiosity.

"Do you recall one of the many women you ravaged several decades ago, one who was called Rosemary? Do you?"

Thinking a moment, Gouroull nodded.

"I thought you would remember. Little did you know that, when you forced yourself upon her, you inseminated her. As if the horror you had inflicted on her weren't terrible enough, she found herself impregnated with your demon seed. Months later, she died giving birth to your unholy offspring. I was told the last emotion she felt before leaving this world was her complete horror at witnessing the gleaming yellow eyes of her son. The same color eyes that you and I both possess!"

After noticing how the hue of Erik's eyes mirrored his own, Gouroull now realized with full clarity that he was standing before his own progeny. The monster grinned.

"Do you have any idea what a nightmare this life of mine has been?" Erik passionately queried. "I inherited your hideous appearance, as well as your longevity, which made me suffer for all too many decades! I have been denied the simple pleasures that most humans take for granted, including the acceptance of a community and the pleasure of being in the arms of women! I may wield much power, but I acquired it by deeds of evil and bloodshed! I hate this world! I hate humanity! I hate myself! And more than anything else, I hate *you* for spawning me!"

Upon hearing those words, seeing tears stream from Erik's flaxen eyes, Gouroull abruptly burst out in joyous, fiendish laughter. As the Phantom gazed at his sire's reaction with utter bemusement, the monster glared back and forced himself to do something he rarely attempted to do—talk:

"This is truly wondrous to hear. I was unaware that my unique physiology was capable of impregnating a human woman. But now, thanks to you, my offspring, I know that I can.

"And you turned out just as I had always hoped an offspring of mine would. You routinely wreak murder and terror upon the human race that I, too, loathe; the race who rejected me just as it did you. I couldn't possibly be prouder of you, my son. You do a great honor to your legacy. *My* legacy. I must continue to inject my seed into as many women as I can find, for the purpose of spawning as many progeny like you as possible, who will be rejected by humanity for their horrid appearance, and will grow up filled with hatred towards men. Each of my children will kill many, out of vengeance or pleasure for as long as they live, much as you have done. The more like you I bring into this world, the more terror will be exacted upon the human race. This is a supremely rare occasion when my heart has actually been gladdened. I will now return to the world of men with renewed purpose. Please continue to make your father proud by doing exactly what you have been doing with such aplomb for all of your putrid life."

Ending his spiel with a demonic laugh, Gouroull turned and began to leave the tunnels. Erik, however, felt on the verge of a breakdown.

"No! You will not carry out that plan! You will not spawn more like me to carry out more death and destruction! My mother was among the few true innocents of this world, much like my dear Christine, and you will not ravage another like them and desecrate her womb with your spawn! I will gladly die myself rather than allow you to leave these tunnels alive!"

Always the master schemer, Erik had had powerful explosives buried under the tunnels prior to leading the monster there, in case circumstances had come to this. Though he knew he would likely be killed as surely as Gouroull, he could not take the chance of the monster escaping to carry out his darkest plan yet. Without the slightest hesitation, the Phantom hit the button that would instantly set off the explosives.

"Good-bye, father," the Phantom quietly said to himself as the caverns collapsed about them. "I shall surely see you in Hell."

One week later, police officer Jules Maigret was among those sifting through the rubble of the tunnels that collapsed in the 16th Arrondissement, due to an explosion of such magnitude that it had startled all of Paris. Hoping to personally see how the investigation was going, the young man approached the medical examiner, Jules de Grandin, who was likewise on the scene.

"Has anything pertinent been discovered, Doctor?"

"Nothing besides the fact that a great number of very powerful explosives were set off. This could be the handiwork of the Red Hand, the Black Coats, the Vampires, or who knows what new organization of terror may have risen to besiege Paris. However, none of them have claimed responsibility as yet. We've discovered two dead bodies under the rubble so far. Their heads were shattered as if crushed between a printing press. Truly ghastly."

"Anything else worth noting, Doctor?"

"Just one thing, actually."

Motioning for the younger Maigret to follow him, de Grandin walked to the far side of the countless tons of scattered debris littering the ground and pointed to what appeared to be a round metallic lid on the floor of what seemed to be all that remained of the destroyed labyrinth's main chamber.

"What is this?"

"As near as we can tell, it appears to be a hatch leading to another network of catacombs, even lower than the tunnels that were destroyed. It could have withstood the collapse, and may have been designed to allow someone to escape, had they ever felt the need to detonate those explosives."

"So you mean to say that someone, perhaps the very individual who initiated the explosion, may have escaped alive?"

De Grandin looked at Maigret and twirled his mustache. "Yes, lad. It's quite possible that whoever perpetrated this atrocity may still be on the loose in our fair city…"

John Peel, a regular contributor to Tales of the Shadowmen *and* Doctor Who *writer extraordinaire, brings together Madame Palmyre, the central character from Renée Dunan's extraordinary supernatural thriller* Baal, *recently released by Black Coat Press, with the ground-breaking Occult investigator Thomas Carnacki, for a story that beautifully recaptures the eerie, otherworldly atmosphere of William Hope Hodgson's universe...*

John Peel: *More Imaginative Sins*

London, 1912

My friend Carnacki was a man of unvarying routine. He would invite the four of us over for dinner after one of his cases, and nothing would be spoken of it until after a fine meal was finished and we had settled in comfortable chairs. Carnacki would light his pipe and then commence telling us of his latest adventures. Those adventures were always of an astonishing nature as he is, by profession, a ghost finder. I firmly believe that Carnacki needed the strictly unvarying routine of that social interaction as a counter to the complete unpredictability of his cases. In some instances he would deduce that a human agency was at work and would supply his clients—and by extension the four of us—with an explanation of how something that appeared to be supernatural was achieved by trickery. But in other cases... well, they were the sort that would make the skin crawl.

This evening, I had been strongly tempted to break the routine as Carnacki looked as shaken and pale as I had ever seen him. Before I could remark on his appearance, however, he had caught my eye and shaken his head slightly to dissuade me from such a course of action. The other three all gave a start when they saw Carnacki, but they, too, received that slight shake and held their peace.

After dinner and a fine brandy, Carnacki consented to speak. We settled into familiar chairs and waited until he had lit his pipe and taken a few puffs.

I know you were all surprised by my appearance (he began). To tell the truth, I've had rather a rough time of it in this last case of mine. I've not spoken much about my neighbors here in Cheyne Walk, but there are some interesting types. One in particular—Sâr Dubnotal. He is in a line of business not too unlike mine, though he tends to travel the world and I like to stay in my own little country. He's been able to offer me advice and a little help from time to time, so I wasn't too surprised when he called upon me and asked me to take on a case for him as a favor. It seems the sister of a friend of his had suffered from a curious affliction. He himself would have investigated, save for the fact that it was imperative for him to be in the South of France the following day on crucial business. Naturally I agreed that I would look into the affair, and he supplied me with an address and a letter of introduction.

As I didn't have much to keep me busy, I went around that afternoon to a place in Eaton Place. It was about what you'd expect—reeked of old money and the tweedy inhabitance of several generations. The owner was a Richard Cardinal and he lived there with his wife, two children, one sister and a barrage of servants. The house had been his father's before him, and the grandfather's before that, so he knew the history of the place back to the days when the first brick had been laid. There had never been the hint of a ghost before this, and no signs of anything out of the ordinary. Any self-respecting haunt would have been bored stiff, most likely, in such a staid household. Save when the gentleman of the house was speaking, the only noises to be heard were the ticking of the various clocks. A place less likely to be an outpost of Hell is hard to imagine.

And yet, that is what it appeared to have become. Cardinal's wife and children were in the country with relatives as they simply couldn't stand the house any longer. At precisely eight in the evening, the terror would commence, and it would last until dawn. The events were wholly centered upon the sister, Agnes. She herself could recall nothing of what transpired in her room between those hours, save that she was exhausted and horrified when they were over. And there were no witnesses to what occurred, at least not directly, because the events happened only inside the room and no one else was able to enter the room once eight had struck until the dawn of the following morning. All that anyone else knew was that poor Agnes would scream and scream in horror, and that there was something else in that room, something that cast a putrid light beneath the door and a foul stench that filled the upstairs corridor. The events had commenced a week prior to my arrival and were repeated without change every night.

Naturally, the thought that first occurred to me was that perhaps the sister should leave the house—or, at the very least, occupy some other room in this house in the evening.

"That has been considered," Cardinal informed me. "But it's simply not possible. We cannot remove Agnes from the room at any time."

I confess, this case was certainly an intriguing one, and I was determined to see for myself what was happening. Accordingly, I asked Cardinal to take me to see his sister.

He consulted one of the clocks in the receiving room. "At this hour, she's probably sleeping," he said. "Whatever it is that happens to her, she's left completely exhausted."

"Then you would not advise my seeing her?" I asked. I know I must have scowled, for it would be a great inconvenience if I could not look over the room and examine the young lady in question.

"Oh, no, you may see her," Cardinal explained. "It's merely that you won't be able to question her. She sleeps very deeply, no doubt worn out from the night terrors." He rang for the butler. When that worthy appeared, he sent the man to fetch a Miss Bolton. "She is my sister's ladies maid," he explained to me. "She will accompany you to my sister's room. I…" He paused and then admitted: "I prefer not to enter the room myself." Seeing my expression, he added hastily: "My sister and I have always been close. It distresses me greatly to see the suffering she is subject to."

That I could understand. Miss Bolton arrived—a sharp, nervous woman in her late forties—and she regarded me with some suspicion before leading me up the stairs. The sister's room was down the corridor to the right and I paused outside the door. "You appear suspicious of me," I commented.

Miss Bolton studied me steadily. "I do not approve of meddling with the occult," she stated flatly. "I've told Miss Cardinal this before. It is against my personal beliefs to trespass in realms we are not supposed to traverse."

"I see." This is a common attitude I find in my investigations. "If it is of any comfort to you, I, too, disapprove of trespassing in such realms. Yet, sadly, people constantly do so. It is my task to attempt to save them from their follies, not to encourage further transgressions."

That seemed to change her opinion of me somewhat. "It's a shame that not everyone shares such beliefs," she commented.

"Including Miss Cardinal?" I prompted.

"I will hear nothing spoken against her," Miss Bolton said sharply. "Only…Well, I did warn her not to see that fortune teller."

I hid my smile. "Though many so-called fortune tellers are nothing but fakes, I doubt one could seriously harm her—except in her purse."

"You did not see the one who came here," Miss Bolton snapped. Then she covered her mouth with a thin hand. "I should not have spoken; I gave my word."

Then I could see how little her word was worth. But this seemed a possible line of investigation, but one I shelved for the moment. I wished my inspection of Agnes Cardinal's room to be unprejudiced by suspicions. Instead, I stood outside the bedroom door and studied it.

"Do you not wish to enter?" Miss Bolton asked.

"Only when I am satisfied there is nothing further to discover outside," I informed her, then dismissed her from my mind for the moment as I examined the framework of the door. If, as Mr. Cardinal claimed, the room was impenetrable from this side after eight, there had to be some reason for this.

So-called magic is simply the manipulation of energies as yet little understood or investigated by man. Many rituals have evolved through trial and error, some of which are effective in working those energies, others of which are not. In order to prevent people from either entering or leaving this room, there had to be some force at work, and as a result there must be something close at hand that could affect and focus that force.

At first glance, there was nothing obvious. That led to only two conclusions: either Roger Cardinal's story was a tissue of lies, or else the obvious was incorrect. I seriously considered the former—not from distrust of my client, but simply as a matter of logic. If Cardinal was lying—why? Why employ me if there was nothing wrong? And why tell a lie that could be disproved so simply as to ask other people in the house what was transpiring? Many thoughts came to mind, though I dismissed them rapidly. Perhaps his sister had money he wished to control and he wanted her declared insane? Then would he not have called a doctor and not an occultist? Perhaps he wished to keep her imprisoned in her room for other reasons? Then why call in an outsider at all? No, he had begged my friend Sâr Dubnotal for help, and that must have been a genuine request. Dubnotal was no fool, and could have told if his friend had been lying. So—if Cardinal had been telling the truth, what I sought was too subtle to spot at first glance.

"Now I will see Miss Cardinal," I informed Miss Bolton. She nodded and tapped gently on the door. There was no reply, but she led the way into the room. It was in no obvious way different from a thousand such bedchambers in the City of London. The centerpiece was the canopy bed itself, with laced curtains drawn about it. There was a ladies' dressing table beside the window that overlooked the street below, and a chair drawn up to it. To one side was a couch with an upholstered chair beside a tea table. Though the room had been fitted for electricity, there was a large candelabra standing in the corner. A door led from the end of the room, clearly to a dressing room beyond. It was a pleasant bedchamber, neat and tidy. It looked normal and most charming.

There was a stench of evil thick enough almost to be touched.

Anyone who works in any profession—from banker to rat-catcher—develops a certain sense of their sphere of interest, things that are immediately apparent to them when an outsider detects nothing amiss. I could quite clearly feel the presence of some inhuman force upon the structure of this room. It was nothing definite and in no way could I define what it was I sensed—and yet any lingering doubts as to Cardinal's veracity were gone in that instant. The otherworldly had entered our fragile realm at this point.

"Is anything ever found in this room in the mornings?" I asked Miss Bolton.

"Nothing physical," she replied. "But there is a most unpleasant odor that lingers a short while."

"Yes, I imagined there might be." Other realms have other atmospheres, not often pleasant to our senses. "And are there marks on the body of Miss Cardinal?"

Miss Bolton drew herself up to scowl at me. "It is not polite to enquire about the form of a young lady," she scolded me.

"Quite so," I agreed. "But perhaps you might consider me a doctor of some sort for the duration of this investigation? My interest in her form is professional, and not salacious."

Miss Bolton considered for a moment. "There are… welts," she finally stated. "They do not persist long."

"Would they be visible now?" I asked.

"Not to the likes of you."

I sighed. "Miss Bolton, do you wish your charge to continue to suffer through her nights, or do you wish her freed from her terrors and pains?"

"Of course I want her to be free," the companion said.

"Then please indulge me and allow me to see some evidence of what is left with her after her trauma."

Miss Bolton clearly struggled with her prudish conscience, but finally her affection for her employer overcame her moral scruples, and she reluctantly led the way to the bed. She glared at me in warning, and then pulled aside the curtain.

My first sight of Agnes Cardinal was quite a shock. She was a young woman of perhaps 23 years, but she looked a decade older. She was drawn and her skin pale, though there were indeed raised welts on her exposed cheek and wrists, welts that had clearly been red and livid, but were dying down. Miss Cardinal was sleeping badly, panting slightly, a sweat upon her brow. From time to time she gave off whimpers, much as a beaten dog might, and thrashed about in her bed. When she was well, she would have been a pleasant, if undistinguished, young lady.

I had seen all I needed, and gestured to Miss Bolton that she might close the curtains again—which she did with an audible sigh of relief.

I considered what I had seen. Miss Cardinal clearly suffered physical assaults in these strange nocturnal occurrences, but the effects were not lasting. The fear and horrors, however, seemed to have ingrained themselves in her soul. The events transpiring in this room were very disturbing, but to be sure of what might be causing them I would have to witness one of the attacks. This left me in something of a dilemma, one I would have to discuss with her brother.

"I have two courses of action here," I explained to him a short while later. "The first is to gather information which may aid me in coming to a method of aiding your sister. This means, however, that we should have to allow another attack on her this evening. The second option is that I can attempt to protect her whilst still being uncertain of the exact nature of the problem."

"Which would you recommend?" he asked me. I could hear the pain and evident concern for his sister in his voice. If Mr. Cardinal was somehow behind these attacks for whatever nefarious reason, then he was a better actor than my ability to penetrate. He seemed utterly genuine.

"I am always in favor of gathering as much information as possible," I responded. "I am, in that way, akin to a doctor preparing for surgery. The dilemma here is that your sister would be forced to suffer more agonies."

"And do you think you can help her now, even being uncertain of the forces at work?"

"I do not know," I admitted. "I have methods at my disposal that might—and I stress *might*—alleviate the problem. They are unlikely to be completely effective, but they may ameliorate the pain."

"In which case," he said firmly, "you must try them. Anything that might help relieve the suffering my sister endures must be my primary concern."

Thus in agreement, we began the preparations for that evening's vigil. Miss Cardinal slept through most of the arrangements, waking only at about six in the evening. She was startled to see me and only calmed down when her brother appeared to assure her that I was a friend who would help her.

"I fear nothing can help me, Roger," she replied, her voice tinged with pain and terror. "I am in Hell."

"Not Hell," I assured her, in as kindly a fashion as I could. "Perhaps an outpost of that region, however." As she ate a light meal, I continued my work. Her eyes darted about, following my work, but she refrained from asking questions, which I found most unusual and welcome in a woman.

I set up my electric pentacle on the floor about her bed. I have spoken of this before, as I frequently find it to be very useful in protecting against the forces of evil. I was not certain how effective it would be in this case, as I still had no clear picture of precisely what was attacking the slender woman who ate and drank sparingly and watched my every move. I then quietly invoked the Aalaaron Ritual from the Sigsand Manuscript as further protection about the bed. This combination ought to provide some protection for Agnes Cardinal, whatever the evil might be. Then I sent her brother from the room, remaining only with Miss Cardinal and Miss Bolton as chaperone.

"If you are up to it," I told the victim, "I should appreciate a little information from you. I thought you might speak more freely if your brother was not present. Please think of me as you would a doctor or a priest—whatever secrets you divulge will not be revealed to your family."

[Here Carnacki paused and regarded those of us who were his audience. "I should add," he said, gently, "that I have changed the names of those involved in the household, as well as disguising its true location in order for me to keep my promise. All other details are quite accurate." He then resumed his tale.]

"I can tell you no more than Roger already knows," Miss Cardinal replied. "I know only that at the stroke of eight some monstrous evil invades my room and I recall nothing more until I awaken the following morning with lesions across my body and in terrible fear and agony. During the day I sleep, which enables me to recover slightly, and in the evening the events repeat themselves. They wear me down," she confessed, "and I do not know how much longer I can endure them." She hesitated a moment. "I have been contemplating a grave sin," she added.

"My dear lady," I told her, "in these circumstances I should be most surprised if the thought of suicide had not crossed your mind. But none of this is what I wished to question you on. Rather, I wish to know about your experiences with a certain fortune teller."

A guilty flush brought brief life to her cheeks, and then it faded. "You know of that?" She glanced in some annoyance at her companion. Miss Bolton had the grace to squirm under the accusing gaze.

"I do not judge you," I informed her. "It is merely that there would appear to be some connection between that event and your current predicament. If I am not mistaken, the person involved visited your rooms here at least twice before your misfortunes began? And both times when your brother was not present?"

"Yes," Miss Cardinal admitted. "But I cannot see what possible connection there might be between the visits of Madame Palmyre and my current situation."

"Nevertheless it is there," I assured her. "You seem to be a well-bred woman, and I doubt you are in the habit of receiving strangers here in your room."

"I am not."

"Then my hypothesis would appear sound—the only stranger to visit you was this Madame Palmyre, and subsequent to her visits you suffer nocturnal attacks. Therefore the two events must be linked. Now—a delicate question, I know—I must ask you to tell me the reason for her visits." As she flushed again, I held up a hand. "I understand that it must be of a delicate nature as you kept the visits secret from your brother. That is why I sent him from the room before talking to you. But if I am to help you, I must have a complete grasp of the facts in the case."

"You will think me foolish," Miss Cardinal replied.

"I repeat, I do not judge; I am here only to help, and in order to help, I need information. Whatever your motivations, they have led you to this state and I must know them." I softened my voice a little. "Besides, there is not one human being who does not behave in a foolish manner at some date in their lives. And some live in a perpetual state of folly. If you behaved unwisely, then it proves only that you are as human as the rest of us."

"Thank you for your kind words," she replied, her head bowed. "Very well, I shall tell you—and you will see why it can have no connection to what is befalling me." She looked up, her indecision fled. "There is a friend of my brother's of whom I am extremely fond. I shall not name him, as that cannot be of interest to you—but he is... dear to me. Yet he has given me no signs that he returns my regard. So..." She gestured with her hand. "I had heard of Madame Palmyre, who visits London for a short while, for her skills." She colored again. "She is not a fortune teller as such, but one who promises to help a person achieve their goals."

I began to understand the picture Miss Cardinal was doing her best to avoid painting. "She offers love potions?" I ventured a guess.

"Yes." She looked down at her hands again. "And she promised me that she could deliver one that would be effective in winning his affections."

I nodded. "Hence the two visits," I said. "The first for the consultation and the second to deliver the philter."

The pale woman looked puzzled. "But how could you be so certain that she visited twice?"

"That will become clear shortly," I promised her. "First, did you use the potion?"

Again that feverish flush of the cheeks, which made her words redundant. "Yes," she admitted. "I was instructed to add a little to his wine and a little to my own. Thus we should be linked, and thus would our affections be linked."

"And did it work?" I asked.

"I do not know," she confessed. "That evening was the first when I was attacked. I have not seen the gentleman since. My brother does not invite visitors whilst I am in this state." She started. "You think that the potion may have caused my troubles? I do not see how."

"Nor do I yet," I admitted. "But given the juxtaposition of the two events, cause and effect does seem to be likely."

"But what reason would Madame Palmyre have for offering me such evil?" she asked, bewildered.

"Again, I cannot see a reason—but reason there must be. It is quite clear that she has a hand in these events. Perhaps when I speak with her she will enlighten me."

"You will go to her?"

"Not today," I said, consulting the clock in the room. "It is already past seven, and I cannot leave you alone this night."

"You cannot do anything else," Miss Cardinal said, sadly. "I cannot leave this room and no one can stay with me past eight. There is some... force that prevents either action."

"A force I wish to investigate," I informed her. "Is it painful for you to attempt to exit your room?"

"No—it is merely impossible."

"This I wish to see, then, with my own eyes." I gestured at the door. "Perhaps you would be good enough to attempt an egress?"

Miss Cardinal paused a moment to gather her resolve and then she stood up and walked steadily to the door. She looked back at me and then attempted to cross the threshold.

I confess, I was taken aback. I had seen nothing like this in any of my investigations. She was caught in the act of walking, one foot raised, as if trapped in an invisible spider's web of tremendous strength. I could see clearly that she was trying to complete her step and that there was some unseen force literally preventing her. I asked her permission and then attempted to push her through the exit. This proved to be impossible—she was not able to move forward at all. Yet, when I tried it, I was able to leave the room without hindrance. I gripped her hands and attempted to draw them after me, but they were completely immovable, though only in the forward direction. As soon as I told her to cease the attempt, she was able to step back into the room without a problem.

"Miss Cardinal," I informed her, "you have certainly shown me something novel."

"Then you do not know what is causing this?" she asked me, disappointment evident in her voice.

"On the contrary, I am certain I know precisely what is causing the problem. I simply have never seen it before."

She blinked and then looked hopeful. "Then you can cure this condition?"

"As to that, I am not so certain." I knelt down and examined the door frame from the hall side of the door, looking for something I was certain had to be there. After a moment, I discovered what I had anticipated—at the base of each side of the frame, two small sections of wooden paneling had been fixed to the door. They were colored so as to blend in perfectly with the existing frame and so would not be evident except to the sort of intense scrutiny to which I had subjected the frame. Miss Cardinal watched me in surprise as I pried the first of these loose from the door and examined it.

As I have said, the outside was camouflaged to blend in perfectly with the frame. On the inside, however, there was an inscription in some language unknown to me—and, I suspect, to most human beings now alive on our planet—surrounding an inverted pentagram. I showed it to Miss Cardinal.

"What in the world is that?" she asked.

"What is preventing you from exiting this room and preventing anyone else from entering during your ordeal," I informed her. "They are called wards, and these are exceptionally powerful ones written in a tongue that was ancient when our world was still a boiling ball of stone. They manipulate the lines of forces of what we call magic and what other intelligences consider their science. They were left here by your friendly Madame Palmyre."

Understanding flooded her features, making her for a moment less plain than she normally appeared. "I see why you knew she must have been here twice, then," she commented. "The first time she would have needed to ascertain the wood for the door frame, and the second time to place those—what did you call them?—wards."

"Correct." I smiled. "It was clear to me that something had to be keeping you in the room, and when I saw your reaction attempting to cross the doorframe, it confirmed my suspicions." I bent to replace the ward where it had been. When I straightened again, I saw the shock on her face.

"If you remove those wards, will I not be able to leave my room?" she asked. "The hour of eight approaches." I could see the terror she felt in her eyes and in the slight tremors of her body.

"Yes," I said gently. "You would be able to leave your room. But so might your nocturnal haunter. I do not understand the language the wards are inscribed with, and they might be all that keeps the horror confined to your room."

"I could not inflict my sufferings on my brother and his family," she said, sadly but firmly. "You are right to leave them in place, then, even though it means another night of agony for me."

"I am hopeful that this may not be the case," I informed her. I gestured to her bed. "My electric pentagram and the incantations I have used have their own power, and I do possess knowledge of my own—not as ancient or as dark as that of Madame Palmyre, admittedly, but it may suffice for us this night."

"Us?" Agnes Cardinal blinked. "But the same force that keeps me here will prevent you from lingering."

"Within my pentagram, I believe the spell ejecting strangers will not work," I said. "And I trust it will keep whatever evil manifests itself in your room from approaching you." As her face lit with hope, I held up a warning hand. "I cannot promise either without trial, but I am hopeful."

"Then so am I," she decided. "Mr. Carnacki, whatever befalls this evening, I offer you my heart-felt thanks for your efforts."

I had almost forgotten Miss Bolton was still present, so silent had she been, but she now stepped forward. "I, too, shall stay," she insisted, with a sniff. "I cannot leave Miss Cardinal without a chaperone."

"Then we shall face this together," I informed them. "First, I must stress this—on no account leave the protection of the pentagram. This has strength only within its confines—if you cross the electric barriers, then you will be subject to anything without. Second, if I appear distracted it will be because I am reciting protective chants to aid us. Try not to break my concentration."

The ladies both signified their understanding, and so we sat tensely awaiting the numerous clocks scattered about the house to mark the appointed hour. It was no long in coming, but the strain made it seem almost eternal. Miss Cardinal was upon her bed, and Miss Bolton was upon a chair within the confines of the electric pentacle. I myself paced up and down, knowing the weaknesses that might prove disastrous. A thousand thoughts and scenarios flickered through my mind, haunting me with possible outcomes. Given that Miss Cardinal had survived every other night, I felt it unlikely she would be harmed any more than usual if my precautions failed us. But as Miss Bolton and I were intruders on an event that its perpetrator seemed eager to keep secret I could not be assured of our own safety.

As the numerous clocks began to strike the hour, we all three stiffened. Now it would begin.

And, indeed, I immediately began to feel the effects of some strange force. It was as if a hundred unseen hands were grabbing at my, tugging me toward the door. Unheard voices seemed to cry: "Leave!" The pressure on me to move was strong and relentless—but not overwhelming. I fought back, struggling to remain rooted in place.

Miss Bolton gave a startled cry and rose to her feet. Shaking, she took a step. Worried, I cried out: "If you leave the pentacle, rush immediately out of the door! You should be safe outside of the room, but do not linger." This warning penetrated the shock, and she shook her head and then reseated herself firmly in the chair.

And then the urge to flee was gone. For a brief moment there was peace—the dreadful tension in the air stilled. But only for a moment.

This time it was Miss Cardinal who gave the warning cry. With a shaking hand, she gestured toward the window, and we both followed her gesture.

It is difficult to describe what we saw. Imagine that the world we see here about us as a painting. Then what we were watching was as if some unseen hand had ripped the painting and was pushing it aside, exposing another scene behind it. In front of the window was a tear in the picture of the world as we know it, and—from some nether dimension beyond—a separate reality was exposed. What that reality was is impossible to describe, because it was something no human eye was ever meant to see. Our senses are too feeble, too ethereal, to be able to grasp the substance of that world. There were colors and shapes and movement, but what any of them were I cannot say. Human mouths and tongues cannot form themselves about the words needed to describe those events. Suffice it to say that there was a second reality temporarily imposed upon ours, a reality that was utterly incompatible with our own realm of experiences. And it was a reality populated with life utterly unlike anything we have ever known.

One of these dwellers was waiting as the breach occurred. We never did see all of it, so I cannot describe the entirety. It sat, or squatted, or stood beyond the rift, and allowed only portions of its immense form to pass through into our world. Tentacles there certainly were, in profusion, writhing and questing as they came. Sections of a leathery hide were visible behind these, but it was impossible to focus on those. Whether the creature had eyes or other senses, I cannot say. The tentacles were the overwhelming substance visible, the more so as they groped toward us.

I have heard that octopi and squids of the seas of our gentle world use their tentacles as hands, able to manipulate them to seize prey and drag it into their maw. This unearthly thing used its appendages to do far more. They reached across the room, writhing and searching, clearly intent upon Miss Cardinal.

Now I was aware again of my companions. Since the tear in reality had occurred, I had barely thought of them, but now Miss Bolton screamed and promptly fainted. My first thought was that this would at least prevent her from attempting to leave the protection of the pentangle. Miss Cardinal was affected

228

in a different fashion, drawing the bedclothes about her as if mere fabric could defend against those questing digits.

"That… that is the thing which has attacked me these nights?" she gasped.

"Evidently," I replied, my own voice far from steady.

"Little wonder my mind has refused to recall it, then," she observed. "Even now, I find it hard to see and understand. Can it… reach us?"

Her question was a good one, for the tentacles had reached the boundaries of my pentacle now and had paused. The tips quivered and moved slowly in the air as if they had come across something solid that barred their way. Then they reared back and struck forward—but recoiled as if they had struck a wall. There was a pause, and then another assault. Again, my protection withstood.

The being beyond the rift possessed intelligence and purpose. It probed and pushed and squeezed, the tentacles whipping about the room, surrounding the bed and striving to reach us—or, rather, Miss Cardinal. I could not be certain it even knew or cared that I was present. It had one objective in mind and focused all of its energies on achieving that end. Strange sounds that had to be the voice of that creature shook the room as it screamed its frustrations.

My incantations and protections held. I cannot describe the relief I felt as I realized this. I meant nothing to that being—if it could reach me it might swat me or squash me or even ignore me. To an intelligence that alien, anything was possible. But it possessed one single thought—to reach Miss Cardinal. To what purpose? Why should a creature from a realm so distant in space and time and imagination concern itself with a weak, terrified human victim? Why should it attack and torture her night after night?

I discovered that I had retreated into the center of the pentacle, which was filled by Miss Cardinal's bed. The edge of it struck the back of my knees, and I fell upon the edge of it. Miss Cardinal grasped me, holding on as if her life and sanity depended upon that link.

"What is it?" she gasped. "What does it desire of me?" I simply shook my head.

The cries of the creature doubled in intensity and fury, and the tentacles lashed and slammed against the unseen barrier preventing them from reaching its prey. I was not thinking logically at that point—in that noise and amidst that insane activity I doubt if any human being could—but some thoughts penetrated the haze of terror and shock.

I recalled that the Bible mentions the early days of the Earth, and that in that dim and distant pass before we humans had built up our defenses that other creatures came to our world in search of women with which to mate. The Bible calls them giants, or *nephelim*, but we have other names for them. One that I knew was Baal. Was it possible that this thing that was attacking us might be one of the surviving *nephelim*, these untold ages afterward? That it still sought to mate with human women? Why it should wish so, I cannot say, but these were the thoughts running through my mind—as much as I was thinking anything at all coherently under that assault. The screams, the frustrations, the desperation to reach Miss Cardinal—all of these pointed to the possibility that my hypothesis was correct. It would explain why she was alive after facing such an inhuman being night after night, and why her tortured mind refused to allow her to recall any details of her encounters. Who on our warm and friendly planet would wish to remember the embraces of such a cold and pitiless demonic entity?

The night passed. I would describe it in more detail if possible, but there is little to say. Miss Cardinal and I clung to each other for comfort as the creature raged and thrashed impotently about. When the dawn came, the tentacles withdrew and the gash between the dimensions sealed itself. The terrible pressure we had felt and the raging fear both subsided and we were able to let our feverish grips on each other go. There was a bond of sorts between us, for we had survived a night such as—thankfully—few other humans ever had. Once again, I was grateful that my electric pentacle had proven to be so efficient.

Miss Bolton was still unconscious—indeed, she did not recover her wits until the family doctor had called and treated her. She then promptly gave noticed and immediately quit the household, refusing to ever return.

Miss Cardinal and I were both strained from the night's events, but there was no thought of sleep for either of us. We both knew that if we closed our eyes, we should see that living nightmare fresh and cold and clear again, so we sought to defer sleep as long as possible.

"You have saved me, Mr. Carnacki," she commented, as we sat to breakfast with her brother. I had removed the wards at her door once again to allow her to leave that haunted room and she had vowed to move to another before the day was through. "I cannot thank you enough."

"I have not saved you, Miss Cardinal," I replied. "Yet. I have merely postponed the evil for a single night. I am certain that the horror will return this evening to that room if I am not able to lay it. Accordingly, I intend to visit your Madame Palmyre today and see if I cannot persuade her to remove whatever spell she has cast upon you." I scribbled a note on the back of one of my calling cards and had the butler send it around to her hotel by one of the footmen. As I had hoped, I received a short note by return.

"*Six o'clock would be convenient. Madame Palmyre.*"

I showed it to Mr. Cardinal and his sister. "Tonight, then, should see the end of this—one way or another."

I arrived at the hotel shortly before six, carrying my equipment bag. Madame Palmyre had rooms on the third floor front, and I was escorted up. I was uncertain what I would find when I arrived, and was quite surprised when the lady greeted me.

She was tall and very beautiful, dressed in impeccable fashion and with little jewelry. With her was a smaller woman, fussy-looking, but clearly quite intelligent and obviously devoted to her companion. "My secretary and companion, Renée," Madame Palmyre introduced her.

I dropped my bag just inside the door, and gestured to it. "I apologize, but I've come straight from the Cardinal household, and had no time to return this home."

"The Cardinals?" Madame Palmyre did not seem surprised to hear the news. "And you came straight here? How... kind of you to call."

"This is not a social visit, I am afraid."

Her eyes gleamed. "I hardly thought it was, Mr. Carnacki, given your profession. Yes, I have heard of you—we have friends in common."

"Really?" I murmured. "I am surprised we have anything in common."

"Now you're being rude, Mr. Carnacki," she protested.

"Madame," I responded, "you have callously dispatched a demonic being to prey upon an innocent young woman, setting both her and her family into nights of terror. I hardly think I am being rude to a person capable of such sins."

"Sins?" She glared at me. "Mr. Carnacki, you English are capable of only pallid sins." She cast a scornful eye over me. "Judging from your waist-line, I was guess that a minor case of gluttony was as serious as you could ever achieve. Do not speak of that which you do not understand."

"I understand evil, Madame," I replied. "I understand wickedness. And I understand selfishness. What I do not understand is why you have inflicted such wanton cruelty on an innocent woman."

"Innocent?" She laughed. "Oh, I think not, Mr. Carnacki. If you read your Bible—and I suspect you do, from your attitude—then you know that we are all of us sinners, and there is not one innocent amongst us."

"You play word games with me when I wish a serious answer."

"I am being quite serious," she assured me. "Agnes Cardinal is not the sweet, gentle girl you take her for. Did she tell you why she sought my services?"

"She spoke of a love potion to be used on a man she admired."

"And did she bother to mention that this man is already married, with two children? I see from the look on your face that she did not." She smiled at me again, the smile of a cat stalking a wounded bird. "Miss Cardinal wished to destroy the lives of a perfectly fine family for her own selfish desires. How, then, is she innocent?"

"I see that you are not a believer in Gilbert and Sullivan," I replied.

She raised an elegant eyebrow. "Musical comedy? My dear Mr. Carnacki, perhaps you are not as dull as I feared. To which of their entertainments do you refer?"

"*The Mikado.*"

"Ah!" She gave another of her delightful laughs. "Let the punishment fit the crime?"

"Precisely. Even if she did seek her own desires through compelling a man to desert his wife and family, that hardly merits long nights of torture."

"Go back to your Bible, Mr. Carnacki," she suggested. "The vengeful God within its pages aims to send all sinners to the eternal fires of damnation. All I did was to give Miss Cardinal a foretaste of what your God plans for her in any event."

"Whatever God may or may not plan for an individual—and one who may yet have remorse for her sins—does not give you the right to assign punishment of your own."

"Perhaps not," Madame Palmyre agreed, casually enough. "But it suited my purposes. And it still does."

"You condemn her to Hell far too casually," I protested. "I have come to ask you to remove the spell upon her that brings that... hideous creature to her every night."

"Ah, I see that you have met Baal yourself, then?"

"Miss Cardinal and I spent the night frustrating his desires."

She laughed again. "Spending the night with an unmarried lady? Mr. Carnacki, you are getting positively naughty!" Then she turned serious. "But frustrating Baal is never a good idea—it merely makes him more determined to achieve his desires. His attack tonight will be even more ferocious—and you are here, with me, and not there to protect Miss Cardinal." She shook her head. "I fear she may not survive the next attack."

"I am here to appeal to you to prevent any further attacks," I informed her.

"It would not be in my best interests so to do," she replied. "You see, I have been the object of Baal's interests in the past."

I began to understand. "I see. And to avoid them in the present you needed a scapegoat with which to keep him occupied."

"Quite so. And I am afraid that Miss Cardinal is still of use to me in that role, so I must reluctantly decline your request." She glanced at the clock on the sideboard. "It is nearing six thirty, and I am due to take my dinner now. It has been a pleasure meeting you, Mr. Carnacki—you amused me, and few people can do that. If you would be so kind as to leave?"

I sat myself in one of the chairs. "I do not aim to leave here until you have agreed to my request," I said, stubbornly.

Her eyes flashed with anger—she was not one used to having her desires denied. "Now you begin to annoy me, Mr. Carnacki," she said. "Very well—if you will not leave, then I shall." She crossed the room and then halted in the doorway. A look of surprise and then concern crossed her face as she discovered she could not approach the door. She turned back to face me, coldly. "What have you done, you wretched little man?"

"I have told you a small falsehood," I replied. "I did, in fact, have the time to go home before I came to see you. And there, in the Aadrach Testament, I found the warding spells you cast upon Miss Cardinal to bind her within her own room." I smiled slightly. "I rewrote your spells a trifle and brought them along with me."

To my immense surprise, Madame Palmyre broke into peals of genuine laughter. "Why, Mr. Carnacki, it appears that I have underestimated you—you are capable of more imaginative sins than I had expected."

"I take that as a compliment."

"It was meant as one." She inclined her head slightly. "But you do understand what this means?"

"It means that Baal will be visiting here this evening instead of the Cardinal residence," I answered.

"It means I am to miss a very fine meal," she answered. "Well, there is always tomorrow—if we survive the night."

"Baal will be coming here?" her secretary asked, anxiously. I could tell from her tone that she had witnessed that being before.

"Thanks to Mr. Carnacki's interference, yes." Madame Palmyre shook her head and then turned back to me. "I do hope you have some sort of a plan for dealing with him. While he will not have the same interest in you as he will have for the two of us, he will not leave you untouched." Despite her brave words, I could hear the fear in her voice. "And he will be angry when he arrives."

"I have a few small weapons," I told her. "And you have your witchery. I had thought we could join our forces together and defeat him."

"You have a high opinion of yourself!" she scoffed. "And of me, it would seem. Mr. Carnacki, Baal is unborn and undying. We are *nothing* in his eyes, beyond sport and perhaps food. Neither we nor any human can hope to defeat him."

"Then perhaps we can simply close the rift that he uses to get from where he dwells to our world?" I suggested.

She considered the idea a moment. "There is a possibility of reversing the spell that calls him to the wards," she agreed slowly. "But it will take time and energy and concentration on my part. I cannot defend myself against his amorous advances and cast the spell at the same time."

"Then allow me to protect us all," I offered.

She gave me an odd look. "Mr. Carnacki, the bindings in my spell only keep us women here in this room. You could leave at any time quite safely."

"I know," I replied. "And whilst the thought has its appeals, unlike you I cannot condemn anyone to suffer at the hands of Baal without attempting to help."

"Ah!" She threw up her hands in disgust. "Now you have quite spoiled my opinion of you—you have an idiotic nobility ruining your soul."

"I find it quite touching and heroic," Renée offered.

"You would." Madame Palmyre shook her head. "Well, if you are to have a visitation in an hour or so, we had better get busy. I suspect the management may well ask us to never return again. And they have such an excellent kitchen, too."

Despite her mocking words, she proved to be a very efficient and careful worker as we prepared for the manifestation of Baal. She consulted texts she carried in her luggage, but much of her preparation was from memory. As I set up my electric pentagram, she paused to examine it.

"An interesting juxtaposition of science and magic," she commented. "If we survive this, I shall have to discuss your researches with you. You are proving less dull by the minute."

We worked carefully but swiftly as the appointed hour approached. Renée fetched books and special inks and paper for her mistresses' wards and spells, and watched us, enthralled, as we prepared. Finally, we were finished, and with barely ten minutes to spare. The three of us took our places inside the pentagram and waited.

"You interest me, Mr. Carnacki," Renee finally observed. "You manage to meld two very different disciplines—science and magic—with apparent ease."

"The ease if only apparent," I replied. "Perfecting my instrumentation has been a matter of long and careful research." I managed a rueful smile. "And a considerable number of failures."

"It had better not fail us this night," Madame Palmyre said sharply.

"It stood the test yesterday," I pointed out.

"But today Baal will be angrier and stronger," she snapped. "Make no unwarranted assumptions!"

At that moment, the hour struck. We glanced at one another, and then felt the tension in the air that signaled the approach of the horror. The compulsion to leave the room struck at me, but I was able to fight it down. Then the lights dimmed as something fed upon the electrical power, drawing it to itself. Again came that slashing in the air as a second world intruded upon our own.

Madame Palmyre was quite correct—this time around Baal was stronger and more furious than ever. The tentacles whipped from the gash, assaulting my shield. They battered against the invisible force generated by the pentacle, writhing, grasping, tearing—but unable to secure a purchase. A stench that burnt the lungs issued from the vent, along with screams and howls of rage and fury.

I recited from the texts again, struggling to retain my composure under the dreadful strain, in order to keep our protections fresh and effective. I was barely aware of Madame Palmyre beside me, muttering and gesturing in her own quest for serenity amidst insanity. The rest of the hotel must have heard the noises and felt the building shake from the attack. I discovered later that the management had believed the building subjected to an earthquake and evacuated it. Thankfully no member of the staff was foolish enough to try opening the door to this room.

Baal raged. Why it should desire to mate with human females is beyond my understanding. Perhaps it was simply some primal drive even Baal could not fathom. But it was clear that frustrating its urges was driving it mad with both desire and anger. Again and again those tentacles struck out, seeking one or other of my companions. If they had been able to connect, neither woman would have been able to survive. Thankfully for us all, the pentagram held fast. But the strain on me was terrible. As you have all noticed, the struggle left me drained of almost all of my strength. Even now, days later, I am not fully recovered. But I held.

And Madame Palmyre came through in her own fashion. I was gradually aware of her voice rising louder and louder, her calm manner giving way increasingly to triumph as she cried out the words of those ancient texts, words that seem to tear from her throat in a voice no human could form. Stronger and stronger she spoke, the beats and stresses in her voice rising and ringing about us.

Baal screamed, and redoubled its efforts, clawing at us—again, without effect. It could not know how close to total collapse I was as I struggled to remain alert and erect, fighting to keep the shield intact. When it seemed as though I could withstand no longer, Madame Palmyre's voice rang with triumph, and she pronounced the final sibilant syllable of her spell.

The gap slammed closed—so fast that Baal was unable to react in time. Three of the lashing tentacles were severed and dropped to the carpet, oozing ichors and writhing for several minutes.

The three of us collapsed also, within the protection of the pentangle. Both women were shaking from strain, exhaustion and shock, and I knew I must look the same. Madame Palmyre finally managed a small, feeble smile. "I suppose the kitchen is probably closed by now?"

The tentacles were composed of some alien ectoplasm, and they dissolved in moments, leaving nothing but a dire stain on the carpet and a stench in the air. When we were certain that the creature was indeed banished back to its dark realm, we exited our protection. I dismantled my apparatus and returned home.

Miss Cardinal has not been bothered again by any nocturnal invaders and has, she assured me, given up her interest in the married man that caused these events. Madame Palmyre and Renée were asked, politely but very firmly, to vacate their suite in the hotel. They plan to return to France shortly. I myself have just about recovered from my ordeal, as you can see. Now (he concluded), I must ask you all to leave because I am expecting a female visitor.

As I have said, my friend Carnacki is a man of unvarying routine. One of his points of insistence is that he will answer no questions once his tale is concluded. He made no exception to his rule this time. We all departed, not knowing who that female visitor was to be.

Dennis Power already described the youth of Jean Passepartout, Phileas Fogg's capable sidekick, in "No Good Deed" published in Tales of the Shadowmen *No.6. He returns to the character to narrate a further adventure of the indomitable sidekick that takes place in the American West during Fogg's famed World Tour and features some very unusual characters...*

Dennis E. Power: *Passing through the Hands of Steel*

December 10, 1872

Hot moist kisses became freezing wet stings.

As the dream arms of a San Francisco belle faded away, Passepartout passed from darkness to blinding light. His eyes stung from the glare of a winter's storm, flesh chilling as sleet and snow covered his hair, exposed skin and sodden clothing. A ceaseless drumming accentuated his throbbing pain.

Patches of dark dry earth and winter browned, frost-tipped grass flitted across his vision at a dizzying speed. Bleary eyes gazed over a horse's curved, muscled flanks. Lying on his right side, he was face down over the back end of a galloping horse. As the pounding in his head subsided, he noticed the pain in his arms, legs, back, hands and feet. He had been what the Americans so charmingly called hog-tied and thrown over the back of a horse. The tied lump of hands and feet had been looped to the rear of a saddle.

His fingers were cold and stiff from the winter's chill, so he flexed and warmed them. Once they were limber, he gingerly felt the rope binding him. The knot was simple. Untying it would take mere seconds, but if he loosened the rope, he could fall and land beneath the horse. Doing this when the horse was galloping would perhaps not be healthy. He ignored the burning strain on his leg and arm muscles and withstood the jarring and bouncing of the horse, waiting for the right opportunity to make his move.

What fate awaited him, he was not certain. Passepartout had been standing on a train car platform when several war-painted savages in buckskins surrounded him and beaten him down. The savages had attacked and overwhelmed the train that he and his employer, Monsieur Fogg, were using to traverse the wilds of America. During their attack, the savages had killed the engineer and fully opened the steam valve, hurtling the unmanned train down the tracks.

Passepartout had clambered over several cars to reach the engine of the runaway train. He had prevented it from being derailed by disengaging the engine car from the rest of the train. Then, he had then fallen prey to the not-so-noble savages and been carried away.

"Was wir sollte, über den Franzosen tun?" (What should we do about the Frenchman?) shouted one of the Indians.

Passepartout barely heard him over the pounding din of hooves crunching through the frozen ground. And so, for a moment, he thought he had misheard.

"Keep him alive until Herr Schultze says otherwise. However, guard the hunchback with your life," answered another Indian in the same language.

Passepartout wondered if the blow to his head had scrambled his brains. The red savages were speaking German! A Mormon missionary's lecture he had recently heard claimed that Indians were of the Lost Tribes of Israel. As such, they might have spoken Hebrew—but their speaking the tongue of Goethe was inexplicable.

"Once Fogg is either killed or captured, we can kill the Frenchy or take him back to Steel City to become a slave," added another German-speaking Indian.

Passepartout was as fluent in German as he was in English. Once the alleged Indians' conversation sank into his muddled mind, he grew infuriated. Passepartout had no love for Germans, especially since the invasion of France two years past. Since he knew he was dealing with bogus Indians, Passepartout decided to escape sooner than later.

Wiggling his fingers free, he then loosened the loops confining his feet. He scooted up to a higher, more horizontal position on the horse's back by shifting his weight slightly. He grabbed onto the saddle and kicked his feet loose. Passepartout then swung his feet about in an arc that gave the unsuspecting rider a clout to the head. Although the blow was relatively weak, the startled rider dropped his reins.

Passepartout pivoted and let his captor have a *revers* to the throat. This prevented the rider from crying out and sent him flying off of the galloping horse. Rolling forward, Passepartout seated himself in the saddle and gained control of the horse with his legs. After he finished untwining the rope from his hands, he took hold of the horse's neck.

The thick snowstorm helped cover Passepartout galloping his mount directly into the path of the nearest horse. This horse reacted to the sudden proximity of another animal and tried to get out of the way. His rider thought his mount was being troublesome and bore down the reins. Passepartout's horse shied away from colliding, but brought Passepartout close enough for a vault onto the other horse.

His feet landed upon a wrapped tarpaulin behind the saddle. He heard a loud grunt. The Indian who had been struggling to regain control of his suddenly difficult horse turned at the noise, shocked to see Passepartout standing on his horse.

He could not have known that this particular valet had once been a circus rider!

Passepartout batted the head of this second faux-Indian with the rope still looped around one wrist. A knotted end struck an eye and the rider clawed at the stinging orb. A follow up blow to the side of the head unmounted him.

Passepartout slipped into the vacated saddle and grabbed the reins. Whipping his head around, he quickly took in his situation.

About 20 yards away ahead was a single rider. The thick snowfall, the clamor of pounding hooves and the howling of the winter's wind had hidden his attacks so the man remained unaware that his two companions had fallen. Off to Passepartout's side, a large body of Indians rode towards the east.

The saddle contained a boot with a rifle and also two bags with ammunition, dried food and water. Passepartout lifted the tarp and looked into the face of a gagged, blindfolded young man. Since he did not have time to free the boy, he covered him back up.

Passepartout turned his horse and galloped off to the west. Although he knew that it was the opposite direction of Fort Kearney, he hoped to gain some distance before his absence was realized. Once he had lost the war party, he would circle back towards the Fort.

Passepartout had gained perhaps a mile before his horse was spotted and given chase. Further off to the west rose a group of hills. Passepartout galloped towards them, wanting to gain the high ground before the savages caught up with him.

However, the gap between he and his pursuers closed far too quickly for his liking. The main body of 40 or so riders were shrouded in a white fog created by the churning of snow and frosted earth, but one lone man outdistanced the main group. As the distance between them closed, Passepartout heard the whoops and cries of the Red Indians intermixed with some Germanic curses.

When he arrived at a small cluster of grass and brush-covered hills, Passepartout urged the tired horse upwards. Near the summit of the largest hill, Passepartout found a hollow with brush cover. He jumped from the horse and, in a short time, untied the captive young man and removed the saddle, rifle and saddlebags. Since there was not enough brush to hide the horse, he reluctantly chased it off. He loved horses too much, however, to shoot it and use it as a barrier. He propped the saddle up over a slight rise in the hollow, spread out the tarpaulin and crawled under it.

The snow quickly covered the oiled canvas sheet and, he thought, would provide some warmth and cover.

The lone rider and the group of Indians swung further west, following the freed horse. It would not take long for them to realize that they had been deceived.

Passepartout loaded and readied the gun, being careful that it remained out of sight.

The young man dropped down beside him and crawled underneath the oilcloth. "Did Mr. Henry send you?"

Passepartout shook his head, "No, Monsieur, I am a victim of circumstance and was captured by the Sioux as they raided my train. They took me prisoner when I stopped the train from being derailed."

"The Sioux!" snorted the young man. "They aren't Sioux, leastways not entirely. That's an unholy mob of renegades and whisky reds from the Sioux, Apache, Arapaho and other tribes. They're led by a man named Santer. I'm Johnny Brainerd."

Although Passepartout inwardly winced at the American brash manner-isms, he smiled and gave Brainerd a slight bow of the head. There seemed very little remarkable about him. He was a handsome youth, despite being small in stature and having a hunched back. Passepartout wondered if the youth had been captured for purposes of ransom.

He barely had time to introduce himself when a rider arrived at the foot of the hill. A cloud of snow and dust indicated that the other riders were not far be-hind. As the man's horse climbed the slope, Passepartout took aim with the rifle's silver blade sight and fired.

He meant to shoot off the rider's hat, but being unfamiliar with the wea-pon, he planted a shot right between the horse's eyes. Man and mount tumbled sideways down the slick snowy hill. A pang of regret washed over Passepartout for killing the beautiful animal. The sentiment faded when Gallic practicality made him concede that, without his horse, the man had become less of a threat.

When the rider stood up, apparently unharmed, Passepartout shot again. This time, he hit what he was aiming for: the ground next to the man's feet. The Indian turned and ran down the hill, not stopping until he had met up with the rest of the band.

"Nice shooting, Mr. Passepartout. My old friend Baldy could not have done any better, God rest his soul."

Below them, the single rider was making gestures to the Indians, motion-ing for them to split into two groups and make their way around the hill.

"Gosh! Santer is going to have them flank us," Brainerd whispered to Pas-separtout, who had come to the same conclusion on his own. He fired the rifle twice, once at either end of the group of Indians, warning them not to move. One of the Indian braves shouted something, raised a spear defiantly at Passepartout, wheeled his horse and made a dash away from the rest of the group and towards their position. Passepartout fired once more and the defiant brave flew from his horse. The remaining group turned their mounts and moved further back away from the hill where Passepartout was positioned. The third German-speaking Indian, whom Brainerd had said was named Santer, followed the rest.

Once they were further away from the hill, the Indians spread out once more. Passepartout shot at their feet. In response, a warrior knocked and shot an arrow. The arrow landed quivering in the dirt a few dozen yards away from where Passepartout and Brainerd were hidden. Santer gave the Indian who had shot the arrow a rifle butt stroke to the face. He screamed orders at the rest. Passepartout assumed that they were being told not to shoot at them.

Santer turned to face the hill, peered upwards and shouted in German accented English, "Give us the boy and we will let you go, Herr Passepartout. We only wished to delay Herr Fogg by taking you. That part of the mission is accomplished, so we do not need you any longer. We want the boy, not you."

The young man regarded him with a trusting face. Passepartout instinctively knew that giving him the boy to Santer was the wrong thing to do. "Why do they want you so desperately? Is your family rich?" Passepartout asked in a whisper.

To Passepartout's surprise, the boy laughed. "Not rich yet, but one day... Once I get my factory set up. I am an inventor, that's why they want me. Or rather, that is why their boss wants me."

"Boss?" Passepartout asked, not certain of this American term.

"Their leader, Herr Doktor Schultze. He is building a city in Oregon named Steel City based on technology and industrialization. He wants me to work for him. Initially, I agreed, but when I learned that his ultimate goal was to create superior weapons of war so that Germany could conquer Europe, I changed my mind. He wants me to redesign my Steam-Man and mass-produce it. When I refused, Doctor Schultze' hired hand, Santer, and his two owlhoots, kidnapped me from my St. Louis home."

At Passepartout's request, Brainerd described the Steam-Man he had built eight years before. A ten-foot tall steam-vehicle, it was shaped like a man with a top hat. The driver sat in the hat. With spiked feet, it could move as fast as locomotive. Its arms could lift great weights and were versatile enough to kill a bear or a buffalo. The Steam-Man's main drawback was that, like a train, it needed to haul its own fuel and did so in a cart, which trailed behind it. This hampered its mobility. Brainerd had been redesigning the engine so that it would use a more efficient fuel than wood, such as whale oil or petroleum.

Passepartout had a horrifying vision of battalions of metallic juggernauts barreling through the French countryside, rolling over the French army and crushing the life and spirit of his beloved country. He became determined more than ever to not let Johnny Brainerd fall into this Santer's hands.

Santer gestured for a couple of his henchmen to move towards the hill and asked with some impatience, "So are you going to give us the boy, or not?"

"I think not, Monsieur!" Passepartout shot at the feet of the Indian who had moved closest to the hill. His shot clipped him against his shin, scoring a deep wound and possibly breaking the leg. His companion scurried back leaving the wounded man on the ground.

Seeing Passepartout's puzzled look, Brainerd said, "The one you winged is a Pawnee; the other one is a Cheyenne. Normally, they are enemies. They work for Mr. Santer, but not with each other, get it?"

"*Oui*", Passepartout murmured. He had run across the same phenomenon recently in his travels through India and Africa. The various native groups were forced into a peace not of their choosing through the imposition of imperial might, or through a mutual hatred of the Colonial powers. He suspected that if the Colonial powers were ever to leave Africa or India, the various groups would almost immediately be at one another's throats.

Over the next hour or so Passepartout and Santer played a game whereby Santer would try to catch Passepartout unaware and send one of his hired men to climb or skirt the hill. Passepartout sent them back with well-placed shots near their feet.

"You know, we aren't going to harm the boy," Santer shouted. "He is just going to work for us—and for a very good sum, too."

Brainerd shot Passepartout a sour look at that.

Santer approached once more. "How much do you make working for that Englishman? He seems to have forgotten you. I doubt if he will come after you!" Although Passepartout could not clearly see Santer's face in the waning afternoon light, there was no mistaking the guile in the next words. "Perhaps you are not as valuable to him as we thought. He holds you in such high regard that he abandons you in this land of savages... We can pay you three times your year's salary if you help us out. Give us the boy and, when you catch up with Fogg, make certain he does not make it back in time to win his bet. Get a little payback for leaving you out in the Great American Desert."

His curiosity piqued, Passepartout could not help but ask, "Why are you so interested in stopping Monsieur Fogg. You cannot be members of the Reform Club?"

"Do you really think the wager is confined to Herr Fogg and that decadent club? *Nein*! The betting has spread over the world. Herr Doktor Schultze has bet against Fogg for quite a sum of money and has taken steps to ensure that the Englishman fails."

Because of the various setbacks that Fogg had encountered upon his voyage, Passepartout had come to believe that a conspiracy created by the Reform Club existed to stop him. For a time, he had believed that their fellow traveler Fix was an agent of the Reform Club, until Fix had revealed that he was member of Scotland Yard on Fogg's trail for a bank robbery.

Passepartout realized now that such a conspiracy did exist, although not specifically from the Reform Club. This Herr Doktor Schultz, through his agents, was probably behind both the Indian attack and the damaged bridge that had nearly stopped the train at Medicine Bow, Wyoming. He wondered if the annoying Colonel Stamp Proctor who had challenged Fogg to a duel was also an agent of this Herr Doktor Schultze.

As the afternoon Sun waned, Santer grew more crafty; he had his hired renegades crawl up the hill on their bellies, making them harder to see and harder to hit. Passepartout responded to this new challenge by also being bolder. He stood on his knees and blasted at the areas near the Indians until he either scored a hit or drove them back. The ammunition emptied from the bags at a furious rate.

Santer had counted upon this. "Herr Passepartout, you cannot hold out much longer. I know how much ammunition Hans and Fritz had. Soon, you will have none and then, *mein freund*, it will be the curtains for you. Give us the boy now, and we will let you leave with your life."

Passepartout counted the remaining bullets and made his decision.

"Pardon me for being blunt, Monsieur Brainerd, but can you run with your condition?"

"You mean, do I lurch and limp like Quasimodo?" Johnny Brainerd answered with a wry smile.

"*Oui*," Passepartout answered, coloring with embarrassment.

"My gait is fairly normal, although the weight of my hump throws my balance a little to the left. Why do you ask? Are we going to make a run for it?"

"I suggest that you do so, Monsieur. I will use what little ammunition I have to hold them off so you can get away as far as you can under the cover of darkness."

Brainerd shook his head and set his chin firmly. "I will not leave you to be butchered by these savages."

While Passepartout admired the young man's spirit, he tried to reason with him and get the young man to accept the reality of the situation. However, Brainerd remained adamant in his refusal to leave Passepartout. His nobility left Passepartout with a moral dilemma.

When Santer and his men overwhelmed their position, as they were certain to do, Passepartout had meant to save one bullet to use on himself rather than be subjected to the tender mercies of the renegades. However, he knew he could not allow Brainerd to fall into their hands either. Although the young inventor would not be killed, he would no doubt be severely tortured until he used his creative genius for this Herr Doktor Schultze. France would certainly be the first target of the madman's quest for domination and so, the first nation to be crushed by Brainerd's juggernauts.

Although Passepartout did not much care for the current leaders of his country, despite his exile, he was still a patriot and still considered himself an agent of France, as he had been for years.

While a young itinerant street singer, Passepartout had aided Chief Inspector Gevrol on several occasions. Chevalier Dupin had also called upon Passepartout's aid. When he was still a child, Dupin had put him in the circus to hone his natural acrobatic and acting abilities.

As Dupin's agent, Passepartout had, while posing as a gymnasium teacher, uncovered and thwarted a Prussian plot to assassinate Napoleon III. Later, while working as a fireman, he had, at Dupin's request, investigated and stopped an arson ring. His efforts were brought to the attention of his imperial majesty and

Napoleon III had personally requested him to undertake a delicate assignment in 1867, which, through no fault of his own, he had failed. As a consequence, he had been exiled.

Passepartout's exile had meant that he was unable to be present to defend France when Germany had invaded. Although Napoleon III had fallen from power, Dupin had informed him that the new government viewed his former agents with suspicion. If Passepartout returned home, he would have an unpleasant welcome. The Frenchman knew that this suspicion would eventually subside, but, until then, he was still effectively exiled.

Monsieur Dupin had suggested that he seek employment with Monsieur Fogg, having known somehow that Fogg would dismiss his previous valet. Although he did not know how Dupin had foreseen the trip around the world, Passepartout realized that he had been sent to aid and guard Fogg,

Although Passepartout considered his connection to the French government finished, he still wanted to do what was best for his country. Despite not being able to return to his homeland, Passepartout had no desire to see it crushed beneath the iron heels of a voracious Germany.

The Sun set and Passepartout realized that, if any rescue were forthcoming, it would have already arrived. He remained convinced that for the sake of France, Jack Brainerd could not fall into Doktor Schultze' steely hands.

So resolved, Passepartout braced himself for the final act. He carefully counted his shots until only two bullets were left. One for Brainerd, and one for himself. Passepartout comforted himself with knowledge that he would not have to live with the consequences of this heinous act; at least, not for very long. Blissfully unaware of what Passepartout planned, Brainerd smiled encouragingly at him, despite knowing that their situation was all but hopeless.

Passepartout closed his eyes and gathered his will to quickly swing the rifle around and shoot Brainerd before his conscience got the better hand, and before Brainerd realized that Passepartout had betrayed him.

A horrendous scream startled Passepartout and his hand twitched, firing the rifle. Passepartout cried "*Mon Dieu!*" as the bullet left the gun.

Tired of the stand off, one of Santer's Indians had decided to make a charge up the hill. He streaked upward screaming a war cry, his spear and tomahawk poised to strike. Fortune's hand guided the unaimed shot, which plowed through the charging brave's chest.

Biting his tongue in self-mortification, Passepartout cursed himself for having wasted one of the two remaining bullets. The deed he knew needed done was going to be even harder to perform now. Passepartout would not only have to live with the guilt of his act, but certainly the enraged Santer would allow his savage minions to do what they wished to him. Doubtless he would suffer for untold hours or days under the cruel ministrations of their barbaric artistry. Yet Passepartout would gladly suffer the tortures of the damned, if it meant that France would live!

Passepartout had once knifed an old man in the back, but never suffered a second's qualm over the act. The old man had been about to torch an orphanage and would have killed dozens of children, not out of malice or hatred, but simply because they were in the way. Yet, killing Brainerd was different. It was an expedient elimination; the sort of killing Passepartout had once vowed never to do. Each time he broke the vow, he died a little himself.

Santer screamed a long string of words that Passepartout could not translate, yet he understood their meaning. Since he knew Passepartout was out of ammunition, Santer told the braves to capture them. As a howl went up from the slopes below, Passepartout bit the inside of his cheeks, he turned, aimed the gun at Johnny Brainerd's head and fired.

The bullet struck the ground about a foot from Brainerd's prone head. Tears stung Passepartout's eyes as he cursed his weakness. He could not bring himself to kill this innocent young man, even though he knew that it could mean the extinction of France.

Brainerd gazed up at Passepartout with a wistful smile on his face; his eyes glimmered with compassion and understanding. Passepartout immediately realized that Brainerd knew that Passepartout had intended to kill him and had understood why. Shame and guilt flared over Passepartout and he turned away from the young man to face the coming onslaught

Suddenly, from out of the night, thunder cracked, and cracked again. At each crack, one of the dim, night-blurred figures in Santer's mob fell. Several voices shouted: "Inya-Nape!" or "Winnetou!"

Passepartout strained to peer through the moonlit darkness until he saw a silvery glint off to the west. His eyes adjusted to the dark and he saw two riders galloping across the plain. One was an Indian dressed in buckskins who rode a horse so black it shone silver in the night. The other rider was a white man, also dressed in buckskins, but wearing some sort of mask across his eyes. Both fired rifles at the Indians who had been charging up the hill. Their rifles seemed to have an endless supply of ammunition. The rapid and continuous gouted flames reflected on the glossy coats of the horses, briefly making them steeds of fire.

A cloud of dust and snow rising behind them, the horses galloped across the plain with such a speed his vision in the dim light had trouble keeping up with them. The Indian raised his rifle and shouted, "*A he ya eh Silberbüchse!*"

As his friend reloaded, the Indian charged forward and fired his rifle with deadly accuracy from a full gallop. Santer's men either scattered or gathered their nerve to attack the new arrivals.

Passepartout was surprised when the masked white man jumped off of his horse without his rifle and fought the Indians with just his bare hands. Yet, at every swing of his fists, an Indian brave sank to the ground unconscious or dead.

Brainerd danced with excitement. "Mr. Henry started using my designs after all!" Brainerd stiffened after a second and peered intently down the hill, moving his head back and forth, "Santer. Where is Santer?"

"Behind you, hunchback!"

Passepartout whirled about. A burly Indian strolled up over the summit holding a rifle on Brainerd and Passepartout. No stranger to disguise, Passepartout realized that the Indian was a white man with dyed skin and warpaint.

Santer smiled as he aimed his gun at Passepartout's stomach. "You should have taken my earlier offer Frenchman, now you will die slowly and painfully"

Brainerd moved in front of the rifle, forcing Santer to jerk his rifle aside to miss him. As it was, the blast seared Brainerd's left shoulder.

Brushing past Brainerd, Passepartout attacked Santer with a kick to the midsection. But Santer was faster than he appeared, and he used the gun to block the kick. However, the kick knocked the rifle out of his hands. Passepartout advanced, bouncing on his toes and heels. Santer pulled a bowie knife out of a sheath on his back and kept the Frenchman at bay with a series of feints and lunges. He scored a slash against Passepartout's chest.

Johnny Brainerd tried to rescue Passepartout once again, thus proving the adage that often genius and common sense do not go hand in hand.

Santer grabbed Brainerd and placed the bowie knife against his cheek.

"I have to bring this *kruppel* to Herr Doktor Schultze alive, but not necessarily in one piece. He has to be able to talk and hear and see and think. Everything else is fair game, like his ears and cheeks. Tie yourself up and I'll not carve up the boy."

Brainerd slammed his head backwards and onto Santer's nose. The knife slashed Johnny's cheek as he jerked away from Santer. Passepartout leapt at Santer knocking him to the ground. They wrestled for the knife. Santer's knee caught Passepartout in the groin and knocked the air out of his lungs. The villain's knife was inches away from the Frenchman's neck when it suddenly flew from Santer's nerveless fingers.

An arrow had transfixed Santer's shoulder, nailing him to the ground. Passepartout pushed away from the villain and rolled to his feet. The masked white man and his Indian companion had arrived. The Indian had knocked another arrow, aiming at Santer's chest.

The short, muscular white man put his hand in front of the bow, "No, Winnetou, do not kill a downed foe, it is not very Christian"

"Very well, Sharli, I will not kill him." The bow sang and an arrow transfixed the other shoulder, nailing that side of Santer into the frozen ground.

"Damn you, redskin, I have a bullet with your name on it!" Santer screamed writhing in agony. His eyes rolled back and he slumped insensible. The falling snow blanketed his still form.

Passepartout felt a flash of shame for enjoying the man's suffering, but only a flash. With a small smile, he turned to Jack Brainerd and said, "Who is that masked man and who is his friend?"

Brainerd laughed, "It's not who you might think. Actually, that's not a mask at all—it's my night-glasses. This here is Charlie, known as Old Shatterhand to the westerners and Indians. His friend is Winnetou of the Mescalero. I met them through Mr. Henry, a gunsmith and inventor in St. Louis who crafted some of my inventions. I designed a rifle that has 25 shots and Mr. Henry made it for Charlie. I also designed these spectacles that allow a person to see at night. How do they work, Charlie?"

"Fair, but not great, Jack." Charlie spoke and to Passepartout's shock, he also had a Germanic accent. "People and animals look like torches against a black night, but they hurt the eyes something fierce." Charlie removed the mask, which was actually a curved band of black glass with a nose bridge. "Henry sent for us when you were kidnapped and we have been trailing you for the last couple of days. We best get you back to St. Louis, and get this fella back to his train." Charlie pulled a half smoked cigar out of his cap and winked at Passepartout as he lit it. Talking around the cigar he said, "Winnetou's got a bet on your Mr. Fogg to win!

Winnetou's hard black eyes bore directly into Passepartout's eyes. "Winnetou be very angry with palefaces if he loses bet. We go now."

Although the stone of Winnetou's face did not move, Passepartout saw a merry twinkle in Old Shatterhand's eyes. Winnetou might have been less than serious.

They left Santer still transfixed to the ground, deep splotches of red staining the snow covering his upper arms and chest.

Winnetou's and Old Shatterhand's lightning-fast horses caught up with two of the errant Indian horses. As Passepartout and Brainerd mounted, shouts and curses came from the top of the hill. Santer stood screaming invectives at them. Although arrows still transfixed his shoulders, he loudly vowed vengeance on Winnetou and his family.

Santer pulled the arrows from his shoulders. He stood, a lone figure in the white expanse, screaming in pain and rage. With a curse, he threw the bloody arrows in Winnetou's direction. Santer's display went unnoticed by Winnetou and Shatterhand for he was only a speck on the horizon by this time.

Shortly after leaving the hills, they encountered another band of Indians, some Arapaho. The Arapaho had three people with them whom Passepartout recognized as his fellow train passengers. The train passengers were bewildered, frightened and confused about what had happened to them.

After a moment's conversation Shatterhand told Passepartout that the Arapaho had come across a small group of Cheyenne and Sioux, who were passing around bottles of firewater while taking turns cuffing and kicking some white men who were bound hand and foot. The drunken Indians also poked them with spears or threatened them with knives to great hilarity. When the Arapaho entered their camp, the renegades had either fled or attempted to fight.

After a short skirmish with the renegades, the Arapaho had picked up the nearly frozen palefaces with the intention of taking them to Fort Kearney. The Arapaho had been at peace with the bluecoats and did not want war again. The

Arapaho agreed to accompany Old Shatterhand, the enemy of their enemies, the Kiowa, to Fort Kearney.

Passepartout knew that Monsieur Fogg must have departed without him, and understood why. Fogg stood to lose everything if he lost the bet. Passepartout vowed to catch up if he could and double his effort to help Monsieur Fogg win the bet. For when Fogg won, Herr Doktor Schultze would lose a fortune. Passepartout hoped it would stop his mad plans to make Germany a world-conquering nation.

Winnetou broke Passepartout's reverie as he pointed to a cloud of white fog with a dark center rolling in from the east. "Cavalry comes."

"Well, this is where we part, Monsieur Passepartout. Them boys look like they are out for blood. The cavalry has a tendency to shoot first and sort things out later. I don't want to end up in a shooting match with some of my fellow Christians, so I will bid you adieu." Old Shatterhand bowed his head in Passepartout's direction and turned his horse towards the west.

Following Old Shatterhand, Johnny Brainerd waved goodbye to the Frenchman who replied in kind. The band of Arapaho joined Old Shatterhand and Winnetou leaving Passepartout and the three other passengers behind.

Brainerd's departure brought a slight sting to Passepartout's eyes. He had grown to be very fond of the young man in the past few hours so renewed guilt flowed through him over what he had nearly done to keep him out of Doktor Schultze' hands. Passepartout was glad that they had safely escaped the clutches of Steel City. He hoped that Brainerd would be safe in Old Shatterhand's custody. He shuddered to think at what devastation Germany could cause if Prussian efficiency was married to such naïve genius.

The United States Cavalry soon surrounded Passepartout and the three other passengers. None other than Monsieur Fogg led the Cavalry!

A mixture of elation and guilt ran through Passepartout when he learned that Fogg had paid the soldiers $5000 to rescue him, and by personally undertaking the mission, had jeopardized his chances of winning the bet upon which his entire fortune had been staked.

The cavalry and Fogg were under the impression that the Indians had turned and run when they saw the soldiers, freeing their captives as they made haste to escape. Not wanting to depreciate his master's sacrifices, Passepartout omitted telling him that the rescue had not been necessary and that the Indians that had turned away from the Cavalry had been friendly ones. He merely told Fogg that he had overpowered three of his captors; Monsieur Verne, elaborated, as he often did.

With the hindsight of history, the stereotypical characters of the Asian detective and the Asian villainous mastermind are more interesting insights into the way popular fiction viewed Asians in less enlightened times, than full-blown, credible representatives of their culture. Pete Rawlik has chosen to gather here five of the most well-known figures of that sub-genre—or, four, since Pete believes that the Mr. Moto of the books and the cinema are two different persons, albeit brothers—for one last confrontation on the eve of World War II...

Pete Rawlik: *Before the War, Five Dragons Roar*

The Pacific Ocean, West of the Territory of Hawaii, December 1939

It was an hour before dawn, and the flagship of the Oceanic Steamship Company, the SS *Claridon*, crashed through the waves, sending a spray of dark water over the bow. The five figures that had arranged themselves on the deck flinched as the cold wind and water whipped around them. There were a Japanese couple, a man and a woman, and two Chinese men. Several yards away stood another man, also of Japanese descent.

The Japanese man with his back to the ocean was suave and well-groomed, with hair cut in the Prussian manner that framed a pair of round wire-rimmed glasses. His black suit blended into the wicked-looking pistol he held in his right hand. Moonlight reflected off his teeth, which some time ago had been replaced with gold duplicates. His smile widened as his partner, a stern and serious-looking young Japanese woman in a conservative black dress, spoke:

"A very clever trap, Mister Chan," there were tones of both respect and sarcasm in the woman's voice. "Tell me if you would, in the interest of science, what mistake did I make?"

Lieutenant Chan shifted his considerable weight and grinned slyly. It was as much a communication to the two foreign agents facing him as it was to the former FBI agent to his left and the other Japanese.

"Your attempts to divert our attention to other suspects were expertly executed, Dr. Yoshimuta," he said. "Unfortunately, both the people you attempted to frame, Mr. Gottfried Venger and Mrs. Nora Charles, had alibis for the night in question. They were engaged in a rather loud and somewhat vicious argument concerning the recent invasion of Poland by Germany. Mrs. Charles was quite enraged by Mr. Venger's support of the German Chancellor. Her husband spent the rest of the evening calming her down with several dozen martinis. Mr. Venger ended the night in the ship's lounge playing cards with Mr. Cranston and Mr. Reid."

"Those men could be lying," she proffered.

Chan's partner, James Wong, waved his gun menacingly. "They could be, Doctor, but we have our reasons for taking them at their word." He was taller than his compatriots, with graying hair and a thin haggard look that made him look older than he was. His voice was cultured and betrayed a cosmopolitan upbringing. "Only you and your friend Mr. Aratomoto—Ichirou Aratomoto that is—had both the means and opportunity to murder the aging Mr. Jak Kim back in Honolulu. Though we are still puzzled as to the motive."

The man standing to the side, nearly equidistant from the opposing factions, cautiously raised his arm. A careful observer would have noticed that he bore a striking resemblance to the man standing next to Dr. Yoshimuta, whom Wong had identified as "Ichirou Aratamoto." The glasses and haircut were the same, as were the general shape of the face and shoulders. Indeed, the differences between the two were only superficial. Kentarou Aratamoto wore a white suit, and was slightly heavier than Ichirou, and he seemed to have all his own teeth.

"Perhaps James, if you please, I can offer an explanation," he said. "Mr. Kim was not as he claimed from Korea, but was in actuality Japan's master spy, Oka Yuma."

His black-suited double, Ichirou, shook his head, though he was careful to keep the gun steady. "You will forgive me, brother," he said, "but I think you would agree that Oka Yuma's days as Japan's master spy were over long ago. He was a relic of a less sophisticated time, the memory of which the Empire would like to erase. It was most unfortunate that he had to be... liquidated."

"Lovely people you are thinking of working for, Kentarou," the prematurely aged Wong sneered. "Killing a man just because he was old."

Doctor Yoshimuta laughed sinisterly. "No, Mr. Wong, I suppose you wouldn't think of us as very nice people. We don't have that luxury. The European powers that have for so long held sway in Asia are failing, falling, fleeing. There is a void and Japan intends to fill it, first in China and then... well, we shall see, won't we? For this, we need the best. We need men who are capable, daring, unafraid, loyal. It has been many years since Kentarou has been to Japan, but he is still a child of the Rising Sun. His mother was a princess, imperial blood flows through his veins. He will come with us and, together, the Aratamoto brothers will help lead the Empire to its rightful place."

Chan lowered his gun. "Kentarou, is this what you want?" he asked. "Who was it that tried to kill you in Port Said? And when you were sick and I took your place in Panama, who was it that tried to kill me? Do you think it would have made a difference if it had been you?"

Wong chimed in, "We're your friends Kentarou. I got you that job at Berkford University, teaching Criminalistics remember? We've worked together. You've just moved to Hawaii, bought a house on Punch Bowl Hill. Charlie got you a job training the state militia. Are you going to throw that all away because this man says he's your brother?"

Kentarou Aratamoto turned to face both Chan and Wong. "You misunderstand, James" he said. "This man, Ichirou, he is my brother, my older twin, born as I was in 1894 in San Francisco. Family honor requires that I owe him some measure of fidelity."

"I am not sure that Mr. Wong understands the concept of fidelity, Kentarou san," cautioned Dr. Yoshimuta. "After all, it was Fu Wong that terrorized the city of San Francisco during the summer of 1935. How many men did your brother kill, Mr. Wong?"

Unable to control himself Chan quoted a long forgotten aphorism, "Families sometimes like large trees, can bear bitter fruit."

Dr. Yoshimuta laughed sinisterly. "That applies to you as well, Mr. Chan. Tell me, before your mother died, did she tell you who your father was?"

Chan tried to stifle his response, but she caught the moment of doubt on his face.

"I see; she didn't, but you've discovered that little secret on your own? Michael Croft is really such a transparent alias, and so easily checked. All the Manchurian had to do was to review the British peerage."

Wong straightened up. "What has the Manchurian to do with this?" he asked. "Is he involved?"

Now it was Ichirou Aratamoto's turn to be sly. "You will find, Mr. Wong, that when it comes to Asia, there is little that the Manchurian does not involve himself in, sometimes to our detriment, sometimes to our benefit. In this case, our recent campaign in Nanking gained us access to one of his strongholds. There, we found references to many things, including the lineage of Mister Chan, and of course your own plans to return to China as the Devil Doctor's ally. We assume that you have achieved what your brother could not, that you have all twelve of the Confucian coins; that you shall travel to Keelat and take up the mantle of Fen Chu? Will you seek to avenge the death of your wife Win Lee on the whole of the Empire of Japan?"

Wong's face turned to stone. "You should not have killed her, Ichirou. She would have given you the map."

Ichirou looked puzzled for a moment. "Oh, I see, it is very funny. I should tell you sometime the story of that map, and the trouble it caused. Many people died trying to find that oil. But you misunderstand; I did not kill Win Lee. Her own father did that, when he learned that she had married you, a man of low standing, a half-breed who freely served foreign masters."

Suddenly Kentarou was in motion, "*James! No!*" he shouted.

But it was too late. Enraged by Ichirou's words, James Lee Wong's gun fired a barrage of bullets at the Japanese agent who dove to the side, grabbing Dr. Yoshimuta and whisking her over the side of the boat into the darkness beyond.

Chan ran to the railing, moving at a speed one would not have thought possible for his size. As he reached the edge of the boat, he led with his gun, usually reluctant to engage in battle, but for once eager to use a weapon other than his mind. He peered over and quickly turned away. Then, like a roaring freight train, he was suddenly on top of Wong and Kentarou, whisking them back in the other direction.

Two minutes later, the deck erupted in fire, twisted metal and wooden splinters that showered down on the three men like an avalanche of destruction.

As the crew dealt with the flames and damage, the three detectives licked their wounds.

"They escaped?" queried Wong.

Chan nodded. "It was waiting for them, a small submarine with a very large gun."

Kentarou Aratamoto was attempting to brush the larger pieces of debris off of his suit. "Please, did you really think I was going to go with them?" he asked.

Wong found that a rather large metal splinter had pierced the skin between his forefinger and thumb. "It was a definite possibility," he replied. "As they said, my own family isn't exactly without its bad seeds. My nephew Richard is following in my footsteps, but my niece is making quite a reputation as San Francisco's Dragon Queen. So when you ask me whether or not I thought you would go with them, I have to say that I thought it was a definite possibility."

Chan found his hat and emptied it of debris. "I think we should perhaps discuss a more serious issue. Must explain to Oceanic Steamship Company and the captain about the hole in the bow of ship, and then tell the passengers that we must go back to Honolulu."

Kentarou smiled, "You are not concerned over what Oka Yuma, Yoshimuta and my brother were doing in Pearl Harbor?"

Chan smiled that sly smile. "Sixty-five summers has taught me much, mostly that knowledge like hole in trousers; will be revealed when time least convenient. Am more concerned with thought that James will be leaving us for dubious venture."

James Wong hung his head. "Sadly, my path is not yet clear. I have all twelve coins, but not yet the will to wield the power they bestow. Right now, though, I could use some breakfast."

Chan nodded. "Captain tells me that ship's cook, Egg Shen, has an excellent supply of Chinese delicacies."

As the Sun rose over the stern, the three men staggered down the deck in search of a warm cup of oolong tea.

Also on the eve of WWII, but taking place on the other side of the globe, this confrontation between heroes and villains (and that ultimately depends on which side of the political chessboard one stands) pits the mysterious Ghost of the Louvre against the French King of Detectives (both creations of Arthur Bernède) and one American Super-Detective...

Joshua Reynolds: *The Carolingian Stone*

Paris, 1940

It was 1940 and night spread across the City of Lights like a shroud. Only the gentle murmur of the Seine broke the quiet of the Rue d'Auteuil, where the growl of motor cars had been banned by government edict. Even the bright lights that set the rest of Parish awash in a fairy-tale glow were absent here, leaving the entire street dark and uninviting.

Bare feet padded across the tiles of the rooftops, their path unhampered by either the darkness or the quiet. With a grunt, their owner sprang across the gap between two buildings in a display of almost simian agility. A bronze hand shot out, latching onto the brick of a chimney and the roof-runner swung about to face his pursuers.

Clad in black, their faces hidden behind grotesque masks, the three hunters would not have been out of place at the Grand Guignol. But the weapons they carried were anything but harmless props and their wary movements bespoke trained killers rather than mummers. Clinging to the chimney, almost invisible in the darkness, their prey watched them, his dark eyes taking in their every twitch and gesture and filing it away for future investigation. As they passed near him, he slunk around and up onto the chimney and sprang off with a predatory grace, tackling the closest of them. A powerful fist cracked a false face and bruised the flesh behind, sending one would-be assassin rolling limply down the slope of the roof.

His two companions spun, raising their weapons. But their target was already up and moving, the downed man's weapon slung over his shoulder. They hesitated for a moment, suddenly uncertain. Then one cursed and descended carefully towards their unconscious compatriot. The other wavered, and then followed.

Their prey crouched not far away on the peaked roof of a garret apartment, watching them. He moved not a muscle until they had departed, their dazed burden in tow. He allowed himself the briefest of smiles and then looked down at the roof. Noiselessly, he scampered down the peak and, clinging upside down to the wainscoting, he picked the lock on the window. Then he slithered inside, landing on the carpet in a crouch.

A light snapped on, nearly blinding him. The click of a pistol being cocked froze him in place. As his vision cleared, he saw an older man, spare of frame with a lupine leanness and clad in a dressing gown sitting in a battered chesterfield armchair in the corner of the attic room. The old man held a pistol in one unshaking hand, and the look in his eyes said that he would not hesitate to put it to use. "I am disappointed," he said. "Is my word not enough? Do you have so little faith in the power of your threat?"

"That's a Galand, isn't it?" the intruder said, relaxing slightly. "1870, I believe? Double action, nine millimeter. The loading mechanism is a bit complicated, but otherwise a fine weapon. A bit out of date, though, for my taste."

The old man's eyebrow shot up. "I am comfortable with its function," he said. "More so, I dare say, than you are with that cumbersome tool you carry. Drop it, if you please."

"Gladly," the other man said, unslinging the weapon he'd taken from his attacker and letting it thump onto the thick Persian carpet that covered the floor. The old man peered at it curiously, and then directed his hawk-like gaze back up at his uninvited guest. He was younger than his host by two decades and tall and broad with an athlete's build and he was clad in loose linen trousers and a baggy sweater of the type often worn by merchant seamen. His feet were bare, but he showed no sign of being uncomfortable.

After a moment, Chantecoq sniffed. "American. You spent some time in the Southwest of that country. The weapon isn't yours as your hands are too large for it. Who are you?"

"Anthony." The man smiled, his sun-bronzed face splitting in a white grin. "Jim Anthony. It's a pleasure to meet you, Monsieur Chantecoq."

The old man blinked. "You recognize me?"

"A man in my trade wouldn't be worth much if he didn't recognize the King of Detectives," Anthony said, dropping onto his haunches with an ease that the old man found slightly off-putting. Hands dangling between his knees, he looked around the apartment, taking in the overstuffed bookshelves and sloppy paper piles. It looked like the residence of a scholar or academic, until you realized that most of the reading material was devoted to identifying types of cigarette ash and bullet calibers, as well as a dozen other topics more suited to a criminalist than to a forgetful professor.

"Anthony, you said?" Chantecoq peered at him and gave a grunt. "Hmm. James Anthony, heir to the Anthony fortune; philanthropist, amateur journalist and murderist of international repute. They call you the—ah, what is it?—the Super-Detective?" Chantecoq's lips quirked in a smile.

Anthony grimaced. "That's the tag they hung on me, yes. And I hardly think owning a newspaper makes me an amateur journalist."

"I was referring to the series of articles you wrote pseudonymously for the *London Times* in which you decry the current political tolerance extended to

253

Germany. Very well reasoned, I thought, without being altogether jingoistic." Chantecoq leaned back in his chair and uncocked the pistol. "Please have a seat."

"I'm quite comfortable, thank you," Anthony said. "I won't ask how you knew that was me."

"Then I won't bother explaining. The rifle is German-made, I notice." Chantecoq gestured with the pistol. "Some type of carbine... a Mauser, I think."

"It's a modified Kar-98k," Anthony said. He tapped the barrel, which had been seemingly replaced with what looked like a thick length of smooth-cut pipe. "A noise suppression system, to go with a barrel altered to allow for a different type of ammunition."

"What kind?" Chantecoq said. He reached into his dressing gown and pulled out a cigarette case. Popping it open, he extracted one and popped it between his lips.

"I was hoping you could tell me, actually. It's why I came to see you." Anthony frowned. "I would have been here earlier, and by a more civilized route, but I was followed."

"Followed? By whom?" Chantecoq said, a lit match held inches from the tip of his cigarette.

Anthony tapped the gun again. "Three men, carrying these. And wearing masks. I think I convinced them to give up the chase though."

"Masks?" Chantecoq said, slowly lighting his cigarette. He puffed quietly for a moment and then said, "Where were you coming from?"

"The Louvre."

Chantecoq froze. "Why?"

"A series of unusual events, why else?" Anthony shrugged. "I'm not surprised you haven't heard. The police have been keeping quite a tight lid on things. Four nights ago, a night-watchman died in the museum. The cause was apparently shock." Anthony made a face. "The other watchmen reported seeing a mysterious figure when they responded to his scream... a figure that vanished in a flash of light. The night after that, they saw the figure again, only this time, they saw it in three different places in the Louvre." Anthony held up three fingers. "All at the same time. The night before last, another guard died, again supposedly of shock. A fellow named de Felipone, the current Director of the Louvre, called for me then, knowing I was in Paris and that this sort of thing is my line. Ostensibly, I'm investigating the haunting, but since it's connected to the deaths..." He looked at Chantecoq. "And I wondered why they hadn't called for you."

Chantecoq was silent. Anthony leaned forward, his eyes narrowing. "They did, didn't they?" he said.

"Get out please." Chantecoq settled back in his chair. "And take that rifle with you. Go as you came in. Like as not, they haven't seen you yet."

"What? Who? Monsieur, I..." Anthony began. He rose to his feet and the pistol in Chantecoq's hand rose with him. The elderly detective cocked the weapon.

"Get out, please," he said quietly.

"I came to get your help, Monsieur."

"Then you have failed, through no fault of your own. I am sorry, but I cannot take the risk."

"Risk what?" Anthony said.

"Risk *who*," Chantecoq corrected. "In my desk is an envelope. Get it."

Anthony did so with haste, Chantecoq's pistol tracking him the entire time. He found the envelope and opened it, extracting the handful of photographs that were inside. A woman and a man, both middle-aged, sat outside a café. In another picture, the same couple was window-shopping in the Rue de Rivoli. He looked at Chantecoq. Before he could ask the obvious question, the other man said, "My daughter Colette and her husband. Someone sent these pictures to me as a warning. They wanted me to know that they can get to her—at any time."

"Who?"

"Turn the envelope over." Anthony did so and grunted as he saw the strange image stamped on the torn flap. In almost every way, it was an exact two-dimensional reproduction of the grotesque masks worn by his attackers earlier in the evening. He looked at Chantecoq. The old detective said, simply, "Belphegor."

"*Gesundheit*," Anthony said.

Chantecoq glared at the younger man. "It is not a joke," he snapped.

"Sorry. Who—or what—is Belphegor?"

"A curse." Chantecoq looked away. "One I thought had claimed its final victim 13 years ago, almost to the day."

"The Simone Desroches case," Anthony said. "That's why I wanted your help though... There are similarities..."

"Of course there are." Chantecoq made a sharp gesture. "It is Belphegor. Go. Now."

"I don't think so. Who were those men following me?"

"I have no idea," Chantecoq said bitterly. "I do not want to know."

"We can protect your daughter," Anthony said.

"I am protecting her," Chantecoq snarled. "Now, will you go? Or must I force you?"

In reply, Anthony lunged towards the older man like a tiger. As he tackled him to the floor, chair and all, the space that Chantecoq's head had occupied was split by the passage of something solid and deadly. The plaster on the wall cracked and dust drifted down. Anthony sprang to his feet, Chantecoq's pistol in hand, and raced to the open window.

The full Moon had turned the rooftops silver and Anthony caught sight of a tall, thin figure as it raced away, a black cloak flaring around it like the wings of some great bat. He took aim, but resisted the urge to fire. He stepped back from the window, eyes blazing with frustration. "I guess they didn't give up after all," he said, his tone half-apologetic. "And I'll bet they haven't now either." He moved quickly to the closest bookshelf and toppled it in front of the window, effectively blocking it.

Chantecoq pounded the floor with a fist. "My daughter! You have doomed her!" he snarled, scrambling to his feet. Anthony stepped back, his hands raised. Old, the King of Detectives might have been, but he was still intimidating, even to a man of Anthony's size.

"Monsieur, we can have someone protecting her within minutes, if you'll just let me borrow your phone!"

Chantecoq swiped a hand towards a cabinet. Anthony hurried to it and pulled out a phone. Swiftly, he rang the hotel he was staying at and rattled off instructions to the voice which answered. Then he hung up and turned back to Chantecoq. The old man had gotten dressed while his back had been turned, and his lean frame was clad in an immaculate suit of expensive, if slightly out of fashion, cut. "Who did you call?" he said, his voice now composed.

"My hotel. I have a friend staying in a room near mine, a fellow named Tom Gentry. An excellent man in a tight spot. When he rings back, I'll have him see to your daughter's safety."

"I trust her husband, Jack, immensely," Chantecoq said. "He is a good man. Strong. And Colette is stronger still, in her way." He took a deep breath. "But I could not risk them." He bent over the desk and scrawled out an address on a loose sheet of paper. "This is their address."

"I understand," Anthony said. "More than you know."

"Yes. How is Senator Colquitt's daughter, by the by?" Chantecoq said, straightening his tie. Anthony blinked and Chantecoq smiled crookedly. "I am not a hermit, Monsieur Anthony. Merely old."

Anthony chuckled and extended the butt of the Galand to its owner. "Isolation has its advantages."

"And disadvantages." Chantecoq turned as the phone rang. Anthony snatched it up and answered. As he spoke to his man, Chantecoq scooped up the rifle and ejected the ammunition clip. When Anthony hung up for a second time, Chantecoq said, "Look at this."

Anthony took the clip. "Tom is heading to their home now, and he'll call the police and let them know. I have special dispensation from the Sûreté after that business with the Vampires in Marseille, so it should be no difficulty in arranging a protective detail. Unless they've been shadowing me since I got to Paris, our mysterious masked enemies will have no idea what Tom looks like, or who he is. It should be easy for him to get the drop on them."

"You have much faith in your subordinates."

"I have faith in my friends," Anthony replied, examining the clip. "Are these bullets? They look like they've been baked out of flour."

"Not flour. Something similar, however." Chantecoq bounced one of the bullets on his palm. "Water soluble, I'd guess."

Anthony went to the wall where the sniper's shot had ended up. Though the plaster was cracked, there was no sign of a hole. Taking a penknife off of the desk, he traced the crack and pried a small soggy lump free of the wall. He made to grab it and Chantecoq hissed, "Don't!" Anthony glanced at him. Chantecoq held up the bullet in his palm. "Smell, eh?"

Anthony did, and grimaced. "Is that what I think it is?"

"The delicate odor of the *Aminata Muscaria*. A hallucinogenic weed. The bullets are crafted from it. On impact, they release their deadly cargo. Diluted, it causes hallucinations. In its concentrated form, it is positively lethal." Chantecoq placed the bullet back in the clip and carefully wiped his palm with a handkerchief.

"I tangled with a Russian who smeared that stuff on his ammunition. Called them *Fear-Bullets*," Anthony said, hefting the rifle. "Why not use regular bullets, though?"

"Regular bullets leave obvious clues. But if a man dies of fright…?" Chantecoq shrugged. "A simple murder becomes something much more complex."

"And this phantom…?"

"Belphegor," Chantecoq interjected.

"Belphegor," Anthony said. "He—or she—Is behind it? That explains the dead men, I suppose."

"You tell me," Chantecoq said. "I have stayed well out of it. What have your investigations uncovered?"

"So far? Most of the museum employees think it is Simone Desroches' ghost come back to haunt the scene of her crime." Anthony sagged back and sat on the desk. Balancing the rifle on his palms, he examined it. "But there are similarities to the case from '27. There is no obvious sign of theft, or tampering, except in the Room…"

"Of Barbarous Gods," Chantecoq finished for him, stroking his chin. "Where two men have died; yes, I see what you mean."

"Add to it this rifle, which is German military issue. The modifications are even more worrying," Anthony said. He ran his fingers along the altered barrel. "The noise suppression system implies that killing was factored in to whatever plan is being played out here. Which implies a certain degree of ruthlessness." He looked up. "The masks aren't holiday rentals either. What happened to Simone Desroches' original outfit?"

"It was destroyed, I assume. But there were dozens of pictures of it in the press, and the statue itself is still there…"

"So someone, or several someones, have taken up Belphegor's mantle. They threatened you preemptively, knowing you'd recognize the similarities, and they're trying to kill me." Anthony stood and looked at the window. "But why kill the guards? What did the guards see that wouldn't have been put down to Simone Desroches' ghost?"

"We won't know unless we look for it ourselves," Chantecoq said, rubbing his hands together.

"We? Does that mean you'll be coming out of retirement then?"

"If my daughter is safe, there is no reason to do otherwise." Chantecoq patted the pistol now holstered beneath his arm. "Besides, this is one demon I intend to see exorcised personally." He looked at the broken window. "They may be waiting for us."

"Oh, almost certainly. Do you have a car?"

"*Oui*," Chantecoq said. "It is parked at the head of the street."

Anthony grinned. "Lovely. They'll be keeping watch on the street. So I'll go out the window."

Chantecoq blinked. Then he chuckled. "So I am to be bait then?"

"Yep," Anthony said.

"Ha! Be careful. I would hate for this partnership to be dissolved abruptly."

"Soul of discretion, me," Anthony said, giving him a salute. Then, as Chantecoq turned off the light, he shoved aside the bookcase and climbed out the window into the Parisian night. Slithering along the edge of the roof, he let his eyes adapt to the darkness. He saw shapes crouching like gargoyles nearby. He felt a flush of satisfaction... he had been right. They were waiting. Inching up, his fingers found the strap of his belt; composed of thick fibers culled from the South American jungles, the belt had the tensile strength of steel but the springiness of rubber. Its ends were weighted with polished river stones and when he pulled it free, it dangled in his grip like a bolo.

Below, on the street, Chantecoq was hurrying towards his car. As one, the men rose with clockwork military precision. There were three of them, as there had been earlier. He wondered if they were the same three. Two of them peeled off and began moving up the slope of the roof, likely searching for him. He grinned mirthlessly and sighted on the remaining assassin and began to whirl the belt over his head. He snapped his wrist forward and sent it slicing silently through the air. It caught the sniper around the throat and he reared up, clawing at his throat. Anthony was on him a moment later, clamping a wide, hard palm over the mouth and nose holes of the mask. Forcefully, he swung the man around and dashed him to the roof, rendering him unconscious. Then he stripped the bolo from around his neck and sighted on the next man.

They had both paused, backlit by the full Moon. He could see every contour of the gruesome masks they wore. Anthony let the bolo fly and one of the men tumbled back down the other side of the roof. The other froze momentarily, which was long enough for Anthony to snatch up the first killer's rifle and fire with the surety of trained marksman. He had learned the art of the rifle at the withered knee of his grandfather Mephito, a Comanche shaman with more white scalps to his credit than Anthony was entirely comfortable with.

The assassin was punched backwards off the roof, and Anthony lunged up and after him. Hopefully one of them was alive. As he reached the crest of the roof, he heard the hiss of a rifle and flung himself aside as the soft, poisonous bullets struck the spot where he'd been standing. The second assassin stood and tore the bolo from around his rifle barrel and fired again. Anthony sprang back and then sent the rifle in his hands spinning at his assailant. The man fell back and rolled off the roof with a despairing scream.

Anthony turned to the other, who lay sprawled on the slope, facedown. He turned him over and stripped the mask away, only to recoil in disgust. Death came in myriad forms, as swift and as certain as the tide, that much Anthony knew. But only rarely had he seen it take such an altogether unpleasant shape. The man's face was contorted into such an expression of abject terror that it was almost painful to look at. He was already rigid, half-curled into a ball, eyes wide, the veins and muscles of his neck bulging with eternal strain. Anthony rose to his feet, disgusted.

He returned to the other side of the roof, slid down it, and then dropped to the street with barely a moment of hesitation. His landing was a thing of feline smoothness. Chantecoq, sitting behind the wheel of his car, shook his head as Anthony trotted towards him. "I've only seen one other man pull a stunt like that, a man named Francis Ardan."

"Puts me in good company then," Anthony said, sliding into the passenger seat. "To the Louvre, and don't spare the horses."

Chantecoq proved to be a wheelman-par-excellence, and the Parisian traffic proved little obstacle. As the shape of the Louvre rose up over the Seine, however, the King of Detectives glanced at Anthony. "We are being followed."

"How long?"

"Since the Rue d'Auteuil." Then, apologetically, "I thought I could lose them. They are persistent however."

"At least, we know where they are," Anthony said. "What's the plan?"

"I thought you had a plan," Chantecoq said.

"Youth defers to age. Besides, you've been through this before."

Chantecoq grimaced. "Not quite. Simone Desroches and her co-conspirators were murderous, but not quite this organized."

"What was she looking for?" Anthony said.

"A treasure. One hidden in the statue of Belphegor."

"What was it?"

"Jewels, nothing more," Chantecoq shook his head. "But there was something else to it besides the so-called Valois Treasure. She never found it, determined as she was however. And she killed herself before I could pry it out of her. I know that it had to do with the mad scribblings of Queen Catherine's astrologer, Ruggieri. But just what it might have been... Who can say?"

"I'd wager our opponents know. Or at least suspect."

"Most likely. Which means we must find it first! *Merde*!" Chantecoq jerked the wheel with the speed of a man whose reflexes had been honed to a razor's edge. The black car narrowly missed them and careened wildly before it righted itself and set off in pursuit. Anthony twisted in his seat and then ducked down as the back window exploded.

"Looks like they've decided to stop following us," he said. "How far is the Louvre?"

"Just across the Pont du Carrousel!" Chantecoq said, jerking the wheel and causing the car to skim up onto the sidewalk as their pursuer tried again to ram them. "Obviously, they're trying to stop us from getting there in one piece!"

"Obviously," Anthony said blithely. A machine-gun chattered and lead wasps perforated the roof and back of Chantecoq's car. "Whatever is hidden in that statue must be important!"

A second car pulled up alongside them, the grim masks of the passengers glaring at them. Anthony cursed and kicked his door open, smashing it into the other car. As it drifted aside, he swung himself out and up onto the roof of the car. Holding onto the top of the door frame with one hand, he dug the other into his trouser pocket, extricating a handful of multi-colored pellets. The pellets contained chemicals of his own concoction, and could be mashed together to create instant smoke or even a choking fog. Without looking, he squeezed the pellets tight, popping them, and then hurled them into the second car as it drew close again. The fuming handful sped through the open window and soon enough the car was filled with purple smoke. It veered off and crashed through the window of a café, sending pedestrians fleeing.

A hornet of fire scraped across Anthony's shoulder and he was nearly flung from his tenuous perch. Falling flat onto the roof, he turned to see a gun-man hauling himself up out through a window on the remaining black car, a pis-tol clutched in one hand. He made to fire again when Chantecoq suddenly drifted towards them, causing the other driver to jerk the wheel instinctively. The car slammed into one of the large Petitot statues at the head of the bridge and crumpled like a child's toy. Chantecoq sped on without slowing.

Anthony pulled himself back inside. "Fancy driving," he said.

"I took second at the last Moroccan Grand Prix," Chantecoq said. They reached the Louvre a few minutes later. It was closed for the evening, but An-thony had been given a set of keys for the duration of his investigation. He and Chantecoq hurried through the silent corridors, towards the Room of Barbarous Gods. "I believe our opponents are more than just simple criminals, Monsieur Anthony," Chantecoq said, puffing as he attempted to keep up. "The lengths they have gone to speak of vast resources, more so than those of any criminal enterprise I have had the misfortune to cross swords with. In fact, I can only re-call one other time that I have faced such odds...during the Great War."

"Espionage?" Anthony said.

"Possibly. We must move carefully. We... Hush!" Chantecoq turned and darted into a side corridor, his pistol in hand. A moment later, a struggling figure was shoved towards Anthony, who caught him.

"Monsieur de Felipone!" Anthony exclaimed. "What are you doing here?"

"He was waiting for us, with this," Chantecoq said, tossing a revolver to Anthony, who caught it and stuffed it in his belt. "This is the man who hired you?"

"Yes. Monsieur Chantecoq, may I introduce you to Director de Felipone... Director de Felipone, Monsieur Chantecoq," Anthony said, holding the man by his collar. De Felipone was a small man, and unassuming in appearance, albeit dark-complexioned.

"I wasn't waiting for anyone! This is an outrage! Let me go!" de Felipone barked, trying to free himself from Anthony's clutches.

"Then why were you carrying a pistol?" Anthony said, releasing the man.

"I was waiting for the Ghost," he snapped.

"I thought you said you weren't waiting for anyone?"

"I... ah..." de Felipone said, hesitating. "I heard a noise," he said finally.

"I think Director de Felipone had best come with us," Anthony said, shoving the smaller man forward. "We can all investigate this noise together."

"But..." de Felipone began, but fell silent as Anthony gave him a dark look.

"He was a look-out," Chantecoq murmured. "And we are being shadowed. Look to the gallery above..."

"I heard them," Anthony replied, his voice pitched low. "Smelled them too; Austrian tobacco has a particular odor, as does the gun-oil the German military utilizes." He glanced upwards. "We're walking into a trap."

"Yes," Chantecoq said, looking peculiarly pleased.

They entered the Room of Barbarous Gods, de Felipone pushed ahead of them, and Anthony looked around at the barbaric effigies that crouched in their assigned nooks and niches and repressed a shudder. The child of two cultures, both of them superstitious, Anthony had found the room and its contents to be as disturbing as any cairn or burial ground the first time, in daylight. Seeing it now at night only increased that sensation.

Chantecoq stopped. "Belphegor," he said hollowly. Anthony froze. The statue that rose up before him had an expression on its face that was both beautiful and hideous, with almost peculiarly malign proportions and fixed grin that seemed to promise infernal delights. Belphegor was a masterpiece of understated terror, something which was at once satanic and sublime. "The fiend in the flesh, so to speak," Chantecoq continued softly. "They found it in a hidden vault in the Cathedral of Dol, in Brittany. A few hundred years ago, some sacristain or other discovered a hidden store of gold in the base. And almost two decades ago, poor Simone Desroches set out to uncover whatever other secrets might be lurking in its stony guts."

"But she found nothing," Anthony said.

"Only death." Chantecoq looked at the younger man. "I have made quite the study of this statue. A puzzle to pass the time. In all those years, I have never come across anything to bear out Desroches' claims that the treasure she found was not the only one."

"Then you were not looking hard enough!"

Both men spun, Chantecoq's hand dipping for his pistol. A demonic shape stood in slash of moonlight which draped across it, revealing a face out of nightmare. Clad in an all encompassing cloak of the deepest black, the hideous figure glared at them.

"Belphegor, I presume," Anthony said. He moved quickly, bounding towards the figure with instinctive speed. However, just before he reached his enemy, there was a bright flash and Anthony found himself blinded. He crashed to the floor, his ears ringing with laughter and his eyes filled with colored blobs.

"Close, but no cigar," the masked figure said, stepping from behind the statue. "You arrived in admirable time, gentlemen... almost to the minute."

"Arrived?" Anthony swung around as dark-clad masked figures stepped out of the shadows, their peculiar rifles aimed at the two detectives. De Felipone snatched his pistol from Anthony's belt as he climbed to his feet, and grabbed Chantecoq's as well. "So it *was* a trap then?"

"Of course," Belphegor said. He spread his arms almost theatrically, allowing the cape to billow and fall just so. "Why else would we dress so gaudily?"

Anthony's eyes narrowed. He looked at Chantecoq. The old man grunted. "They did not choose the costumes to frighten, but to intrigue us. And the threat to my daughter?" he said, directing the latter towards Belphegor. "A double-blind, to make me lower my guard and dull my suspicions?"

"Oh, very clever," Belphegor said, clapping mockingly. "Your daughter will die, have no doubt about that. But not because you investigated...no, she will die because she has been marked for death from the beginning, even as you have been, King of Detectives!" Belphegor looked at Anthony and chuckled. "Very clever, sending your man, by the by. Luckily for us, we had tapped Chantecoq's phone line. My men will be well-prepared for your Mr. Gentry, never fear. But you, Mr. Anthony...a far worse fate awaits you." He removed his mask and grinned crookedly at Anthony. The latter repressed a bestial snarl.

"Mayen," Anthony growled. Jan Mayen, detective and inventor bowed floridly and laughed. The Austrian was as famous on the Continent as either Anthony or Chantecoq, though the associations with his name were much darker these days. Mayen, it was said, had fallen in with bad company—the National Socialist German Workers Party, as well as the shadowy *ubermensch*, Sun-Koh. Anthony knew that that last one was no rumor, much to his regret.

"Hello again, Jimmy, long time no see, eh?" Mayen said.

"The last time I saw you, you were leaving Vienna with your tail between your legs along with your master Sun-Koh," Anthony said, his hands clenching. "I still owe you for kidnapping my fiancé..."

"Sun-Koh is hardly my master," Mayen said, obviously more sharply than he'd intended. "More of an interested co-conspirator. And considering that you destroyed my Viennese residence, we'll call it even, shall we?"

"Those rifles are your work then?" Anthony said.

"Yes. And I'm quite proud of the flashbulb effect I designed. It makes it easy for the 'ghost' to make his exit." Mayen turned to the men and snapped, "Bind them!" As they advanced, he smiled again at Anthony. "Sun-Koh is eager to get reacquainted Jimmy. It's your physiology, you see...obviously superior despite coming from inferior stock. A modern day Bran-Mak-Morn, one could say." He turned to the statue and gazed at it admiringly. "But now to claim our true prize."

"Prize?" Chantecoq said.

"Of course. You didn't think this was just about revenge, did you?"

"Careful, Mayen. The stone belongs to my Order as much as the Thule Society," de Felipone snapped.

"Order?" Chantecoq's eyes widened as de Felipone made a strange gesture towards him and smiled grimly. "Rosicrucian... I should have guessed."

"Desroches was our servant, and a good one until her baser desires got the best of her," de Felipone said, glaring at Chantecoq. "It took me almost a decade to work my way up to a position to get close to the statue."

"Of course, we could have saved you Rosy Cross fellows a bit of bother if you'd simply come to the Thule Society in the first place," Mayen said as he strode towards the statue. "Now you'll have to share the prize."

"A small price to pay," de Felipone sniffed. "Without us, you cannot get to it. And without you, we would not be able to have our revenge on an enemy, if unknowing, of our Order."

"There is nothing in the statue," Chantecoq said. "This was all for nothing!" He made to step forward, but several men grabbed him. He and Anthony were bound quickly and painfully.

Mayen didn't turn around. "Of course there's nothing in it. That would be ridiculous. But under it is a different story. Isn't that right, *Herr* de Felipone?"

De Felipone didn't answer. Instead, he went to the statue and squatted down. His hand slithered across the base of the statue and something rumbled softly. "This statue has been here for centuries. Indeed, this room was built to hold it specifically. It is a marker, you see...an 'X' marking the spot of France's greatest treasure, even as it once did in the Dol Cathedral," he said.

The statue began to slide back from its spot with a terrible grinding noise, revealing a hollow half-bubble set into the stones of the floor. "The Thule Society has searched for it for decades, as have our cousins in the Rosy Cross," Mayen said breathlessly as de Felipone stepped back.

"Only a brother of our Order can unlock the secret of the statue," de Felipone said.

"Paracelsus studied it, and it gave shape to his theories on matter alteration. Before him, the Carolingian Dynasty used its secrets to drag Europe kicking and screaming from the Dark Ages after Rome's fall," Mayen continued, ignoring his co-conspirator. Almost reverentially, he dipped his hands down into the crevice and pulled a misshapen lump free. "The legends say that it was all that remained of the star-stone that Weyland wrought his mighty weapons from. Roland's Durandal was crafted from it, as was Joyeuse. Charlemagne built his empire on its back, even as we will build ours...behold, the New Metal! Behold, the Carolingian Stone!"

"Very dramatic," Chantecoq said. The old man smiled. "And thus an old mystery is solved."

Mayen turned. "What?"

"Years I have spent puzzling over it," Chantecoq said. "I found the mechanism mere months after Desroches' death. But I could not work out how to open it without destroying the statue. Nor, in truth, was I sure I wanted it opened. But when I received the photos you sent, I knew I would finally discover the mystery of what Desroches was searching for all those years ago."

"You...knew?" de Felipone stuttered.

"Pah. Am I not the King of Detectives?" Chantecoq said. "You wanted me here to witness this. Why threaten, when you could simply have snuck in? No, this plan was, from the beginning, about flaunting your victory." He smirked at de Felipone, and then turned to Mayen. "Thus, I contacted the police as soon as I opened that cursed envelope. And then I played the part of the reluctant hero until it was my turn to spring *my* trap on you!"

The wail of sirens suddenly filled the air, echoing around the room. "What the Devil?" Mayen said, looking around.

"The police, of course. Likely, they have those of your men you sent to kill my daughter and Monsieur Gentry in custody already," Chantecoq said mildly. "I would suggest surrendering."

"No! No!" de Felipone whirled. "We must return it to its hiding place! Unbelievers must not have it!" He aimed his pistols at Mayen, who rolled his eyes in disgust.

"And on that note, I believe our partnership is at an end." So saying, Mayen drew the Mauser holstered on his hip with the swiftness of a striking snake and fired. De Felipone staggered with a wild cry. Mayen watched him fall and laughed softly. He held up the Stone. "With this, Sun-Koh shall remake the world in his image...an unyielding *Reich* which will hold the world in its grip like Atlantis of old..."

"I'm thinking not so much." Anthony lunged to his feet and smashed into Mayen, driving him back into a statue of Bal-Sagoth crouching nearby. The statue toppled over with a crash as both men rolled aside. Anthony slit his bonds on a chunk of stone and tackled the Austrian as he got to his feet and took aim with his pistol.

Chantecoq, meanwhile, cut his own bonds with the thin blade he kept concealed in his coat sleeve. Without a second thought, he whipped the blade into the throat of the closest guard and then dove for de Felipone's forgotten pistols. Reclaiming his Galand, he rolled onto his back and plugged another guard.

The sound of yelling filled the room as a tide of blue burst through the doors and invaded the Room of Barbarous Gods. Policemen swinging truncheons overwhelmed the panicked Germans, bearing them under. Chantecoq was on his feet a moment later, desperately searching for the Carolingian Stone amidst the chaos of the mêlée.

Elsewhere, Anthony and Mayen traded blows beneath the gazes of Rhan-Tegoth and Nodens. Mayen, hampered by his costume, soon slumped back, lip busted open and one eye already swelling shut. Anthony advanced on him.

"Stay back, Anthony! I'm warning you!" the Austrian barked. He raised one voluminous sleeve and there was a soft rattle. Anthony dove aside as several poisonous balls smacked into Nodens' stony features. He sprang to his feet and charged towards Mayen. There was a sudden flash of light and Anthony staggered, momentarily blinded. When his vision cleared, Mayen was gone.

"Anthony?"

Anthony spun to find Chantecoq behind him, pistol in hand. "Where is he? Did you see him?" he said, looking past the older detective.

"*Non*, he is gone I'm afraid," Chantecoq said. He holstered his pistol. "But he did not get what he came for. That much, at least, we accomplished."

"What happened?" Anthony said, as they moved back towards the police.

"De Felipone," Chantecoq said simply. He gestured. De Felipone lay near the statue in a pool of blood. Red smears decorated its base, showing where he had re-sealed it. "In the confusion, he managed to place the Carolingian Stone back in its crypt. And good riddance to it."

"How can you say that?" Anthony said, staring at the statue. "If it truly was what they claimed...imagine what could be learned from studying it."

"Oh, I can, Monsieur Anthony. I can indeed. I know first-hand what such knowledge would be used for at the moment, with the Great Powers snapping and snarling at one another, and I say again...good riddance," Chantecoq said firmly.

Anthony nodded after a moment, and smiled ruefully. "When de Felipone tried to get you involved, you recommended me to him, didn't you?"

"I might have said something, yes," Chantecoq said.

"Why?" Anthony asked, looking at the King of Detectives, who was busily lighting a cigarette. He chuckled at the question and gave Anthony a thin smile.

"Why...you're not the only one who knows how to bait a trap, Monsieur Anthony."

Frank Schildiner has made it his habit to spotlight the character of 1950s archeologist Jean Kariven, created by French sf writer Jimmy Guieu. In Frank's fourth contribution, Kariven, still unearthing evidence of hidden extraterrestrial activities, encounters the unflappable and quintessentially British, Albert Campion...

Frank Schildiner: *The Death Bird*

London, 1954

"It's a rum thing, I know, to drag you away from your conference and all that, but needs of the Crown and all," Albert Campion intoned, his light tone belying his pompous sounding words. He was a tall, thin figure of a man with lank blonde hair who carried himself with an air of unintelligent affability that fooled most people, until you looked past the owl-shaped glasses and into the keen intelligent eyes that never missed a detail.

Jean Kariven smiled, remembering Campion's habit of behaving as one to be discounted. It led those in the French Resistance with less perspicacity to underestimate the brilliant, soft-spoken man who served in British counter-intelligence. Four of the best Nazi traitors were captured thanks to Campion, leading to some of the most impressive false-flag signals sent to the hated German foes.

Kariven himself was a tall, lean man with dark hair and eyes and a thin pencil mustache that gave him a slightly rakish air. His movements were energetic and caused most people to believe, despite the slightly prominent ears and sharp nose, that he was a stage actor, someone used to having attention cast upon them at all times. Nothing was, in fact, further from the truth. Jean Kariven was one of the world's leading archaeologists, a renowned expert on ancient artifacts who was called in to consult by universities and governments all over the world.

"Not at all, Campion," Kariven replied, lifting the sherry in his hand and taking a small sip. "A repeat of old beliefs by men who know too little! I would enlighten them, but they would not even understand what I told them... It would be like discussing submarines with Neanderthals!"

"Jolly good then," Campion replied, raising his voice slightly, "Lugg? Lugg, here!"

"Wot now?" Magersfontein Lugg called out from the other room, pushing inside the drawing room, a dishcloth in hand. A large ungainly man with a shiny bald head and a large white mustache, Lugg moved with a surprising nimbleness that belied his form. Formerly one of London's top burglar's, he was retired and had acted as valet for Albert Campion for well over a decade.

"The etching on my desk. Bring it here for Dr. Kariven." Campion said, his voice still light, though a slight edge had entered his words.

Lugg walked out, reappearing a moment later, a yellowing folder in hand. "Looks older than the 'ills. Even if it's a Sexton Blake, you could get some bread and honey for it."

Kariven stared for a moment at Lugg, clearly not following the larger man's statements. "Sexton Blake? The famous detective? Bread and...? Forgive me, my friend, but I did not follow a word you said."

Lugg grunted, sounding as if he expected nothing less, "Speaking English, wasn't I? To freely translate for the foreign gent, Sexton Blake means fake. Bread and honey means money."

Campion sighed, his air that of one used to being oppressed. "You must forgive Lugg, he often forgets his manner. He was speaking in a form of English known as rhyming slang. Just ask for a translation if it ever gets past you, I've long since ignored it."

Handing the folder over to Kariven, Lugg sniffed and said, "I'll just get back to the washing up, if 'is Nibbs don't mind."

Kariven watched Lugg leave and smiled again. "An excellent man, for all his air of insolence. Now, let us see what you bring to me today!"

Opening the folder, Kariven started slightly but otherwise remained perfectly still. For a full half hour, he did not even seem to breathe, studying the page before his eyes with an almost unapproachable intensity. Finally, he looked up and his eyes were hooded and wary.

"Albert," he began softly, "where did you find this particular item?"

Campion's attention had been unwavering; if anything, his countenance seemed to grow as time passed. The blank expression of inoffensive blandness was gone, replaced by a controlled power that was always hidden beneath the surface. This was the man of authority and action who had solved terrifying murders and fought Nazi agents who attempted to undermine the Allies' war efforts.

"From a man named Tobin, a Yank chap who was on the side of Uncle Adolph. He owned some property here and this was unearthed by a friend of mine the other day. And I'm guessing, based on your rather fierce reaction, that I did the right thing." Campion's words sounded relaxed again, but with an undertone of concern and readiness.

Kariven nodded, standing and pacing as he looked back at the document. The page was a modern blueprint of a very ancient piece of art, with detailed descriptions of the item in German and English. At the top corner was a frightening reminder of the war and the dreadful men that promoted terror on a world-wide scale—the stamp of SS Reichsfuher Heinrich Himmler himself!

The blueprint showed an odd-looking bird, with straight, equally sized wings and a tail also geometrically shaped. The details surrounding the drawing suggested the model was approximately three feet in length and was made from an unknown metal.

"This is the Saqqara Bird," Kariven explained, pointing to etching. "Or at least, a representation of the artifact in larger scale than the one that sits in the Cairo Museum. You see, the Saqqara Bird that most are familiar with is a balsa wood model built in approximately 200 B.C. The original has never been found... except it appears to have been discovered by this American!"

Campion seemed to accept that and stated, "Looked rather like a glider to me, not at all like something Egyptian."

Kariven let out a long breath. Deciding he needed Campion's help, he came to the conclusion that deception would not be useful. "No, in fact this was not built on Earth. This is of Polarian design, a humanoid race which has used our world as a battleground..."

"...With the Denebians," Campion finished, amused by the shocked expression on Kariven's face. "Forgive me, old top, but I've had a few shaky moments myself, thanks to those blighters."

"I, as well," Kariven replied, shaking his head. The war between these two alien races was one of the reasons he was discounted by many of his fellow academics. Few believed that much of humanity's history was tied to Outer Space.

The Polarians and Denebians had been locked in an interstellar war for an untold number of centuries. Earth was unfortunately all too often used as a pawn in their schemes, with both powers affecting the course of history thanks to their many devices and experiments left behind. But there were differences between the Denebians and the Polarians, radical ones that had often impacted Jean Kariven's life over the years.

The Polarians, who outwardly resembled humanity, were essentially a benevolent people, rarely wishing to involve mankind in their struggle. They looked upon the people of Earth with a patronizing amusement, viewing them as backwards and foolish, but good-hearted despite their lack of intelligence.

The Denebians, on the other hand, were a green-skinned race with sharp demonic ears and an open loathing for all other types of life. An advanced, warlike culture, they viewed humanity as potential slaves, or tools to be used in their crusade. Many Earth legends of demons and monsters who sought to enslave or destroy humans came in contact with them were the product of Denebian interference throughout history.

"Then I suppose we had best get a move on to Herr Tobin's domicile. Lugg! Get the car, if you please." Campion said, standing and reaching for his jacket. A short time later, they were off, speeding through the London streets towards Surrey.

Lugg, at the wheel of Campion's fast and well-built roadster, called back, "Would one of you mind tellin' me why we're been hivin' to bloody Surrey again?"

"I have to assume you wish to know the hurry, Mr. Lugg," replied Kariven. "It is this: according the hieroglyphs on the side of the Saqqara Bird, this is a weapon. Most would be unable to interpret the pictographs. The writing is in the style of Pre-Dynasty Egypt, possibly that of King Ka who came before the uniter of those lands, Narmer." Kariven held tight as Lugg skirted around a slow moving lorry with inches to spare.

"A bit small for a weapon to cause you such concern," Campion observed.

Kariven nodded, "Yes, but apparently this flying machine is capable of destroying life instead of buildings and the like."

"Dangerous," Campion agreed, "But no more so than the majority of the devices used by the Royal Air Force... Perhaps less so, I should think."

Kariven chuckled, without any trace of humor. "You mistake my meaning, my friend. The Saqqara Bird's duty is to destroy life on a planetary scale. It is the ender of *all* life—not merely human. The hieroglyphs state how worlds attacked by the Saqqara Bird are reduced to lifeless deserts. I believe this weapon is the reason vast areas of the Earth went from fertile lands to deadly deserts devoid of life."

"Bit more bustle may be called for, Lugg." Campion called out and was already braced as the roadster's speed jumped to even greater heights.

After a time of silent speeding along the roads, they turned off the main streets, arriving at the small town of Lower Gatton. Once a rotten borough that provided two seats in Parliament, the village consisted or 20 small cottages and a 15th century manor house which loomed above the community with an authority based in old world noble values.

"Upper Gatton Park," Campion identified the mansion as it loomed above them on a large hill. As it grew larger in their view, an oppressive feeling engulfed all present in the car. It was almost as if the building disapproved of their uninvited presence.

"Gives me the right cobblers, that drum does," Lugg added, nodding at the approaching location.

Upper Gatton Park was a large rectangular building made from white stone which made the house even more imposing as one approached it. The scrollwork on the outside was simple, yet impressive, and the stone pillars on the front of the façade gave one the impression this was a location where great events should, and would, occur.

The building itself was of little interest to Kariven. His thoughts were on the infamous Mocata family that had built the manor back in the days of Henry VI. The Mocata clan were reputed to be wizards and warlocks of the worst order, and at least four were burned for witchcraft throughout English history. The last Mocata to inhabit Upper Gatton Park was a learned man who was a member of the highest social circles. He had died a strange death, reputedly engaging in a bizarre occult ceremony with his friends and colleagues over 20 years earlier. The scandal was an embarrassment for many of his social set, one quickly forgotten in favor of other titillating piece of gossip.

"Be very careful," Kariven warned as all three climbed out the vehicle, now parked by the enormous dark wooden doors. They looked as if they were made from a material that absorbed light, the black surface almost caused one to recoil at the sight.

"Wise advice as always, Kariven," said a man who stepped around the pillar and regarded them behind sunglasses almost as dark as the door. He was tall, thinly built but moved with a smooth grace that seemed almost too agile and perfect.

Kariven snorted with annoyance at the sight of the man. "Polarians, of course. Will I never escape your constant meddling in my life?"

"Doubtful," the Polarian stated. His voice was clipped and accent-free, like that of a BBC Radio newsreader. "Your presence has prevented the Denebians from seizing many important weapons in their war to destroy all life other than theirs or their slaves."

"Cor," Lugg breathed, shaking his large head mournfully, "it's like you aliens has got the same Morning Glory."

The Polarian frowned a moment and said, "Morning Glory…your rhythmic talk is a rather interesting aspect of humanity. Morning Glory, in the context, would translate to mean 'story,' I assume. Therefore, you are saying all Polarians say the same thing. Very perceptive—and also quite true. We are careful about what we can tell your people. You are so backward and so willing to try violence…"

"A rather verbose way of agreeing with my man Lugg, I should say." Campion observed, peering through his glasses and attempting, once again, to appear inoffensive and bland.

"I think we've chatted rather enough," Kariven snapped. He turned to Lugg. "Sir, I believe you are the expert at entering locations *sans* key. If you will?"

With a frown, Lugg stepped up to the door and glanced at the lock. With a shrug, he pushed it and it swung slowly open, revealing a well-lit hall. The floors were made from a pink-colored marble and the walls were devoid of any form of decoration. A sweeping grand staircase of black stone spiraled upwards to a huge landing on the second floor. Like the outside, the inside of the manor had a striking, off-putting air.

"I've searched this building for three days," the Polarian said, pushing past the three humans and looking at them with resignation. "The death bird is not within."

"You had best hope it is, slave! Otherwise I will make your deaths slow and agonizing!" a harsh, grating voice snarled from above. Looking down on them from the second floor was a tall woman with long black hair, pale green skin and red eyes that were too large for her face. Her ears were sharply pointed and she was clutching an orange staff that pulsed with energy. She was a Denebian.

The Polarian reacted instantly, stepping between the three humans and raising an elegant-looking pistol made of what seemed to be colored glass. He fired a lance of green energy just as the Denebian pressed a button on her staff. A beam of red light struck the Polarian just as his ray hit the Denebian, causing both to topple over and lay unmoving.

"Dead," Campion pronounced, not sounding particularly aggrieved. "I do wish they would behave that way more often. Saves us from listening to long Polarian speeches."

"Not to mention streams of insulting comments from the Denebians," Kariven added.

He looked about the large, imposing manor house. Then, an idea struck him, a means of discovering the Saqqara Bird's location. Though filled with good intentions, the Polarians were unable to think like a human being, not to mention a deceptive one like the late unlamented spy, Mr. Tobin.

"Mr. Lugg," he said, smiling at the former burglar with amusement, "if you needed to hide an object the size of the Saqqara Bird here, where would you place it?"

Lugg frowned and ran a hand over his bald head as he considered the question. "If I was thinking the John Hops might be after me, I'd hide it somewhere you wouldn't look. Because it would be in danger of getting destroyed by an idiot what don't know it's there."

Campion smiled and nodded. "I think I have just the location. Follow me, Doctor, we'll require your expertise in the handling of this device."

"Handling?" Kariven asked and suddenly looked very determined. "No, my friend. I have a different plan for this infernal device."

It was Kariven who discovered the Saqqara Bird, having been told by Lugg that the coal scuttle by the fireplace was an ideal hiding spot. The artefact was hidden under a thin layer of soot, but even that could not hide the beauty of this terrible, world-destroying machine.

"Don't touch it," Kariven warned. "Some Polarian and Denebian devices are not as dormant as one would hope. Best to destroy it here and now."

Lugg stepped forward, reaching into his pants and pulling out a small box of matches. "I'm on it, gents, best to leave it to me. There's an art to the blaze. Done wrong an' yer liable to destroy the whole building."

Campion nodded and waved Kariven out ahead of him. They headed towards the roadster, secure in their belief that this would be the end of the terrible Saqqara Bird.

"One question, old chap," Campion mused. "Why do these alien blighters insist on using our world as their Roman Arena, for lack of a better term?"

Kariven shook his head, but the expression on his face was not happy. "I'm not sure, Albert, but you can be assured I am making this question my mission from now on…"

Brittany-based French writer Michel Stéphan has made excellent use of iconic characters in his previous contributions to Tales of the Shadowmen. *In his latest tale, he pulls several heroes from the 1960s, plus Madame Atomos (whom he had already depicted in "The Red Silk Scarf" in Volume 6) and then boldly crosses media lines for an unexpected ending which we wouldn't dare spoil here...*

Michel Stéphan: *With the Compliments of Nestor Burma!*

Paris, 1960

It was a morning like any other at the Fiat Lux Agency (confidentiality guaranteed). I was trying to break the Laws of Physics by stretching my legs as far as I could on my desktop, while keeping my posterior still comfortably stuck in my chair. The sound of my secretary Hélène typing on her battered Underwood was music to my ears. I wondered if she was really trying to catch up with the mail, or if, like me, she was just pretending to work. My hands comfortably tied behind my head, I let myself become lost in fundamental existential questions like that.

"Have you taken a look at the Floutard file?"

Hélène's voice pulled me out my reverie and I almost fell off my chair. I realized that she had come into my office without me noticing. Either she was very silent, or I had fallen asleep. I managed to avoid the humiliating fall and grabbed the green folder she was thrusting at me.

"The Floutard file?" I repeated, pretending to know what she was talking about.

"Yes, the Floutard file," she said again. "That's the bald guy who thinks his wife is cheating on him with the former Maître D' of *Picratt's*. You're the one who did all the surveillance."

"Oh, right! Now I remember him."

"Well, the file is closed and ready to be sent to the cuckold with the invoice. I just need your signature."

"Hélène, you're an angel!"

"That's not all. There's a woman in the waiting room who wants to see you."

My smile froze. All my generous thoughts towards Hélène flew out of the window.

"A client is in the waiting room and you didn't show her in?" I exclaimed. "Do you know how many customers we've had this month? Are you trying to bankrupt the man who feeds you so lavishly?"

Hélène looked at me with the same cool expression as usual, but I thought I could discern a slight hint of annoyance, or perhaps condescension, in her eyes. She did not even try to apologize.

"If I had a new typewriter," she went on, "I'd have more time to take care of the clients."

I was about to respond to her unjustified attack when I heard a slight cough coming from the threshold. The woman in question had decided to not wait for the end of our family tiff and had let herself in. I admired her initiative—as well as her tall, lithe body and elegance. I hastened to offer her a chair. That back-stabbing Hélène seized the opportunity to slip out of the room and I found myself alone with the woman. She neither sat nor responded to my smile, but instead politely offered me a rather dry hand to shake.

"Monsieur Burma?"

"Just like it says on the door," I said. "Please, do sit down, Madame…?"

To my great relief, she responded:

"Leni Riefenstahl. The name might mean something to you?"

"Yes," I replied, trying desperately to remember if I had had any dealings with the German movie industry during the War.

My thoughts lingered for a brief moment on a Belgian actress whom I had met in Bordeaux who was now working as an extra on an Emile Couzinet film. Leni Riefenstahl was in a different class entirely. Judging from the perfect cut of her suit, and her beautifully-manicured nails, she was more likely to be featured in *avant-garde* cinema as opposed to the last séance at the Midi-Minuit.

"As you know, I'm a filmmaker—or rather, I was. Today, I'm a photographer. I've just returned from the United States where I've sold photos of the Masai tribes of Africa to *The National Geographic*…"

"This is very interesting," I said, "but surely you haven't come here to sell me pictures of whirling dervishes?"

She made a frown that quickly turned into a small smile, the first I'd seen cross her lips. Fraulein Riefenstahl must have been very beautiful once and, despite the fact she was now over 50, she still exhibited a certain charm.

"No, of course not, Monsieur Burma. I've come to you because I heard you were both capable and the soul of discretion."

"Has my reputation spread to America?"

"I'm prepared to pay you 3000 francs to meet someone, give him the confidential documents I have here, and, most especially, not ask any questions."

"But why…?"

"I said, no questions, Monsieur Burma. Is the fee adequate?"

"Could I at least know where I'm supposed to meet this guy?"

"Certainly. Rue de Tolbiac, in front of the café *La Petite Vitesse*, in 24 hours.

Leni Riefenstahl deposited a briefcase on my desk, disturbing my precious pile of paperwork.

"Wait a minute," I said. "I want to know the contents of that thing. I won't do anything illegal, even for 3000 francs."

She pressed on the suitcase's two snaps and the lid opened as quickly as a jack-in-the-box, revealing a sheath of papers written in a language unknown to me.

"OK, at least, it won't blow up in my face. And it doesn't look like there's any illegal merchandise in there. I suppose these papers could be top secret documents on the German V2, program, but the war has been over for more than a decade now, so they can't be worth very much today," I said, with a snicker.

Obviously, she didn't find my joke funny.

"Are you willing to take the job, Monsieur Burma?" she asked.

I nodded. She then handed me an envelope full of crisp, new banknotes.

"You can count them, if you like."

"No need. I trust you," I replied, pocketing the money.

From the window, Hélène and I watched Leni Riefenstahl's tall figure disappear around the corner. I had resisted the temptation to count the money in her presence, but as soon as she left, I did. The count was indeed correct.

"Leni Riefenstahl!" said Hélène, admiringly. "She's a great woman. I bet she's gone through tough times since her days in Berlin..."

"I'm all in favor of forgiving, but not of forgetting," I said, stuffing the money into my wall safe.

"Come on, Nestor. She was vindicated after the War, and she had a tough time getting any recognition from her peers."

"Maybe, but she still broke bread with Hitler."

"She's a great filmmaker. No one can deny the undeniable qualities of her *Triumph of the Will*."

"I'll never watch any anti-smoking film," I replied, happy to finally have had the last word with my secretary.

The next day, I stood as instructed in front of *La Petite Vitesse* in the 13th Arrondissement. I'd been waiting for 15 minutes when I saw a black sedan stop across the street. A man—an Oriental—got out. Judging from the size of the car and its dark-tinted windows, I figured he hadn't come alone.

He seemed rather harmless. Having spotted me, he beckoned to me and instructed me to get inside the car. If life had taught me anything, it was to not get into a car full of dubious-looking strangers, so I shook my head and offered him the briefcase. But suddenly, a pair of hands grabbed the case from inside, while the man standing outside shoved me into the back.

Before I realized what had just happened to me, I found myself in the back seat of the car, facing, as I had guessed, several other Orientals. It was like a casting call for a Yellow Peril movie. I didn't have time to defend myself or try to get out. I just felt a dark veil come over me, my sight grew dim and I slowly sank into unconsciousness. My last thoughts were for mother, Hélène any my new mattress at home, not necessarily in that order.

I had slept like the proverbial baby, a deep, restorative slumber and woke up in a good mood, all things considered. I found myself in a luxurious room that would not have been out of place at the Hotel George V.

A change of clothes had been neatly folded over a genuine Louis XV chair positioned near the bed. They weren't the clothes I'd been wearing when I'd been kidnapped. They were much too nice and smelled fresh. They were the type of clothes one might have worn for an evening soirée in Neuilly. I have absolutely nothing against duds like that, and they fit me pretty well, but in my business, they would be a handicap. Can you imagine me dressed like that tailing a punter through the streets of Belleville?

I got up and instinctively looked for my pipe, which seemed to have disappeared, like the rest of my personal effects. That irritated me a little, but I grudgingly put on the new clothes and, now dressed like a notary on the town, I decided to take a good look around.

Surprisingly, the door wasn't locked. What I found on the other side left me speechless: a vast corridor lined with mirrors, with high ceilings, lit by a series of crystal chandeliers. It looked like a miniature Versailles. There were doors on one side and French windows on the other, but not a single human being in sight. I looked through one of the windows and saw a large park with symmetrical alleys lined with endless rows of trees, all perfectly trimmed. In the center was a basin whose dimensions were that of a bird bath for giant rocs.

I found my way to the ground floor by walking down a grand staircase. I noticed that, despite the opulence of the house, it was largely unfurnished. But since I wasn't there to play real estate agent, I continued my investigation. I turned right into a salon where I immediately saw a man, dressed in a tweed jacket, who stood by a side window, looking outside.

I coughed, hoping that he would turn around and notice me, but he didn't react. I walked towards him and tapped him on the shoulder. He then turned to meet me. He was a funny-looking little man, with a round face, and kind, intelligent eyes. His hand came out to shake mine. It was a firm and friendly handshake, which I took as a sign that he was trustworthy. I was about to ask his name when he beckoned me to look outside.

"Do you see it?" he asked.

I approached the window and looked at the gravel path alongside the mansion. A Renault 4L van was parked right in the middle, clearly unattended. I was surprised not to find a more luxurious vehicle like a Citroën DS or a Mercedes in such a place, but its ordinary, streetwise look somehow made it a more reassuring sight.

"Do you see it?" he repeated.

I nodded, a thousand questions buzzing through my head.

"I checked it out this morning," the man continued, with an accent which I clearly identified as British. "For three hours, I turned the engine on and off. I checked under the bonnet, in the boot, under the chassis... There is no trap. The car is in perfect working order and the gate outside is open. We only have to drive it and go."

He stared at me and laughed, waving a set of car keys.

"Because, you see, Mr. Burma, the keys were on the mantelpiece!" he said, pointing at the fireplace. "I found them there this morning."

"You know my name?" I asked.

"I knew Leni couldn't come. She sent word that she was sending someone in her place—you. But I'm afraid you might be too late..."

I was going to ask him to explain himself more clearly when he feverishly grabbed me by my arm.

"You do know how to drive, don't you, Mr. Burma? I'll tell you everything once we're out of here."

I sighed and took the keys from his trembling hands.

Five minutes later, we were inside the 4L. As I was about to start the engine, I noticed that my new companion seemed increasingly agitated and panicky. I could see beads of sweat on his forehead. I wasn't unhappy about it because I thought it might make him more malleable.

"Don't make that face!" I said. "You told me you checked every inch of this car yourself. Besides, if there's a bomb somewhere on board, we won't even feel the explosion!"

I turned on the ignition. The 4L's engine started the first time and, a few minutes later, after driving through an impressive metal gate that had been left wide open, we found ourselves on a small country road. My companion kept looking behind us to see if anyone was following us, but we were alone as far as the eye could see.

"Stop fidgeting!" I said. "No one's following us. Now I'm waiting for the explanations you promised me. Start with who you are, and what you were doing in that empty castle."

There was a moment of silence during which I imagined my companion was marshalling his thoughts. Then, he began to speak, at a much greater speed than the average man. But, despite that and my rusty English, I managed to understand what he said, even if it wasn't always easy.

"I'm a British astrophysicist. I live in Highbury in North London. Three years ago, I was asked by the Americans to join a small taskforce to combat the greatest terrorist menace bent on attacking America the world has ever seen. I, alone, managed to infiltrate that organization and discover some of its best-kept secrets..."

The first thought that crossed my mind was that he needed a good psychiatrist, but I restrained myself and let him continue.

"That organization is named Atomos, after its leader. For a year, I have been working for them, while secretly passing along information to the OSS using Leni Riefenstahl as a conduit. I've risked my life every day. The Atomos Organization is merciless when it comes to punishing traitors. Eventually, I couldn't take the pressure anymore, and I told my superiors that I wanted out. Using a third-party organization, SMOG, an exchange was arranged. The Atomos Organization would let me go in exchange for some information SMOG has collected on the mysterious 'Black Knight' satellite that was detected two years ago. Leni gave you that information and, in exchange, the Atomos Organization let me go."

"Your plan worked perfectly, it seems. Your terrorists even left us a car in perfect working order. So what are you afraid of?"

"You don't know the Atomos Organization, Mr. Burma. In the last year, I've learned much about them, their plans, their secret bases inside the United States. I know enough to allow the Americans to deal them a fatal blow before they're ready to move ahead. What if they found out that the deal with SMOG is phony? That dreadful woman will never let me live with all that knowledge in my head!"

"Woman? Atomos is a woman? You're kidding me?"

"It's not funny, Mr. Burma. You don't know her as I do. And I envy you your ignorance. When Madame Atomos' minions brought you here last night, I believed the exchange was on. But this morning, finding the castle where I'd been working in isolation until now deserted, with this car waiting in the garden... It was all too much. I know Madame Atomos. She likes cat and mouse games. It amuses her to let me believe until the last moment that I've gotten away, and then..."

At that moment, I saw a small café, no more than a truck stop, coming up on the side of the road, just as we were approaching a village.

"I tell you what—how about stopping for a drink to lift your spirits?"

The little English scientist nodded. I parked the car alongside the café, we got out and went inside. I ordered two Calvados, which were promptly served by a gruff, taciturn man with a rubicund face.

After finishing his drink, the little man's face looked less pale and pinched. He seemed more relaxed and appeared to have regained some confidence.

"I'm supposed to meet my superiors at a *lieu-dit* called Bel Air, five kilometers east of Senlis. Our rendezvous is at noon. Can you take me there, Mr. Burma?"

"You'll be there early!" I replied.

As we approached the rendezvous, my companion grew more silent, if not downright gloomy. I was just happy at the thought of being able to return to my office after delivering him into the hands of the spooks.

Just ahead of us, I saw several army vehicles parked on the roadside. Then, everything happened very quickly. I hardly had time to stop before a squad of soldiers surrounded the car. Two men, dressed as civilians, but who had the unmistakable look of being in charge, opened the door on the passenger side and let my friend out. The way he reacted to them and their friendly greeting reassured me that this wasn't a trap an Atomos Organization trap.

"Thank you for everything, Mr. Burma," said my companion as the soldiers took him to an armored vehicle, presumably to start his debriefing.

The two civilians came towards me next. One of them was well known to me.

"We owe you a sizeable debt, Burma," said Bob Morane. "This is Hubert Bonisseur de la Bath, from the OSS," he said, introducing the other man.

"You've done a great service to the United States, Mr. Burma," said the OSS Agent. "Thanks to you, we will soon have the information we need to bring down the Atomos Organization before it can do evil."

"So what the little guy told me was all true?" I asked.

"The 'little fellow' is one of the greatest astrophysicists in the world, Nestor," said Morane, smiling.

"But if that Atomos Organization is so powerful, and your scientist so valuable, why did they agree to this exchange? Why didn't they neutralize him before we got away?"

"You're correct, Mr. Burma," said the OSS Agent. "Perhaps we have overestimated their capabilities, or…"

Suddenly, a soldier came running towards us.

"Sir! Sir! Come quickly!"

Morane and Bonisseur de la Bath followed him. After a few seconds, shrugging, I decided to go and see what was going on.

There were only a few people outside the armored truck which was full of electronic equipment. Inside, sitting on a fold-out chair, was my erstwhile companion. But he now looked dramatically different.

There was nothing in his eyes but emptiness, a void so profoundly intense that it froze my blood. This man, who had had one of the best minds in the world, had become a moron. And the worst part of it was that he recognized me. I saw him making inane, smiling faces and uttering friendly grunts and snickers at me. What, at another time, might have been funny was now unbearably tragic.

I understood that he would never speak again and that the world would soon hear from Madame Atomos in a big way.

"Did he have time to say anything?" I asked.

"Nothing," said the OSS Agent. "Apparently, it happened just as he was about to speak."

"We found traces of a drug we can't identify in his blood," said a man dressed like a doctor. "We believe he was poisoned less than a couple of hours ago."

The Calvados! My friend had been right: Madame Atomos liked cat and mouse games...

Nobody said anything. Everyone was still in shock. After a moment, I managed to speak:

"I didn't know him very well, but he was a swell guy. I never learned his name..."

"Professor Bean," said OSS 117. "But he didn't like the title, so we just called him Mister Bean."

(English adaptation by Jean-Marc & Randy Lofficier)

Michel Vannereux is the French translator of the German Perry Rhodan *series;
he has also written a few science fiction stories for our sister imprint, Rivière
Blanche. This tale features "Cal de Ter," the hero of five famous French sf novels penned by P.-J. Herault between 1975 and 1984. Sometime in the future, a
bloody war has erupted between Earth and its Martian colony. During one of
the battles, a military strategist named Cal is forced to go into a hibernation life
pod, condemned to drift into space forever. Thousands of years later, the pod
lands on the planet Vaha, still in its primitive stages of evolution. Cal emerges
and eventually comes across a deserted alien base, left by the long-lost, advanced race of the Loys. He uses its resources, including its giant computer HI
and a squadron of sentient androids, to monitor Vaha's progress and safety
throughout its history...*

Michel Vannereux: *The Warlord of Vaha*

Planet Vaha and Mars, The Future

Cal

The continent of Gol on Vaha always awakened in me a feeling of desola-
tion and despair. I felt just that way, as I flew over an immense steppe burned by
the Sun, skirting the line of the equator. I didn't dare imagine the heat which
must have reigned below, without any trees to provide shade. And yet, there
were people who lived down there. Nomads. Their lifestyle was too primitive to
constitute a real danger to the rest of the civilized people on the planet, but I
would nevertheless recommend to HI to keep a periodic eye on their progress. If
these people—they call themselves the Nochis—someday managed to cross the
ocean, I feared that my poor, peaceful Vahussi might get into serious troubles.

The steppe below was gradually replaced by an undulating prairie; then, a
big city came into view. It was the largest one that I'd ever seen on Vaha. I
made an unhappy face. If the source of the signal HI had detected came from the
heart of that sprawling metropolis, it wouldn't be easy to get close to it. Especially since the natives were unlikely to prove very friendly. Unless they'd im-
proved since my last visit, which I strongly doubted.

"Cal?"

Lou's calm voice tore me away from my thoughts. My copilot was pointing out a large, isolated building next to a cliff that would make a discreet landing spot. It was an imposing fortress, rather severe looking. A good section of it
appeared to have been demolished; recently judging from the smoke. Houses
located on either side were in the same state. I might have attributed that to an
earthquake if I didn't know that a rain of meteorites had fallen in that area.

And, of course, the mysterious signal was coming from there! When I thought that I could have been relaxing peacefully at the Base!

That was the plan, in fact, just before the Loys' supercomputer HI had told me that it had detected a powerful transmission coming from the very heart of Gol. At first glance, it looked like it might have come from some kind of Loys device, but HI quickly reassured me. He had not detected any starships entering the Oma system. On the other hand, a shower of meteorites had fallen on the area in question during the last few days. Upon further analysis, it turned out that what had caused such an unusual event was the passage of a rogue planet in our skies.

I decided to go and investigate what had happened, taking two of my android servants, Lou and Salvo, with me.

John Carter

As I advanced carefully though the deserted streets, I could feel the weight of the centuries on my shoulders. A million years ago, the water of the mighty Throxeus river had irrigated the proud nations of Barsoom, and the ruined city where I presently stood had been a thriving harbor.

The two moons, Cluros and Thuria, illuminated the night sky, enabling me to see as if it were daylight. It was the first time that I'd come to this section of Mars. For three long months, I had been busy with endless trade negotiations between Helium, Toonol and Sinharat. More than once, my blood had begun to boil and I had been within an inch of using my sword to slice through the issues on the table. I am, after all, a warrior, not a diplomat, but Tardos Mors, Jeddak of Helium, thought that only I, John Carter, Warlord of Barsoom, could impose his will on the rulers of these remote city-states. Finally, wishing to relax my temper, which had been severely tested, I had decided to leave on an adventure. I had lived on Mars for decades, and yet, there still existed entire sections of the planet which I had never visited. This time, I had chosen to cross a vast desert beyond which, according to some legends, was the mythical land of the Erloors.

Eventually, I had come across this deserted city. I had wondered whether it might not be the legendary Loï, one of the strongholds of the Orovars, the former masters of Mars. I decided at once to explore it.

A dark opening in the ground attracted my attention. Being by nature curious—a curiosity which had often gotten me into trouble!—I entered and followed a paved pathway that led underground. After a few minutes, I arrived in a great rotunda from which many tunnels radiated. Strangely, it was bright even though I failed to see any artificial lamps or torches. The light seemed to emanate from the ceiling itself. I spent some time observing a very peculiar carving which occupied an entire wall. It was a large and very intricate heptagonal design, made up of countless small triangles intersecting one another in an incomprehensible pattern that almost made one dizzy just by looking at it. I examined it a long moment, vainly seeking to understand its meaning.

Then I returned to my exploration; the gallery continued for approximately 50 meters, then made a sharp turn to the right. I came out into a room with a high arched ceiling. Against its walls were shelves filled with many strange instruments and ancient scrolls, which, I was certain, would crumble into dust at the least contact. My eyes were drawn to an object occupying the center of the room: a large metal cylinder which shone softly. After all these centuries, this artifact, which undoubtedly dated back to the time of the Orovars, still functioned, although I couldn't determine its function.

Cal

As night fell, taking advantage of the dark, the three of us entered the fortress. We had dressed like the natives, in order to not attract attention. HI had made a precise scan of the place and located precisely the source of the mysterious energy source: a large interior courtyard, located right in the center of the destroyed section of the building.

Any normal human being would have quickly lost their way in the maze of corridors, stairs and galleries, but I had my infallible androids. Lou swiftly guided us to a balcony which overlooked the courtyard in question.

The ground was strewn with fragments of rock and huge blocks of stone. The surrounding walls were either broken or in bad shape. The meteorites had inflicted severe punishment on the entire building. During our descent, I heard a vague clamor. It turned out to be a small crowd joined together in prayer at the foot of an enormous statue half-hidden in the darkness. Considering their richly decorated attire and the fact that they kept repeating the same incantations, it could be only worshippers praying to their local god. I could easily imagine their panic when they saw their city struck by what must have seemed to them the wrath of the sky gods.

They were positioned in a semi-circle in front of a stone altar. I repressed a curse. On the altar was a young girl dressed in a white tunic. She was still, but the heaving of her chest indicated that she was alive.

The bastards were about to make a human sacrifice. I feel my blood boil in my veins and my hand tightened on the pummel of my sword. In my rage, I felt that that primitive weapon would serve better to punish these murderers.

"Cal, did you see?" said Lou.

"Yes, they're about to sacrifice that girl..."

"No. The statue. Look."

My attention had been entirely focused on the girl and I had ignored the statue. I squinted to take a better look at it. At first, I didn't understand what Lou wanted me to see. Then I saw it! By the Cosmos! I knew that creature—oh how well I knew it! And it wasn't a statue! No, it was... a *dijar*!

John Carter

While I observed the strange artifact, I heard a small noise behind me. In a flash, I grabbed my sword, turned around, and was able to block the vicious attack by one of the gigantic, four-armed Green Martians who haunted the dead sea-beds of Barsoom. I saw at once that he was a Warhoon. He was truly hideous, with his right eye missing and an ugly gash crossing the face.

I didn't know why he was there. He must have been exiled by his clan, because if he had come with them, I would have noticed their tracks. We crossed swords for long minutes. Ordinarily, I would have easily dispatched him, but here, the ground strewn with debris obstructed my movements. Once, I stumbled on a metal cylinder and lost my balance. The one-eyed creature took advantage of it and launched an attack which almost ended my life, but I managed to parry it. Carried by his speed, the Green Martian tripped over the cylinder and fell to the ground.

Unwittingly, he must have activated some long dormant mechanism, because, suddenly, there was a flash and an incandescent vortex formed in the air before us. I had never seen anything like it before!

Surprised by this turn of event, I made the mistake of dropping my guard. My foe jumped on the occasion. He sprang up and charged me. His sword left a bloody cut on my right hand. In his mad launch, he had, however, neglected his own defense. I plunged my own blade straight into his heart.

The Warhoon looked shocked, hiccupped in pain and, taking me completely by surprise, stunned me with a violent blow of his lower arms, before collapsing, dead at my feet. But his attack had propelled me right into the fiery vortex. Then, I lost consciousness.

Cal

A *dijar* was a Loys shuttlecraft. What was it doing there? For a brief moment, the notion of a return of the Loys to Vaha preyed on my mind, but looking at it more closely, I realized that ship was ancient. Its hull had a dull color which made it look like stone, which is why I hadn't immediately identified it earlier. It was clearly a wreck dating back several millennia, now worshipped as a god by the natives. Because of its relatively small size, I thought the *dijar* was a recon ship. The section of the wall that had crumbled enabled me to notice a large gash in its belly.

"I get it now," I whispered to my two androids. "When the meteors struck, they damaged the *dijar* and it started to emit some kind of energy signal. We should be able to fix it if we can gain access to the ship..."

To get a better view, I leaned over the parapet, forgetting how damaged the entire structure was. Suddenly, I fell the ground give way under my feet. I noisily tumbled down to the courtyard. The priests stopped their ceremony and all the faces are turned in my direction. *So much for discretion*, I thought.

The man who seemed to be their leader barked an order. Sprouting out of nowhere, a squadron of guards rushed towards me, swords raised. I tried pulling out my blaster, but I discovered that the holster was empty. I'd lost it during my fall!

Fortunately, my androids were there. A volley of fire hit the first soldiers in the legs, and they dropped to the ground, hurling curses. Lou and Salvo were doing a fine job.

Since I had no other choice, I drew my sword. I blessed fate that I had had the forethought of getting a memory update with all the fencing skills necessary to survive in a medieval society. I was thus able to disarm my next attackers with a master stroke.

From the corner of my eye, I saw Lou and Salvo aiming their blasters at the rest of the soldiers, but luck wasn't with us that day, because the remainder of the balcony suddenly collapsed with a loud crash, burying my two androids in the rubble. Lou's last beam missed its target, passed whistling above the head of the priests—who had now thrown themselves to ground in panic—and hit the *dijar*.

The result was devastating. A violent explosion blinded us all for a few seconds. The ship broke apart in a hellish din, raising a cloud of dust which covered the entire courtyard. When it had dissipated, I saw that it lay broken in half, on its belly. Its hull was traversed by random energy discharges. The most surprising, however, is that the explosion had created a large ring of fire in the air, whose center was absolute darkness—a tear in the very fabric of space.

I looked at this strange phenomenon with amazement, forgetting the battle. I had a vague idea of what might have caused it. Lou's blaster beam had hit the damaged engines and caused some kind of tear in the space-time continuum.

"Lou? Salvo? Are you OK?" I asked.

No reply.

I felt cold sweat running down my back. I saw my two androids totally still lying partially buried under the rubble…

However, I didn't have time to check them out. The priests might have still been paralyzed by fear, but the soldiers, like myself, had had time to recover and showed signs of wanting to start the battle again.

There were too many for my chances to be any good. This time, I needed a miracle to save my precious skin.

And the miracle occurred!

John Carter

I felt as if I was sinking into a bottomless pit. It was as if the universe itself was whirling around me, a completely different sensation from what I had experienced when I had been transported from Earth to Mars.

Then, abruptly, I again felt solid ground under my feet.

I was inside a courtyard, the architecture of which I didn't recognize. I took a step forward and I knew at once that I was no longer on Barsoom. Gravity was different here. But if that place was foreign to me, the drama which was unfolding in it looked very familiar.

The motionless body of a young woman was lying on an altar, with several individuals crouching around it, one of them holding a long knife. Without being even conscious of it, my right hand went to my sword...

My eyes then fell onto a man whom surrounded by a dozen of threatening soldiers. He was completely surrounded. I didn't know who he was, I knew that he would soon perish if I didn't come to his rescue. A smile formed on my lips. John Carter, Prince of Helium, Warlord of Barsoom, was ready to fight!

I jumped into the middle of the combatants and my blade quickly found its first victim. Three men already lay dead at my feet before the soldiers understood what had happened. I'm afraid that this confrontation won't add to my glory and I don't take any pride in it when I think back about it. Whether it was my superior fencing skills or the fact that the soldiers saw me as some kind of avenging god who burst out of nowhere, we won the fight easily. The surviving soldiers and priests, as if by mutual agreement, ran away as fast as they could and I saw them disappear under a porch.

I then approached the man whose life I had just saved. Perhaps he could tell me where I was and how I had arrived there. I was unaware, of course, of the local language, but some gestures are universal. I struck myself in the chest and said:

"I'm John Carter."

And, although I thought it might be pointless, I repeated the sentence in French and Martian.

Cal

"I'm John Carter."

Hearing the newcomer speak English was a revelation. How could anyone know English on Vaha? Unless that tear in the space-time continuum had somehow opened a gateway to the Earth... But how could that be? Earth was long gone! I decided that the best way to find out the answer was to respond.

"My name is Cal" I say. "Where the Devil do you come from?"

"I come from a world called Barsoom, but don't ask me how I arrived here. I have no idea myself."

At least, this Carter was familiar with the concept of space travel. He looked at the *dijar* whose entire hull was now vibrating and shaking. We were going to have to do something about those engines fast.

"We" reminded me of my androids.

I looked at the place where Lou and Salvo had been partially buried, and I discovered, to my great relief, that they were extracting themselves from beneath the rubble. Lou was the first to stand upright and, after shaking the dust off him as if nothing had happened, he said quietly:

"A minor malfunction caused by the fall. My systems are now fully operational again."

He looked at John Carter. I briefly told him the strange circumstances of his arrival. Carter was still holding on to his long sword; I saw from the vigilance in his eyes that he was always on his guard. This was good because, sooner or later, the soldiers might return.

With a few words, he described the strange artifact which he had discovered on Barsoom, as well as the circle of fire which had formed in the air, just like here.

"I can see only one explanation," said Lou. "For reasons yet to be determined, that artifact and the *dijar* entered into a resonance state through space and time and established some kind connection between them, like a subspace corridor."

"HI is sending me a transmission," interrupted Salvo. "It has detected an abnormal energy spike in subspace that could affect Vaha's gravitational field and have catastrophic effects. This 'corridor' must be closed at once."

"Yes, but how?" I said

"By shutting off the energy supply. Only, that must be done at the same time at both ends, otherwise the corridor will open again."

"That doesn't sound too difficult."

" 'At the same time' means within a tenth of a second, Cal. No human could be that precise."

No human? Could he mean?...

"I shall have to travel to Barsoom," continued Salvo. "My android brain can be synchronized with that of Lou here. We will be able to act at the exact same time."

"But once the subspace corridor is shut, you'll be stranded there forever!"

"I am sorry, Cal, but there's no other way."

"You're insane! You can't do that!"

"I must, Cal."

As hard as it was to accept it, I could see that he was right. It was the only solution. Clenching my teeth, I notified my agreement with a short nod.

At that moment, I saw Carter raise his sword. I turned around and couldn't repress a curse. Ten soldiers were running towards us. They had apparently recovered from their earlier panic, or else the exhortations of their superiors and the priests had provided them with the required incentive.

Lou and Salvo came to stand in front of us in order to protect us, according to their programming, but I objected:

"No! You have a mission to complete. Go ahead, I order it! I'll keep these men busy."

The two androids did not raise any objections. They heard the tone of my voice, and understood there was no room for discussion. They ran towards their respective targets: the *dijar* and the subspace corridor. To my surprise, I saw that Carter had remained with me.

"Why are you still here?" I said. "If you don't go home now, you won't be able to return—ever!"

A smile appeared on his lips

"It won't ever be said that John Carter, Jeddak of Jeddaks, Warlord of Barsoom, has abandoned a brave man to face a superior enemy alone!"

Then, the soldiers were on us.

John Carter

Cal and I fought our enemies back to back. It was a tough, harsh battle; had there been any witnesses, no doubt this might have been turned into an epic to be sung throughout the ages. Our two blades lashed and twisted and turned into the air, hacking the soldiers like so many corn rows.

From the corner of my eye, I had seen the one Cal had called Lou disappear inside the wreck of the alien ship and Salvo jump into the ring of fire.

A single adversary proved to be a challenge. He was a scraggly, red-haired giant. When the battle had begun, I thought it would quickly be over, but that man was made of a different cloth than the other soldiers. He parried my first blows without difficulty, then tried to pin me through the chest like a butterfly. I barely escaped by sliding aside at the last minute. Our blades clashed and we fought silently for a long time. Then, he made one mistake, but it was enough to cost him his life. He attacked too strongly and, as a result, lost his balance. In a lightning flash, my sword neatly cleaved his head and separated it from his body. Then, ignoring the still twitching body, I went to assist Cal who handled his weapon with incredible dexterity.

I knew nothing about him, yet I felt he was an exceptional man—a true Jeddak.

And finally we came to that miraculous moment: Cal and I still stood, the winners, in the midst of a bloody battlefield strewn with corpses. Against logic, against superior numbers, we had carried the day. We remained still for a moment, not daring to believe that the battle was over.

Cal looked around, making sure there were no more enemies lurking somewhere. Then, he pointed at the circle of fire which was still there.

"The subspace corridor is still open. Take it. It might close any minute."

"I shall. I am happy to have known to you, Cal."

"Me, too, John Carter, but hurry up, will you? And take care of Salvo."

We shook hands and then, without further ado, I jumped into the gateway.

The dizziness that I had experienced earlier seemed shorter this time. A lightness in my limbs told me that I had returned to Barsoom. If I had the slightest doubt about it, the corpse of the one-eyed Warhoon was there to confirm it.

Salvo was waiting for me, next to the strange cylinder which was still shaking. He didn't seem surprised to see me.

"I am now ready to deactivate this device. I only feel regret that I do not have more time to discover how a Loys portable generator has ended up on your world."

So that was the nature of the artifact! I wonder if there was a connection between the Loys and the Orovars? I was going to ask Salvo when a new, violent jolt made the walls tremble. It was urgent to sever the connection between Barsoom and Vaha.

The android must have read my mind, because he lowered a tiny lever. The light which enveloped the generator vanished, but the vibrations became even more intense.

"Run, John Carter!" said Salvo. "The generator is about to blow..."

A that moment, a section of the ceiling loudly collapsed and I lost sight of Salvo. I realized at once that he must have been buried under tons of rock. I turned around and ran as fast as I could towards the exit.

Once I had reached the outside, I looked with sadness on what would now be forever the tomb of the artificial being which had sacrificed his own existence to save two worlds.

Cal

It was with a heavy heart that I looked at the tear in space through which had stepped John Carter, but also my faithful Salvo, whom I would never see again. Of course, HI could build me a new Salvo, but he wouldn't have all the experiences we had so often shared together. It would be as if his heart was missing.

I was exhausted after this epic battle. When I looked at all the bodies lying all around me, I could barely accept that it was over.

A violent jolt tore me out of my contemplation. The ground shook, then an entire wall collapsed within a few meters from me.

The subsequent minutes passed with frustrating slowness. What had happened to Lou? No more priests or soldiers dared show up. They were probably too terrified to launch a new offensive. It is only then that I realized that the girl who was going to be sacrificed had gone too. Had she found time to flee, or had the priests carried her away, saving her for another ceremony? I would never find out the answer...

As I was seriously beginning to worry, the circle of fire vanished. Lou came out of the *dijar* running.

"Get out of here! Fast!"

"Why? You've successfully closed the subspace corridor."

"Yes, but the engine has gone critical. It's going to explode in a few minutes."

We used our Anti-G harnesses to leave the courtyard as fast as possible. While flying over the outside walls, I saw a panicked crowd which undoubtedly believed it was the end of the world, including two exterminating angels.

As we landed near a fountain, a terrible explosion shook the night. We threw ourselves to the ground and heard debris whistle past our heads. A few minutes later, I looked up. The fortress was nothing more than a huge cluster of smoking ruins. I thought of the number of people still inside and grimaced. No one could survive such a cataclysm.

No one?

I suddenly saw a limping silhouette in the middle of the smoke. At first, I grabbed my sword, before a moonbeam illuminated the face of the newcomer. I felt a burst of joy and elation.

"Salvo!"

As incredible as it seemed, it was indeed Salvo whom I had thought was lost forever. I was about to run towards him, when Lou intervened:

"More guards are coming! Let us not waste time here!"

During our return flight, Salvo explained how, during the twin explosion, there had been a feedback effect which had restored the subspace corridor for a few seconds, which he had used to get back to Vaha.

I wonder what, of all this, I should consign in our archives. This adventure seemed so incredible, with this warrior of legend, this Warlord of Barsoom... No one will ever believe me...

(English adaptation by Jean-Marc & Randy Lofficier)

Credits

Don Camillo and the Secret Weapon

Starring:	Created by:
Don Camillo	Giovanni Guareschi
Peppone	Giovanni Guareschi
Smilzo	Giovanni Guareschi
Avakoum Zahov	Andrei Gulyashki
Miss Hutchens	John Hermes Secondari
The British Agent	Ian Fleming
Mr. Hawthorne	Graham Greene
Eva Kant	Angela & Luciana Giussani
Princess Ann	Ian McLellan Hunter
	& John Dighton
And:	
Clerville	Angela & Luciana Giussani
The Satan Bug	Alistair MacLean

Matthew BAUGH is an ordained minister who lives and works in the Chicago area. He is a longtime fan of pulp fiction, cliffhanger serials and old time radio. He has written a number of articles on characters like Zorro, Dr. Syn, Jules de Grandin and Sailor Steve Costigan. He has had stories published in *The Green Hornet Chronicles, More Tales of Zorro, Six Guns Straight From Hell, The Avenger Chronicles* and *The Phantom Chronicles*. He is a regular contributor to *Tales of the Shadowmen*.

The Elphberg Red

Starring:	Created by:
Rudolf Rassendyll	Anthony Hope
Colonel Sapt	Anthony Hope
Queen Flavia	Anthony Hope
Prince Rupert of Hentzau	Anthony Hope
Dr. John Watson	Arthur Conan Doyle
Sherlock Holmes	Arthur Conan Doyle
A.J. Raffles	E.W.Hornung
Bunny Manders	E.W.Hornung
Countess Cagliostro	Maurice Leblanc
Inspector Mackenzie	E.W.Hornung

Baird	E.W.Hornung
Sir Edward Lytton	Blake Edwards
	& Maurice Richlin

Nicholas BOVING lives in Toronto. He was formerly a mining engineer and traveled the world widely. He also worked from time to time as a docker, fruit inspector and forester. His books and screenplays draw on these experiences to provide characters, backgrounds and scenes. He is the author and publisher of the *Maxim Gunn* series of action/adventure books. He has also written some fifteen other novels and screenplays which follow the central character to countries and places where the forces of nature as much as people provide the conflict. This is his first contribution to *Tales of the Shadowmen*.

The Most Dreadful Monster

Starring:	**Created by:**
Madame Atomos	André Caroff
Bruce Banner	Stan Lee & Jack Kirby
Co-Starring:	
Gojira	Shigeru Kayama, Takeo Murata
	& Ishiro Honda
Rodan	Ken Kuronuma, Takeo Murata
	& Takeshi Kimura

Matthew DENNION lives in South Jersey with his beautiful wife and new baby daughter. He currently works as a teacher of autistic students at a Special Services School. Matt has been a huge fan of the works of Edgar Rice Burroughs ever since he first picked up *A Princess of Mars*; he is also a big follower of Sherlock Holmes, Doc Savage, Spider-Man, Batman, and James Bond. He is a regular contributor to *Tales of the Shadowmen*.

Marguerite's Tears

Starring:	**Created by:**
Violet Clarke Holmes	Philip José Farmer
Siger Holmes	based on Arthur Conan Doyle
Sir Percy Blakeney	Emmuska Orczy
Marguerite Blakeney	Emmuska Orczy
Alice Clarke Raffles	Philip José Farmer
Fitzwilliam Darcy	Jane Austen
Colonel Bozzo-Corona	Paul Féval
Lecoq	based on Paul Féval
	& Emile Gaboriau

Lupin	based on Maurice Leblanc
Duke of Holdernesse	Arthur Conan Doyle
Baron Tennington	Edgar Rice Burroughs
The Delargardies	Philip José Farmer
Drummond	based on Herman Cyril McNeile
Joseph Balsamo	Alexandre Dumas
Kramm	based on Gustave Le Rouge
De Winter	based on Alexandre Dumas
Gerolstein	based on Eugène Sue
John Gribson	Philip José Farmer
Charles Bingley	Jane Austen
Lord Richard Selwick	Lauren Willig
George Knightly	Jane Austen
Snuff Box Man (Von Hessel)	Philip José Farmer

Co-Starring:

Countess Nadine Carody	Jaime Chávarri, Anne Settimó & Jess Franco

Also Starring:
Napoléon Bonaparte (Lupin's half-brother)

Win Scott ECKERT Win Scott Eckert holds a B.A. in Anthropology and a Juris Doctorate. He is the editor of and contributor to *Myths for the Modern Age: Philip José Farmer's Wold Newton Universe*, a 2007 Locus Award Finalist for Best Non-Fiction book. Win's latest books are the encyclopedic two-volume *Crossovers: A Secret Chronology of the World*, and the Wold Newton novel *The Evil in Pemberley House*, about Patricia Wildman, the daughter of a certain bronze-skinned pulp hero (co-authored with Philip José Farmer). He is immensely pleased to appear in all eight volumes of *Tales of the Shadowmen*.

Leviathan Creek

Starring:	**Created by:**
Joseph Rouletabille	Gaston Leroux
Herbert Brown	Jules Verne
Kapitan Mors	Anonymous
Neb Jnr.	based on Jules Verne
Elena Brown *née* Fairchild	John Prebble, Daniel B. Ullman & Crane Wilbur
Jaws	Peter Benchley
Co-Starring:	
Cyrus Smith	Jules Verne

Captain Nemo	Jules Verne
Robur	Jules Verne
Harold Dobey	William Blinn
Professor Stangerson	Gaston Leroux
Also Starring:	
Jean Jules Jusserand	
Michael Schleisser	

Martin GATELY is the author of the comics novella *Sherwood Jungle* in the *Phantom: Generations* series. He is a regular contributor to the UK's journal of strange phenomena *Fortean Times*, for which he also created the *Cryptid Kid Investigates* comic strip. His writing career began back in the 1980s when he wrote for D C Thomson's legendary *Starblazer* comic-book. He lives in a decaying mansion in Nottingham that has a view of a former insane asylum. This is his first contribution to *Tales of the Shadowmen*.

Slouching Towards Camulodunum

Starring:	**Created by:**
Becky Sharp	William Makepeace Thackeray
Sâr Dubnotal	*Anonymous*
Helen Vaughan	Arthur Machen
Clarke	Arthur Machen
Villiers	Arthur Machen
Jacques Courbé	Clarence A. "Tod" Robbins
Naïni	*Anonymous*
Rudolf	*Anonymous*
Annunciata	*Anonymous*
Francis-Aytown	Bram Stoker
Lord Henry Wotton	Oscar Wilde
Randolph	Lloyd C. Douglas
Charles Delaware Tate	Dan Curtis, Sam Hall
	& Violet Welles
Co-Starring:	
Dr. Robert Matheson	Arthur Machen
Richard Upton Pickman	H.P. Lovecraft
Basil Hallward	Oscar Wilde
Pierre Rodin	Micah Harris
	based on Robert Bloch
Minuette	Micah Harris

Micah HARRIS is the author (with artist Michael Gaydos) of the graphic novel *Heaven's War*, a historical fantasy pitting authors Charles Williams, C.S. Lewis and J.R.R. Tolkien against occultist Aleister Crowley. His most recent publication is the novella "On the Periphery of Legend" in Volume 2 of *Jim Anthony, Super Detective* for Ron Fortier's Airship 27 Productions. 2010 will see the release of his first comic *book* book (as opposed to *graphic novel* comic book), *Lorna, Relic Wrangler* with Loston Wallace, illustrator of Harris's *The Eldritch New Adventures of Becky Sharp*. He is a regular contributor to *Tales of the Shadowmen*.

In the Caves of the Serpent

Starring:	Created by:
El Borak (Francis Xavier Gordon)	Robert E Howard
Masa	Robert E Howard
Orlando	Virginia Wolfe
The Serpent Men	Robert E Howard
The Wandering Jew	Paul Féval
Lotte	Paul Féval
The Dark Elder Gods	Robert E Howard & H.P. Lovecraft
Co-Starring:	
MacLeod	Gregory Widen
Sâr Dubnotal	*Anonymous*
Doctor Omega	Aenould Galopin
And:	
Hattori Hanzo sword	Takao Okinaga

Travis HILTZ started making up stories at a young age. Years later, he began writing them down. In high school, he discovered that some writers actually got paid and decided to give it a try. He has since gathered a modest collection of rejection letters and had a one-act play produced. Travis lives in the wilds of New Hampshire with his very loving and tolerant wife, two above average children and a staggering amount of comic books and *Doctor Who* novels. He is a regular contributor to *Tales of the Shadowmen*.

Sleep No More

Starring:	Created by:
Richard Wentworth	Harry Steeger
Nita Von Sloan	Harry Steeger
Harry Dickson	*Anonymous*
Georgette Cuvelier	*Anonymous*
Natasha	Paul Hugli
Tang-Akhmut	Norvell Page

Jeffrey Fairchild (Dr. Skull)	Randolph Craig
Robert Fairchild	Randolph Craig
The Scorpion	Randolph Craig
The Pods	Jack Finney
Billy Brown (CLASH)	Franco Frescura
	& Giorgio Trevisan
The Shop	Stephen King
Ted White	Lina Buffolente
Carrie White	Stephen King
Co-Starring:	
Stanley Kirkpatrick	Harry Steeger
Leo Saint-Clair	Jean de La Hire
Imhotep	John L. Balderston
Dr. Anton Phibes	William Goldstein
	& James Whiton
	& Robert Fuest
Kent Allard	Walter Gibson
And:	
The Interocitor	Raymond F. Jones
Also Starring:	
William Randolph Hearst	
Marion Davies	
Liserl	

Paul HUGLI has a degree in Zoology, and has written for everything from *Cracked* magazine to general interest pamphlets, and for most of the first, second *and* third tier adult magazines. He is the author of three published "adult fantasy" novels, and the acclaimed *Traci Lords Companion*. He has also been employed as a science/math instructor, and as a "Floor Manager" at a local "Gentleman's Club." In addition, he once owned/managed Destiny Bookstore, which dealt in SciFi, comics and adult "fantasy" magazines, for 30 years. He now has three novels in the works. He is a regular contributor to *Tales of the Shadowmen*.

Vampire Renaissance

Starring:	**Created by:**
Addhema	Paul Féval
Marcian Gregoryi	Paul Féval
Janos Szandor	Paul Féval
Dracula	Bram Stoker
Co-Starring:	
Armand Tesla	Griffin Jay, Kurt Neuman

	& Randall Faye
Count Yorga	Bob Kelljan
Great Old Ones	H.P.Lovecraft
Slidith the Drac (Draco)	Lin Carter,
	Peter Tremayne,
	Sylvie Miller
	& Philippe Ward
Yiggurath (Yig)	H.P. Lovecraft,
	Zealia Bishop
	& Robert Bloch
Tiamit of Arabu	Robert E. Howard
Adana	Abraham Merritt
Set (Great Serpent)	Robert E. Howard
Serpent Men	Robert E. Howard
	& Clark Ashton Smith
Werewolf Folk	Robert E. Howard
Akaana	Robert E. Howard
Red Brotherhood	Lin Carter
Dragon Kings	Lin Carter
Rammon	Robert E. Howard
Akivasha	Robert E. Howard
Simon the Mage (Simon of Gitta)	Richard L. Tierney
Gilles Grenier	Clark Ashton Smith
Also Starring:	
Matthias Corvinus	
Pontius Pilate	

Rick LAI, a regular contributor to *Tales of the Shadowmen*, is a computer programmer. During the 1980s and 1990s, he wrote articles expanding on the Wold Newton Universe concepts which have since been collected by Altus Press as *Rick Lai's Secret Histories: Daring Adventurers, Rick Lai's Secret Histories: Criminal Master Minds, Chronology of Shadows: A Timeline of The Shadow's Exploits* and *The Revised Complete Chronology of Bronze*. Rick resides in Bethpage, New York, with his wife and children.

Satan's Signature

Starring:	**Created by:**
Auguste Dupin	Edgar Allan Poe
Sherlock Holmes	Arthur Conan Doyle
Solar "Sunny" Pons	August Derleth
Mr. Bunbury	Oscar Wilde
Dr. Henry Jekyll	R.L. Stevenson

Mycroft Holmes	Arthur Conan Doyle
Bancroft Pons	August Derleth
Colonel Moran	Arthur Conan Doyle
Bisclavret	Marie de France
Co-Starring:	
Marquis Eric (The Beast)	Marie Le Prince de Beaumont
Lord Ruthven	John William Polidori
Alinska	Etienne-Léon de Lamothe-Langon
And:	
Miskatonic University	H.P.Lovecraft

Joseph D. LAMERE is a middle school English teacher and closet Francophile. He commutes to work each day by bicycle. He is married to Emily and is the proud father of Ella and Sofia. He wishes to dedicate this story to them, as well as his fellow Midwesterners, the late, great August Derleth and Philip Jose Farmer. He also wants to thank his mom for those miniature *Illustrated Classics* she used to buy him at K-Mart. He would have been a different kid—and man—without them. This is his first contribution to *Tales of the Shadowmen*.

Lost in Averoigne

Starring:	Created by:
Jules de Grandin	Seabury Quinn
Henry Jones, Sr.	George Lucas & Menno Meyjes
	& Philip Kaufman & Jeffrey Boam
	& Steven Spielberg
Azedarac	Clark Ashton Smith
Jirel of Joiry	Catherine L. Moore
And:	
Averoigne	Clark Ashton Smith
Book of Eibon	Clark Ashton Smith
Yog-Sothoth	H.P. Lovecraft
Shub-Niggurath	H.P. Lovecraft
Tsathoggua	Clark Ashton Smith

Olivier LEGRAND is a French literature teacher who lives in Caen, Normandy. He is a fan of RPGs, comics, and, in his spare time, the writer of the excellent Holmesian graphic novel series, *Les Quatre de Baker Street*. This is his first contribution to *Tales of the Shadowmen*. He has also contributed a *story to Doctor Omega and the Shadowmen*.

The Affair of the Necklace Revisited

Starring:	Created by:
Richard Benson	Paul Ernst
Pierre Duchêne	Jean-Marc Lofficier
The Dreux-Soubize	Maurice Leblanc
Commissaire Gilles	Jacques Decrest
Baruch Jorgell	Gustave Le Rouge
Judex	Louis Feuillade & Arthur Bernède
Co-Starring:	
Alice Benson	Paul Ernst
Victoria Benson	Paul Ernst
Arsène Lupin	Maurice Leblanc
Zigomar	Léon Sazie
Fantômas	Pierre Souvestre & Marcel Allain
Belphégor	Arthur Bernède
Ténébras	Arnould Galopin
Dr. Cornelius Kramm	Gustave Le Rouge
And:	
The Queen's Necklace	Alexandre Dumas & Maurice Leblanc

Jean-Marc & Randy LOFFICIER, the editors of *Tales of the Shadowmen*, have collaborated on five screenplays, a dozen books and numerous translations, including *Arsène Lupin, Doc Ardan, Doctor Omega, The Phantom of the Opera* and *Rouletabille*. Their latest novels include *Edgar Allan Poe on Mars* and *The Katrina Protocol*. They have written a number of animation teleplays, including episodes of *Duck Tales* and *The Real Ghostbusters*, and in comics, such popular heroes as *Superman* and *Doctor Strange*. They created the Mayan detective series *Tongue*Lash*. Randy is a member of the Writers Guild of America, West and Mystery Writers of America.

Catspaw

Starring:	Created by:
Harry Paget Flashman II	based on George MacDonald Fraser
Sgt. Ballantine	based on Henri Vernes
Jean Saint-Clair	Jean de La Hire
Karram Khan	Talbot Mundy, Ivan Goff & Ben Roberts
Dr. Moreau	H.G. Wells

Co-Starring:
Oxus   Jean de La Hire
Fulbert   Jean de La Hire
The Hictaner   Jean de La Hire
Dr. Jekyll   R.L. Stevenson

David McDONALD is a professional geek from Melbourne, Australia, who works for an international welfare organisation. When not on a computer or reading a book, he divides his time between helping run a local cricket club and working on his upcoming novel. He is a member of the Melbourne-based writers group, SuperNOVA, and the Australian Horror Writers Association. This is his first contribution to *Tales of the Shadowmen*.

Patricide

Starring:	**Created by:**
Erik (Phantom of the Opera)	Gaston Leroux
Gouroull (Frankenstein Monster)	Mary Shelley
	& Jean-Claude Carrière
Bouzille	Pierre Souvestre
	& Marcel Allain
Dr. Cornelius Kramm	Gustave Le Rouge
Fritz Kramm	Gustave Le Rouge
Hélène Gurn	Pierre Souvestre
	& Marcel Allain
Florence Drummond (The Flame)	Carroll John Daly
Brianna "Bri" Warren	Constance M. Burge
The "Angels of Music"	Kim Newman
Cochenille	Jules Barbier
	& E.T.A. Hoffman
Jules Maigret	Georges Simenon
Jules de Grandin	Seabury Quinn
Co-Starring:	
Christine Daae	Gaston Leroux
Dr. Septimus Pretorius	William James Hurlbut
Heinrich Van Drummond	Calvin Kelly & Ed Jurist
The Black Coats	Paul Féval
The Vampires	Louis Feuillade

Chris NIGRO is a writer of both fiction and non-fiction with a strong interest in the pulps, the comic book medium, and fantastic cinema.*Patricide* is his debut appearance in print. However, he may alreadybe known to some in the field of fantastic fiction by his extensive writings in cyberspace, including his websites

The Godzilla Saga and *The Warrenverse*, as he is an authority on the subject of dai kaiju eiga (the sub-genre of sci-fi cinema specializing in giant monsters), and all the series characters featured in the now defunct but fondly remembered comic magazines published by Warren Comics. He presently works as a website administrator for a small business when he isn't writing, and resides in Buffalo, New York. This is his first contribution to *Tales of the Shadowmen*.

More Imaginative Sins

Starring:	Created by:
Thomas Carnacki	William Hope Hodgson
Madame Palmyre	Renée Dunan
Baal	Renée Dunan
Co-Starring:	
Sâr Dubnotal	Anonymous

John PEEL was born in Nottingham, England, and started writing stories at age 10. John moved to the U.S. in 1981 to marry his pen-pal. He, his wife ("Mrs. Peel") and their 13 dogs now live on Long Island, New York. John has written just over 100 books to date, mostly for young adults. He is the only author to have written novels based on both *Doctor Who* and *Star Trek*. His most popular work is *Diadem*, a fantasy series; he has written ten volumes to date. He is a regular contributor to *Tales of the Shadowmen*.

Passing Through the Hands of Steel

Starring:	Created by:
Jean Passepartout	Jules Verne
Johnny Brainerd	Edward S. Ellis
Santer	Karl May
Old Shatterhand	Karl May
Winnetou	Karl May
Phileas Fogg	Jules Verne
Co-Starring:	
Doktor Schultze	Jules Verne
Fix	Jules Verne
Stamp Proctor	Jules Verne
Gévrol	Emile Gaboriau
C. Auguste Dupin	Edgar Allan Poe
Also Starring:	
Napoleon III	

Dennis E. POWER has a B.A. in History and lives in Saint Louis, Missouri. In 1998, his interests in history, popular entertainment and literature led to the creation of the second internet site dedicated to Philip Jose Farmer's Wold Newton Universe concept. The site hosts essays with diverse subjects such as Phra the Phoenician, Dr, Jekyll, The Invisible Man, The Cartwrights and Fu Manchu. He was a contributor to *Myths for the Modern Age* and is a regular contributor to *Farmerphile: The Magazine of Philip Jose Farmer*. He is a regular contributor to *Tales of the Shadowmen*.

Before the War, Five Dragons Roar

Starring:	**Created by:**
Charlie Chan	Earl Derr Biggers
Dr. Yoshimuta	André Caroff
Ichirou Aratamoto (I.A. Moto)	John P. Marquand
Kentarou Aratamoto (Kentarou Moto)	John P. Marquand & Norman Foster
James Lee Wong	Hugh Wiley
Co-Starring:	
Gottfried Vanger	Stieg Larsson
Nora Charles	Dashiell Hammett
Mr. Cranston	Walter B. Gibson
Mr. Reid	George W. Trendle & Fran Striker
Oka Yuma	*Anonymous*
Fu Wong	Harry Stephen Keeler
The Manchurian (Fu Manchu)	Sax Rohmer
Fen Chu	Georges Fronval
Win Lee	Hugh Wiley & Ralph Gilbert Bettison
Richard Wong	Lee Fredericks
Dragon Queen	David Axelrod, Stan Burns & Jerry Sherlock
Egg Shen	Gary Goldman, David Z. Weinstein & W. D. Richter
And:	
S.S. *Claridon*	Andrew Stone
Berkford University	Hugh Wiley
The Map	Hugh Wiley & Ralph Gilbert Bettison & Kim Ji-woon & Kim Min-suk

Twelve Coins of Confucius	Harry Stephen Keeler
Keelat	Harry Stephen Keeler

Pete RAWLIK holds a B.S. in Marine Biology and manages monitoring projects in the Florida Everglades. He has been a fan of the Lovecraftian fiction since his father sat him on his knee and read him Lovecraft's *The Rats in the Walls*. His fiction has appeared in *Talebones, IBID* and *Crypt of Cthulhu*. His literary criticism has appeared in *The New York Review of Science Fiction* and in *The Neil Gaiman Reader*. He is a regular contributor to *Tales of the Shadowmen*.

The Carolingian Stone

Starring:	**Created by:**
Jim Anthony	Victor Rousseau Emmanuel
Chantecoq	Arthur Bernède
Belphégor	Arthur Bernède
De Felipone	based on Ponson du Terrail
Jan Mayen	Paul Alfred Müller
Co-Starring:	
Tom Gentry	Victor Rousseau Emmanuel
Colette Chantecoq	Arthur Bernède
Senator Colquitt	Victor Rousseau Emmanuel
The Vampires	Arthur Bernède
Francis Ardan	Guy d'Armen
Sun Koh	Paul Alfred Müller
Bran Mak Morn	Robert E. Howard
Also starring:	
Paracelsus	

Joshua REYNOLDS is a freelance writer of modest ability and exceptional confidence. His sword & sorcery novel, *Knight of the Blazing Sun,* is due for publication by Black Library in 2012. Also to-be-released 2012 is *Out of Black Aeons*, the first book in *The Adventures of Charles St. Cyprian* from Pro Se Press. In other interesting facts, he was once bitten by a snake. It subsequently died. This is his first contribution to *Tales of the Shadowmen*.

The Death Bird

Starring:	**Created by:**
Jean Kariven	Jimmy Guieu
Albert Campion	Margery Allingham
Magersfontein Lugg	Margery Allingham
The Polarians	Jimmy Guieu

The Denebians	Jimmy Guieu
Co-Starring:	
Mr. Tobin	Peter Viertel, Joan Harrison,
	Dorothy Parker
	& Alfred Hitchcock
Mocata	Dennis Wheatley

Frank SCHILDINER has been a pulp fan since a friend gave him a gift of Phillip Jose Farmer's *Tarzan Alive*. Since that time he has published articles on *Hellboy*, the Frankenstein films, *Dark Shadows* and the television show's links to the H.P. Lovecraft universe. He is a Senior Probation Officer in New Jersey and a martial arts instructor at Amorosi's Mixed Martial Arts. Frank resides in New Jersey with his wife Gail and two cats. He is a regular contributor to *Tales of the Shadowmen*.

With the Compliments of Nestor Burma!

Starring:	Created by:
Nestor Burma	Léo Malet
Hélène Mora	Léo Malet
Atomos Organization	André Caroff
SMOG	Henri Vernes
Bob Morane	Henri Vernes
OSS 117	Jean Bruce
Mister Bean	Rowan Atkinson & Ben Curtis
Also Starring:	
Leni Riefenstahl	

Michel STEPHAN was born and lives in Brittany with his wife and two children. He has been a fan of science fiction, fantasy and horror since age 10. He loves Universal monster movies (especially the *Frankenstein* series), sci-fi serials and collects Aurora model kits. He has submitted stories to Black Coat Press's French sister imprint, Rivière Blanche and has previously contributed to *Tales of the Shadowmen*.

The Warlord of Vaha

Starring:	Created by:
Cal	P.-J. Herault
Lou	P.-J. Herault
Salvo	P.-J. Herault
John Carter	Edgar Rice Burroughs

And:

Vaha	P.-J. Herault
The Loys	P.-J. Herault
Barsoom	Edgar Rice Burroughs
Helium	Edgar Rice Burroughs
Sinharat	Leigh Brackett
The Erloors	Gustave Le Rouge

Michel VANNEREUX has been a science fiction fan since he discovered Dan Barry's *Flash Gordon* in *Le Journal de Mickey*. He is one of the French translators of the German series *Perry Rhodan*, and edits two fanzines: *La Tribune des Amis d'Edgar Rice Burroughs* and *Le Météore*, devoted to popular science fiction. He works in computers for a major telecom company and lives in Paris with his wife and two children. This is his first contribution to *Tales of the Shadowmen*.

WATCH OUT FOR

TALES OF THE
SHADOWMEN
VOLUME 9: LA VIE EN NOIR
TO BE RELEASED EARLY 2013

TALES OF THE
SHADOWMEN

Volume 1: The Modern Babylon (2005)
Matthew Baugh, Bill Cunningham, Terrance Dicks, Win Scott Eckert, Viviane Etrivert, G.L. Gick, Rick Lai, Alain le Bussy, Jean-Marc & Randy Lofficier, Samuel T. Payne, John Peel, Chris Roberson, Robert Sheckley, Brian Stableford.

Volume 2: Gentlemen of the Night (2006)
Matthew Baugh, Bill Cunningham, Win Scott Eckert, G.L. Gick, Rick Lai, Serge Lehman, Jean-Marc Lofficier, Xavier Mauméjean, Sylvie Miller & Philippe Ward, Jess Nevins, Kim Newman, John Peel, Chris Roberson, Brian Stableford, Jean-Louis Trudel.

Volume 3: Danse Macabre (2007)
Joseph Altairac & Jean-Luc Rivera, Matthew Baugh, Alfredo Castelli, Bill Cunningham, François Darnaudet & J.-M. Lofficier, Paul DiFilippo, Win Scott Eckert, G.L. Gick, Micah Harris, Travis Hiltz, Rick Lai, Jean-Marc Lofficier, Xavier Mauméjean, David A. McIntee, Brad Mengel, Michael Moorcock, John Peel, Chris Roberson, Robert L. Robinson, Jr., Brian Stableford.

Volume 4: Lords of Terror (2008)
Matthew Baugh, Bill Cunningham, Win Scott Eckert, Micah Harris, Travis Hiltz, Rick Lai, Roman Leary, Jean-Marc Lofficier, Randy Lofficier, Xavier Mauméjean, Jess Nevins, Kim Newman, John Peel, Steven A. Roman, John Shirley, Brian Stableford.

Volume 5: The Vampires of Paris (2009)
Matthew Baugh, Michelle Bigot, Christopher Paul Carey & Win Scott Eckert, G.L. Gick, Micah Harris, Tom Kane, Lovern Kindzierski, Rick Lai, Roman Leary, Alain le Bussy, Jean-Marc Lofficier, Randy Lofficier, Xavier Mauméjean, Jess Nevins, John Peel, Frank Schildiner, Stuart Shiffman, Brian Stableford, David L. Vineyard.

Volume 6: Grand Guignol (2010)
Matthew Baugh & Micah Harris, Christopher Paul Carey, Win Scott Eckert, Emmanuel Gorlier, Travis Hiltz, Rick Lai, Roman Leary, Jean-Marc Lofficier, Randy Lofficier, Xavier Mauméjean, William P. Maynard, John Peel, Neil

Penswick, Dennis E. Power, Frank Schildiner, Bradley H. Sinor, Brian Stableford, Michel Stéphan, David L. Vineyard.

Volume 6: Femmes Fatales (2011)

Roberto Lionel Barreiro, Matthew Baugh, Thom Brannan, Matthew Dennion,
Win Scott Eckert, Emmanuel Gorlier, Micah Harris, Travis Hiltz, Paul Hugli,
Rick Lai, Jean-Marc Lofficier, David McDonnell, Brad Mengel, Sharan New-
man, Neil Penswick, Pete Rawlik, Frank Schildiner, Stuart Shiffman, Bradley H.
Sinor, Brian Stableford, Michel Stéphan, David L. Vineyard.

Doctor Omega and the Shadowmen (2011)

Matthew Baugh, Thom Brannan, G.L. Gick, Travis Hiltz, Olivier Legrand,
Serge Lehman, Jean-Marc & Randy Lofficier, Samuel T. Payne, John Peel, Neil
Penswick, Dennis E. Power, Chris Roberson, Stuart Shiffman.

The Nyctalope Steps In (2011)

Matthew Dennion, Emmanuel Gorlier, Julien Heylbroeck, Paul Hugli, Jean de
La Hire, Roman Leary, Randy Lofficier, Stuart Shiffman, David L. Vineyard.

www.ingramcontent.com/pod-product-compliance
Lightning Source LLC
Chambersburg PA
CBHW030344020726
47493CB00003B/679